S0-BAT-481

DARK DESTINY

Edited by Edward E. Kramer

WHITE WOLF
PUBLISHING

Dark Destiny I is
a product of White Wolf Publishing.

For information write: White Wolf Publishing, 780 Park North Boulevard, Suite 100, Clarkston, GA 30021.

The characters and events described in this book are fictional. Any resemblance between the characters and any person, living or dead, is purely coincidental.

The mention of or reference to any companies or products in these pages is not a challenge to the trademarks or copyrights concerned.

Because of the mature themes presented within, reader discretion is advised.

White Wolf is committed to reducing waste in publishing. For this reason, we do not permit our covers to be "stripped" in exchange for credit. Instead we require that the book be returned, allowing us to resell it.

Printed in Canada

Dedication

THIS BOOK IS DEDICATED TO ROBERT BLOCH, GRANDMASTER OF DARKNESS. MAY THE BLOOD DRAWN FROM YOUR TYPEWRITER'S KEYS SUSTAIN US ALWAYS.

Acknowledgments

THE EDITOR WOULD LIKE TO THANK STEWART WIECK AND MARK REIN·HAGEN FOR SHARING THEIR *WORLD OF DARKNESS* WITH US. YOUR INNER VISIONS REVEAL A SENSE THAT WE MAY ALL ONE DAY PERCEIVE.

Contents

Foreword

Growing up strips away children's innocence along with their belief in such icons as Santa Claus, the Tooth Fairy and the Easter Bunny. Few adults today retain these mythological symbols of hope — but fear is a completely different emotion.

It is perfectly natural for a child to fear the darkness and the creatures concealed within. Nightmares, as some call them, are often filled with vampires, werewolves, and other terrors of the dark. The funny thing is, as we grow to adulthood, these monsters don't dissipate along with our other childhood fantasies — they simply mature.

The stories contained in this volume are just that — stories. At first glance, they bear little resemblance to life itself, or certainly not to real life as we presently understand it. Each story is set in White Wolf's *World of Darkness* and focuses on the vampires, werewolves and mages that have inhabited this fictitious world — not ours — for all eternity. But as you read these accounts, you can't help but notice the striking similarities between the *World of Darkness* and the world in which we live today.

Of course, in our world, the undead fail to prosper and secret societies don't even exist. And we aren't really losing ground to nuclear waste and destroying endangered species in record numbers. Gangs of inner-city youth don't roam the streets at night looking for bodies to break and blood to drain. And vampires, werewolves and mages aren't real....

Or are they?

If one were to accept, by even the most remote possibility, that creatures from the Netherworld do share our world with us, then many of society's most intrinsic aberrations could well be explained.

And all those childhood nightmares founded.

And life would become a greater challenge — as death no longer becomes the ultimate escape.

Pleasant dreams.

— *Edward E. Kramer*
June, 1994

That Evil Stuff Again

An Introduction
by John Mason Skipp

This world is a comedy for those who think and a tragedy for those who feel.

—Horace Walpole

I know a number of people—some of whom I love very much, some of whom I love very little, all of whom come equipped with a potent persona that sets them apart from the normative herd— and these people, whatever I may think of them, share one ideological linchpin in common.

They believe that life is essentially cruel. That we're basically fucked, and that's all there is to it. That any warmth, success or happiness we manage to enjoy is, in essence, a temporal, fleeting thing: clawed by dint of sheer will or trickery from the earth's begrudging breast, then yanked back away at the earliest opportunity.

They sincerely believe, in their heart of hearts, that we were born to fight and die in a world that loves us not at all, and cares for us even less.

Frankly, it's a hard case to argue against. I am not one of those people, but I sure as hell know what they mean. If it's not the axle itself, then cruelty is *certainly* one of the primary spokes at the hub of firmament. The food chain is rooted in teeth and terror, churning animate acids that take a live wire and reduce it to a nice fat steaming turd in the time it takes to watch your average Hollywood movie (and gee, I wonder where *that* metaphor came from?). And the world of Man and Womankind is a hothouse of mayhem and willful mendacity, throttling and thriving like kudzu in spring, never resting until every last inch has been claimed.

It is not hard to know these things; and yes, that's just the way it is. Once you bite into the apple—or the apple bites you—you can never unsee. You can only stop looking. You can only forget or deny, let the two feed on each other, as they so often do.

But for those who find honor in wide-open eyes, it can then become astonishingly difficult to trust: a Promethean endeavor which—if these folks are to be believed—pretty much guarantees you an eternity strapped to the screaming, bleeding rock. Sporting a little sign that reads, "SUCKER!!!"

(It should be noted, at this point, that people—*particularly* those in question—are notoriously cruel to those who cross or disappoint them.)

So. If life has hammered you brutally somewhere along the line, and you have been paying attention, it's not a big stretch to wrap oneself in this kind of functional fatalism.

This working, acquiescent embrace of one's own dark destiny.

But here's the problem. If you hold in your soul that these truths are self-evident—true as the highest expressions of the holies and *maybe even more so*—then what on earth is stopping you from being the biggest bastard that this world has ever seen?

The question becomes: Why *not* be a monster? Why *not* just go and take anything you want? Why *not* be the thing that waits in no lines, that takes no prisoners, that suffers no fools, that rips every raw dripping chunk of pleasure from this planet's bleeding bosom and then wallows in the gore? Why *not* be the cool vampiric presence that savors the blood of its enemies, plucks virgins off the vine, rapes and drains them, then feeds them back to Gaia or, better yet, turns them into blood-hungry monsters just like you?

Why *not* join the ranks of the great Illuminati, lording fiercely hoarded knowledge and power over the great blank bleating hordes? Why *not* sit back and cackle with your other evil cronies, enjoying the best things that power can buy? Why *not*, if the tides have turned redly in your favor, seek out a life as everlasting as you can possibly snag, ward off the ultimate failure that we know as *true death* for as long as your wiles and your viciousness can sustain you?

Why *not*?

Because it makes you an asshole, that's why.

Because it feeds the flow of true evil into our world.

And believe you me, there is true evil in this world; and I've found that the people arguing most strenuously against that are either just about to start some, or are already in over their heads. I don't care how cool you think you are, or how cool you think the stance might make you: if you do the things you think about in your most pissed-off imagination, you are performing evil magick.

And you're an asshole then.

Okay?

Let's take the case of John Wayne Gacy: a serious asshole, if ever one was. This is a guy who ran a bunch of Kentucky Fried Chicken franchises, ran some weasely contracting firm for ten years after that, made himself look legit through the Jaycees or some other such civic flamdoodle, and just generally wagged his tail so well that, once, he actually scarfed himself a photo op with then-First Lady Rosalyn Carter. He was the ultimate definition of a low-rez wannabe thunkhead Illuminatoid, lording *all this great power* over his piddly little realm.

And what did he do with his leisure time? Well, he got thirty-three strapping boys to come back to his shack. He got 'em high, he showed 'em porn, he got their little motors revving. And then he showed them the Handcuff Trick, which was this: there is no trick. Except that now you're in handcuffs, and I'm gonna fuck you for a while, and then I think I'll throttle you until you black out, and then I think I'll fuck you some more.

And then I think I'll throttle and fuck you some more until I'm bored or you're dead, whichever comes first, but guaranteed you'll be dead, and then I'll drag you to my crawlspace—which got so septic with human decay that the cops had to wear fucking spacesuits to keep from dying themselves as they crawled around in there, exhuming the dead—and somehow, as a result of all this, I'm suddenly a *cool guy* with pen pals across the nation, and people buy my shitty paintings, and I'm a goddam household word.

Did it piss you off when his death knell rang, and they treated this guy like a fucking prince, and they gave him a nice hot chicken dinner and let him take a few calls and then just kinda waltzed him down to a room where they laid him out and fed him a needle full of death so humane it practically sweet-talked his ass into the Great Hereafter?

Man, I'll tell ya: it's times like that that make me pray there is a Hell; and that the first thing that smacked his beady little eyes was the sight of some demon so horrific, so *mind-blastingly bad*, that he was screaming even *before* they ripped that fucking chicken dinner right out of his ass, then proceeded to pork him till the cows came home. With not just a little bit of throttling on the side.

But hey: that's just the monster in me.

And so, yeah, I admit it. I'm a goddam monster, too. And the fact of the matter is that all of us are. Whether you want to admit it or not—and certainly whether or not you care to *embrace* it—there is an inescapable part of us that rages and wails and capers on the graves of those who try or do us wrong.

And let's be honest: fact is, half the time it doesn't even need a reason. It's rarin' to go.

It'll do it just for fun.

There is also a part of us that knows and understands this, and it is constantly under the whip. It is restrained by the part of us that bristles at the recoil; that does not love the pain; that knows that payback is a bitch. It is kept back by the leash and threat of tenfold retribution.

But is that all that holds us back?

No.

That is not all there is.

Because there are other reasons for not getting lost in the beast within. There are many other reasons for decency above and beyond the norm. And chief among them is the understanding that true coolness, true decency, comes from staring down that impulse at the core of your being, and then fighting it down in your actual life. So that you don't become a monster. So that you're not a total dick. You make your peace. You come to terms.

But you do not let it win.

As far as we can discern, the sole purpose of human existence is to kindle a light of meaning in the darkness of mere being.
—C. G. Jung

I love horror stories. I always have. And I spent a good bit of the last ten years with them as my constant companions: writing them, selling them, swimming in them, and letting them keep me alive. It was, all in all, an astonishing phase in my own little journey, and I have no regrets.

But for now, at least, it's pretty much over and done.

These days, I mostly like to sing with this cool band I'm in. We write songs, and they play, and I sing, and it feels great. These days, I often go for weeks on end without having to murder a single person. And ya know what? Without conceding an inch to my old adversaries, I must admit that it's immensely refreshing. I find myself addressing strata of my soul that had seemed to lay fallow for years upon years; that didn't quite fit in with the parade of squirting organ meats and exploding heads required to maintain my zippy li'l splatboy cachet.

So now I just swim and I swim in the music; and when I write—and you should know that I am writing all the time—it's pretty much exclusively about love.

Not that I'm reduced to gloopy greeting-card crap. I didn't get a lobotomy; I just shifted gears. These days, I write about my love for the sheer groove itself; my love of the dance, and of the waves that shape and sway us. I write about the love that I continue to find at the heart of all creation: no matter *who* tries to tell me it's all shit in the end; no matter *how* nasty or psychotic things get.

I write about heartbreak, about loves lost and dreams shattered.

I write about falling in love again.

I write about the passionate drive to be recognized for who you are, and the terrible perversities that both rejection and hubris can bring . . . because when the power of love becomes the mere love of power, then you're a sellout and a monster and you can fucking kiss my ass.

And lastly, I write about the terrible love I cannot help but feel.

For the terrible monsters we cannot help but harbor within.

That, for me, is the crucial link between the guy I used to be and the guy I am today. It's the thread of continuity that lets the center hold. Because I *love* those monsters, so romantic and so debased, trying to seize their shreds of meaning in a world gone mad with pain. And writing those horror stories was always like surfing a razored bannister, sliding down and down a cutting edge and going, *"WHOOO-EEEE!!! Are we havin' fun yet?"*

And I remember times when I was so pissed off that I was thinking, *man, if I didn't have a place to put this shit, I don't know what I'd do. I'd have to kill, and kill again.*

It is the great redeeming value of a well-told horror tale.

Because the monster needs to prowl. It needs to feed. It needs to howl. It needs to grab us by the throat and let us know how bad things are. If we don't give the beast its due, it has no choice but to devour us. And who could blame it? I can't. I know exactly how it feels.

But I have to admit that I'm lucky as hell, because I have what writer Michael Ventura calls "the talent of the room." I can sit by myself for hours on end, with nothing to distract me but my own weird thoughts; and after hours of frenzied gnashing and flailing about, I can come out with a piece of something that expresses how I feel.

And it doesn't matter, at that point, if I can't write my way out of a paper bag (as one thimbleweight critic has been kind enough to suggest). Because I have written my way out of Hell; and *that's* the thing that matters.

But not everyone is quite so darned lucky as me. Not everyone has a semi-commercial artform that lets them raise hell on the inner plane and still meet half of their bills. Not to mention being a halfway decent person on the flipside.

And that, I suspect, is where little things like reading and gaming might come in.

And now for a word from our sponsor.
                    —TV

Dark Destiny is a book that's just chock full o' monsters. In fact, most of the heroes (and virtually all of the villains) are steeped in vile hungers they cannot deny. It's a common point of view in macabre entertainment; and its tropes—vampire, werewolf, mage—are staples of the field, here subtly but deeply reworked by the context through which they are presented.

Because this is the first original anthology released by White Wolf; and the matrix of mythos playing out in these pages is derived—sometimes loosely, sometimes straight by the book—from the guidelines laid out by the White Wolf Game Studio. Since 1991, if my information serves, they have engaged in the aggressive production and dissemination of cool monster-based roleplaying games like **Vampire: The Masquerade** and **Werewolf:**

The Apocalypse. (In fact, they prefer to refer to these items as "storytelling games of personal horror," a euphemism I personally like quite a bit.) And their success has been such that they are now publishing fiction; not just this, but many others.

Keep 'em comin', I sez.

Having leafed at great length through their gaming materials, I am forced to conclude that they are hep as all get-out. A profound amount of loving labor has been expended in getting the details just right. For bright, imaginative folk who know the dream inside out, these games might just be the ticket: they offer full-on immersion in story and character, active personal involvement, and a chance to hang out with your friends! This, to me, is one excellent combination. It makes me itchy to play some. Invitations? Feel free.

It's no surprise, I hate to say, that they have met with some resistance. Some dork offs himself cuz he thinks he's a wizard, and it's a new epidemic: D&D as HIV. I would like to suggest that these games are *profoundly* healthy: that they give our monsters romping ground in the fun-filled arena of friendly play. And though this may seem glib in the extreme, you know that it's not *entirely inconceivable* that if John Wayne Gacy had brought those boys home to a nice game of **Mage: The Ascension** instead, they might still be alive today. And I wouldn't be dreaming about his ass, roasting on a spit. Forever and ever. Amen.

Having read these stories, in fact, I'm not entirely convinced that reading them is more fun than just playing the games. But rest ye assured: there's some big fun to be had.

For one thing, there's a new Harlan Ellison story. And lemme tell you something, peoples: that bad boy is *back*. He isn't playing by the rules—but then again, has he ever?—and his "Sensible City" is an awful lot like manna from Heaven to me.

Past that, there is "One of the Secret Masters", a Darrell Schweitzer romp set superbly in that place where H. P. Lovecraft and Robert Anton Wilson meet. There's a nasty little number by the great Robert Bloch, which sports the finest nonculinary use of vinegar I think I've ever seen. Nancy A. Collins waxes grand on "The Love of Monsters", and it's a lovely thing, steeped in vile history and doomed, transcendent romance.

But that's not all. Nancy Holder gets to play "Leaders of the Pack"; Lisa Lepovetsky sets "Vampire Lovers" to sweet, spare verse; C. Dean Andersson posits a refreshing speculation on the *actual* relationship between vampires and crosses; and I suspect that I will be honestly haunted forever by the ghostly slaughterhouse lowings of "Go Hungry", written by the incomparable Wayne Allen Sallee.

From there, you're on your own; and if there's a moral to this story, I suspect that it is this:

Yes, life sucks; and yes, it's a shame; and yes, we all die. But then, maybe we don't. There's a lot more to all this than Horatio dreamt of. So snuggle up to your beast. But keep the reins in your hand.

And when it's all said and done, just *be nice* to each other. It's not too much. It's all I ask.

Just be nice, okay?

Be nice.

Let us endeavor so to live that when we come to die even the undertaker will be sorry.

—Mark Twain

John Mason Skipp is a renaissance mutant: best-selling novelist and editor, screenwriter, songwriter, musician and performer of stage and screen. As one-half of Skipp & Spector, he helped radicalize contemporary horror fiction with novels like *The Light at the End* ('86) and the George Romero-inspired anthology *Book of the Dead* ('89). He appeared in Clive Barker's Nightbreed and had a brief screenwriting fling with the late Freddy Krueger. John now writes and performs with the L.A. band Mumbo's Brain; their first album, *The Book of Mumbo*, has just been completed.

Sensible City

by Harlan Ellison

uring the third week of the trial, sworn under oath, one of the Internal Affairs guys the DA's office had planted undercover in Gropp's facility attempted to describe how terrifying Gropp's smile was. The IA guy stammered some; and there seemed to be a singular absence of color in his face; but he tried valiantly, not being a poet or one given to colorful speech. And after some prodding by the Prosecutor, he said:

"You ever, y'know, when you brush your teeth . . . how when you're done, and you've spit out the toothpaste and the water, and you pull back your lips to look at your teeth, to see if they're whiter, and like that . . . you know how you tighten up your jaws real good, and make that kind of death-grin smile that pulls your lips back,

with your teeth lined up clenched in the front of your mouth . . .
you know what I mean . . . well . . ."

Sequestered that night in a downtown hotel, each of the twelve
jurors stared into a medicine cabinet mirror and skinned back a
pair of lips, and tightened neck muscles till the cords stood out,
and clenched teeth, and stared at a face grotesquely contorted.
Twelve men and women then superimposed over the mirror
reflection the face of the Defendant they'd been staring at for three
weeks, and approximated the smile they had *not* seen on Gropp's
face all that time.

And in that moment of phantom face over reflection face,
Gropp was convicted.

Police Lieutenant W.R. Gropp. Rhymed with *crop*. The meat-
man who ruled a civic smudge called the Internment Facility when
it was listed on the City Council's budget every year. Internment
Facility: dripping wet, cold iron, urine smell mixed with sour liquor
sweated through dirty skin, men and women crying in the night.
A stockade, a prison camp, stalag, ghetto, torture chamber, charnel
house, abattoir, duchy, fiefdom, Army co-op mess hall ruled by a
neckless thug.

The last of the thirty-seven inmate alumni who had been
subpoenaed to testify recollected, "Gropp's favorite thing was to
take some fool outta his cell, get him nekkid to the skin, then do
this *rolling* thing t'him."

When pressed, the former tenant of Gropp's hostelry – not a
felon, merely a steamfitter who had had a bit too much to drink
and picked up for himself a ten-day Internment Facility residency
for D&D – explained that this "rolling thing'" entailed "Gropp
wrappin' his big, hairy sausage arm aroun' the guy's neck, see, and
then he'd *roll him* across the bars, real hard and fast. Bangin' the
guy's head like a roulette ball around the wheel. Clank clank, like
that. Usual, it'd knock the guy flat out cold, his head clankin' across
the bars and spaces between, wham wham wham like that. See

his eyes go up outta sight, all white; but Gropp, he'd hang on with that sausage aroun' the guy's neck, whammin' and bangin' him and takin' some goddam kinda pleasure mentionin' how much bigger this criminal bastard was than *he* was. Yeah, fer sure. That was Gropp's fav'rite part, that he always pulled out some poor nekkid sonofabitch was twice his size.

"That's how four of these guys he's accused of doin', that's how they croaked. With Gropp's sausage 'round the neck. I kept my mouth shut; I'm lucky to get outta there in one piece."

Frightening testimony, last of thirty-seven. But as superfluous as feathers on an eggplant. From the moment of superimposition of phantom face over reflection face, Police Lieutenant W.R. Gropp was on greased rails to spend his declining years for Brutality While Under Color of Service – a *serious* offense – in a maxi-galleria stuffed chockablock with felons whose spiritual brethren he had maimed, crushed, debased, blinded, butchered, and killed.

Similarly destined was Gropp's gigantic Magog, Deputy Sergeant Michael "Mickey" Rizzo, all three hundred and forty pounds of him; brainless malevolence stacked six feet four inches high in his steel-toed, highly-polished service boots. Mickey had only been indicted on seventy counts, as opposed to Gropp's eighty-four ironclad atrocities. But if he managed to avoid Sentence of Lethal Injection for having crushed men's heads underfoot, he would certainly go to the maxi-galleria mall of felonious behavior for the rest of his simian life.

Mickey had, after all, pulled a guy up against the inside of the bars and kept bouncing him till he ripped the left arm loose from its socket, ripped it off, and later dropped it on the mess hall steam table just before dinner assembly.

Squat, bulletheaded troll, Lieutenant W.R. Gropp, and the mindless killing machine, Mickey Rizzo. On greased rails.

So they jumped bail together, during the second hour of jury deliberation.

Why wait? Gropp could see which way it was going, even counting on Blue Loyalty. The city was putting the abyss between the Dept., and him and Mickey. So, why wait? Gropp was a sensible guy, very pragmatic, no bullshit. So they jumped bail together, having made arrangements weeks before, as any sensible felon keen to flee would have done.

Gropp knew a chop shop that owed him a favor. There was a throaty and hemi-speedy, immaculately registered, four year old Firebird just sitting in a bay on the fifth floor of a seemingly-abandoned garment factory, two blocks from the courthouse.

And just to lock the barn door after the horse, or in this case the Pontiac, had been stolen, Gropp had Mickey toss the chop shop guy down the elevator shaft of the factory. It was the sensible thing to do. After all, the guy's neck *was* broken.

By the time the jury came in, later that night, Lieut. W.R. Gropp was out of the state and somewhere near Boise. Two days later, having taken circuitous routes, the Firebird was on the other side of both the Snake River and the Rockies, between Rock Springs and Laramie. Three days after that, having driven in large circles, having laid over in Cheyenne for dinner and a movie, Gropp and Mickey were in Nebraska.

Wheat ran to the sun, blue storms bellowed up from horizons, and heat trembled on the edge of each leaf. Crows stirred inside fields, lifted above shattered surfaces of grain and flapped into sky. That's what it looked like: the words came from a poem.

They were smack in the middle of the plains state, above Grand Island, below Norfolk, somewhere out in the middle of nowhere, just tooling along, leaving no trail, deciding to go that way to Canada, or the other way to Mexico. Gropp had heard there were business opportunities in Mazatlan.

It was a week after the jury had been denied the pleasure of seeing Gropp's face as they said, "Stick the needle in the brutal sonofabitch. Fill the barrel with a very good brand of weed-killer, stick the needle in the brutal sonofabitch's chest, and slam home the plunger. Guilty, your honor, guilty on charges one through eighty-four. Give'im the weed-killer and let's watch the fat scumbag do his dance!" A week of swift and leisurely driving here and there, doubling back and skimming along easily.

And somehow, earlier this evening, Mickey had missed a turnoff, and now they were on a stretch of superhighway that didn't seem to have any important exits. There were little towns now and then, the lights twinkling off in the mid-distance, but if they were within miles of a major metropolis, the map didn't give them clues as to where they might be.

"You took a wrong turn."

"Yeah, huh?"

"Yeah, *exactly* huh. Keep your eyes on the road."

"I'm sorry, Looten'nt."

"No. Not Lieutenant. I told you."

"Oh, yeah, right. Sorry, Mr. Gropp."

"Not Gropp. Jensen. Mister *Jensen*. You're *also* Jensen; my kid brother. Your name is Daniel."

"I got it, I remember: Harold and Daniel Jensen is us. You know what I'd like?"

"No, what would you like?"

"A box'a Grape-Nuts. I could have 'em here in the car, and when I got a mite peckish I could just dip my hand in an' have a mouthful. I'd like that."

"Keep your eyes on the road."

"So whaddaya think?"

"About what?"

"About maybe I swing off next time and we go into one'a these little towns and maybe a 7-Eleven'll be open, and I can get a box'a Grape-Nuts? We'll need some gas after a while, too. See the little arrow there?"

"I see it. We've still got half a tank. Keep driving."

Mickey pouted. Gropp paid no attention. There were drawbacks to forced traveling companionship. But there were many cul-de-sacs and landfills between this stretch of dark turnpike and New Brunswick, Canada or Mazatlan, state of Sinaloa.

"What is this, the Southwest?" Gropp asked, looking out the side window into utter darkness. "The Midwest? What?"

Mickey looked around, too. "I dunno. Pretty out here, though. Real quiet and pretty."

"It's pitch dark."

"Yeah, huh?"

"Just drive, for godsake. Pretty. Jeezus!"

They rode in silence for another twenty-seven miles, then Mickey said, "I gotta go take a piss."

Gropp exhaled mightily. Where were the cul-de-sacs, where were the landfills? "Okay. Next town of any size, we can take the exit and see if there's decent accommodations. You can get a box of Grape-Nuts, and use the toilet; I can have a cup of coffee and study the map in better light. Does that sound like a good idea, to you . . . Daniel?"

"Yes, Harold. See, I remembered!'"

"The world is a fine place."

They drove for another sixteen miles, and came nowhere in sight of a thruway exit sign. But the green glow had begun to creep up from the horizon.

"What the hell is that?" Gropp asked, running down his power window. "Is that some kind of a forest fire, or something? What's that look like to you?"

"Like green in the sky."

"Have you ever thought how lucky you are that your mother abandoned you, Mickey?" Gropp said wearily. "Because if she hadn't, and if they hadn't brought you to the county jail for temporary housing till they could put you in a foster home, and I hadn't taken an interest in you, and hadn't arranged for you to live with the

Rizzos, and hadn't let you work around the lockup, and hadn't made you my deputy, do you have any idea where you'd be today?" He paused for a moment, waiting for an answer, realized the entire thing was rhetorical – not to mention pointless – and said, "Yes, it's green in the sky, pal, but it's also something odd. Have you ever seen 'green in the sky' before? Anywhere? Any time?"

"No, I guess I haven't." Gropp sighed, and closed his eyes.

They drove in silence another nineteen miles, and the green miasma in the air had enveloped them. It hung above and around them like sea-fog, chill and with tiny droplets of moisture that Mickey fanned away with the windshield wipers. It made the landscape on either side of the superhighway faintly visible, cutting the impenetrable darkness, but it also induced a wavering, ghostly quality to the terrain.

Gropp turned on the map light in the dome of the Firebird, and studied the map of Nebraska. He murmured, "I haven't got a rat's-fang of any idea where the hell we *are*! There isn't even a freeway like this indicated here. You took some helluva wrong turn 'way back there, pal!!" Dome light out.

"I'm sorry, Loo – Harold . . ."

A large reflective advisement marker, green and white, came up on their right. It said: FOOD GAS LODGING   10 MILES.

The next sign said: EXIT   7 MILES.

The next sign said: OBEDIENCE   3 MILES.

Gropp turned the map light on again. He studied the venue. "Obedience? What the hell kind of 'Obedience'? There's nothing like that *anywhere*. What is this, an old map? Where did you get this map?"

"Gas station."

"Where?"

"I dunno. Back a long ways. That place we stopped with the root beer stand next to it."

Gropp shook his head, bit his lip, murmured nothing in

particular. "Obedience," he said. "Yeah, huh?"

They began to see the town off to their right before they hit the exit turnoff. Gropp swallowed hard and made a sound that caused Mickey to look over at him. Gropp's eyes were large, and Mickey could see the whites.

"What'sa matter, Loo . . . Harold?"

"You see that town out there?" His voice was trembling.

Mickey looked to his right. Yeah, he saw it. Horrible.

Many years ago, when Gropp was briefly a college student, he had taken a warm-body course in Art Appreciation. One oh one, it was; something basic and easy to ace, a snap, all you had to do was show up. Everything you wanted to know about Art from aboriginal cave drawings to Diego Rivera. One of the paintings that had been flashed on the big screen for the class, a sleepy 8:00 AM class, had been *The Nymph Echo* by Max Ernst. A green and smoldering painting of an ancient ruin overgrown with writhing plants that seemed to have eyes and purpose and a malevolently jolly life of their own, as they swarmed and slithered and overran the stone vaults and altars of the twisted, disturbingly resonant sepulcher. Like a sebaceous cyst, something corrupt lay beneath the emerald fronds and hungry black soil.

Mickey looked to his right at the town. Yeah, he saw it. Horrible.

"Keep driving!" Gropp yelled, as his partner-in-flight started to slow for the exit ramp.

Mickey heard, but his reflexes were slow. They continued to drift to the right, toward the rising egress lane. Gropp reached across and jerked the wheel hard to the left. "I said: *keep driving!*"

The Firebird slewed, but Mickey got it back under control in a moment, and in another moment they were abaft the ramp, then past it, and speeding away from the nightmarish site beyond and slightly below the superhighway. Gropp stared mesmerized as they swept past. He could see buildings that leaned at obscene angles, the green fog that rolled through the haunted streets, the shadowy

24

forms of misshapen things that skulked at every dark opening.

"That was a real scary-lookin' place, Looten . . . Harold. I don't think I'd of wanted to go down there even for the Grape-Nuts. But maybe if we'd've gone real fast . . ."

Gropp twisted in the seat toward Mickey as much as his muscle-fat body would permit. "Listen to me. There is this tradition, in horror movies, in mysteries, in tv shows, that people are always going into haunted houses, into graveyards, into battle zones, like assholes, like stone idiots! You know what I'm talking about here? Do you?"

Mickey said, "Uh . . . "

"All right, let me give you an example. Remember we went to see that movie *Alien*? Remember how scared you were?"

Mickey bobbled his head rapidly, his eyes widened in frightened memory.

"Okay. So now, you remember that part where the guy who was a mechanic, the guy with the baseball cap, he goes off looking for a cat or somedamnthing? Remember? He left everyone else, and he wandered off by himself. And he went into that big cargo hold with the water dripping on him, and all those chains hanging down, and shadows everywhere . . . *do you recall that?*"

Mickey's eyes were chalky potholes. He remembered, oh yes; he remembered clutching Gropp's jacket sleeve till Gropp had been compelled to slap his hand away.

"And you remember what happened in the movie? In the theater? You remember everybody yelling, 'Don't go in there, you asshole! The thing's in there, you moron! Don't go in there!' But, remember, he *did*, and the thing came up behind him all those teeth, and it bit his stupid head off! Remember that?"

Mickey hunched over the wheel, driving fast.

"Well, that's the way people are. They ain't sensible! They go into places like that, you can see are death places; and they get chewed up or the blood sucked outta their necks or used for kindling

25

. . . but I'm no moron, I'm a sensible guy and I got the brains my mama gave me, and I don't go *near* places like that. So drive like a sonofabitch, and get us outta here, and we'll get your damned Grape-Nuts in Idaho or somewhere . . . if we ever get off this road..."

Mickey murmured, "I'm sorry, Lieuten'nt. I took a wrong turn or somethin'."

"Yeah, yeah. Just keep driv –" The car was slowing.

It was a frozen moment. Gropp exultant, no fool he, to avoid the cliché, to stay out of that haunted house, that ominous dark closet, that damned place. Let idiot others venture off the freeway, into the town that contained the basement entrance to Hell, or whatever. Not he, not Gropp!

He'd outsmarted the obvious.

In that frozen moment.

As the car slowed. Slowed, in the poisonous green mist.

And on their right, the obscenely frightening town of Obedience, that they had left in their dust five minutes before, was coming up again on the superhighway.

"Did you take another turnoff?"

"Uh . . . no, I . . . uh, I been just driving fast . . ."

The sign read: NEXT RIGHT 5O YDS. OBEDIENCE.

The car was slowing. Gropp craned his neckless neck to get a proper perspective on the fuel gauge. He was a pragmatic kind of a guy, no nonsense, and very practical; but they were out of gas.

The Firebird slowed and slowed and finally rolled to a stop.

In the rearview mirror Gropp saw the green fog rolling up thicker onto the roadway; and emerging over the burm, in a jostling, slavering horde, clacking and drooling, dropping decayed body parts and leaving glistening trails of worm ooze as they dragged their deformed pulpy bodies across the blacktop, their snake-slit eyes gleaming green and yellow in the mist, the residents of Obedience clawed and slithered and crimped toward the car.

It was common sense any Better Business Bureau would have

applauded: if the tourist trade won't come to your town, take your town to the tourists. Particularly if the freeway has forced commerce to pass you by. Particularly if your town needs fresh blood to prosper. Particularly if you have the civic need to share.

Green fog shrouded the Pontiac, and the peculiar sounds that came from within. Don't go into that dark room is a sensible attitude. Particularly in a sensible city.

Harlan Ellison's writing career has spanned over forty years. He has won more awards for his 45 books, 1300+ stories, essays, articles and newspaper columns, two dozen teleplays and a dozen motion pictures than any other living fantasist. Harlan has served as creative consultant on the revival of the series *The Twilight Zone* and presently as creative consultant for *Babylon 5*. He can also be seen weekly as host of Sci-Fi Channel's *Sci-Fi Buzz*.

Dreaming Saturn

by James S. Dorr

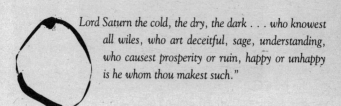

Lord Saturn the cold, the dry, the dark . . . who knowest all wiles, who art deceitful, sage, understanding, who causest prosperity or ruin, happy or unhappy is he whom thou makest such."

From Franz Cumont, *Astrology and Religion Among the Greeks and Romans* (New York: Dover, 1960)

It was blood that kept them together,
blood at first,
but later they discovered men's dreams and preyed, also,
      on fear.
Their numbers were always small — one dozen, two dozen —
they waxed and waned, though always their strength grew,
their own blood-lust dreaming.
They devoured their children.
They lived in the cities, cities they helped build, where
      hope congregated,
feeding at random,
building nests underground where blackness reigns
even at highest sunlight,
where they could hollow vast pens in the virgin earth
interconnecting with tunnels and walkways,
hollows to keep their slaves,
parody-dwellings to rise from at night when,
singly or in rare pairs,
they sought the warmth of their victims' drowsing.

———

Slaves, yes! They packed bodies into their earth homes,
sometimes eating them after they'd bred them —
but later, as they grew in their power,
they learned to influence men's minds directly,
to serve them, unshackled,
as beasts, self-slaughtering at their masters' whim.

———

They changed their names often.

———

These were the child-eaters, the dream-destroyers,
the dark creators:
Saturn, the Black Sun, called Kala-Siva,
worshiped as Lord of Death;
Rhea, his sister-wife;
Mimas, the ruler of Earth's volcanoes;
two-faced Iapetus who, out of Gaea, was sire to Prometheus,
      himself twice traitor;
foolish Pandora, who loosed pain and longing;
moon-strider Phoebe;
vampyr; vrykoklass; others, named old and new —
bee-goul Melissa and Annchuck, the night-seeker;
Kestrel and cat-Bast;
Enceladus; Dione;
Armida;
Coyote.
Female, they sought youth, channeling night-fears,
guised now as *Lamiae*, snake-limbed seductresses,
draining the breath of life, leaving behind shriveled flesh
      and cold ashes;
as male they were vanquishers, ravishing whom they would —
scattering seed husks.
They taught men cave-dwelling;
they taught the need for protection from darkness.
They built the first weapons.
Later, when they fought their twins, the Olympians, and
vanquished themselves were cast down from the Heavens,
they stole fire down with them and taught men to work
      bronze,
to cast shields and spearheads.
They reveled in slaughter.

———

Prometheus. Pandora. Giver and taker.

Nephew and niece to the first generation.

Saturn, destroyer, father of all who, master of time and yet
fearing the future,

devoured his own children until Rhea, angry, secreted one in
a cave,

naming him Zeus and feeding him bee-milk,

honey and pollened wax,

spurting her own milk across the sky of stars.

Saturn returning, she swaddled a boulder;

she gave it up to him telling him, "Here, Lord. Take this,
the greatest of all your children."

And Saturn took it into his arms and rocked it gently.

He held it out from him and raised it slowly above his head,

and gazed at it, loving it in his way,

then stretched his jaws and thrust it down into him,

gulping and swallowing,

into his gut where it swirled with the others — the others
of his flesh he'd eaten before it —

and caused him to vomit.

He spewed forth his progeny in bile and hatred,

in blood and acid:

fat, ox-assed Hera, the vain, the vindictive;

Hestia;

Demeter — she of the mare's head;

wealth-loving Pluto, who clutched even past the grave;

greed-filled Poseidon, who raped his own sister, then built
and betrayed Troy

— children and grandchildren —

Athena, owl-bitch;

whore Aphrodite;
crippled Hephaestus who, for his deformity, was later cast
      down by his own natural mother . . . .
He laughed when he saw them lie, bile-drenched, before him;
when tyrant Zeus, unscathed, emerged from his cave-bunting;
because he knew in time they would wane also,
all but forgotten,
while he and *his* cohorts would always endure.

———

Earthbound, all godhood lost, they, once called Titans,
      became man's protectors.
Remained his destroyers — the givers and takers.
They taught him to forge iron, to make swords and later
      guns.
They taught him how to build dwellings together to form the
      first cities at bases of mountains —
Aetna, Vesuvius,
Idhi and Fuji —
to dredge the first harbors.
They helped him to build Pompeii, City of Mimas,
Ur, Maracandra, Sodom and Jericho,
glittering Babylon,
Cusco and Changan.
They helped and they waited, skulking in alleys, biding
      their own time in darkened earth-burrows.
They taught him to smelt gold,
to raise the first armies.
They waited and watched as the world exploded.
They wallowed in blood-roil.
They breathed fire and sulfur —
City of Mimas! —

33

as mountain tops shattered,
towers fell, walls crumbled,
flesh cauterized to bone, bubbling and blackening,
drowning out even screams,
even the stench of women's hair burning.

———

As later, in masks of ghouls, they sifted through an entire
    city's wreckage.
Oh, yes! they were stronger now. Sifting through ash, they
    read the inscriptions,
graffiti of nations:
Cunnus polosus melior est quam cunnus abrasus —
melior, better than, that which is hairless in style of the
    plucked and perfumed *hetaeirae,*
the temple prostitutes,
minions of Saturn who giveth.
Who taketh . . . .
Blood and semen.
Incubi, succubi.
Burnt blood of witches.
Phoebe in new dress.
Rhea, the bitch-mother, cast as a madam,
a spread of diseases.
Prometheus, fire-bringer.
Desert air split as a miniature sun burst,
firing dust upward.

———

A four-engine bomber droning, alone, through cerulean skies,
    lifting over Hiroshima.

Bright Nagasaki.
A shadow, in white, etched on flame-blackened walls, of a
child, arms raised upward,
a woman running.
A fire-melted tower, its steel frame twisted.
And, after, the living, tortured breath rasping as flesh
    still courses from carbonized bone,
lungs too collapsed to scream,
skin boiling, agonized,
begging with blinded eyes only for death-mercy
— *Age of the Atom!* —
while, slowly, through ashes,
sift Saturn and Rhea,
Phoebe,
Enceladus,
Mimas and Dione, Iapetus, Tethys,
the Siva-Destroyers,
the dark persuaders,
the feeders on men's souls.

———

They still walk among us.

James S. Dorr is a full-time free-lance non-fiction writer and a
semi-professional musician with Die Aufblitzentanzetruppe (*The
Flash Dance Band*). He is a two-time Rhysling Award finalist for
his poems "Dagda" (*Grails*) and "A Neo-Canterbury Tale: The Hog
Drover's Tale" (*Fantasy Book*). His chapbook of horror poetry is
entitled *Towers of Darkness*.

The Scent of Vinegar

by Robert Bloch

Every Saturday night Tim and Bernie went bowling at the whorehouse.

"It didn't look like a whorehouse," Bernie said. "At least not any more than the places most of us lived in back then. And the damn thing was perched so high above Beverly Hills you'd have to look down to see King Vidor's spread." The old man glanced at Greg, the cigar in his hand semaphoring apology. "Sorry, I keep forgetting we're talking 1949. You've probably never even heard of the man."

"King Vidor." Greg paused. "He directed *The Big Parade*. And Bette Davis in *Beyond the Forest*, the picture where she says 'What a dump!' Right?"

Bernie aimed the cigar at Greg. "How old are you?"

"Twenty-six."

"I'm seventy-six." Bernie's eyes narrowed behind his hornrims. "Where'd you hear about Vidor?"

"Same place I heard about you," Greg said. "I'm a student of Hollywood history."

"And whorehouses." Bernie's dry chuckle rose, then ceased as pursed lips puffed on the cigar.

Greg Kolmer grinned. "They're part of Hollywood history too. The part I couldn't find in books."

Bernie was nodding. "In those days everything was hush-hush, and if you didn't keep your mouth shut, Howard Strickling shut it for you."

"Wasn't he publicity director at MGM?"

"Right again." Bernie's cigar gestured benediction. "He's the guy who said the first duty of a publicity man is to keep the news out of the paper." Another chuckle. "He knew everything. Including where Tim and I did our bowling."

"Was it really that big of a deal? I mean, all those stories about living it up out here —"

"— are true." Bernie said. "You think sex was invented by Madonna or some hot-dog computer hacks over at Cal Tech? Let me tell you, in the old days we had it all. Straights, gays, bi-, tri-: anything you wanted, you could get. You bring the ladder, we furnish the giraffe."

"Then why were you covering up?"

"Censorship. Simple as that. Everybody knew the rules and cooperated, or else. Tim and I were in management at the same studio; not top-level, but our names were on parking slots. So we weren't going to risk the 'or else' part, if you follow me."

Greg nodded, concealing his impatience. Because that was the only way to get Bernie to tell him what he really wanted to hear. And Bernie would tell him, sooner or later, because he had nothing else to do, sitting in this rundown old house on the wrong side of Wilshire with no friends to talk to, because you can't talk to the dead. Which is probably why he'd agreed to talk to Greg, was talking to him now.

"You take the stars," Bernie was saying. "The smart ones never fooled around with anybody under contract on their own lot. Getting involved with somebody you were liable to see every day was too risky; too much pressure, and you couldn't just walk away. So they patronized the hook-shops." Bernie's face crumpled in an old man's grin. "What do you suppose the folks in Peoria would say if they knew their favorite loverboy had to pay to play, just like the guy next door?"

"I doubt if many people in Peoria went to brothels in those days," Greg said.

"Maybe not." Bernie flicked cigar ash as he spoke. "But we did. Tim and I hung out at Kitty Earnshaw's. Great old broad, a million laughs."

Greg leaned forward. *At last. Now it's coming.* "The one who had this house up in the hills you were talking about?"

"Right. Kitty was the best. And her girls were user-friendly."

"Where was this place?"

Bernie spiraled his cigar in a northerly direction and more ash fell carpetward. "Way off Benedict Canyon somewhere, past Angelo. Been more than forty years since I've been up there, I don't remember —"

"Why'd you stop going?"

"Kitty Earnshaw retired, got married or religion or something. The new management was different, everyone Oriental. Not just Japs or Chinese, but girls from places like Burma, Singapore, Java, all over. Woman in charge never showed her face when I was there, but I heard stories. Marquess de Sade, that's what they called her."

"Marquis de Sade?"

39

"Marquess. A gag, I guess. But the place was getting a little too kinky for me. Like the night I met some drunk down at the bar and he says, 'You pick a girl yet? Take the one with the glass eye — she gives good socket.'"

Bernie shrugged. "Maybe that was a gag too, but I saw enough to make me start wondering. The chains and bondage scene — you know, with the little whips and the handcuffs on the bedposts, all four of them, and the Swiss Army knives. Anyhow, I stopped going there."

"And your friend Tim?"

"I don't know. Studio dropped him when television took over out here. What happened to him after that I can't say."

"Did you ever try to find out?"

The old man stubbed his cigar in the ashtray. "Look, Mr. Kolmer, I'm getting a little tired, so if you don't mind —"

"I understand, sir." Greg smiled. "And I want to thank you. You've been very helpful." He rose. "Just one other thing. The location of this place we've been talking about. If you could be more specific —"

Bernie frowned. "All I remember, it was east of Benedict. Dirt road, probably been washed out for years now." He hesitated. "Come to think, the place must have been burned out in that big fire back in the Sixties."

"I could look it up," Greg said. "Fire Department records."

"Don't waste your time. The place wasn't even in Beverly Hills city limits, or L.A. either. Area up there is no-man's-land, which is why the house could operate. Nobody was sure who had jurisdiction."

"I see." Greg turned. "Thanks again."

The old man walked him to the door. "Don't do it," he said.

"Do what?"

"Don't try going up there. Look, it's none of my affair. But for your own good I'm telling you —"

"Telling me or warning me?"

"Call it advice. From somebody who knows."

"Knows what?"

The old man smiled, but his voice was somber. "That house up there is no place to take a bowling ball."

Greg didn't go up there with a bowling ball.

He didn't even take a Thomas map, because the place Bernie Tanner had told him about wasn't on the map. The area was blank, which meant there was no access unless Greg could locate that dirt road, which might or might not still exist.

It took Greg almost two hours of cursing up and down Benedict before he found the path. And it was scarcely more than that, at best a winding trail. The entrance was so overgrown with scrub that it couldn't be seen from the lane leading to it, and the stretch spiraling around the hillside was invisible from below, choked with weed and sage.

At first Greg wasn't sure it was wide enough even for his small car, but he had to chance it; chance the ruts and ridges and clumps of vegetation that punished tires and driver alike as the little hatchback went into a slow low. Without air conditioning it was like trying to breathe with a plastic bag over your head, and by the time he was halfway up the hillside he wished he hadn't started.

Or *almost* wished. Only the thought of what might be on the summit kept him going, through the stifle of heat and the buzz of insect swarm.

The car stalled abruptly, and Greg broke into panic-ooze. Then the transmission kicked in again, and he sweated some more as a bump in the road sent the hatchback veering left, pitching Greg against the door. Beneath underbrush bordering a curve he caught a sudden sickening glimpse of the emptiness just beyond the edge, an emptiness ending in a tangle of treetops a thousand feet below.

Greg fought the wheel, and the car lurched back on an even

course. The road must have been better in the old days: even so, it was one bitch of a trip to make just to go bowling. But that was Bernie Tanner's business and Bernie Tanner's road.

Greg's own road stretched back a lot farther than the bottom of this hill, all the way back to Tex Taylor, a onetime cowboy star at the Motion Picture Country Home. He had all those stories about the old days in Hollywood, and that's all Greg had wanted at first: just some kind of lead-in he could work up into a piece for one of those checkout-counter rags. He'd been selling that kind of stuff long enough to get used to the idea he'd never win a Pulitzer Prize.

But what the dying western wino told him gave sudden startling hope of another kind of prize — one that might have awaited presentation for nearly half a century up there at what Tex Taylor called the House of Pain. That's what he said its name was, after the Asian woman took over and began to give quality time to S-and-M freaks. Maybe it was all a crock, but it sounded possible, certainly worth a trip up there to find out.

Trouble was that Tex Taylor was borderline senile and couldn't remember exactly where this weirdo whorehouse was located. But he did, finally, come up with the name of somebody he'd seen there in the glory days. And that's how Greg got hold of Bernie Tanner.

Greg wondered if Bernie had any money. Today anything with a Beverly Hills address could probably fetch a mil or so on the current market. Maybe Bernie would pay him a mil or so just for old time's sake, just out of pride.

And there were others like Bernie still around, stars and directors and producers who were bankable way back when; some of them had saved their money or put it into real estate and led comfortable, quiet lives in Bel Air or Holmby Hills. If Bernie would pay a million, how much would all the others be willing to fork over, given the proper motivation?

Greg grinned at the thought. And then, as the car swung around the last curve, his grin widened.

He had reached the summit. And on the summit was the house.

Hey, it wasn't the Taj Mahal or Buckingham Palace or even the men's washroom at the Universal Tour. But the bottom line was it hadn't burned or gone down in an earthquake or been bulldozed by a developer. It was still here, standing in shadowy silhouette against the late afternoon sun.

Greg took a flashlight from the glove compartment and clipped it to his belt. Then he reached into the compartment again and found there was just enough left in the envelope for a little toot, enough to keep him bright-eyed and bushy-tailed while he did whatever he'd have to do up here. He waited for the rush, then got out and lifted the hood to let the steam escape. There'd be no water up here, and probably no gas or electricity; they must have had their own generator.

He stared up at the two-story structure. Frame, of course; nobody could have hauled machinery here for stone or concrete construction. The roof had lost its share of shingles, and paint peeled from boards that had once been white, but the building's bulk was impressive. Half a dozen boarded-up windows were ranked on either side of the front door: tall windows for a tall house. Greg closed his eyes and for a moment day was night and the windows blazed with the light of a thousand candles, the front door opened wide in welcome, the classic cars rolled up the driveway, headlights aglitter, wheels gleaming with chrome. And off behind the distant hills the moon was rising, rising over the House of Pain.

It was the toot, of course, and now moonlight shimmered into sunlight and he was back in the teeth of searing heat, radiator-boil, insect-buzz.

Greg walked over to the double door. Its weathered, sun-blistered surface barred intrusion, and at waist level the divided doors were secured by lock and chain. Both were rusty; too much to expect that he could just walk up and yank his way in.

But it happened. The chain gave, then came free in his fist, covering his palm and fingers with powdery particles of rust from the parted links. He tugged and the door swung outward. Hinges screeched.

Greg was in the house and the house was in him.

Its shadows entered his eyes, its silence invaded his ears, its dust and decay filled his lungs. How long had it been since these windows were first boarded, this door locked? How many years had the house stood empty in the dark? Houses that once were thronged with people, throbbed to their pleasure and their pain — houses like this were hungry for life.

Greg withdrew the flashlight from his belt, flicking it on and fanning the beam for inspection. *What a dump!*

He was standing in a foyer with a solid wall directly ahead, archways opening at left and right. He moved right, along a carpet thickly strewn with dust long undisturbed, and found himself in a room that he imagined must take up most of this wing. A huge Oriental rug covered the floor; its design was obscured and fraying, but Greg thought he could detect the outline of a dragon. Sofas and chairs were grouped along three sides beneath gilt-framed paintings which, Greg noted, might have served as centerfolds for the *Kama Sutra*. Angled at the far corner was a piano, a concert grand. Once upon a time somebody had spent a lot of money furnishing this place, but right now it needed maid service.

Greg's flashlight crawled the walls, searching for shelves and bookcases, but there were none. The fourth side of the room was covered by a row of tattered drapes hung before the boarded-up windows. The drapery may also have displayed the dragon pattern, but outlines had faded; its fiery breath was long extinguished.

Greg crossed the foyer and went into the other wing. It turned out to be a bar, and at one time may have resembled Rick's place in *Casablanca*, but now the set was struck. The room was a tangle of upended tables and overturned wooden chairs, flanked by booths on two walls and tattered drapery on the third. Along the fourth wall was the bar, with a big mirror behind it, bordered on both sides by shelves and cupboards that had once displayed bottles and glasses but now held only heaps of shard. The mirror itself was cracked and mottled with mold. *Here's looking at you, kid.*

At one side of the bar a door led to what must have been the kitchen; on the other side an archway framed the base of a staircase beyond. Skirting the maze of tables and chairs, Greg headed for the archway.

Upstairs would be the bedrooms and maybe the private quarters of the Marquess or whatever she called herself. The place looked as if it had been abandoned in a hurry; the padlocked door and boarded-up windows may have been the results of a return visit. But why leave all the furnishings? Greg had no answer, but he hoped to find one. And find what else might also have been abandoned.

The stairs' worn padding muffled his footsteps, but creaking began when he reached the long hallway off the upper landing. It echoed again as he opened and closed the doors lining both sides of the corridor.

All led to bedrooms, each with its own indecorous decor. Here lay a round bed surrounded and surmounted by mirrors, but the sumptuous bedspread was riddled with moth-holes and the mirrors reflected only the light of Greg's flashlight beam. In another room stood a bare marble slab with metal cuffs and an assortment of chains hanging from ends and sides. The marble top was flecked, the metal attachments reddened with rust, not blood. And the whips on the wall rack dangled impotently; the case of knives and needles and surgical shears held pain captive through the empty years.

Empty years, empty rooms. Wall mural obscenities turned into absurdities by the crisscross of cracks, the random censorship of fading over decades of decay.

But where were those private quarters: an office, someplace to keep the books, the files, the cash, and maybe — just maybe — what he was looking for? He hadn't gone through all this just to chase shadows. What the hell was he doing here anyway, prowling through a deserted whorehouse at sunset? The johns didn't come to these places looking for starkness and desolation; tricks were supposed to be welcomed. But what had he found except rot and ruin, a bar full of broken bottles, a parlor piano that grinned at him with keys like rows of yellowed teeth? Damn it, why didn't somebody tend to a customer? *Company, girls!*

Greg came to the end of the corridor, reached the last room on the left. There'd been nothing here now and maybe ever. Tex Taylor was lying, the old rummy had no proof, and he was just doing a number like the old ham he was, using Greg as an audience for the big deathbed-revelation scene. Who said people had to tell the truth just because they were dying?

He opened the door on a bedroom just like all the others, dark and deserted: bare walls and bare bureau top, empty chair and empty bed.

At least that's what he thought at first glance. But when he looked again he saw the shadow. A dark shadow, lying on the bed.

And now, in the flashlight's beam, the shadow turned to gold.

There was a golden girl lying on the bed, a golden girl with a jet-black halo of hair framing an almost feline face — slanted eyes closed in slumber above high cheekbones, coral curvature of lips relaxed in repose. The flashlight beam swept across her nudity, its light lending luster to the gold of her flesh.

Only one detail marred perfection. As Greg stared down he saw the spider. The big black spider, emerging from her pubic nest and crawling slowly upward across her naked belly.

Greg stifled his gasp as he realized the girl was dead.

She opened her eyes.

She opened her eyes and smiled up at him, opened her mouth and flicked a thin pink tongue in a sensual circle over the coral lips. Her smile widened, revealing twin razor-rows of teeth.

Now, still smiling, the girl sat up. She raised both arms, hands coming to rest on either side of the throat hidden by the dark tumble of her hair. The long fingers splayed, tightening their grip as if trying to wrench the head free.

Then the girl tugged, lifting her head off her neck.

She was still smiling.

And Greg was still gasping as he turned, stumbled from the room, down the hall and the stairs, through the littered bar below, the cobwebbed foyer. Then the door at last: *open fast, don't look back, slam it tight.*

The house had been dark, but now it was dark outside as well, and Greg was grateful he'd somehow managed to retain his flashlight. He ran to the car, keyed the ignition, sent the hatchback circling to the spot where the road wound down, down in the dark, around narrow curves, twisting trees. It didn't matter as long as he kept going down, going away from there, that place and that thing he'd seen —

Or *thought* he'd seen.

Someone doesn't just reach up and lift her head off her neck; nobody can do such a thing, loosening the red, blood-choked strands of the arteries and the darker filaments of veins all twined against the central cord of the esophagus with a flashlight beam shining on its coating of slime. You don't imagine details like that, you have to see them. And he *had* seen, it had happened, this was real.

But what was it?

Greg didn't know, but Bernie would. That had to be why the old man warned him about going up there, going to where it waited in the dark.

The clock on the dash told Greg it was 9:30. Most elderly people go to bed early, but a few stay up for the news. And tonight Bernie would be one of them, because Greg had news for him.

It took a half-hour to get down, but by the time he pulled up, parked and knocked on the front door his course was clear: this time he was going to get some answers.

The door opened on Bernie Tanner's startled stare. "Mr. Kolmer?" There was surprise in his voice, whisky on his breath.

"Didn't think I'd be back?" Greg said. "Thought she'd get me, is that it?"

"I don't know what you're talking about."

"Don't hand me that!" Greg's voice rose.

"Please, not so loud. I got neighbors —"

"You'll get new ones in Forest Lawn if you try to dump on me again." Greg tugged at the door. "Open up."

Bernie obeyed quickly, then closed the door even more quickly after his self-invited guest had entered. Turning, the old man lurched toward his chair. Greg noted the bottle on the table and the half-filled tumbler beside it. The old man picked up his glass and gestured. "Drink?"

"Never mind that." Greg seated himself on the sofa; its faded fabric reeked of alcohol and stale cigar smoke. "Let's have it," he said.

Bernie avoided his gaze. "Look, if something's wrong it's not my fault. I told you not to go up there."

"Sure. But it's what you didn't tell me that made trouble."

The old man shook his head. "I didn't think you'd go. I didn't think you or anyone else could find the place, even if it was still standing after —"

"After what?"

Bernie tried to push the question away with his hand. "Look, I told you all I can —"

"Maybe you'll have more to say after I steer the law up there to take a look around."

Bernie gulped air, then gulped the contents of his glass. "All right, I'll level. That place didn't close down because the madam got married. She got murdered."

"Keep talking."

The old man poured himself another drink. "This fella Tim,

the one I told you used to go up there with me. I said I didn't know what became of him after I quit going. Well, I lied."

"Why?"

"I didn't want to get involved. It happened so long ago and it wouldn't do any good. You'd figure I was crazy, the way I figured Tim was when he told me."

"Told you what?"

"About the hookers up there, the Orientals the new madam brought in. He said they were some kind of vampires. If you dozed off, fell asleep, they'd suck your blood." The old man paused. "He showed me toothmarks on his neck."

. "He should have gone to the police."

"Do you think they'd believe him any more than I did? Instead he went to Trenk, Ulrich Trenk — you wouldn't remember him, he did some horror flicks for the indies back then."

"*Blood of the Beast.*" Greg nodded. "*Crawlers.* I know the titles but I never saw them."

"Nobody did," Bernie said. "They got shelved before release. And so did Trenk. His stuff was too strong for those days. Trouble with him, he believed in what he did — not the lousy scripts, but the premises. Ghosts, vampires, werewolves, all that crap. And he believed Tim, because he'd heard some other things about the place up there, about the way bats flew around and —"

"Never mind that. Tell me what happened!"

Bernie reached for his drink. "Word was that Trenk went up there with Tim and three other guys who'd been customers and got suspicious; of what, God only knows. But there was some kind of hassle and the bottom line is the place closed down, everybody left, end of story."

"I thought you said the madam was murdered."

Bernie frowned. "Tim told me he'd been the one who killed her. He told me because he was dying down at the old Cedars of Lebanon hospital, with what they thought was some rare kind of blood disease. They'd only let me talk to him for five minutes; when I leaned on him for details he said to come back tomorrow."

"And —?"

"He died that same night." The old man swallowed his drink. "Maybe it's just as well I didn't hear the rest. Nobody else who went up with Tim ever said a word about it. Trenk went back to Europe, but he'd kept his mouth shut, too."

"What about those bats?"

"All I know is what Tim told me, and what he said didn't make much sense. Don't forget, he was dying, probably hallucinating."

"Probably," Greg said. He wondered if he should ask another question, but it wasn't worth the risk. The way Bernie talked, it didn't sound as if he even suspected, and if that was the case there was no sense giving him a clue.

The old man thought Tim was hallucinating. If Greg told him about the girl in the house, would he say that was a hallucination too?

Could be. After all, Greg did have himself a toot before going in, and it wasn't as little as he liked to tell himself it was. Maybe that washed-up cowboy actor was on something too — either that or just jiving him. But the cowboy was dead, Bernie's friend was dead, and Bernie looked as if he'd stayed up way past his bedtime.

Greg stood up. "I'll be going now," he said.

Bernie blinked. "Aren't you going to tell me what happened to you up there?"

"Nothing. It's just a spooky old house, and I guess I got carried away." Greg walked to the door, opened it, then glanced back at the old man slumped in his chair. "Just in case you've been worrying, let me relieve your mind. I didn't see any bats."

So much for his good deed for the day.

Now it was time to do a good deed for himself. It had been a long time since lunch. Driving off, Greg turned onto Olympic and headed for a mini-mall offering a choice of franchised junk food. He chose the place with the best grease-smells and wolfed down more than his diet dictated: two burgers with everything, extra fries, coffee and a shake. He hated pigging out like this, but right now it was all he could afford. If tonight had been different he might be eating at Morton's.

As it was, perhaps he ought to consider himself lucky just to be alive. There was no sense stewing about the rest.

Driving home he reached his decision before he reached his destination. Whether what he'd seen was real or the product of his imagination, one thing was certain: he didn't want to see it again.

When Greg pulled into his parking space under the apartment it was close to midnight. The close-to-witching hour when the unholy hosts rise from their graves — Leno, Letterman, Arsenio, reading their ad-libs to the cackling crowd, welcoming their guests with all the grace of Dracula greeting Renfield, then draining their blood —

Now where had all that come from? Riding the elevator up to the third floor he had the answer. Damn Bernie and his vampire talk. And as for what Greg had seen, or thought he'd seen, there was an answer for that too — an answer he'd have to face sooner or later. And after tonight he knew it had better be soon. When the spiders come out of their hiding places and the sleeping beauties start taking off their heads, you'd better stop. Going up there had been enough of a bad trip in itself.

First thing he got into the apartment, he'd flush the rest of his little stash down the tube. If not, he'd be going down the tube himself one of these days. The time to think about it was over; this was *do it* time.

Only it didn't quite work out that way. When Greg opened the door and reached for the light-switch, a voice from the dark said, "Freeze!" and that's what he did.

Footsteps sounded softly behind him and a faint gust of air fanned his neck as someone closed the front door.

Beside him a switch clicked on. Against the background of

the cluttered little living room, the light of a lamp in the corner framed the outline of a man wearing jacket and jeans. But Greg's attention focused on the glint of a gun in the intruder's hand.

The gun gestured.

"Hands behind your head. That's right. Now move to the sofa and sit."

As Greg obeyed he got another glimpse of the gun. *Piece like that could blow your head off. God, what's happening? I need a fix.*

The intruder edged into a chair on the other side of the coffee table, and now the lamp highlighted eyes and cheekbones and skin tone.

For a moment Greg evoked an image of the golden girl he'd seen — or had he? — earlier this evening. But what he was seeing here was unquestionably real. A middle-aged man with coarse, close-cropped black hair: obviously an Asian or Asian-American, obviously not the friendly type. A man with an attitude, and a gun.

Just a snort, a sniff, anything —

The man's stare was cold. So was his voice. "Put your arms down. Both hands in your lap, palms up."

Greg complied and the man nodded. "My name is Ibraham," he said.

"Abraham?"

"Perhaps it was once, when Muslim rule began. But I'm called Ibraham in Kita Bharu."

"I don't know that country."

"It's a city. The capital of what used to be Kelanton, in Malaya." The man frowned. "I'm not here to give geography lessons."

Greg kept his palms up, his voice steady. "What are you here for?"

"I want you to take me to the house."

"House? I don't know —"

"Please, Mr. Kolmer. Your friend told me you went there earlier this evening."

"When did you see Bernie?"

"About an hour ago. He was kind enough to furnish your address, so when I found you were not home I took the liberty of inviting myself in."

The bathroom window, Greg told himself. *Why do I keep forgetting to lock it when I go out?*

That wasn't the question which needed answering at the moment. There was another one more important, so he asked it. "What did Bernie tell you?"

"Everything he knew." Ibraham's slight shrug didn't cause his aim to waver. "Enough for me to guess the rest." A nod didn't jar the gun either. "That story about researching an article — it's not true, is it, Mr. Kolmer? You went to that house looking for something you didn't find."

"How do you know?"

"If you found it you wouldn't have gone back to Tanner. Of course he didn't know what you were looking for, or he'd have told me that too." Ibraham lifted his gaze: eyes of onyx in slanted settings. "Tell me what you were after."

"I can't," Greg said. "Swear to God, I don't know."

"But you have some idea?" Ibraham leaned forward. "The truth — now."

Greg stared at the gun and its muzzle stared back. "The cowboy who told me about the place said there was a blackmail operation. This new madam was bugging rooms, getting pictures, filming with hidden cameras, using two-way mirrors and whatever else they had back in those days.

"There was a market then; magazines like *Confidential* paid plenty for such stuff, particularly if stars were involved. But nothing about the place ever showed up — I know, because I waded through library files. So my hunch was the material — photos, film, audio tape, whatever — never was submitted. Something happened to close the house down before the stuff could be peddled. Which meant —"

"It could still be there," Ibraham said, and nodded.

"How did you hear about all this?" Greg asked.

"From my mother. She was there when it happened."

"At the house?"

"She worked as a maid." For the first time there was a hint of amusement in Ibraham's eyes. "You must understand she was very young. The lady, the one they called the Marquess, adopted her after both my grandparents were killed in the war. When my mother came with her to this country she was only fifteen. Some of the other girls, the ones who did what was expected in such a place, weren't much older. But the Marquess protected my mother from everything, including full knowledge of what she was involved with. Of course she learned in time. But when she did, it was too late." Ibraham's eyes were somber now. "She was lucky. On the night everything happened she wasn't at the house. The Marquess' chauffeur had driven her down to a Westwood laundromat. I don't know how they found out about what took place, but news got to them somehow and they never went back. The chauffeur had a substantial bank account; he'd been the Marquess' lover. On the journey back to Kelanton he became my mother's lover as well. He died in a Johore brothel the day I was born.

"I never knew any of this until just before my mother died, several years ago. What she told me made me suspect the same thing you did, but I couldn't get over here immediately." Ibraham glanced at the gun. "In my country there is still a war going on."

"You're in the army?"

"The military became my career after I graduated from university in Singapore. Now I wish to retire."

Greg shifted cautiously. "Look, do you have to do this *shtick* with the gun?"

Ibraham lowered the weapon. "Probably not. After all, we're partners."

Greg fought for self-control, and lost. "No way!"

"It's the only way," Ibraham said. "You know how to find the house. And my mother told me what's hidden there. We go together. Tonight."

Greg shook his head. "Didn't Bernie tell you what happened to me — what I saw?"

"I know." Ibraham seemed to have no problem with self-control, Greg noted — but then, he had the gun. "My mother warned me. I know what to do."

Greg took a deep breath, "Maybe so. But do it tomorrow, when we can go up there in daylight."

"No. We can't afford delay."

"Do you think Bernie might start talking —"

"Only through an *ouija* board." Ibraham glanced down at his gun. Fear iced Greg's spine. "Why?" he murmured.

"The old man was the only one who'd know where we were going. No sense taking chances."

"How can you say that, knowing what we might run into up there?"

"What we're going after is worth the risk. I'm sure you're aware of that or else you'd never have gotten into this in the first place. That house holds a fortune, and we're going to get it."

Greg glanced at the gun. "And when we get it, you'll get me," he said.

"I give you my word." Ibraham rose. "Either go with me or stay behind. Like Bernie."

Greg swallowed hard, "Look, man, I've had a rough night, you know? Let me get my medication —"

"What are you on?"

Greg told him, and Ibraham gestured quickly. "You're not going up there stoned," he said. "Could be bad for your health."

A muzzle moved to press against Greg's spine; that was bad for his health too.

"Move," said Ibraham.

And they did, in Greg's car, with him behind the wheel, Ibraham at his side, and the gun riding against his rib cage. The midnight air was humid; both men were perspiring moments after the car swung out into the deserted street.

"Roll down your window," Greg said.

"Don't you have any air conditioner?"

"Can't afford it."

"You can, after tonight."

Ibraham was smiling, but Greg frowned. "This thing I saw up there — what is it?"

"*Penangallan.* A kind of vampire, but not exactly."

"Meaning what?"

"A *penangallan* doesn't need to rest in grave-earth or a coffin. Like your western vampires it seeks human blood for nourishment, but it can hibernate for years if necessary. Maybe the difference is in their metabolism. Vampires require a greater supply of energy to walk abroad each night. But the *penangallan* survives indefinitely in some sort of suspended animation. And when it does move, it flies."

Greg nodded. "You mean it turns itself into some kind of a bat."

Ibraham shook his head. "That's just superstition. The *penangallan* still retains human form — or part of its human form."

"I don't get it."

"These creatures can detach their heads from their bodies. And the head has the power of flight. When the head is removed, the stomach and intestines are pulled out and stay attached to it, receiving the blood it drinks."

The words triggered Greg's memory — just a flash, but enough. *The golden girl, sitting up and lifting her head from the open stump of the neck.* He'd seen it. It was true.

He felt a jarring movement and beside him Ibraham stirred in his seat. "Watch what you're doing," he said.

What Greg was doing was turning onto the concealed side road. Had they really come this far this quickly? Of course there was no traffic up here, no lights. Strange how easy it was to locate the hidden opening this second time around, even in the dark. But then again, it was associated with something he wasn't likely to forget.

The car entered and moved upward in a tunnel formed by the overhanging trees lining the roadway. Greg switched headlights, but even the brights were of little help here. Then the trees thinned, but the underbrush thickened and the car began to lurch around the sharp curves.

"Watch it!" Ibraham warned.

But Greg had already warned himself with the memory of what lay ahead. A *head* —

"I can't cut it," he said. "We've got to wait. Tomorrow. We'll do it tomorrow."

"Now." The gun jabbed against his ribs; Ibraham's voice jabbed his ear. "You're going now. Either behind the wheel or dumped in the trunk."

"You're bluffing —"

"That's what the old man thought."

Greg's hands were wet on the wheel, but they stayed there as the car inched forward over the rutted roadway and climbed around a curve. Now he glanced at the Malayan. "Suppose we're wrong. Suppose we don't find anything there?"

"I told you what my mother said. It's there and we'll find it."

"One thing I don't understand," Greg said. "If the stuff they had on their customers was so valuable, why wasn't it used?"

"My mother wondered about that too, but she didn't learn the plan until later, from the Marquess' lover."

"Plan?"

"Bit by bit the pieces fit together. The Marquess had bought the place with more than just profit in mind. Back in Kelantan she had a reputation as a *pawang* — a sorceress, you'd call it — and she gathered together and brought the *penangallans*, which

57

she controlled for her own purposes. Which were to use blackmail money to take over other vice operations and gradually gain political power in the area. The *penangallans* would deal with those who stood in her way. She was ready to carry out her plan when the end came. You know the rest."

Greg frowned. "Your mother could have gone to the police —"

"She was a fifteen-year-old girl, an illegal immigrant with forged papers, who spoke almost no English. Even if she'd found a way to contact the authorities — do you think anyone would go along with what she said about hookers who remove their heads, and all the rest of it?"

Greg had no answer for that, only another question as they angled up the torturous trail. "The thing I saw," he said. "Why would it still be there after all these years? Why didn't it leave the place when the Marquess was killed?"

"The *penangallan* flies low," Ibraham said. "It can't soar like a bat, and it must protect its dangling stomach sac and intestines from harm. In Malaysia, homes are often guarded by garlands of *Jenyu* leaves hung on doors and windows. The *penangallan* fears the *Jenyu* plant's sharp thorns." He glanced at the looming pines and the clumps of underbrush clustered beneath them. "Here your hillsides are covered with cacti and all kinds of spiky vegetation. It would rip the creatures' guts if they tried to escape."

"But they wouldn't have to fly," Greg said. "They could go down staying in their bodies just as they did up there."

Ibraham shrugged. "A *penangallan* preserves its body by drinking fresh blood. Without it the body will decay just like any other corpse. So if they did try to come down in human form before decay set in, there'd be problems. I don't think they'd last very long if word got out that human heads were flying around Beverly Hills and sucking blood in Bel Air. Besides, they'd have to have a place to hide. And to store the vinegar."

"Vinegar?"

"If the *penangallan* flies, its entrails swell up when exposed to the open air. So afterward it must soak its lower parts in a jar or vat of vinegar to shrivel the stomach and bowels to normal size. Then it fits them back in the body when the head is replaced."

No way, Greg told himself. *Either this guy is crazy or I am. There are no such things, no such place, no house —*

They rounded the turn and there it was.

If the place had looked ghostly by day, it looked ghastly in the grayish shroud of moonlight filtering through lowering clouds. Its dark silhouette seemed to slant toward them as the hatchback halted amidst spirals of steam from the hood. Greg stared numbly at the house. If it was real, then what about the rest —

"Out," Ibraham said.

Greg hesitated, then took a deep breath. "Look, I've told you everything I know, everything that happened. There's no reason for me to go in again with you now."

"What about the material you were looking for?"

Greg took another deep breath. "I've changed my mind. I don't want any part of it."

"Afraid?"

"After what you told me? Damned right I am."

"You expect me to go in by myself?" Ibraham asked. "So you can drive off and leave me stranded?"

"I'll wait, I swear it. Hey, you can take my car keys —"

"I'm taking you."

The gun rose, and so did Greg. Ibraham tensed as Greg's hand went to the glove compartment, then relaxed as the younger man brought out his flashlight.

Together they left the car and moved to the entrance in silence. Even the sound of the wind had died; everything had died here.

Greg halted before the door, and his companion eyed the broken lock. "You're making a mistake," Greg said. "If what you told me is true, a gun won't protect us from that thing I saw."

"There are other ways," Ibraham said, raising the weapon as he spoke. "Inside."

Inside was pitch blackness pierced by the pinpoint flashlight beam. Greg adjusted it so that they stood in a wider circle of radiance, but the light was dim against the darkness beyond. The silence itself seemed more intense than outside; there was nothing to disturb it here, nothing until they came.

"Leave the front door open," Greg whispered. "We might want to get out of here in a hurry."

Ibraham shrugged. "As you wish." Moving forward, he peered toward the right archway. "What's in there?"

Greg described the parlor, and his captor nodded.

Now he glanced to his left. "And here?"

"The bar."

The two men halted just past the archway as the flashlight beam roamed the room.

"All that damage," Ibraham said. "This must be where the fighting took place." He peered at the stairs on the far side.

Greg spoke quickly. "You don't have to go up there. I told you there's nothing in those bedrooms."

"Except the last one," Ibraham countered. "That's reason enough. We've got to go up."

"You know what's there. You admitted your gun won't help."

Ignoring him, Ibraham scanned the tile shambles of the littered floor. His eyes swept over the toppled tables, overturned chairs and broken glass. His eyes halted. "This will do," he said.

Greg followed his gaze to a chair turned upside down, two of its legs wrenched half-free from the base of the seat. "What do you mean?"

Ibraham told him what he meant. He told him what to do, then watched, gun in hand, while Greg did it. Getting the chair leg loose wasn't difficult, and locating a sharp knife in a drawer behind the bar wasn't a problem for him either. The hard part was whittling away at the wooden chair leg until the end was trimmed into a tapering shaft with a narrow point. It was Ibraham, rummaging through shelving beneath the bar counter, who came up with the bung-starter.

"Good," he said. "We're ready."

Greg didn't feel ready. He felt he needed out of here. Ibraham had already goaded him to the base of the stairs, and it was there that he turned.

"Hey, man," he said. "I thought we came here to look for that stuff."

"We will."

"You're wasting your time. It's not upstairs."

"But something else is. And we won't be safe looking around here until we dispose of it."

The gun muzzle guided Greg up the staircase. In the upper hallway the floorboards creaked, and so did the doors as Ibraham opened them in turn. But it was the sound of his own heartbeat that Greg heard as they reached the end of the hall and stood before the last door on the left.

It was Greg who opened the door, but Ibraham was the one who gasped as the flashlight beam encircled the burnished golden beauty of the naked girl on the bed.

Her eyes were closed, and this time she did not stir. Ibraham gestured impatiently, but Greg stood immobile at the bedside, staring down at the golden girl.

This was what he'd needed. Proof that he hadn't freaked out from dropping acid, that what he'd seen here before was real.

And if it was real, then so was the rest of what he'd seen, what had sent him screaming down the hillside. That's why he was standing here now, holding the sharpened stake. He knew what he must do, and this was the worst reality of all.

He took a step backward. He couldn't go through with this, no way, now was the time to get out of here —

The muzzle of the gun bit against his spine. Greg heard the faint click signaling the release of the safety catch.

The girl on the bed heard it too, for she stirred for a moment, stirred but didn't awaken.

Once she did, once she opened her eyes, it would be too late. Greg remembered the rows of pointed teeth, remembered the hands that tugged the head away from the neck swiftly, so very swiftly. Which meant he had to be swift too.

He belted the flashlight.

He lifted the stake with both hands.

Gasping with effort, he plunged it down into the cleft between the golden breasts.

Then her eyes did open, wide. Her lips retracted and he saw the teeth, saw the talons rise to slash at his face, claw at his wrists as he held the stake fast.

Snakelike she squirmed, and like a snake she hissed, but Ibraham was standing on the other side of the bed and he brought the broad head of the bung-starter down, driving the stake deep.

The golden hands tore frantically at the shaft imbedded between the golden breasts, but Greg's grip remained unbroken. He held the stake firmly as Ibraham hammered it home. There was a single shattering shriek as a gout of crimson geysered upward, then sudden silence.

Talons loosened their hold; the golden face fell back on the pillow, its slant-eyed stare veiled by the billowing black hair. No sound issued from the open mouth, and the blood around the base of the stake ceased further flow. Mercifully, there was no movement or hint of movement to come. The golden girl was dead.

Greg turned away, panting after his exertion, filling his laboring lungs with the acrid odor of blood. His stomach cramped and for a moment he thought he might pass out. Then he became aware that Ibraham was speaking.

"— not finished yet. But it should be safe to go now."

Greg unhooked his flashlight. "Go where?"

"To get what we came for." Ibraham motioned him to the door and Greg noticed that he was again holding the gun.

So nothing had changed, really. Except that they'd come here this crazy midnight to pound a stake into the heart of a dead girl or an undead girl; it didn't matter which, because she was dead now. *We killed her and the stake went in and the blood spurted out just like in those horror movies only this wasn't a movie just a horror God I need a fix —*

But there was no fix, not in the hall or on the stairs or down at the bar.

Ibraham's gun urged him along to the hall before the mottled mirror on the back wall. "Should be just about here," Ibraham said. He reached out and ran his free hand across the inner edge of the bar, muttering, "If my mother was right." A panel under the bar slid back silently, revealing a black rectangular opening.

"She was," Ibraham said.

Greg's flashlight dipped toward the darkness. "Lower," his captor said. "Must be some stairs."

There were. Greg descended first, beam fanning forward until he reached the bare stone surface below the fourteenth step. Ibraham followed, but this time his gun wasn't aimed at Greg. Like the flashlight, it swerved and circled, as if seeking possible targets in the cavernous cellar before them.

The two men moved slowly, silently. Nothing to hear but the thud of their own footsteps, nothing to see but the beam tracing a path along the stone floor beneath their feet.

Here the air was cooler, but the odor it carried, a mingling of dust and decay, was almost stifling. There was another smell, faint but pungent, which Greg couldn't identify.

Now Ibraham identified it for him. "Vinegar," he said. "Remember, I told you the *penangallan* shrinks its entrails in vinegar in order to squeeze them back down into the body? I was wondering where they kept their supply."

"But we didn't find any others —"

"My mother thought there could be a dozen among the Marquess' girls."

Greg started to speak, but Ibraham waved him to silence. "The scent is almost undetectable here. Probably evaporated."

"I'm not worried about the goddamn smell," Greg said. But if there are more of those things down here —"

Suddenly his foot struck something, something that clattered as he stumbled back. The flashlight beam dipped down toward the stone surface, sweeping over the sprawled length of arm and leg bones, the ridged rib cage and nacreous neck of the skeleton.

It had no skull.

The rush came so quickly that Greg almost dropped the flashlight. Its beam wavered because his hand was shaking. No skull. No head. It was one of them.

Ibraham moved forward; his harsh whisper echoed through darkness: "Here's another."

Greg raised the flashlight, semicircling its dim beam, then wished he hadn't.

The floor ahead was littered with bones. Some, heaped against the walls, were partially joined: a leg attached to a pelvis, a collarbone to a humerus, radius and ulna to the metacarpals. Two other skeletons were fully articulated but, like the first, they lacked skulls. Greg's stare swept across the scatter, but Ibraham's attention was elsewhere. He skirted the bonepile, threading his way between heaps and jumbles, then approached the makeshift wooden shed rising along the right side of the cellar. More skeletal fragments lay there, piled almost at random, amidst shreds of rotted cloth.

There was a door at the far end of the shed's wall, and Ibraham pulled it open slowly, revealing the wooden shelving ranged along the far side within.

"Get some light over here," he said. Greg started toward him, raising the flashlight. Its beam sought the shelves — long, low shelves bearing wide-mouthed, deep-bodied clay bowls. There were perhaps a dozen pots of them resting side by side like the pots in a florist's shop, but what bloomed in each were not flowers.

Greg stared at the rows of human skulls. And they grinned at him in greeting, grinned as though sharing some grisly secret that only the dead can know.

Ibraham moved beside him. "You see what's happened here? Those bowls must have been filled with vinegar."

"To shrink the intestines." Greg nodded. "But why didn't it work?"

"You can't store liquids in leaky containers," Ibraham explained. "And every one of these bowls is cracked."

Now, peering more closely, Greg could see what he meant. Most of the cracks were visible just above the base of each bowl to form a pattern, almost as though they'd been gouged out by some sharp tool or instrument.

Greg frowned. "Didn't they realize it was wrong to use these?"

"They had no other choice," Ibraham said. "She must have broken them after the raid. Probably that's how they escaped the madam's fate — they hid down here while the raid was going on. Maybe the raiding party killed the bartender too. Stands to reason they took the bodies away and got rid of them." He glanced down at the scattered bones. "But the *penangallan* were safe here. They must have stayed in hiding a long time, and when they came out they were hungry. And you know what happens when there's no food in the house."

Greg nodded. "You go out to eat."

"Exactly. They flew off to try their luck at hunting. But there's not much around, just birds and perhaps some small game. Since they couldn't fly down from here, that's all they could find. The only way they could survive was to hibernate." Ibraham gestured. "The one upstairs was smarter. She must have known how little success they'd have out there, because she didn't go. And when they returned and came down here she had a surprise for them."

"Like you said, she'd broken the bowls."

"That's what I figure. While their bodies rested out in the cellar, they settled their heads and entrails in the bowls here, but most of the vinegar leaked out quickly; before it could be effective it was gone. The girl we saw upstairs was gone too, after locking them in. She probably had her own bowl and vinegar supply tucked away somewhere upstairs, because she'd already planned what she was going to do."

"But what *could* she do?" Greg said.

"You still don't get it." Ibraham glanced down. "Don't these bones and skeletons tell their own story? The heads rested helplessly in those dried-out jars while the stomachs burst and rotted away. And trapped out here, the headless bodies, blind and squirming in the dark."

Greg grimaced. "And the thing upstairs —?"

"She ate them," Ibraham said. "That's what kept her alive all these years." He nodded at the skeletons and the piles of bones. "She didn't need to fly in search of food. Not with a dozen bodies down here, bodies that still moved, bodies filled with blood. She stripped the flesh from these bones bit by bit, sucked arteries and veins dry. It must have been done over a long period, and most of the while she slept, just as we found her."

Greg's stomach knotted convulsively. "I'm outta here," he panted, turning to seek the stairs.

"First we get what we came for." Ibraham's weapon pressed against Greg from behind as he climbed. And back upstairs the gun prodded Greg to the rear of the room.

"Take a look behind the staircase," Ibraham ordered. "The madam could have had her office under there."

Greg swore silently. Of course the office would be in someplace like that, close to the action but not easy for outsiders to spot. If he'd only looked around more carefully before going upstairs on the first visit, chances are he might not have had to go upstairs at all. The office would be where the madam kept the stuff. If he'd used his head and thought things through, he wouldn't be here now in the middle of the night, middle of nowhere, this crazy house with that crazy thing upstairs and a crazy gook downstairs pushing a gun into him for half of what they'd find.

"Let's go," the crazy gook was saying. "I tell you it's got to be here."

And that's where they found it, under the stairs. The door was metal, closed but unlocked, and behind it was the office. Or had been, until the intruders burst in, tore the drawers out of desks and filing cabinets, smashed them with crowbars and an ax that still lay atop shelving wrenched from a battered bookcase on the right wall.

Across from it, on the left wall, was an open safe.

Open, and empty.

Greg blinked at the bare steel shelf. "Gone; those bastards took the stuff with them —"

"Take another look," Ibraham said softly.

Greg followed his gaze, traveled with it across the bare concrete floor to the center of the room. His eyes followed a paper trail — or a trail of what had once been paper. Now it was just a brownish-gray muddle of charred shreds speckled with tiny glints from flecks of burned photos. From the trail rose an odor, faint as the scent of vinegar; the reek of long-dead ashes in which all hope lay buried.

"Outta here," Greg whispered.

Ibraham shook his head. "You think I don't know how you feel? I want to forget it ever happened. But before we put it behind us, there's one more job. The *penangallan* —"

"It's dead," Greg said. "We killed it. You know that."

"Not so. Remember, the *penangallan* isn't like other bloodsuckers. As long as the head remains attached to the digestive tract it can still fly and feed. A stake is not enough."

THE SCENT OF VINEGAR

"It's enough for me," Greg told him. "I'm not going to tangle with that thing."

"The stake probably paralyzes it, at least for a time," Ibraham said. "But we can't take chances. We must cut off the head."

"Forget it. I'm finished."

Ibraham ignored him, but his weapon did not.

Would he shoot? Greg thought of Bernie Tanner for a moment and he didn't need an answer. Instead he asked another question. "What do you want me to do?"

Ibraham nodded toward the toppled shelving at his right. "Over there," he said. "Get the ax."

Greg turned, imagining the impact of a bullet in his back. And perhaps it wouldn't have been imagination if they'd found that blackmail material intact. No reason for Ibraham not to shoot him then, kill him and take all the loot; nobody'd ever know. But that could still be true now. If they got rid of the *penangallan*, Ibraham would get rid of him too — because Greg was the only one who could tie him to Bernie Tanner's murder.

So there really wasn't much choice but for Greg to do exactly what he was told: reach out and pick up the ax. But it was his own idea to turn swiftly, raise the ax and bring it down right between Ibraham's eyes.

The gurgle was still dying in his victim's throat as Greg ran, reeling through the office doorway, the barroom, the hall, the open front door.

He squeezed into the car, fumbling for his keys, cursing the broken air conditioner but grateful for the breeze from the windows. The air was still warm and moist, but it was clean, free of must and dust, the scent of vinegar, the mingled odors of stale ashes and fresh blood.

Blood. He'd killed a man; he was a murderer. But nobody knew, nobody would ever know if he played it cool. Even if somebody wandered up to the house there was nothing to connect him with what they'd find. Get himself a set of tires tomorrow and the old tread marks wouldn't match the new. They might get prints off the doorknobs and ax handle, but they'd have nothing to match them with either; he'd never been fingerprinted. And they wouldn't be looking for him in the first place, with nothing to go by.

So he was home free, would be now that the car had started, now that he was wheeling down the hillside with every twist and turn taking him farther away from that damned house and that damned thing; taking him closer to the lights and the streets, streets where you could find a fast fix, find it and forget what had happened. It would just be like a bad trip, he didn't really kill anyone, and there wasn't really anything like that thing with the golden face and the almond eyes and the gleaming, pointed teeth in the crimson mouth he was seeing now in the rearview mirror, rising up from the back seat.

Greg screamed, and so did the brakes of the car as he spun the wheel, spun and lost because there was no way to win, no way to turn from that narrow, tangled trail.

And then the thing was hovering behind him, rising up and swooping forward, its viscera lashing and looping.

The slimy coils twirled and tightened around Greg's neck, and from the stalklike stem above it the golden face dipped, lips fastening on Greg's flesh as the fangs found his throat. Ibraham had been right, after all.

Now Greg knew why a stake through the heart was not enough.

Robert Bloch writes: "Chances are, my friends, that I was a published writer long before you were born. I sold my first short story a full sixty years ago, and since then I've been active in books, magazines, radio, television, and films. So far I've never been a tagger, but I'm not making you any promises. I still enjoy writing stories today and hope you enjoy reading them, because it's a bit late for me to try learning a useful occupation."

In the Garden

by Esther Friesner

The poet strolled among the roses, feeling the summer night surround him like a velvet skin. Everywhere the overwhelming scent of the flowers hung upon the air, filling the young man's head with dreams of beckoning lips, fair white arms wreathed around a lover's neck, reckless promises whispered in the warm shadows of a ducal throne while empty-headed courtiers passed so close that lover and beloved might have reached out and plucked at the brocade of a passing sleeve, tweaked a feather from a nodding headdress.

Will she come? His heart beat faster. *She said at midnight.* The sundial in the garden's midst cast a shadow of black ice that told the anxious lover nothing. The moon's face was hidden by the green mist of a willow tree.

The poet drifted aimlessly up and down the paths of crushed stone, letting his fingers trail through the silken blossoms of roses red as blood. Each petal's lingering caress thrilled him from his fingertips to the depths of his soul with memories of her kisses, deep and sweet as the wine at the goblet's heart. Once he paused, gazing up at the ducal palace where lights still burned brightly in the high windows.

Has he summoned her to his bed? The thought was gall. *But she will elude him, she will make some plausible excuse — the moon's phase, a woman's indisposition — and retire to her own chambers. Then, when the path is open, she will come. Love has taught her guile. Love for me.* And pride swelled him like a berry ripe with juice that wants a single touch of the teeth to bleed it dry.

The moon sailed free of the net of willow leaves, mounting the sky like a grand lady. *I have misjudged the time*, the poet thought, gazing up at her cold beauty. *It wants an hour of midnight. I will go to the place agreed upon and wait. She must not find me wandering or she may turn from me. Not this night. Not with all she has promised.* And his heart kindled like an ember that holds a city's death by flame at its core.

The nodding heads of roses dipped and lifted in a graceful pavanne. The poet paused by a perfect rose and plucked a single blossom from its stem as a present for his love. The flower bled over his fingers, a single bead of clear liquid like a tear that fell from the torn stem to bedew his finger. He gazed at the crystal droplet and saw that it held the moon.

The gardens of the Duke of Este were a wonder by day, a labyrinth of shadows by night. The poet moved with ease through a world of dreaming flowers, himself anointed with the scent of costly musk and ambergris, her gift to him. He still recalled her words to him that first night in my lord of Este's palace, that night he realized that all his life before had been less than a dream:

72

"You are mine, poet," she whispered. He stiffened where he stood; her breath was so close, so hot he felt it stir the small hairs at the back of his neck. He was enclosed by shadows — a poet must lurk as unseen as the buried dead until summoned back into being by his patron's whim — a slender shape behind a pillar's stolid bulk. Her voice came to him out of the shadows, out of the night where fragrant beeswax candles guttered and died like common tallow dips, and torches raised flags of impotent flame against the all-enshrouding dark.

"My lady —?" He did not turn. He did not dare to turn. If he moved, if he stirred so much as a finger she might be gone, vanished like a fever dream. But then, he did not need to see her face to know it was she. Her voice he knew; he had schooled himself to know it. How many times had his lord the duke commanded him to recite his latest work for the entertainment of disinterested dinner guests? And how many times had he seen her there, the Duchess Lucretia, pale and radiant at her husband's side? Always when his recitation was done her voice was the first to ring out with a bold word of praise, rousing those noble guests who had sooner been seduced by sleep than by poetry. Yes, her voice he knew.

"Poet, do not question me." Her words stole over him, the burning cloak Medea wove to devour her rival's living flesh. "I know your desire. You govern your tongue as you can never hope to govern your eyes. I have seen myself naked and wanton in their depths. I have seen what you wish to make of me."

"My lady, on my honor —"

"It is what I wish you to make of me." And then her hands were on him, roughly, violently. She spun him around to stand lips to lips, heart to wildly beating heart as she ravaged a hundred kisses from his lips there, in the shadows, in the very throne room of her lawful husband.

Since then, a score and more of meetings. Always kisses, and sometimes the eager thrust of hands, seeking, finding, kindling flesh into flame. Her little breasts were hard and sweet as apples, the milky skin between her thighs a silken glove welcoming his hand.

But nothing more. Too many accursed obstacles intervened: the hour; the place; an unlooked-for servant's approach; a summons to her husband's presence; a pledge to be elsewhere that she could not, in honest duty, defer.

Until tonight. She had promised him much; she would vouchsafe him all.

The poet drifted in dreams that burned away all pretty rhymes, leaving behind only the flesh and its immediacies. There was a certain place in the gardens, a place she had named and one he knew well. A bench of marble, cool and white as the slab of a noble's catafalque, hid itself away beneath a hedge where white roses like stars were held in a heaven of glossy green leaves. Rampant lions bore the slab upon their backs, their paws raised in challenge to all comers, their lips curled back in fearsome snarls.

It was here that she would find him, in that part of the gardens farthest from the palace. The poet sat down upon the bench to wait.

The pale moon offered him her silvery face to contemplate, whiter than bone. He dreamed his lady Lucretia's face held fast in the shining circlet of the moon. The white roses trembled in a warm breeze that spread their perfume over the garden like a silken shawl. The poet dreamed the scent of his lady's hair, the all-pervading attar of her flesh. *Madonna* Nature opened a hundred gateways into the beauties of the night for his eyes alone; yet all he saw, all that held him by a cold iron chain, was the dream of Lucretia.

A wayward moth, dancing with a moonbeam, cartwheeled before his sight like a tatter of white samite. Its headlong tumble through the rose leaves ended in the gossamer toils of a spider's web. The poet watched, indifferent, as the small soul's struggles roused the drowsing black monster from the center of its lair. The spider scuttled forward with indecent haste, eyes glowing red with greed. It sprang upon the hapless moth and sank its fangs into that fragile, quivering body until the last shudders stilled. The poet sat as if he were one of the lions beneath him, watching the spider gorge on its victim's blood.

"What are you watching so intently, sir?"

That voice! His heart slammed against the ribs' ivory prison. "My lady —!" he gasped, and turned with all haste to welcome her into his arms. He rose from the bench and cast himself on the cloaked figure before him as if he had been lessoned by the spider's example of all-driving, all-devouring greed.

She gave a little cry and crossed her hands before her face, warding him off. "I asked a simple question, in all courtesy. What is the meaning of this insult?" she demanded, although there was too much terror limning her voice for it to be a true demand.

He stepped back, abashed. "My lady, don't you know me?" He glared up at the treacherous moon. "Ah, but this light — yes, there's the fault. It is I, Pietro. Oh, my love!"

Again he attempted to take her into his arms and again she shrank away from him as if she had seen Death's own grinning skull beneath the velvet cap, the fringe of chestnut hair. "Do not touch me." It was a plea, a whimper in the dark. "I will summon help if you do." She did not sound as if she herself believed that threat.

The poet laid a hand to his heart as if all the prettily rhymed lies of his own spinning might prove true and that much-lauded organ would break of thwarted love. Was this madness? Well he knew the evil rumors of his lady's family — may God have mercy on him for harkening to such talk of His Holiness, Pope Alexander! Much ill was spoken of the Borgia brood. Ill? That was too mild a word to describe the heinous crimes of which they stood accused. It was said that her brother Cesare had played Cain; that he had plucked the strings of conspiracy that shamed Lucretia's first husband with the taint of supposed impotence and slain her second lord outright; that he and their common father had shared more than a few murders — some by venom, some by blade. Some said too that they had shared Lucretia.

And could this be so? Were the wild tales of night-long orgies in the papal palace true? Such unnatural revelry must surely drive a woman mad. Had father and brother conspired to enjoy his lady's white-and-gold beauty as they might share the favors of a common whore? No. His soul cried out against such calumny. If such things could be, then men were animals indeed, and animals had no need of poetry.

He took her hand in his, and for all her fruitless struggles would not relinquish it. "My lady, you are unwell," he said. "What else but some fever could have driven me from your mind, your heart? That, or some unwholesome water was poured into your cup to dilute the wine, and from this taint you have somehow lost all remembrance of me." He raised her hand to his lips, tasting their softness, their whiteness. "Let me help you to remember." He pulled her, protesting, into the shadow of the roses.

She struggled vainly, slim arms and legs no match for any hale man's strength. He bore her to the earth beside the bench while the lions looked on with empty eyes. Her dark cloak fell away, releasing the bright torrent of her golden hair. He tore aside her gown, a fragile wisp of fabric more like a night robe than any manner of highborn lady's dress. His ravished senses could not dare to guess which was the whiter: her gown, her breasts, or the roses. He buried his mouth against her neck and murmured poetry against the leaping pulse; all the while his hands tangled to free himself and her from the encumbrance of cloth keeping them apart.

She screamed when he took her. He covered her mouth with his and drank down her cries like wine, hot and spiced. His head swam with the pleasure that was all of his own taking, and when the final shudder came between them, he thought that those poor poets who called it "the little death" did it an injustice beyond name.

"What, my friend? So eager?" A voice as twisted and bitter as an old root broke over the poet's ebbing ecstasy. "You could not wait for me?"

The poet started like a hare. The moon's cold light outlined the shape of another hooded figure now blocking the entrance to the little arbor. Pale hands floated up to pull the hood aside, and he saw a face staring down at him that was twin to the frozen mask staring up.

"What have you done to my poor little poppet?" the woman in the arbor asked. She sounded almost amused. Her hand fell on his bare shoulder, and her fingernails were a raptor's talons piercing the flesh, pulling him away from the limp creature still pinioned beneath the weight of his body. The poet grabbed for his discarded clothing, rearranged the disorder of those few garments he had not entirely tossed aside in his frenzy.

Meantime the woman stood gazing down at the still, white body beneath the roses. She knelt, and the shimmering fall of her own tresses made a veil of modesty between the poet and the lady with whom he had so lately lain.

"Did he hurt you, my dear?" The woman spoke without concern. All the emotion that the poet heard in her voice was the idle curiosity of a child who plucks the legs from ants just to observe what they will make of their new state. She slipped her arm beneath the other woman's neck and forced her to sit upright. "This is your own fault, you know. I told you never to leave your place after dark."

And she slapped her once, sharply, so that even the poet cringed with pain.

The other gasped and tried to stammer some reply, but the woman was bundling her back into her discarded cloak as a little girl might stuff an unwanted doll into a chest or beneath a bed until she desired to play with it again. She helped her to her feet, and now that the two of them stood side by side the poet could see that the one with whom he had lain was smaller, slighter than the newcomer, with a face incapable of holding more than fear.

"Perhaps this will teach you a lesson, little fool," the taller one was saying, prim and very much the pedagogue. "If sleep eludes you, keep to your rooms. Have you forgotten our pact? Obey me and all will go well for you. You shall have your pretty clothes and your gauds, as suits a duchess, and the homage of all who come here to lick the dust before your lordly husband's throne by day. Was daylight not a grand enough realm for your vanity? Would you also dream of usurping the hours of night, the hours that are mine? Ungrateful child. I have saved you from so much. My kind are not the only ones whom the moonlight transforms into beasts of prey. I have spared you from your husband's voracious attentions, from the imperious demands that your blood kin placed upon your flesh in Rome…until I arrived. Have you forgotten how much you owe me?"

The poet's victim shivered and shook her head violently. "Lady…my beloved lady, I have not forgotten. That night in Roma when you came to me as I lay sobbing for my soul's sake — ah, God, what they had made of me, my own father, my brother —! That night when you offered me the rescue of my body, the saving of my soul, I gave myself freely into your hands. I cannot forget my debt to you; not while there is breath in my body can I ever forget."

The stronger woman's eyes narrowed, and an unearthly flame kindled there. The poet saw the crimson glow and knew himself the captive of a nightmare. He prayed that he had fallen asleep while awaiting his sweet mistress and that her awakening kiss would ransom him from the terror gripping his heart. The iron bonds of dreams held him to the spot, unable to move.

"That's my good girl," she said, and held out her hand. The smaller woman rubbed her face against it like a cat seeking to ingratiate itself with its mistress.

"Who — who are you?" the poet faltered. Both women turned

their faces toward him as if he were some strange new breed of plant lately sprouted by moonlight in the ducal gardens. Blue eyes and crimson rested their gaze on him until the silence behind that double stare filled his veins with ice.

Then the taller laughed. "Fool! Do you not know your own duchess?" She handed the smaller woman forward, almost into his arms, as if she were conducting her into the first figures of a courtly dance. And having done this, she too stepped forward so that they stood hemming the poet in on either side. Her hand darted out to clasp his beardless chin in a grip of astonishing strength, forcing him to meet her eyes alone. "Do you not know your own true love?"

"Who are you?" This time the question escaped the poet's lips as a whisper that died as the moth died, held fast in the spider's jaws.

"We are Lucretia." The answer came as if it were a matter of the most supreme indifference. "We share a name, if not a skin, and we share more. This little sister I have made my own knows at least as much of men's uncaring appetites as I, although I came to that knowledge earlier. Proud Tarquin shamed my marriage bed, threatened me with death and scandal if I refused his passion. I bowed my head, accepted — because I believed a woman had no choice but to accept! After he had satisfied himself and gone, I rose from the befouled couch and stepped into the night. I had a dagger in my hand, one I had taken from my absent husband's store. I intended to end a life no longer to be borne, but I could not do it under the roof where I had been so used. So I sought out the gardens, the night. Oh, the kindly night! I wished it might devour me and my shame, but more, I wished that it would give me a dagger long enough to plunge into my despoiler's heart."

"Tarquin…" The poet could not credit what his ears had heard. "Lucretia…" That was the duchess' name, but she was namesake to that Roman matron whose honorable death by her own hand proved the charge of rape against the last king of the Seven Hills and birthed the Republic. This was the stuff of legend, yet here was legend given unnatural life, speaking of the events of centuries long dead as if they had happened only yesterday.

"Do you pity me, my love?" the woman said, twining her arms around his neck. "Or do you feel that I was wrong to lust after vengeance? That is not a woman's right, by your lights, is it? Well, you are not the only breed of man that stalks in gardens by moonlight."

She smiled, and her teeth were white and keen. The poet's eyes shone still whiter in the moonlight when he saw the length, the edge, the points of two teeth in particular that better belonged in the mouth of a she-wolf than of a woman.

"I never knew his name," she was saying, and hot breath hissed over her fangs. "He found me in my misery, the dagger in my hand, and heard me pour out the sorrow of my heart. He took the dagger from me with a strength beyond any man of natural birth. Only then did he offer me the gift. Oh, the gift! I took it, because it gave me all I might desire of revenge — revenge to span the ages. Yet it had its price: as great a violation of my body as Tarquin's evil, and yet what promise of joy to come after I had passed through the scarlet veil! So you see, the night gave me my dagger after all."

"This is madness," the poet said. He tried to squirm out of her embrace, but he was bound by slim white arms stronger than any iron fetters. "Ah, in heaven's name —"

"Do you cry for mercy, poet?" the lady asked. "Do you expect to receive what you would not give? I am surprised that you, with your fine Classical pretensions, your vain fancies that you are heir to the laurels of Rome's ancient bards, do not find this amusing."

The poet jerked his gaze away from those burning eyes, seeking the more human face of the woman he had ravished. "Lady —" he gasped. "My lady duchess, if you are truly she, call off this fiend! Do this by the powers of dark magic all your family must possess, and I swear I shall be your slave forever."

"A slave may own no slave," the duchess murmured, and her head drooped like a wilting flower.

"The Borgia own no magic," the crimson-eyed Lucretia snarled. "Fool to believe such tripe! But the Borgia do own power, worldly power, and that is magic enough for me. From the papal throne, from the heart of Rome their net spreads out, and I — I mean to hold it by a single strand. By day this child of their begetting plays the pretty doll-wife, but by night I slip into her place, I whisper my desires into the duke's ear and he obeys. I send my artful messages by courier to Rome and touch the very heart of His Holiness, Alexander — the pitchy soul of subtle Cesare. Though their hands wield the sword, the poison vial, the pen that changes the world, in the end it is my hand that rules!"

"They will not touch me again," the duchess said, her voice still low, as if she feared to draw notice. "She has given me back my body and promised to leave me my soul."

"And what will you leave me?" the poet asked, feeling every word scrape along his throat like flint. "Soul or body or…neither one?" For now he truly knew himself to be caught in the toils of a monster.

But the crimson-eyed lady only laughed. "What use have I for your soul, poet? It is made of paper; it would perish in my flame. And as for your body, I find it sweet to see, but you have given it away too recklessly. One woman is the same as another to you, no matter how you bray your verses protesting that we are each unique as crystal specks of snow."

"Then…you will let me go?" The poet tried to keep his heart from leaping at this sudden change in his fortunes. "Despite — this?" He gestured toward the duchess.

"'This'?" Another laugh, like a crackle of wildfire. "Is that how you speak of what the lady has given you, willingly or no? Has her favor gone so swiftly from grail to clog?" She shook her head. "Have no fear, little man; your sins are of concern only to those who still own souls with which to judge you. I free you of it."

"Ah!" The breath of the night was sweet in his lungs again.

"But I do not free you of this."

And she was upon him with the speed of the spider, her hair slithering over his face like a nest of golden serpents as she bore him to the ground. The last thing he recalled was a stab of pain at the springing of his neck, and then night without stars.

He awoke to the cold dew of morning on his face and the light-headedness of too much wine. But no wine had passed his lips, he was sure of it. He was sure of nothing else.

"I...dreamed," he told the new sun, passing a trembling hand across his brow. His bones ached from a night spent out-of-doors, and his neck was particularly affected. His wandering fingers discovered two small wounds on the tender flesh. He recalled the spider and cursed all that noxious race as he hauled himself onto the bench of the stone lions. He sat with his head hanging between his legs for a time while the young sun warmed the garden and purged it of the last midnight dews.

At last he was himself again. He rose from the bench, sparing only a moment to indulge a fit of pique, tearing away the spider's fragile web and smearing the silken ruin on the rose leaves. It was a petty act, but it made him feel somewhat better about the wasted night.

"She did not come after all," he said to the awakening garden. "The devil take her."

In the ducal palace, much was astir. The servants dashed here and there, making and doing. The duke's *majordomo* caught sight of the poet as he strolled through the halls at leisure, his clothing still dirty and awry.

"You there!" he called. "My lady Lucretia wants you. You are to go to her chambers at once."

"Me?" For an instant the poet felt a stab of fear, although he was at a loss to explain why the mere mention of the lady's name should affect him so. It might evoke anger, yes, or wounded pride, but fear? Still he went.

He found her among her ladies in the solar, all of them dutifully laboring over their needlework, for the common knowledge since Aristotle teaches that women are light-minded and must be kept from great mischief by an unending succession of petty tasks. The lady looked a trifle pale, but her smile was brilliant as she invited him to seat himself on her footstool. Wine was brought; she poured it for him with her own hands, the rings on her fingers twinkling over the dark red stream.

And then he remembered. In the wine's bloody course his memories of the night before came flooding over him with dread. He felt the color leave his face. The hour was daylight; this was the duchess and not the monstrous creature who had fed upon him. For that mercy he said a small thanksgiving prayer to the Virgin.

But...does she remember too? And with that thought his bowels froze.

"*Signor* poet, did you not hear me?" the lady was saying, her hands a nest of ivory and gold in which the wine cup brooded. "I said that since my dear brother comes to dine with us this night, I would have you compose a rhyme in the lord Cesare's honor. Will you do this?" She pressed the cup into his hands.

The poet's spirits soared. *Was this all the reason for my summoning here? A poem to welcome her brother? Then she does not recall! And perhaps — perhaps there was nothing to recall. Perhaps it was but a midnight fancy. Did not the great Florentine, Alighieri, figure all the hosts of heaven and hell in his mind's eye? Then why might I not create a single she-demon in mine?* And he drank the cup to the dregs eagerly. "It shall be done as you desire, *madonna*," he said.

"Yes," she replied, still smiling. "It shall."

That night the banquet hall rang with revelry. The poet waited in the shadows for his time. There sat Duke Alfonso d'Este, garbed in splendor as befitted a man of his birth and breeding, and there by his side sat the Duchess Lucretia.

Except she was not the duchess.

The poet's skin crept over his bones. Seeing her again, that other Lucretia, there was no room for doubt. She had been no illusion, although she was illusion's mistress. He marveled that neither the other courtiers nor the duke himself seemed in the least suspicious of her presence in their true lady's place.

Were they all so blind? Could none of them see the monster behind the mask? The differences between the true duchess and that dark counterfeit — now laughing at the duke's latest sally, now inclining her fair head to whisper secrets with my lord Cesare — were as day and night. His heart urged him to speak, to reveal the whole obscene charade to his lord the Duke of Este. Prudence counseled otherwise: The duke might believe none of it, condemn him for a madman, and besides, what lasting harm had been done?

What harm? He knew. His neck still throbbed from the creature's assault. How could he forget such an outrage or allow it to pass unavenged? She had dared invade his body, and though he risked the duke's wrath for it, he would speak out against her. *Perhaps if I first obtain a hearing from the Church…* he mused.

And then he heard his name being called by my lord of Este's *majordomo*. He stepped into the middle of the banquet hall and bowed to the dais where the ducal couple and their guest sat waiting. His verse in praise of my lord Cesare was flawless, flattering. In the poet's mouth the Borgia heir became by turns a princely garden whose beauteous roses hid martial thorns, a basking lion whose regal bearing still concealed a deadly retribution for his enemies, a bear whose slumberous looks belied the swift judgment of his powerful paws.

After the applause had died, my lord Cesare beckoned the poet to approach. A gold chain traded necks, lord to lackey. "My friend," said the Borgia jovially, "I thank you for your tribute. Was it not a fine poem, Lucretia?"

The lady on the throne nodded, her smile tight. "Although he might have done better than that reference to the bear," she said softly.

The poet's eyebrows rose in inquiry. My lord Cesare's roaring laugh shook him. Had he unwittingly offended? But now the Borgia was clapping him on the back and beckoning him to incline his ear still nearer. "My sister is too sensitive," my lord Cesare murmured. "No matter what she may imagine, the whole world does not know the meaning of the bear."

"Meaning —?" the poet dared to whisper.

"A jape. A jest. A rumor wilder than the German forests. It's said we Borgia have our…ways of dealing with our enemies, even to the creation of our own black pharmacopoeia. Have you heard of *la cantarella*, poet? A venom that exists nowhere save in the mouths and minds of the credulous. They claim it is a devilish poison that lets us choose the hour of our victim's death, and they say we make it ourselves, from the body of a bear." His teeth showed almost as white and sharp as those of the lady on the throne. "Have you ever heard the like?"

The poet laughed courteously. Having done this, he was dismissed. He left the banquet hall and the ducal palace entire. He needed to wash the reek of wine from his head.

Moonlight called. He stumbled from the gilded trap of palace walls into the freedom of the night. His stomach churned; his head swam. The dew had not yet formed on the petals of the roses, but a cold mist veiled his brow. He stumbled over the graveled paths, pursued by a lion, a bear, a knight armored all in roses.

He found the arbor before he fell, sprawling over the slab of the stone lions. Spiderwebs, holding a host of glittering crimson eyes, flung themselves between his eyes and the moon. He saw her face leaning over him, the tumble of her hair burning his flesh like molten gold. He tried to cry out, but his tongue had swollen in his mouth and all he could do was moan.

"What has happened to you, my little poet?" she asked. "You did not wait for me." Her fingers brushed the twin swellings at his neck where she had feasted the night before. One touch told all: "Ah." She nodded. "So the little doll has teeth too. I will have to speak with her of this. Vengeance is only mine."

Vengeance? The poet could not move, could not speak, but his thoughts screamed within his skull. The moon turned from silver to scarlet through the roses, the scarlet of a brimming cup of wine. *La cantarella…lets us choose the hour of our victim's death.*

He made a heroic effort to speak, to move, and only succeeded in stretching out the quickly chilling fingers of his right hand. Accident let them snare a fold of her cloak. She turned to go and was held back by that weak, almost imperceptible tug at the fabric. She looked down.

"Mercy?" she asked. His eyes implored her. "Even at the price of your soul?" Again his eyes pleaded, offering nothing but surrender.

She knelt before the slab as if she were a petitioner at the cathedral altar. Between her steepled hands she held the opened blossom of a white rose. She scattered the fragrant petals over the cold skin of his throat and smiled with the secret knowledge.

There could only be red petals in the gardens of my lady Lucretia.

Esther Friesner received her M.A. and Ph.D. in Spanish from Yale University. She taught Spanish there for a number of years before going on to become a full-time author of fantasy and science fiction. Her short fiction and poetry appears in numerous magazines and anthologies. To date, she has twenty novels to her credit. Esther lives in Connecticut with her husband, two children, two rambunctious cats, and a fluctuating population of hamsters.

"But I feel the Bright Eyes...."

by Bill Crider

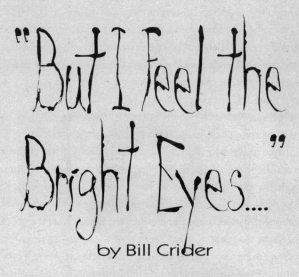

altimore, January 19, 1994.

It was quite cold in the Westminster Presbyterian Church Cemetery at the corner of Fayette and Greene Streets, not unusual considering that it was nearly midnight in the middle of winter. Somewhere out in the dark street a homeless man yelled incomprehensible words in a strangled voice.

Roger Bryce ignored the cries and checked his camera again, just to make sure that the battery was all right. This was one picture he didn't want to miss. Every year on Edgar Allan Poe's birthday, someone put a bottle of brandy on the monument dedicated to Poe's memory, but no one had ever been able to find out who was putting the brandy there, or why. Bryce wanted to know, and he wanted a picture. It would make an interesting addition to the doctoral dissertation he was writing on Poe's life.

Something scraped against the graveyard's iron gate, and Bryce whirled around. There was no one there, but Bryce had heard that sometimes homeless people climbed the gate and slept in the relative comfort of the tombs. According to Bryce's research, the same thing had happened during Poe's lifetime, and more than one person had suffered premature entombment thanks to ingenious spring locks that trapped them in the crypts.

Bryce shivered inside his sheepskin-lined leather coat. It wasn't the thought of early inhumation that had disturbed him. Suddenly, the temperature in the graveyard seemed to have dropped by ten degrees, and a thick fog came out of nowhere, dimming the streetlamps and muffling the sounds from the other side of the iron gate.

Something rasped along the wall of a nearby sepulchre. Bryce almost dropped his camera from his trembling fingers as he brought it up to his eye. There was nothing in the shaky viewfinder except the dark entrance of a tomb. On one side was a woman of frozen stone, holding aloft a winged hourglass. Bryce lowered the camera.

The wind in the bushes, he told himself. And then, when he realized that there wasn't any wind, he said aloud, "Maybe a cat." Thinking of Poe, he added under his breath, "A black cat."

He looked down at his wrist and pressed the button that lit his watch dial. It was eleven forty-five.

No one's coming, he thought. *It's all just a hoax.*

And then it abruptly got colder still, and the lights dimmed yet again, and an arm as cold and hard as the iron of the graveyard gate circled Bryce's neck and crushed inward, cutting off his breath.

Bryce's fingers went slack and dropped the camera, but he didn't even hear it hit the ground.

Philadelphia, 1841.

I learned of the Kindred in Monk Hall, that crumbling building of more than one hundred rooms inhabited mostly by the derelicts and outcasts of society—lunatics, beggars, thieves, prostitutes, and other such pariahs—who had no place else to go.

I was at Monk Hall to visit George Lippard, who for some reason chose to dwell in a chamber that made the sometimes grotesque settings of my own stories look drab by comparison.

The building dated from Colonial times and had been long abandoned by the respectable citizens of Philadelphia. Why Lippard chose to set up an apartment there, I had never understood, but every man to his own tastes.

I walked past a besotted man leaning against a wall, his eyes unfocused, saliva dripping from a corner of his pale lips and into his matted beard. The smell of the man was almost overpowering. Spiders webbed the corner of the ceiling near him as if weaving a shroud that caught the moonbeams through broken window glass.

In another room a tramp, or a madman, knife in hand, crouched over a rat that squealed and struggled as it tried to bite the hand that gripped it. The man's head twisted around at my entrance, his eyes feral with hate.

I strode resolutely forward. "I have no designs on your repast, if that indeed is what it might be. Pray continue."

The madman grunted in reply and moved the knife toward the hairy body. In one quick motion, he severed the rat's throat. Bright blood spurted onto the dusty floor, and the man lowered his head, making growling sounds deep in his chest.

I swallowed hot bile and passed through a door into another room where two women, their hair and eyes wild, their clothing tattered and patched, fought silently and furiously over a crust of bread. In the corner, wrapped in rags, a baby cried. The women paid no attention to me, and I paced briskly by them.

I passed next through an empty apartment and then I was at Lippard's room. I knocked, and Lippard called to me to enter.

Lippard was seated at a table near the window, the pale moonlight that filtered through the wavy glass of the window giving an almost golden glow to his sallow complexion and delicate features.

"Good evening, Edgar. I see that you are punctual."

I inclined my head in a semblance of a bow. "And what is this news you have for me? You said that it would be of some interest."

"Oh, it will," Lippard said. "I can assure you. But first let me offer you a drink."

He indicated a bottle on the table. It was filled with red liquid that somehow reminded me of the fluid from the throat of the madman's rat, as did the liquid in the glass beside Lippard's hand.

I confess that I stiffened at the invitation. "You know that I cannot accept. I have a particular weakness that I cannot now afford to indulge."

Lippard smiled. "Of course. I forgot. Forgive me. But I thought you might need a bit of fortitude for what I have to say."

"I have all the fortitude necessary," I said, wondering what Lippard had to tell me. His note had been quite mysterious. "You may proceed."

Then it was that Lippard told me of the Kindred.

Long ago, he said, they had lived in the caves along Wissahickon Creek in houses they had built themselves, perfecting their ancient wisdom and keeping well away from normal human society.

"Unless, that is, they had need of us," Lippard said. With a colorless napkin he wiped a red stain from his lips. "And they *did* have need of us, my dear Poe. Oh, yes, they did."

I was seated in a chair across the table from my friend. "I have never heard of these people, these...*Kindred*, and I fear that I do not yet grasp your meaning in telling me of them."

Lippard sipped from the glass that he held in his fine-boned hand. "Have you ever heard of the region of Transylvania?"

I sniffed. "My knowledge of geography is quite sound. Transylvania is situated—"

"Never mind, Edgar." Lippard waggled his fingers. "Everyone knows of your vast learning; the question was merely rhetorical. The Kindred came here from Transylvania in 1694, led by a man named Johann Kelpius. I say 'a man,' though that is not what Kelpius was. No, he was something else. Something else entirely."

I sat silently. I did not know where the conversation was leading, but I knew that Lippard would eventually make his point.

Lippard refilled his glass with the viscous red liquid. "Are you certain…?"

"I am certain," I said with disdain. "Please continue." *Or not*, I thought. Lippard was beginning to annoy me.

Lippard took a sip. "Very well. As I said, Kelpius was not a man, though once he had been. Now he was changed. Now he was something more than human. He was *nosferatu*."

And then in the eerie undersea light of that room, while a madman dined on a rat outside the door, Lippard told me a story that filled even me, a writer of gothic tales, with horror.

———

"They rule the world, you see," Lippard said in conclusion. "We humans think that we are in control of things, but that is merely an illusion that they allow us. They are the ones who manipulate us for their own ends, who command the flow of events, who manage the continuum of history. We—ah, we are merely their puppets."

It was a tale as fantastic as any that I had ever composed or thought of composing. I leaned forward in my chair. "And why did you tell me of this?" I asked.

"I wanted you to meet someone," Lippard said.

I felt an unaccountable apprehension, a *frisson* of terror. "And who might that be?"

"His name is one that I have already told you. Johann Kelpius."

I arched an eyebrow. "But my dear Lippard, this Kelpius must have died quite a long time ago. A hundred years or more."

Lippard smiled. "Died. Yes. He died. In a sense, he is dead even now."

"Then," I said, "it is plain that he cannot be *here*."

"Oh, but he can. I tell you that he now stands without the door."

"Very well," I said, sitting straighter in my chair, ready to see the game through to its conclusion. "Pray ask him to come in."

Lippard inclined his head. "I shall," he said, and though he did not rise from his chair, though I heard no door open or close, another man was with us in the room.

The lamplight revealed that Johann Kelpius was tall, thin, and pallid, except for his eyes, which glowed as brightly as those of a cat when the light struck them.

"Good evening, Mr. Poe," Kelpius said with something of a Slavic accent. His voice was deep and clear, and it echoed as if from the stone walls of a tomb. There was the sound of eternity in it, and it chilled me to the bone.

Suddenly, hearing that voice and seeing those eyes, I believed that every wild word that Lippard had spoken was absolutely true. This man was nosferatu. The evil in his soul was now plain on his countenance.

Although I felt as cold as the grave, I began to sweat from every pore. I tried to rise from my chair, to escape those eyes, but I found that Kelpius' gaze pinned me there.

"You needn't try to leave, Edgar," Lippard said. "It's no use, you see."

"What... is... in... your... glass?" I said, my words moving as slowly as glacial ice.

"Oh, it's not what you think," Lippard said. "Not yet, I should say. Soon, however. Soon."

"Con-consumption," I said.

Lippard smiled. "No, though that is what so many believe afflicts me, thanks to the paleness of my skin. But you need have no fear for my life, friend Edgar. The 'disease' that I have does not consume me. Far from it. Is that not true, Johann?"

"True enough," Kelpius said. "The worms will never feed on George."

"Nor on you, either, Edgar," Lippard said. "Not if you agree to join us."

"N-never," I gasped.

I was many things, not all of them good, but I was never evil. And Kelpius was evil in the flesh. True enough, I sought immortality, but the immortality I sought was that of the printed page, the kind that would keep me alive in the minds of men for centuries, not the kind that would turn me forever into a thing of fear and darkness.

"I believe that you will change your mind," Kelpius said. "You really have no choice."

"Wha—wha—"

"What do we want from you?" Kelpius asked. "That is quite simple. We want you to serve us."

"H—how?" My speech was slow, but not my mind. What service could I possibly do for these creatures?

"You have already written tales hinting that you have knowledge of us," Kelpius said. "One such is 'The Fall of the House of Usher.'"

I tried to shake my head in protest, but Lippard said, "Really, Edgar. How can you deny it? Madeline is clearly a vampire, draining the life from her brother. And does she not rise up from her tomb and destroy him at last?"

What Lippard said was true, in its way, but I had never intended for my tale to be taken as a fable of vampire morality. I tried to say as much, but I could not make my lips form the words. I knew then that I was under the influence of some dread and malign power and that I would be forever lost if I did not manage somehow to escape it. But how?

Kelpius tried to look charming, though he failed most miserably. "You are going to have the opportunity, Mr. Poe, to change the literary history of the world. We of the Kindred are going to give you the opportunity to present our case to humankind."

I struggled to refuse, but I could not form the words. Kelpius ignored my efforts and continued.

"From this point forward," he said, "you will write stories to make the preternatural seem less terrifying. Instead of instilling fear, you will give to the Kindred, through your fictions, a kind of domestic familiarity, so that people will come to see us as harmless chimeras at best, feeble charlatans at the worst. It should be an easy task for a man of your talents."

"You see," Lippard interjected. "I told you that they had uses for us, Edgar. You would be surprised at the ways they have of controlling things. Literature is but one of them. If I could only tell you of the legislatures—"

"Those are state secrets," Kelpius said, cutting him off. "Now, Mr. Poe, what say you to our proposal?" He paused and stared at me. "We are quite literally giving you an opportunity to change the very history of the world."

It was the eyes, I thought, ignoring his words as best I could. The eyes were holding me in the uncanny paralysis in which I struggled. If only I could do something about the eyes.

"My... choices?" I moved my right hand slowly, ever so slowly, toward the glass that sat in front of Lippard.

Kelpius smiled, his teeth white in the lamplight. "As George has told you, there really is none. If you refuse us, of course you must be punished. And punished you will be."

The thought of punishment had no appeal for me, and I had to admit to myself that somewhere deep inside me there was a strange desire for what the vampire offered: to live eternally, not only through my writing but in my flesh—unchanged and unchanging; to dwell, as it were, with the dead; to lie down by their sides in their tombs by the sounding sea, in their sepulchres there by the sea...

No! Something, that better part of me that was always there even if buried in the recesses of my consciousness, screamed the word in my mind, and my hand shot out with all my remaining strength, closed around the glass, and threw its contents into Kelpius' face.

The vampire hardly blinked, but it was enough. His gaze was distracted, and I slid from the chair, scuttled across the room and fled.

They were after me in an instant, but as I ran, I cried out to all the loathsome inhabitants of Monk Hall: "The fiend, the foul fiend! He pursues me!"

The madman dropped the carcass of the rat. The drunken man rose up. One of the women grabbed up the child. All of them joined together in my wild flight, and they in turn were joined by others—pickpockets, panhandlers, whores, and vagrants—in a rush that soon resembled a macabre dance of the doomed, a dance that hastened on its lunatic way through the decaying corridors of Monk Hall and into the streets of Philadelphia.

In the ensuing confusion, I escaped to a brightly lit tavern, where, surrounded by convivial companions, I drank wine until the break of day.

Philadelphia, January, 1849.

I escaped the Kindred in Monk Hall all those years ago, and I had escaped them often in the years since. I had even written against them all I could, disguising my moral as best I was able, but at the same time making it obvious to those who had eyes to see. It was there in "The Conqueror Worm," and it was there in "The Facts in the Case of M. Valdemar." It was there in "Ligeia." And in others of my works. It is a clear warning of the Kindred that exist among us, working their will on the human race. You can read it there even now.

But no one saw, because I was too afraid for my worthless life to speak bluntly, and those who did see simply disregarded the message as another outrage from the pen of the drunken Poe. And drunk I was, for from that fateful night at Monk Hall I began a slow descent into the bottle from which I never quite recovered. In the best of times I could drink but little, and now that I drank to forget what I had seen and heard in that terrible place, I drank too much, far too much.

And, too, I drank to forget everything the Kindred took from me, for that was their way. They did not destroy *me*. Rather they took from me everyone I befriended or loved.

They took Griswold, under the guise of consumption, and made him one of their creatures. I had trusted the man, even liked him, but now he had become an enemy to be avoided at all costs. Later he was to blacken my name and cast disparagement on my work so that no reader would give credence to my warnings of the Kindred.

Then they had taken Virginia. Sissy! That was the worst blow of all. I myself had escaped them, but Sissy had not! They had taken her body, and, I was very much afraid, they had taken her soul as well. As far as I *knew*, she rested quietly in her grave, but what I *suspected* was much worse.

And now they were closing in on me.

It was my acute hearing that gave the men away. They were sitting well behind me on the train, but I could hear their every word, though they spoke in whispers.

The one with the knife scar just under one eye said, "He's the one, right enough. Can't miss that fancy mustache."

"What about his valise?" asked the other. He had a whiskey voice and rheumy eyes. "We gotta get our hands on that valise."

I put down a hand and touched the carpetbag between my feet. How could they know? How could they *possibly* know?

"If we kill the little ninny, the valise won't matter," Scarface replied. "He won't be giving the talks if he's dead."

I trembled. They knew for a certainty. The carpetbag contained the manuscripts that I had prepared for two lectures, lectures based on knowledge I had gained of the Kindred over the years. At long last I had decided to speak out, though I feared that all my hearers would simply think me mad.

In these lectures, I would at last give the world the truth, and in doing so I would openly expose the Kindred and their evil machinations. Through careful research among those who dealt in arcane secrets and esoteric wisdom, I had learned how the Kindred manipulated and controlled the destinies of those who thought themselves free.

Suppose that the Pilgrims who landed at Plymouth in the year 1620 had reached their true destination in Virginia. Can you but imagine how their austere religion might have thriving there and how it would have assaulted evil? But suppose again. Suppose that the navigator of their ship was of the Kindred! (Oh, do ask of the deaths on that voyage. Not all of them were of the kind that you in your ignorance might have imagined!)

Suppose that George the Third had not been old and mad, dying and blind, ruled by his ministers and their sycophants. What might America have become under a benign British king? And then suppose that George the Third was not dying in the usual way, but at the hands (and the teeth, dear God! the teeth) of the Kindred.

Supposing only those things, which were true and verifiable with the evidence in my valise, you can see why the Kindred believed that I must be stopped.

But I would not be stopped.

I knew that the two men behind me were not themselves of the Kindred, for the Kindred sought the darkness. No, these two would be what the Kindred called *ghouls*, men who had not the powers of the others, yet who served them willingly in the hope of becoming like them. Lippard was such a one. I knew that I must *not* allow them to have the manuscripts, and I began to plan.

The train slowed on its approach to the city. I waited until someone rose to find a suitcase on an overhead rack and thus shielded me momentarily from the eyes of the two men. Then I grabbed the handle of my valise and hurried down the aisle.

"Damn!" the whiskey-voiced man said. "He's gettin' away."

I did not wait to see if they followed. I flung open the door to the landing. Hardly daring to look before I leapt, I tossed the carpetbag off the train. Then I jumped after it.

I hit the ground with a jolt, going to my knees. Throwing my hands in front of myself to break my fall, I felt the skin abrade on my palms, but I had no time to worry about such minor matters. I grabbed up the carpetbag and began to run.

"There he goes, the son of a bitch!" the scarfaced man yelled. "Jump, Simkins! Jump!"

We were on the outskirts of the city, some blocks from the station, not the choicest of real estate. I ran past rickety tenements and through dingy alleyways filled with the smell of garbage and privies. My foot squished in something soft and rotten that gave off the sweet odor of decay.

I heard a cry behind me.

"That way, Simkins! Into that alley!"

They were behind me, then. Where could I turn?

To my right there was a half-open door. I plunged through it, banging my shoulder on the decaying wood.

Something skittered away in the sudden darkness, and I thought I saw the shine of eyes. Rat's eyes.

There was a board on the floor, and I tripped on it. Dropping the valise, I crashed into the remains of an old table. Rats squeaked in terror, and their claws scratched across the floor.

"In there, Simkins!" Scarface yelled from the alley.

I struggled to my feet. My hand found the board that had tripped me, and when Simkins came incautiously through the doorway, I slammed the board across the man's face.

There was the appalling crunching noise of a breaking nose, followed immediately by Simkins' howl of pain and rage, a howl that was cut short when I slammed the board into his head again. Simkins fell to his knees and then sprawled face-forward on the floor.

I was not ordinarily a man of violence, and I looked down at Simkins, dismayed at what I had done, momentarily forgetting that Scarface must be close behind his friend.

Remembering, I jerked my head up, but it was too late. Scarface was through the door and upon me, bearing me to the floor under his weight.

We crashed down on my valise, breaking our fall, and I discovered that I was still holding the board. I tried to smash it into the side of Scarface's head, but I could get no leverage.

Rats squealed in panic at the commotion around them, and one of them ran across my hand. I snapped up my head in fear, accidentally hitting Scarface on the point of the chin. I heard a grunt of pain as the man's teeth clicked together. Taking advantage of my luck, I dropped the board and pounded my fist again and again into Scarface's ear as hard as I could.

Scarface groaned and rolled aside, and I sprang to my feet. Sprinting for the door, I stepped on Simkins' fingers, grinding them into the floor, but this time I did not hesitate to ponder the results of my violence. I fled down the alley and ran toward the railway station, where friends were awaiting me.

However, when I reached the station, panting and out of breath, my friends were not there. The train had arrived, passengers had disembarked and had departed, but I had not been among them. My friends, knowing my erratic habits, no doubt decided that I had missed the train, and after a brief wait, they left.

My clothing was disheveled and torn, and I had a cut on my face. I knew that I must look like a beggar or a sot. Not wanting to draw attention to myself, I left the station quickly.

Wrapping my coat tightly about me, I wandered the city, trying to decide what to do next. After nearly an hour of aimless walking I encountered John Sartain, one of those who was to have met me at the station. Sartain seemed surprised at my appearance, and I tried to explain what had occurred.

"There were two men, one of them with a scar, on the train," I said. "They are trying to kill me."

Sartain leaned close and sniffed.

I drew myself up with what dignity I could muster. "I am not besotted, Sartain. I tell you, there are two men trying to kill me." A sudden horrible realization dawned on me. "And they have stolen my carpetbag, my lectures!"

This latter thought, along with my recent violent experiences, was too much for me, and I began to weep.

"You must hide me from them, Sartain," I said. "We must go to your apartments. Do you have a razor?"

"What for?" Sartain asked, surprised. "Do you intend to fight them with it?"

"No, no, no!" I said. "I wish to shave off this cursed mustache! That is how they recognized me!"

Sartain put out a hand and touched me on the shoulder. "Calm yourself, Edgar. Calm yourself. Look around you." He pointed down the street. "There is Independence Hall. You are surrounded by the citizens of Philadelphia. Can you believe that any of them wishes to kill you?"

My head turned to the left and to the right. I could see no one among the pedestrians on the street who showed any interest in me, and none of them looked like the two men from the train, but that meant nothing.

"They might be anywhere," I said. My mind was whirling. Why could Sartain not understand? "They could be hiding in the alleys, lurking in doorways. They want to kill me, I tell you!"

"Now, Edgar," Sartain said placatingly.

He put out his hand again, but I drew back. Was there not something strange about Sartain's skin? Was there not a certain *paleness* to it that I had never noticed before? As Sartain tried to draw me to him, I broke away and ran wildly down the street, heading for the woods along the Schulykill River. There, perhaps, there among the trees, I could hide from my enemies.

—

There was only one place in Philadelphia to go for aid. I thought of it the next morning, after a horribly cold night rolled into a tight knot at the base of a tree, trying to cover myself with leaves while fending off the squirrels.

People drew aside as I strode down the streets, as much because of the mad light in my eyes, I am sure, as because of my unkempt clothing and the twigs caught in my tangled hair.

I had to ask directions of several shopkeepers, all of whom looked askance at me, but I found the place without much difficulty. It was only a few blocks from where I myself had lodged with Sissy in happier days, and it was a far cry from Monk Hall. I climbed the steps and knocked loudly on the door.

"By the great Satan," George Lippard said when he saw who

his visitor was. "You do look terrible, Edgar. Won't you come in?"

I brushed past Lippard and into the foyer of the house. "Are your companions here? Do they still seek my life?"

"Dear me," Lippard said. "You were always impetuous, Edgar. What? No 'How have you been, George?' No 'I've been following your career, George.' Just right to business?"

I threw myself into a chair without awaiting an invitation. "You see what I have become," I said, waving a hand at my filthy clothing. "You know my situation. Therefore I have come to ask that you stop harassing me. Let me live my life as I see fit, and I will not bother you or yours any longer."

Lippard stood near my chair, his willowy figure encased in a robe of scarlet silk. "Ah. And what makes you think you are a bother?"

"Simkins and his friend," I said. "They stole my valise."

Lippard smiled. "Oh, yes, your valise. It is quite safe. I have it right here." He walked to another room, but he was back in an instant, my carpetbag dangling from his slim hand. "Of course, it is not now quite so heavy as it was when you saw it last. Wasn't it thoughtful of us to relieve you of some of your burden?"

I shook my head sadly. "What have they promised you, George? What have you gained?"

Lippard shook a finger at me in mock reproval. "You know very well what I hope to gain, Edgar. It could have been yours, too." His eyes grew hard. "But not now. Now you will die as all humans die. And sooner than you think."

"That is all I ask," I said. "Stop this damnable toying with me and finish it. Now."

Lippard picked up the valise and thrust it into my lap. "Go, Edgar. What happens to you is for others to decide, not I. And you have only yourself to blame."

I clutched the carpetbag to me and rose like an old and very weary man. "I know," I said. "I know."

—

Richmond, September and October, 1849.

I left Philadelphia in despair, but my arrival in the South cheered me considerably. The South was different, I told myself. There was something brighter and cheerier about it, something beyond the mere fact that the sun shone longer and more often. Could it be possible that Kelpius' influence and that of the Kindred did not reach this far?

Months passed, and I was not disturbed by the sight of a single sallow face. I began to hope that I might have a life ahead of me after all. I even stopped drinking and went out into society. When I met Elmira Royster Shelton, a sweetheart from my youth, my memories of Sissy faded so far as to allow affection to blossom in my heart. The fact that Elmira was wealthy and could afford to back me in a publishing venture that was dear to my heart might also have had something to do with it, though I did not like to think of myself as being quite so mercenary.

Life was, in fact, so good that I almost began to believe that all that had gone before was nothing more than a dreadful nightmare.

And then one day I saw Scarface.

The man did not see me, for I shielded my face and drew back into the entrance of a mercantile store, but there could be no doubt about who it was.

I stood in the doorway for a few moments, until a patron brushed past me with an odd look. I put a hand to my face and found that my cheeks were wet with tears. They were here, the Kindred were here after all, and they would find me sooner or later. Worse, much worse, they would find Elmira and take her as they had taken Sissy.

I knew that I could not allow that, though what could I do?

After only a moment's thought, I knew the answer to my

question. I could leave Richmond, making my plans public, and draw my pursuers away.

But I would run no more. If I could not escape them, I would make a stand and make an ending.

———

"You do not have a fever, Mr. Poe," Dr. Carter said, "though you do appear unnaturally flushed. Is there some undue excitement in your life?"

"None, none," I assured him, though it was far from the truth. "But I felt unwell and thought it best to see you before embarking on a journey of any length."

Dr. Carter smiled. "Indeed. And you want to be in good health for your marriage to Mrs. Shelton, as well."

"Of course," I said with an answering smile, knowing well that both my trip and my imminent marriage were nothing more than merest shams. "I am glad to hear that I am sound."

I left the doctor's offices, and in an apparent mistake took the doctor's malacca cane, leaving behind the walking stick I had taken to carrying. But it was no mistake. Carter had confided in me during an earlier visit that the cane concealed a sword.

"Of the very finest British steel," Dr. Carter said. "One never knows what sort of villains one might encounter on the streets of Richmond."

No, I thought now as I walked away from the doctor's offices. *One never knows.*

———

Early on the morning of September 27—leaving my trunk behind, knowing that I would most likely never need it or its contents again—I boarded the steam packet *Curtis Peak* and embarked for

Baltimore. Under the pretense of doing some editing work, I was to continue to New York, but when I reached Maryland, I saw that the two men from the train were aboard the boat with me. They kept well away from me, and mingled with the crowd of passengers, but there was no mistaking them.

Well, I thought, *why not make my stand in Baltimore?* There was, after all, a certain fitness in it. I had lived there in happier times. And were not my brother and my grandfather buried in the Poe family plot there? If I should be buried there as well, I could ask for no better companions.

I left the boat in Baltimore, making my departure obvious to all. I wanted to be followed. I was far enough from Richmond that none of my friends would be harmed, whatever might befall my own person. I tapped the sword cane lightly on the cobbles as I strode away from the docks. Let them come. I was ready.

But they did not come. For days I wandered the city, staying first at one inn and then another, leaving a plain trail behind me. Yet no one inquired for me. No one followed me in the streets. I wondered if I had, without intending it, eluded my pursuers.

I had not, of course. They were but awaiting their time, a time that came on a night in the lonesome October. I was on my way to yet another hostelry, when I realized that I was near the family burial plot. I bethought me to visit the cemetery containing the graves of my kin in order to pay my respects, and I turned my steps in that direction.

There was a church under construction beside the cemetery, but the place was otherwise unchanged from the last time that I had seen it. It was a place of huge tombs that showed starkly white in the moonlight, and I wondered if the students from the nearby Medical College still indulged themselves in the sport of robbing graves. I myself had accompanied several of them on one such expedition in earlier times, though the police had arrived on the scene and thwarted us in our attempts to remove the cadaver from its resting place.

I walked in among the tombs and the shadows, seeking my brother's grave. I had not gone far when I heard a noise, a sound of soft laughter.

It was a sound that I knew well, and when I looked up, I saw her. I thought instantly of a line from a poem I had written many years earlier: *For the moon never beams, without bringing me dreams…*

"Hello, Eddie," Sissy said, for it was she indeed: her smile, her hair, her bright, bright eyes.

And the stars never rise, but I see the bright eyes…

She stretched her arms toward me. "Eddie," she said. And again she said, "Eddie."

I wept. But not because of what I saw. I wept because of what I knew. They had annihilated her soul, just as I had feared, for this was not Sissy. No, this was nothing human; this was *nosferatu*.

I looked wildly around, the tears streaming down my face. "Why did you send *her*, Kelpius?" I cried. "Why not come yourself?"

There was no answer except the wind, the wind and Sissy's smile and those large bright eyes, brighter than ever they were in life, as she came forward, her arms inviting me to let her enfold me as she drained my life. I knew that I must resist, but the eyes—the eyes!

And so, all the night tide, I lie down by the side

Of my darling—my darling—my life and my bride…

I turned to flee and found my way blocked by the iron door of a sepulchre. As I shoved it open, it groaned on its hinges like a soul in torment. I slipped inside the tomb, closing the door behind me with a reverberating clang. High on the wall, a narrow window admitted the moonlight and showed a wildly carved coffin that rested near me.

I know not what happened then. I know only that at one moment I was alone in a cold, dark tomb, and the next there was someone—some*thing*—with me. It was not possible, yet

Sissy was there.

I stared at her wordlessly for a moment, and she moved toward me. I backed up to the door, pressing against it, trying to get it open, and then—though how, I know not—I was in her cold embrace.

And, strange to say, I did not fear it. No! Say, rather, that I *desired* it with a hot desire. And her mouth was soft on my neck, and I felt— something, I know not what—and I was unaccountably weak and happy at the same time, and pleasure and terror washed over me in equal waves as I shivered in the wintry clasp of her icy arms.

But there was this in the back of my mind: There was the thought of Kelpius, the knowledge of what he was and what he was doing to me, the knowledge that he was going to win in the end.

I knew that it must not be.

The covering of the sword cane clattered on the ground as it dropped away. Sissy did not seem to hear.

Though I was growing weaker with each passing moment, I somehow managed to raise the sword.

"Sissy," I said, but still she did not hear. Her eyes were closed in a transport and profanation of passion. "For God's sake, Sissy!"

I was weeping again, but I knew what I must do. I put the sword to her breast and thrust it in, leaning toward her with all the strength that was left in my nearly drained body.

She shrieked and drew back her head. Her mouth was covered in blood—my blood—but blood of her own crimsoned her chest as she fell away from me.

"Sissy!" I said. I still could not believe what had happened, what she had done, what *I* had done.

"Take it...out, Eddie," she said. "It hurts me so."

My hand moved toward the sword as if of its own volition. It was almost more than I could do to will it back to my side.

"Please...Eddie."

"No, my dearest Sissy. I cannot. I will take your blood and

free your soul."

How little I knew. I believed every word that I spoke.

"Please, Eddie. If you cannot take it out, then kiss me. One last farewell."

And, God help me, I did. I bent down and touched my lips to hers, and her arms came up around my neck and pulled me to her as tightly as ever bands of steel bound a trunk of wood. I struggled, but it was no use. Her hands found the back of my head and forced my mouth to hers. She held me until I must perforce open my lips, and in that one unholy kiss she sealed my fate.

She opened her arms then, and I sprang free, but it was too late—far, far too late—for me.

"You have taken my blood, Eddie," she said.

"No!" It was a scream. "No!"

A voice came from behind me. "Ah, but you have, you know."

I whirled around. It was Kelpius.

"You are one of us now," he said. "Or soon will be. There is no turning back, not now."

I thrust my finger down my throat and gagged. A sickly green bile spewed out, followed immediately by the remains of the supper I had recently eaten.

"That will do you no good," Kelpius said with a smile. "No good at all. No more good than your lectures will do, though you could have harmed us then had you delivered them. It would never do to have the puny humans know how we use them for our own ends."

He walked over to Sissy and pulled the sword from her breast, cleaned it on her skirt, and put it back into the cane. Sissy looked at him gratefully; then he handed the cane to me.

"I am sorry you chose not to join us willingly, Mr. Poe," he said. "But you have joined us in the end."

"No," I said, but this time it was not a scream. It was a whisper of fear.

Kelpius put down a hand and drew Sissy to her feet. "Oh, but you have. Soon now. Soon. You should be happy, Mr. Poe. You will join your beloved Sissy again."

Sissy smiled at me, her mouth rimmed with my blood. She wiped it with the back of her hand.

"No," I said, and this time there was resolution in my voice. "I will defy you, Kelpius. Even in death, I will defy you."

He gave me a scornful look. "It can be done. It even has been done. But not by the likes of you."

I clasped the sword cane. "We shall see." I turned to go, then turned back. "Good-bye, Sissy," I said.

She looked at me with something that might have been sadness. "Good-bye, Eddie."

Opening the door of the tomb, I walked away into the bitter October night and left them there among the graves.

———

The next days were filled with pain, pain to the most intense degree one can experience and yet remain alive. The sun, weak as it was behind the clouds, burned me intolerably, and though I resolved to bear it, it sickened me... maddened me. I reeled through the streets of Baltimore as a drunken man might stagger in the throes of delirium. I raved as a lunatic might rave, though of course I was neither demented nor intoxicated.

God knows how my old friend J. E. Snodgrass found me. Perhaps he was passing by the saloon on Lombard Street where I had finally taken shelter from the sun; perhaps someone fetched him there. It matters not. I tried to tell him what had happened, but the events were too incredible, and I was hardly coherent. He must have thought me deranged.

Somehow he got me to the University Hospital, where a doctor examined me to see if I was in the throes of *delirium tremens*. Of course he found no trace of alcohol, for I had consumed none, and I am certain that whatever he did find, he kept to himself. For he must have found something. I was going through a change that was both horrifying and terrible, in the literal sense of that overused word.

Of course the *physical* change must not truly have begun at that time. For that, I had to die.

I was in the hospital for four days, tormented by visions.

I saw Sissy, her mouth crimson with blood, her bright eyes shining with ungodly joy.

I saw George Lippard as he swooped like a gigantic bat through the corridors of Monk Hall, blood dripping from his ensanguined fangs as the appalled inhabitants fled, shrieking in terror.

I saw Johann Kelpius and Rufus Griswold as the two of them rent a living body limb from limb and then held up the head for me to see. It was the head of my beloved Muddy, and my screams then were louder than at any other time, though they were loud enough all the day long, and all the night.

Then the moment I had dreaded came at last. I had never been a religious man, but I knew now the terrors that awaited me on the other side of the grave. I looked into the vague faces that seemed to float above me.

"Lord help my poor soul," I said.

And then I died.

—

I did not stay in the grave, of course.

When they came to move my bones and place them at the foot of the monument that bears my name, they found nothing, not even the ashes and dust to which we are all said to return.

But I did *not* join Johann Kelpius. I found the strength to become something other than what he was.

I say *was* because he no longer *is*. I devoted myself to his destruction and to the destruction of those like him, for they *can* be destroyed.

It is not easy, however, for they are everywhere; they control more than you can know, more even than my lectures were to reveal, and they are clever and strong.

Sissy, for one, was even more clever than Kelpius, than Griswold, than Lippard. Them, I found. Her, I have not found, though I have sought her down through the long years, the long, unending years. I pray to see her bright eyes once more, once more before I lay her to her final rest, a rest that *will* come for her as one day it may come for me.

May the grave that receives me then not give me up again forever.

———

Baltimore, January 19, 1994.

The man who held the bottle of brandy to Roger Bryce's mouth was small, with eyes that were both bright and dark. He also had a dark mustache and cold, cold hands.

"I am sorry if I hurt you," the man said. He had a soft Southern accent. "I thought you must be…someone else."

Bryce was leaning against a tomb. He could hardly speak through his bruised throat, but he told the man his name. "I was here to see who put the bottle on the grave. It's been happening for so long."

The man smiled. "I know. It is a sort of joke I have with myself. I loved brandy once. It helped me forget. I only wish that I could drink it now."

"Why?"

"Let us say simply that I never drink…brandy."

"What's your connection with Poe? I'm very interested. I'm

a student at Johns Hopkins, and I'm writing a dissertation on him and his life."

"I see. If that is true, then perhaps you are the one I can trust with this document." The man reached inside his coat and brought out a manuscript. "I have been carrying it for years, waiting for the right person. I hope that I am not making a mistake."

For some reason, Bryce wanted desperately to assure the man that he was not making a mistake. "I'll take care of it, I promise."

"Perhaps you would. I will entrust it to your care."

The man handed Bryce the manuscript, and then he was gone. Bryce didn't see where the man went, but he took the manuscript home and read it. He also took the brandy, and now he had another drink of it.

He knew that no one would ever believe a word of the manuscript. He wasn't even sure he believed it himself, though it went a long way toward clarifying a great number of things about Poe's life—and his mysterious death—that no one had ever been able to explain satisfactorily.

But other parts of it were even more incredible. Lee Harvey Oswald, a tool of the Kindred? What had Poe called him? A ghoul? And that was the least of the manuscript's wild claims. If the author of the manuscript, Poe or not, was correct, then the entire history of the world was being controlled by a group of vampires!

Taking that into consideration, it might yet be worthwhile, Bryce thought, to take the manuscript to a handwriting expert. Even if it were declared genuine, however, there was sure to be endless controversy. Poe had been a lover of hoaxes, and this could simply be another hoax.

But what if the material about the Kindred, as incredible as it seemed, was true? And even if there was only a small chance of that, the world had to be told. Bryce was sure of that. Maybe somehow he *could* get the manuscript published. It would be a wonderful curiosity, if nothing else.

He would begin trying in the morning. And who knew? Maybe someone would even believe it. Whatever else, it explained a great deal about seemingly inexplicable historical events that many people had always wondered about. Yes, maybe people *would* believe it, after all.

At that moment, there was a noise outside Bryce's window. He glanced up, and for the merest fraction of an instant he thought he saw the face of a woman. He almost thought he recognized her.

She was very pale, pale as the moon, and she had bright, bright eyes.

"But I Feel the Eyes...."

Bill Crider is the author of more than twenty mystery and Western novels, including *Blood Marks* and *When Old Men Die*. As Jack MacLane, he published five horror novels with Zebra Books, among them *Goodnight Moon* and *Blood Dreams*. His short stories have appeared in numerous anthologies, including *Dark at Heart*, edited by Joe and Karen Lansdale, and *Obsessions*, edited by Gary Raisor.

Vampire Lovers

by Lisa Lepovetsky

I.

(Virginia — the morning after)

He strutted easy and blue
   under empty moons,
   eyes cold slag
   from the city dump
   and his tongue
   so rough it chewed
   through women like
   a bulldozer through mud.

His voice sent slivers
of frozen glass
so deep in my gut
I burned like acid
and paled white as
a frog's wet belly;
he smelled of old love
and the watered-down prayers
my mother muttered.

His kisses burned my flesh
like Arctic nights,
and bruised off target
to the curve of my throat.
The edge of his laugh
when he loved cut an arc
through the air to land
like incisors on my mouth
and tear me wide open.

He was dark in the day
like the whispered threat
you need and fear
and his breath
so hot it seared
the center of my soul,
and his smile
sliced thinner than light.

But he loved like a razor
clean, cold, and fast,
and the scars he left
on my mind still itch
me wild some nights

when the moon won't sing,
and I chew my lips
for the blood.

II.
(Edythe — from the asylum)

Madder eyes scream hungry
and silent above mouths
that open too wide,
too red in the night.
White skies disappear
behind whiter curtains,
flaccid and cold
hiding air and iron mesh
as I wait for you.

Blind and dumb
though my voice
is never silent,
I'm as embarrassed
as the rabbit snatched
from a magician's top hat.
I sit naked in the light
listening to my own breath,
my heart pecking
holes through my ribs.

Though dusty bevels
of gilt-framed mirrors
ache to trap us
in their rectangular depths
in their hungry glass,

the room reflected
is empty and still
but for one dark shudder.

III.

(Lilith — one of us)

You thrust the iron bolt home
and cloak your windows
with red velvet eyelids
to keep the night at bay
when stars retreat
and the moon refuses to smile.
You think houses
can keep you safe.

I drift through the fog
and like fog
nothing keeps me away
when the sun deserts his post
on the western hills.
I know where you live,
I laugh at steel
and the games
men play at night.

You need to want me
more than meat or wine
or slumber's brief death.
I burn in your veins
the purest drug
you ever knew
and the taste of me

melts your tongue
like lye.

Memories of me drift
like hemp around you
twisting your limbs
in rough Gordian riddles
till breath sends spikes
through your lungs
and your heart
shrivels to a bullet.

When I leave at dawn
all other women fade
like old parchment,
and you wait in alleyways
your fists clenched white
in empty pockets
needing flesh
under your fingernails
and hot blood to warm
the chill in your soul.

Lisa Lepovetsky has written public service spots for television and a screenplay for a short horror film. She writes murder mystery dinner theatre plays for restaurants and teaches writing classes for the University of Pittsburgh (at Bradford). Lisa has already written three novels and is currently working on novels four and five. Many poems of her creation have been in publications like *Grue*, *Not One of Us*, *Deathrealms*, and *Dreams and Nightmares*.

In the Forests of the Night

by Robert Weinberg

iger, Tiger, burning bright,
In the Forests of the night.
What immortal hand or eye,
Could frame thy fearful symmetry?"

— William Blake

1.

The door to McCann's office wasn't locked. Grimacing, the big detective put his keys back into his coat pocket and reached for his gun. Then, with a shake of his head, he shoved the automatic back into his shoulder holster. Twisting the doorknob, he entered the outer office. If whoever waited inside wanted to catch him by surprise, they could have bolted the door after entering. It was a subtle but effective way of indicating to McCann that no place was safe. But the detective knew that already.

The reception area was deserted. The door leading to the inner office gaped. Inside, a figure moved in the darkness. "McCann," rasped a voice like a file scraping metal. "About time you got here."

"Sorry," said the detective, stepping into his sanctum. The figure bulked huge in the dim glow of the streetlamps streaming through the windows. The speaker's features were invisible in the darkness. McCann suspected his visitor wanted it that way. The detective made no move to turn on the lights. "If I had known company was waiting, I would have skipped dessert."

"My kind," said the stranger slowly, "need no food. Only drink."

"Fresh blood," said McCann, his voice flat. "What do the Kindred want with me?"

The figure's head nodded. "I was told you were quick-witted. And that you know of my race. Good. That makes life simpler. We can dispense with the usual explanations. I'm looking for a certain object — an ancient relic. I want you to find it for me."

"Sounds like a job for an archaelogist, not a detective," replied McCann. "I don't know the first thing about artifacts. Why come here?"

"You'll know the answer to that soon enough," said the stranger. "I don't make mistakes."

"And I don't work for vampires," said McCann.

"You haven't heard my price," said the stranger.

"Blood money," said McCann. "I can't be bought."

"Your life," said the other, as if the detective hadn't spoken. "That's the reward I offer. Perform this task for me and I'll leave you alone. Fail me and I'll make you wish you'd never been born."

The Kindred's voice sank to a low whisper. "Would you like

to live forever, McCann? Never die, eternally tormented by a dark thirst that can never be quenched? It's not a pleasant existence. Disappoint me and I'll hunt you down and turn you into one of us. I swear it."

"Rules are made to be broken," said McCann, his voice sounding only slightly less confident. "Even my own. How do I - contact you once I locate this treasure?"

"I'll take care of that," said the stranger.

McCann frowned, his eyes narrowing. He blinked, then shook his head in disbelief. The figure in front of him appeared to be shrinking, crumpling inward like a deflating balloon. Already it was half the size of a man, and continuing to shrivel.

"One more thing, McCann," said the stranger, its voice barely audible. "I'd advise you to keep this meeting strictly between the two of us… for your own safety, not mine."

Then the other inhabitant of the chamber was gone. For a brief instant, in his place, swirled a cloud of red mist. Then it too was gone. McCann was alone in his office.

"Nice trick," remarked the detective, switching on the light. At least he knew how his visitor had gotten past the front door without a key. Sighing, McCann settled into the leather chair behind his desk. Somehow, he felt sure there would be more visitors this night. And more threats.

2.

They arrived at midnight. It was a dramatic entrance. The door to McCann's office banged open though untouched by human hand. A cold wind swept through the chamber and the lights dimmed. A wolflike *something* howled in the distance. McCann, sitting behind his desk, folded his arms across his chest and waited.

A whisper of motion announced the arrival of two visitors. They moved with incredible, inhuman speed. McCann caught a bare snatch of movement before the pair were stationed at each side of his desk. His eyes narrowed as he turned his head from one figure to the other. One tended to think of vampires with dark, swarthy features, a prejudice fostered undoubtably by the image of the fictional count from Transylvania. These two bodyguards, as they could be nothing less, definitely countered that impression.

Clad in white leather jumpsuits that clung to their voluptuous figures like second skins, the two women were nearly identical platinum blondes. High cheekbones, dark eyes, and wide sensuous lips gave them a predatory look that both repelled and yet strangely fascinated McCann. Though they carried no visible weapons, the detective felt sure that these white-clad vixens were very, very deadly. As was the case with most species, among the Kindred females were much deadlier than males.

"You like my twins, Fawn and Flavia, Mr. McCann?" rumbled a deep bass voice from the doorway of the investigator's office.

"I find them....disappointing," said McCann evenly, sizing up the new arrival. Tall and aristocratic, the man was clad in a black tuxedo with a ruffled white shirt, blood-red bowtie and matching cummerbund. His eyes, set deep in a face that could have been carved from weathered stone, glowed with a darkness deeper than the night. McCann knew without asking that this had to be Alexander Vargoss.

The Ventrue clan ruled St Louis's netherworld. Their prince, Alexander Vargoss, was known as a dandy with a flair for the spectacular. As a Fifth Generation Kindred, Vargoss possessed arcane powers to do just about anything he wanted.

"Disappointing?" repeated the vampire, rolling the syllables over his tongue. "How so?"

"I know sex means nothing to the Kindred," replied McCann. "And with these two it seems a great waste. Very disappointing, to say the least."

"A typical kine thought," sneered a second vampire standing slightly behind and to the side of the Ventrue clan chief. A short, squat figure, with thick black hair and shaggy black beard, he was clad in a dark pinstripe suit and carried a narrow, silver-capped walking stick. "Food and sex is all they every think about. Animals."

Vargoss chuckled. "Mosfair finds humans distasteful," said the prince. "Except when blood calls to him. I think sometimes he forgets his origins."

Mentally, McCann checked off a mark on an inner checklist. Vargoss's closest advisor and confidant was a member of the notorious Tremere clan of vampire mages. The detective had heard unconfirmed rumors months ago of a new alliance between the Ventrue and the Tremere. The two groups already controlled the Camarilla, and thus the Masquerade. If they combined forces, they would be an unstoppable force in the secret world of the Kindred.

Vargoss dropped into the red leather armchair directly facing McCann. Mosfair assumed a position at his right side.

"Your name is well known among the Kindred, McCann. You have been mentioned to me by several Midwest princes as a man of astonishing talents. Tonight, I have need of such a man."

"What if I'm busy?" asked the detective, with a faint smile.

The prince smiled back, then casually gestured with one hand. Instantly, McCann found his shoulders pinned to the back of his chair, held there by one of the blonde twins. The other stood directly in front of him, the first two digits of her right hand pointed like steel pins inches away from his eyes.

"Do not mistake my favor for friendship, human," said Vargoss pleasantly. "To me, you are little more than a worm. I need your services this evening. But, if you annoy me too much, there are other worms. One word from me and Flavia will drive her fingers into your skull…and tear off your face."

The vampire prince snapped his fingers and the twin blondes

were back in position. Gingerly, McCann rubbed his shoulders. His bones felt like they had been gripped by a steel vise.

"You've made your point," said the detective. "What do you want me to do?"

"You are acquainted with a Professor Sullivan of the Oriental Institute?" asked Mosfair.

McCann nodded. He knew better than to deny a fact that could easily be verified. "We've met."

"Perhaps he is the one who imparted to you the secrets of the Kindred," continued Mosfair. "The professor is reputed to be the leading human authority on our race. He has studied vampires for the past thirty years."

"Perhaps," replied McCann, seeing no reason to say any more. "He knows quite a bit about the occult."

"Too much, perhaps," said Mosfair sourly. "About a month ago, Professor Sullivan departed from the Institute on an archaeological dig. His destination was not revealed, but rumor has it that he had located the lost city of Enoch."

McCann knew the name. The fabled "First City" according to the fragmentary *Book of Nod,* it was the original dwelling place of Caine, the progenitor of the entire vampire race. It was there that the Second Generation and the Third Generation of vampires once lived, until the metropolis was destroyed by the Great Flood. And, perhaps, by another, less natural disaster.

"I haven't talked to the professor in months," lied McCann calmly. He wondered what the hell was going on. Sullivan wasn't due to surface for another three days. Something wasn't right. He wondered just how much Vargoss and Mosfair suspected. Were the vampires baiting him, or were they truly ignorant of the professor's scheme? The less he said, the detective decided, the better. "I didn't even know he had left town."

"He's back," said Vargoss, his eyes glowing with hellfire. "He returned yesterday. Along with a certain fabled treasure he claims to have found at Caine's temple in the heart of the First City."

"A treasure?" asked McCann, a sinking feeling growing inside him. This was wrong, all wrong.

"Lamech's..." began Mosfair before Vargoss, with an angry glance, cut him off in mid-word.

"None of your concern, human," said the prince. "All that matters is that Sullivan possesses an extremely valuable relic that he has offered to me for sale. The exchange is to take place tonight. The professor has made it quite clear that he will not deal directly with any of the Kindred. I want you to act as my go-between."

"Sullivan returns yesterday and the deal is tonight," said McCann, licking his lips nervously. "That's rather fast negotiating."

"I am anxious to obtain the relic," said Vargoss. "And there are....others....also interested in it."

"The Sabbat," said McCann without thinking, instantly regretting his words.

"You know far too much for an ordinary human, McCann," said the prince. Without warning, his dark eyes peered deep into the detective's. McCann was helpless to turn away. It was like looking into the hypnotic glare of a gigantic poisonous snake.

"Nothing," said the vampire after a few seconds. "I am of the Fifth Generation. Nothing living or dead can hide secrets from me." The prince shook his head, almost as if in disappointment. "From time to time, there are rumors of the Methuselahs—the ancient members of the Fourth Generation—stirring up trouble amongst the Kindred, their descendants, for unknown reasons. But your mind reveals no such knowledge."

"He recognized the Sabbat," snarled Mosfair.

"As would hundreds of other humans," replied Vargoss with a shrug of his shoulders. "Many kine are aware of the war between the Sabbat and the Camarilla. McCann may be merely mortal but he is no fool."

The prince stared at the detective. "A word of warning, human. The Sabbat worships death, and its members hate the living. They consider mankind cattle, suitable only for food. If the sect obtains Sullivan's treasure, all of humanity will suffer."

The telephone on McCann's desk rang shrilly. "Don't pick it up," warned Vargoss as the detective reached for the receiver. "That is the signal. Sullivan's assistant is on the way. She will meet you in front of the building in five minutes. There is just enough time to explain to you these computer access codes."

"Sullivan's assistant?" repeated McCann, dumbfounded.

"A human female," said Mosfair. "She's been the one handling the negotiations. We've never once talked to the professor. He has stayed hidden in the background, letting her take all the risks, relaying all of his instructions through her. For a kine, she sounds quite competent."

"Enough chattering," said the prince harshly. "The exchange will take place at Sullivan's hideaway. Afterwards, the girl will drop you off somewhere in the city, close to a public phone. Call us immediately. My brood will be waiting for your message. So far, we have been able to keep our dealings with Sullivan secret from the Sabbat scum. Hopefully, we will be able to do so a little longer."

McCann, remembering his earlier visitor, suspected otherwise. However, he knew better than to say anything. His night was already filled with surprises. There had been no girl in the plan he had concocted with Sullivan. Whoever she was, this unknown accomplice added a whole new dimension to a very dangerous undertaking. But there was no backing out of it now. Besides — the detective smiled to himself — he had a few surprises of his own.

3.

As soon as he saw the girl, a number of McCann's questions were answered. Short and slender, she was dressed in a short black skirt, dark stockings and a tight black pullover. Her jet black hair was cut punk-style close to her skull, and her cheeks were so crimson they almost appeared painted on her pale skin. She had thick, sensual, blood-red lips and startling white teeth that flashed in the moonlight. Though she was definitely human, the girl looked more like a vampire than the Kindred upstairs.

"Get in, get in," she urged as he stood looking at her through the open door of Sullivan's battered old Buick. Her voice, as he expected, was husky and deep, with the barest trace of an accent. His years of investigating the Kindred had made the professor a sucker for Blood Dolls. Usually, though, he liked them a little older. This girl looked young enough to be Sullivan's grand-daughter. "We don't got all night."

"Sure we do," said McCann as he slid into the passenger seat and pulled the door shut. With a roar, the car spun away from the curb and into the late-night traffic. Lips pressed tightly together, the girl continued to check her rear-view mirror for signs of pursuit. The detective grinned as he settled back onto the cushions. She might look like a vampire, but she obviously didn't know much about the Kindred and their weaknesses.

"Head for a city parking garage," he advised. "Go in one entrance and out another. It'll shake anyone tailing us. Guaranteed."

Wordlessly, the girl did as she was told. Twenty minutes later, they were cruising along the Inner Drive with no pursuers in sight. Not that McCann actually suspected Vargoss of going to the trouble of having them tailed. The prince was much too smooth to resort to such simplistic methods. But he saw no reason to tell the driver that.

"What's your name?" he asked pleasantly.

"None of your business," she snapped back. "You're just a messenger boy. So just sit back and stay quiet." She paused for an instant. "Vargoss gave you the computer codes, right?"

"Of course," said McCann, smiling. "Otherwise, this whole trip would be a waste of our time, wouldn't it?"

When the girl didn't reply, the detective continued. "Have you worked very long for Professor Sullivan?"

"Long enough," the woman answered curtly. "Keep your mouth shut. This ain't no twenty questions."

"I'm surprised," said McCann, ignoring her hostile look. "Professor Sullivan and I go back a long time. And I don't remember him ever mentioning a female assistant looking like you." His voice suddenly grew cold. "Not once."

The girl was good, very good. Except for the slightest tightening of her hands on the steering wheel, she didn't evidence any of the panic she had to be experiencing. "My name is Leslie Hill. I only teamed up with the professor recently," she admitted. "We met a few weeks ago. In Las Vegas."

McCann nodded, more to himself than the girl. The pieces of the puzzle were falling into place now. And the pattern emerging was one of the oldest in the world.

"You worked there" — it was a statement, not a question — "as a hooker catering to men with bizarre and outlandish tastes. People like my friend the professor, who was so obsessed with vampires that he often fantasized about making love to one. Even though he understood that sex meant nothing to the Undead."

Leslie licked her red lips nervously. "An old boyfriend of mine was a witch-hunter. He taught me all about the Kindred. When we broke up, I started dressing like a vampire just to spite the bastard. It caught me totally by surprise when guys started hitting on me for sex because of the way I looked. Opportunity knocked and I answered. The money was great and my clients weren't very demanding. My appearance, not my talents, drew them to me. Sometimes when we did it, they wanted me to bite them, but that was as kinky as it got."

"Why did you kill Sullivan?" asked McCann quietly.

The girl gasped in shock. Stunned, she momentarily lost her

grip on the steering wheel. For an instant, the auto swerved out of control, skidding onto the road's shoulder. Reacting instantly, McCann grasped the wheel and turned the car back onto the pavement. Cursing, Leslie regained her composure and command of the vehicle.

"I didn't kill him," she declared heatedly. "I swear it."

"But Sullivan's dead," said McCann. "Don't deny it. Otherwise you wouldn't be here. The professor never relied on anyone else for help. Least of all a hooker."

The girl's face was white beneath her makeup. "It was an accident. He paid me good money, up front, and demanded the full treatment. I never expected him to kick off in the middle of things. He didn't say nothing about having a bad heart."

She hesitated. "It was the ice cube trick that did it. I should've been more careful with an old guy like him, but he seemed so virile. Damn. Sure scared me cold sober when he collapsed so sudden-like. It was a hell of a way to end a session."

McCann couldn't help but smile. "I can think of worse ways to die. Much worse. What did you do then."

"What do you think?" replied Leslie, making it clear the answer was obvious. "I pushed him off me, got dressed and checked out his pockets. The professor paid me in cash from a big roll. I figured after the shock he gave me I earned a tip. When I found his hotel key in his wallet, I thought I'd do a little exploring before I called the cops about his body."

"You weren't worried about being picked up on manslaughter charges?" asked McCann.

"Nope," said Leslie. "The professor rented the motel room. No one ever saw me. It's a procedure all the girls use. The place was booked for the whole afternoon. It gave me plenty of time to dash over to his room and search the place. That's when I found his notes about this scam."

The detective shook his head in annoyance. "Sullivan was a

brilliant man. One of the smartest I've ever met. But he had a terrible memory and he knew it. Damned fool insisted on writing notes about everything. Including stuff that should never have been put on paper."

"I'll say," agreed Leslie. Steering the car off the drive, she slowly edged it down a desolate South Side street. Up ahead loomed a massive old apartment building. From the outside it appeared deserted. "Nobody messes with the Kindred and gets away clean. Especially not to the tune of twenty million bucks!"

The girl parked the car in front of the dilapidated structure. "Sullivan's hideaway is in a rear apartment on the fourth floor. There's a direct link to the national telephone computer net in the front room. That's where we can feed in those access codes Vargoss so nicely gave you."

"We?" questioned McCann, raising his eyebrows in mock astonishment. "Who made you a full partner?"

"I did," the girl replied confidently. "I'm taking Sullivan's place. One word from me and the whole sting collapses. Deal with it, McCann." Pouting, she rubbed her body against his. "Besides, I have a lot more to offer than the professor."

Nonchalantly, McCann placed his arms around the young woman. Her fingers twined their way through his hair and started to pull his face down to hers. Then she stopped, as she found his hands pressing against her throat.

"I could just kill you," he declared coolly. "That would simplify matters considerably."

"You couldn't," sputtered Leslie, her eyes full of fear. "You wouldn't. You're not that type of guy."

McCann grinned and removed his fingers. "You're right. I'm not a cold-blooded killer. But don't try anything funny. I make a very bad enemy. A very bad one."

The girl nodded. "I wasn't lying," she said, stepping back from the detective. "I'm the only one who can break into the computer banking system. Sullivan wrote the necessary codes in his notebook. After memorizing them, I destroyed the sheets. Without me, you can't access the network. You wouldn't be able to touch a penny of the funds. Like I said, you need me."

The detective nodded. The girl was right. He did need her. But not for the reason she thought.

4.

They rode a rickety old elevator up to the fourth floor. Wheezing, the doors opened onto a dirty, debris-infested hallway. A thick layer of dust coated everything. "The building's deserted," said Leslie. "But," and she pointed to an ancient broom resting against a nearby wall, "I sweep away my footprints every time I leave. Just to stay on the safe side."

Together, they marched down to the fifth apartment from the lift. Leslie pushed open the door. "Welcome to the electronic wonderland," she declared cheerfully.

Not sure what to expect, McCann peered into the apartment. It was as messy, if not worse, than the hall. Books and papers were scattered across the threadbare carpet. In one corner, a black obsidian paperweight shaped like a pyramid rested on a stack of old newspapers. Dozens of maps of Asia and Europe were pinned with thumbtacks to the walls. Except for the remnants of a half-devoured sandwich, there was nothing to indicate anyone was living here. Then he noted the glowing computer monitor and PC in the far corner of the chamber.

"That's it?" he asked, doubt ringing in his voice. "That's all you need to use the access codes?"

"Right as rain," said Leslie, dropping into a chair in front of the keyboard. "Don't judge a computer by its size. This baby is loaded with the proper software necessary for it to plug into major financial networks throughout the world. And it handles bank transfers through an indirect system that makes tracing the source location impossible. After seeing how this machine works, I'm convinced that the desktop computer is the extortion method of choice for the mid-1990s."

Reaching into his coat pocket, McCann pulled out a sheet of numbers. "Vargoss gave these figures to me. I assume you know what to do with them?"

Eagerly, Leslie snatched the paper from McCann's fingers. "Come to Mama, honey," she crooned as she scanned the page. "These are the access codes to the Ventrue bank account containing the twenty million. Once I enter these files into the computer, the money will be immediately transferred into five untraceable Swiss bank accounts in Sullivan's name. With the correct identification numbers, we can draw on those funds from any ATM in the world. In five minutes, we'll be rich."

McCann nodded. "Just as the professor planned. You understand exactly what to do?"

The girl grinned. "Before I started turning tricks, I worked as a keyboard operator. Jobs like this are a piece of cake."

Leslie flexed her fingers, then started typing. She worked slowly, checking the numbers carefully. "Can't afford to make one mistake," she said. "Otherwise, I'll have to start all over again."

"Don't screw up," McCann cautioned, "but enter the information as fast as possible. Vargoss isn't the trusting type. Somehow or other, he's going to trace us here. And when he discovers that the Ventrue paid twenty million for an imaginary treasure, he's not going to be very pleasant."

"That's one thing not in Sullivan's notes," said Leslie, continuing to enter numbers. "What item's worth a fortune to the Kindred?"

"You ever hear of Lamech?" asked McCann.

"No," said Leslie. "Should I?"

"Not unless you're an expert on vampire lore," replied the detective. "It took Sullivan ten years to piece together the legend surrounding him. That's when he came up with the idea for this swindle.

"According to the Old Testament, Lamech was Caine's great-grandson. Thus, in the tradition of the Kindred, he was a member of the Methuselahs, the earliest of the Fourth Generation. Reputed to be the most powerful sorcerer ever to walk the face of the Earth, Lamech was a mysterious, mythical figure even to those of his own kind. No one knew anything about him, other than that he was a rebel, seeking absolute power over both mankind and the Kindred."

"My ex-boyfriend told me about the Methuselahs," said Leslie. "They're the incredibly ancient Kindred, supposedly still alive and manipulating the entire vampire race in some sort of secret war."

"The Jyhad," confirmed McCann. "Sullivan found a long-lost section of *The Book of Nod* that detailed the source of that conflict. It told how Lamech discovered the lost city of Enoch, and there, using secrets he found in Caines' temple, developed his greatest discovery — a magical elixir that artificially induced *Golconda*.

"That's the state of being in which the Kindred are free from their lust for blood," said Leslie. She pondered over McCann's words for a minute. "It's what every vampire wants. Immortality without the guilt. No wonder Vargoss is willing to pay so much for the formula."

"The potion is worth any price," said McCann. "Whoever controls it, dominates the entire Cainite race. No vampire would dare risk being denied the elixir. The owner of the draught would soon become absolute master of the Kindred."

"So you and Sullivan baited this sting with the one thing Vargoss couldn't resist. Absolute power."

"Correct," said the detective. "The Kindred have been searching for the secret of Lamech's elixir for thousands of years. Sullivan and I started planting phony clues six months ago. We carefully built up a web of circumstantial evidence that we carefully fed in small doses to Kindred informants. It was a master plan, perfectly executed. When the professor left the city, supposedly on a secret expedition to Enoch, the final phase of the scam was set into motion." McCann chuckled. "No one ever guessed he was actually hiding out in Las Vegas. Too bad Sullivan never got to see how well our plans worked."

"His loss was my gain," declared Leslie, lifting her hands from the keyboard. "All done. We're rich."

The girl arched an eyebrow. "So neither you nor Sullivan actually had the elixir. It's all bluff."

"Right," said McCann. "It disappeared with Lamech into the sands of time millennia ago. It's like the Maltese Falcon, the stuff dreams are made of."

The detective's eyes narrowed. "Did you hear something outside?"

Not waiting for a reply, he rushed over to the windows looking out onto the street. One glance was enough. His hands clenched into fists as he watched Alexander Vargoss and his twins climb out of a shiny black limo.

"Company's here," McCann announced harshly. "And they don't look happy. Somehow they traced your computer connection."

"Impossible," said Leslie, joining him at the window. "Besides, that would mean they were monitoring my entries from their car. That can't be done."

McCann scowled. Then, angrily, he glanced at his shirt where Fawn had earlier pinned him against his chair. "Microchip transmitters," he growled, ripping the miniature metal pins off his clothing. Dropping them to the floor, he ground the two instruments beneath his heel.

"Too late for both of us to run," he declared. "If Vargoss finds this place empty, he'll guess the truth and start the hunt immediately. We'd never get out of the city. Our only chance is for me to stall him long enough for you to escape. Hopefully, I'll be able to convince him that Sullivan's still in the building. During our search, I'll make my exit."

"You'd take that risk for me?" asked Leslie, her tone puzzled. "Why?"

"Because," said McCann, "I'm that type of guy. The one who doesn't leave a lady, even one who's not much of a lady, in the lurch. Hurry up and get moving. I assume you've got another car parked in the back? Good. I'll meet you in Vegas in a week. Twelve noon in the lobby of the Luxor Hotel."

"You're nuts," declared Leslie, with a shake of her head, "but I'm not one to argue."

Impulsively, she threw her arms around the detective's neck and kissed him hard on the lips. "That's a downpayment on what I owe you. I'll deliver the rest in Vegas."

And then she was gone.

McCann smiled. He knew that the chances of the girl showing up for their rendezvous were one in a million. Or, more precise, one in twenty million. Which suited his purposes perfectly, since he had no intention of being there either.

5.

Once he felt sure Leslie had left the building, McCann walked over to the pile of newspapers on the floor. Gently, he lifted the obsidian pyramid off the stack. Examined up close, the structure showed signs of incredible age. A thousand tiny hairline cracks covered its surface. The Antediluvians built well, but nothing lasted fifty centuries without some wear.

The detective nodded in satisfaction. The best place to hide something valuable was in plain sight. Tucking the dark pyramid under one arm, he stepped into the hallway leading to the elevator.

Sullivan had known the truth but there had been no reason to reveal the facts to Leslie. McCann had never planned leaving the city. Money meant nothing to him. He strived for a much more satisfying goal. One that was nearly complete.

Dust swirled on the floor ten feet ahead of the detective. He halted, immediately guessing what was happening. A spot of darkness formed at the center of the whirlwind. It spiraled upward, like black smoke pouring out of a genie's bottle. In seconds, it had taken form and shape. Where there was nothing, now stood one of the Kindred.

"I told you I'd make contact at the necessary time," said Mosfair, extending a hand. "Give me the relic, human."

"I knew it had to be you," replied McCann, making no move to hand over the pyramid. "Why keep your features hidden from me that first meeting in my office unless I was due to see you again? Evidently, the alliance between the Tremere and Ventrue clans is not as solid as everyone thinks."

"My clan?" said Mosfair, with a laugh. He took a step forward, his hand still outstretched. "Those fools mean nothing to me. Only the Sabbat matters! With Lamech's Elixir in our possession, the true children of Caine will come into their own. Give me the relic, human. *Now!*"

Smiling, McCann tossed the obsidian object to the vampire. Eagerly, Mosfair grabbed it with both hands. "Lamech's secret," he exalted. "Back in Kindred hands after thousands of years."

"You twist the corners of the pyramid to reveal the hidden chamber," said McCann. "Unfortunately, you'll find it's empty. The elixir was removed a long, long time ago."

"What!" shrieked Mosfair. Powerful hands wrenched at the relic in the proscribed manner. With a whir of hidden mechanisms, it opened smoothly to reveal...nothing.

"How — how did you know?" asked Mosfair, bewildered.

"You and the prince made one terrible mistake," said McCann. "You assumed that Sullivan told me the secrets of the Kindred. Not true. I told him."

"A trick," snarled the vampire. "I have been betrayed."

Eyes burning with fury, Mosfair tried to step forward, his hands like claws extended to rip McCann limb from limb. And found himself unable to move. It was as if an invisible barrier cut him off from the detective.

"What?... Who?" the vampire stuttered, sounding terribly unsure of himself. Confused, he stared at the detective. "It cannot be. Vargoss probed your mind. I saw him."

"One of the unique powers of the earliest of the Fourth Generation," said McCann, revealing a hint of his true essence, "is their ability to completely take possesion of ordinary humans. It is a trick that enables the Methuselahs to carry out their plans under the very eyes of their unsuspecting descendants, the Kindred."

"The Jyhad," whispered Mosfair, his voice filled with fear.

"The eternal war," said McCann, smiling. "A complex, hidden struggle between immortals bored with life but afraid to die. You see, Mosfair, *Golconda* muffles the bloodlust. But it leaves ambition untouched. Only one can reign supreme. That is what the Jyhad is all about."

Unable to move forward, Mosfair took a step back. Then another. Then yet another. Anxiously, he waved the hand not holding the pyramid in an intricate series of motions, while muttering a few words beneath his breath. The vampire's eyes widened when nothing happened.

"Sorry," said McCann, shaking his head. "But I can't have you using that trick to depart. You'll have to exit the normal way."

Howling in fright, Mosfair turned to the elevator. Just as the door to the lift opened, revealing Vargoss and the twins.

The prince took in the whole scene in an instant. Mosfair, standing there, caught by surprise, the relic beneath one arm. McCann, seemingly dazed and confused, slumped against a wall at the end of the hall. There was only one conclusion to be drawn and it was an obvious one.

"Kill him," said Vargoss angrily, pointing at Mosfair. "Kill the Tremere traitor."

"No!" screamed Mosfair as the pyramid in his grasp suddenly burst into flame, sealing his doom. There was no time for him to say anything else. As if by magic, a long oak stake appeared in Fawn's hands. With incredible strength, she thrust it into Mosfair's chest and through. Seconds later, the long steel sword in Flavia's hands sliced his head from his shoulders.

"He...he ambushed me," said McCann, stumbling forward, his voice shaky. "Ripped the pyramid right out of my hands."

"Professor Sullivan?" asked Vargoss, staring with unconcealed despair at the ashes of the relic.

"Gone," said McCann. "His assistant muttered something about South America."

"No matter," said the prince. "I do not begrudge him his money. The professor kept his end of the bargain. As did you, McCann. How ironic. Mere humans turned out to be more honest than this Tremere turncoat."

Vargoss' dark eyes blazed with unholy fire. "I should have known better than to trust the mages. They are too ambitious to be loyal allies. A few words from me to the other Ventrue princes, and this foolish alliance will be no more."

McCann said nothing. But deep within his psyche, the part of him that was Lamech smiled in satisfaction.

Robert Weinberg is the only two-time World Fantasy Award winner to be chosen as Grand Marshal of a Rodeo Parade. He is the author of six non-fiction books, five novels, and numerous short stories. His *Louis L'amour Companion* was a best seller in trade paperback and was recently reprinted. His latest fantasy novel, *A Logical Magician*, was published earlier this year. As an editor, Bob has put together nearly a hundred anthologies and collections.

J. Cobb

Leader of the Pack

by Nancy Holder

And the last battles? How were they fought?

How were they won and lost?

The millennium fell. The bombs, and then the cities fell. From the glowing sickness, anarchy rose, and those with passions grabbed history, seized the world, and altered it forever. And among them, the darkest passions were the fiercest, and they triumphed: fury over reason, hatred over love, and revenge over loyalty.

This, then, is the story of Shiloh, whose other name was Vengeance.

They were outlaws among outlaws. They started out by running *from* — then something happened, something bad, something that could never be forgiven — and then they were running *to*, as fast as they could. They were like guided missiles as they screamed in formation through the desert, the wheels of their bikes crushing sagebrush and cow skulls and grinding them into sand. And the sand flared into smoke that streamed behind them like flares that spelled out their name in the wide desert sky: WOLFPACK.

They were outlaws, and their leader was a woman who was still practically a girl. When she was in human form, she was small-boned and fragile, with black, flashing eyes and blue-black hair streaked with white down the center. When she wasn't wearing her human skin, she was magnificent, over eight feet tall, her body lean and muscular, her coat silver and black, her eyes flashing and red. She was only nineteen; she had inherited the lead bike and all that went with it. She'd been on the road for over a century, and her name was Shiloh Marie.

But her pack name was Vengeance, and she was the Mother of Vengeance.

Her brother, Lance, had had the bad sense to fall in love with a woman — a human — so deeply and completely that he had told her something about them — exactly what, the pack didn't know, but it had been enough to send the town on the edge of the stinking, clogged sea after them in a surprise attack, shrieking like banshees. Her brother was killed. Shiloh shook the rest out of their panic and rage and got them onto their bikes, leading them as far away from that cursed little village as possible.

She figured that if the humans knew about them, then everyone knew about them — including the One they had betrayed. That night, under the stars, in their wolf forms, she cursed her brother's name and said that anyone else among them who fell in love with a human would be both traitor and outcast, and she would personally rip them to pieces. No one in Wolfpack doubted where Shiloh's loyalties lay, and that was when they made her their leader.

The desert they now roamed in had once been a paradise. Now there were poisons that glowed in the plants, and glass in the sand, from megaton explosions; More proof of the evil the humans had wrought upon the land, evidence that they all deserved whatever it was they had coming to them.

Whatever Shiloh said they had coming to them.

———

So on their rides through the desert, they began gathering up the humans — a lone man here, a newlywed couple on a journey across the country. The others wanted to kill them then and there, but Shiloh decreed that they would round them up like the sheep they were and then decide what to do with them.

"But how many, Shi?" asked Cutter as they sat together under the moon. They'd made a fire; they both loved the flames and smoke. His face rosy with flickering orange and scarlet, Cutter wore black leather and had the slash of a wolf paw shaved into his black hair. He was young and baby-faced. He had an English accent Shiloh could imitate perfectly. Seated across from her Indian-style, he sharpened a skinning knife against a leather thong. He had a lot of knives...not that he needed any, but he liked their gleaming blades and heavy handles made of bone and leather. He said he liked dead things, and Shiloh knew that was true. He had steel knives and silver ones; he most prized the silver. Most of Wolfpack carried silver.

Swap, swap, swap, the flashing knife blade ran against the leather. "How many of them do we round up before we do something, eh? I mean, something brilliant and bloody?"

Shiloh licked her lips. She didn't know how to answer. As they looked from the mesa down on the compound of humans, she saw the prisoners milling in their compound. On Shiloh's orders, they had erected their own prison, a fence of chain link. Inside were primitive lean-to's they had constructed as shelter. Shiloh made them bargain for food and water. Most of them lived in a perpetual state of terror, but she kept them alive. Now and then one might be taken; she allowed that. But the group…no.

"Do be quiet, Cut," she said gently, and rose to her feet. Inside she was raging. As she stood with her back to him, struggling to compose herself, her black duster grazed the tips of lizardskin cowboy boots. Her jeans were tight, the knees ripped and torn. Cutter grunted and went back to sharpening his weaponry. He was growing impatient. They all were.

Shiloh walked down the mesa, never losing her balance, enjoying the sensation of the sand granules beneath her cowboy boots. The air blew chilly and breezy, like the kisses of ghosts, and her hair wafted behind her like a black and silver pennant.

There he was.

The rough-hewn silhouette of the man was etched in bold relief against the velvet night. He rested one gloved hand on the chain link, and his head was tilted upward as he stared at the stars. They had dragged him off a Harley a week ago. She froze, staring at him, feeling the stirring deep inside. Was it a sickness that ran in her family? A weakness they carried in their hearts? If the others knew, if they had the slightest inkling…

She drew nearer, stealthily, stalking him. At the crunch of her bootheel, his head turned sharply in her direction. She heard a whimper in the shadows. One of the humans said, "Sssh." She could smell their fear.

The man walked toward her, meeting her on the side of the fence closest to her. He squared his shoulders, trying to appear unafraid. His white-blond hair cascaded over his shoulders, and deep blue eyes glowed almost feral in his sun-darkened face. It could never be, and yet she dreamed of ripping the gate open for him and leading him away, deep into the gorges and canyons, and staying with him there forever.

"Good evening," he said coldly.

She made no answer, only stared at him. Like her, he had been elected the leader of his pack. It seemed he never slept. Her sentries reported that he was always watching, always on guard. The good shepherd. She could almost laugh.

Almost.

"We have a sick man in here," he said. "He needs medicine." Still she remained silent. "Damn it! I know you speak English!"

Fury welled inside her. She raised her hand as if to strike him. Her eyes narrowed and she could feel herself quivering, her body straining for release in the freedom of her wolf form. She snarled, "Don't you ever speak to me in that tone again."

"Or what?" He lifted his chin. Clearly he was as angry as she.

"Or I will tear out your heart."

She lowered her hand. They regarded each other. In the distance a coyote howled and she cocked her head, wolf-like.

A grim smile flitted across his features. "I don't think you would. I don't think it's in your nature."

She started. Perhaps he knew more about her than she realized. But that couldn't be. "You don't know anything about us." She kept her tone strong and steady, but she was rattled.

"About *you*, I do," he retorted.

"Don't toy with me." Her voice was low. Her mane of hair rippled and began to stand on end. "I don't have the patience, and I doubt you have the life span."

She saw him stiffen, and was both sorry and glad. Maybe in another place, another time....

Never.

"He's an old man. He's sick."

"Then you should stop feeding him and give his share to

someone stronger. For the good of the pack."

He blinked. "I don't believe you really think that."

She gave her head a little shake. "I do."

"Good grief. Werewolves are Japanese."

This time she did smile. "Your kind would have a better chance if you banded together against us, rather than separate yourselves into meaningless nationalistic groups."

"You sound like a revolutionary."

"Maybe I am."

He crossed his arms. "But if there are only a dozen or so of you, I don't think we have to worry."

"Your arrogance —" she began angrily, but he held up his hand.

"You never have company. Your group never communicates with anyone else. I'd hazard a guess your band is the sum total of the…problem."

"We're enough." He'd struck another nerve; he did it often and well, with the skill and grace of a brain surgeon. Wolfpack was violating all kinds of laws by allowing these humans to live. Her brother's stupidity had already signed their death warrants. Outlaws among outlaws. She hated living like this. There was no one she could confess that to. She was their fearless leader.

"What are you thinking?" she asked him abruptly, in case he could see the wistfulness on her face.

"That I wish I had a cigarette. It's been forever since I've smoked."

"Yeah, me too." Now they both smiled. His was weary, and hers, nervous, edgy. She couldn't let herself get too close to him. But she loved how he looked. She loved how he moved. How he smelled — like more than prey. "Back when I was born, ladies didn't smoke."

He whistled through his teeth. She balled her fists; she'd said too much. She shouldn't talk to him at all.

After a time, he said, "Could I barter something for cigarettes?"

She shrugged. "Depends on what you've got."

"What about medicine for the old man instead?" He narrowed

his blue, blue eyes at her. She wondered what he'd been before. In a way, he had been changed in an extreme fashion. Caged beast. She shuddered. She would rather die.

She rolled her eyes. "You don't give up, do you?"

"No. It's a human trait." He threaded his fingers through the fence. She drew herself inward. The rage began to build again; he was trying to manipulate her. Perhaps he could sense her interest in him. Desire. Her kind could.

He was interested. He desired her.

"I can't get him medicine." She swung away. "You're all lucky to be alive."

She loped away from him. The moonlight shone overhead. Atop the mesa, Cutter sat in the smoke as it rose around him like steam. The blades of his knives glinted like stars. He inclined his head.

"I'm hungry," he said.

She shrugged. "I'm tired."

"Yeah." He didn't look at her as he put the wicked-looking knife in a hand-tooled sheath. She saw his anger in the ripple of his hair, the tightness of his jaw. This wasn't what they'd wanted, baby-sitting humans. There was no reason for it. They were beginning to say she was weak and sentimental like her brother. Sooner or later there would be a confrontation.

Unless she acted soon.

"I'm turning in," she said tersely.

He bobbed his head and reached for another knife.

The full moon waxed, and waned.

The old man who had needed the medicine died.

The other man — the leader of the human pack — was speechless with rage. Shiloh sensed a change in him as his emotions gathered, grew, burst to new intensities, new heights. He was on edge, ready to dare unthinkable acts, take chances that could be fatal. His people were the same.

And her people were the same.

She was going to have to kill *him*.

"Shiloh, something's going down. Something's wrong," Cutter said as they sat beside one of their campfires.

"Yeah," she said, grateful.

"Someone's betraying us. I was watching the day guards come off duty. They were nervous. Avoiding me."

"You doubt their loyalty?" She was astounded. A weakness in the line…

They looked at each other. Cutter put out a hand. "Shiloh, I know you…know. "

That Cutter loved her. She sighed. He must also know that she didn't love him in return, the way he wanted her to. And yet, it would be perfect. They could lead the pack together. He was brave in battle and more important, merciless.

"I fear for you," he went on.

"Thanks." She tossed pieces of tumbleweed into the fire and watched them catch like fireworks. "I know you have cause."

"I don't understand…."

"I'll take care of everything," she promised.

He raised his dark brows. "When?"

"Soon." That wasn't good enough. "Tomorrow night."

"Do it now." He leaned forward and laid his hand over her wrist. She knew what he wanted to share. She felt danger swirling all around her.

"Let's ride." She shredded the rest of the tumbleweed into the fire and wiped her hands on her jeans. Cutter made as if to protest, but got to his feet.

"I'd like to ride straight out of here and never come back," he muttered.

Sometimes Shiloh thought he could read her mind.

They rode deep into the desert night, their bikes roaring beneath them. Free, free, Shiloh thought as she threw back her head and bayed at the moon. Free of all the wrongness of their kind, and of the sight of the devastation around them. Free of the glow from *his* blue eyes.

"*Auuooooo!*" she howled. Cutter laughed and howled back. She yipped; he answered. He screamed up beside her and hailed her.

"It's going to be all right now!"

She made herself smile.

They rode for hours, perhaps until midnight. When they got back to the mesa, his face fell but he said nothing when she told him she was exhausted and wanted to go to sleep early. Finally he licked his lips and said somberly, "Say good-bye to him, Shi. Don't make the same mistake your brother did."

"Too right." She tried to joke by imitating his accent, but he turned on his heel and stomped away.

———

She went to the compound. He stood silently by the fence. He had been waiting for her.

She moved to the gate and put her hand on the lock. She could rip it open. She could let him out.

He didn't move.

She wanted to kiss him, run her hands through his hair. She wanted to spare his life.

She could do none of this.

"If you have a god," she said, "pray to it."

"I have a god." His gaze never wavered from her face. "Do you?"

She didn't answer.

She didn't know anymore.

———

She slept fitfully, unused to the early hour. Then the rock cave she had chosen as her shelter filled with shouts and gunshots. She pushed the stone away from the entrance and ran into the night.

The fence was down and the humans were pouring out. Men, women, little children. They were waving guns. They were shooting.

Wolfpack bikes were flying toward them, circling them, trying to run them over. A bike went down — she thought it was Fang, who had joined only a few months before — and the gas tank exploded. Fang crawled from the wreckage, cursing but unhurt.

"I told you!" Cutter was beside her. He pushed her forward. "Let's get our bikes."

They dashed to their machines. Her engine blasted into life and she careened through the confusion. The humans were shooting at them. She felt a bullet hit her, felt the pain, felt the healing begin.

Past the smoking bike she slammed over the downed fence. She drove wildly. Another bullet hit her. She recoiled from the impact and nearly fell off, but gripped her fists around the handlebars and accelerated to over a hundred.

He stood in the middle of the compound, poised to shoot. He stared at her and she could almost hear the click as he pulled back the trigger. He was going to shoot her. He thought it would kill her.

He thought he was going to end her life.

She smiled grimly and drove straight at him. He didn't move. Nerves of steel, she thought.

Or of silver.

She swerved before she hit him and shot out her arm. She threw him across the bike and shot away from the compound, the smoke, and the shouts.

—

She screamed into the canyons, gripping him around the neck when he struggled. He grunted when she threw him to the ground and stopped her bike, and towered over him. He rolled onto his back like a submissive animal, and for a moment she felt utter contempt for him.

"What the hell were you trying to do?" By now all the other humans must be dead.

"Silver bullets," he said. He was out of breath. "Your people who guarded us. We — somehow we won them over. We got some of your knives."

She was shocked. "They stole from us, for you?"

"A couple of them. That guy you hang out with. He gave us a lot of silver."

Her mouth dropped open. "You don't mean Cutter."

He smiled grimly. "We figured werewolves, silver."

"He crossed you." She wiped her forehead and licked her lips. Suddenly she was very tired, and very hungry. "He was forcing my hand, that's all." He blinked. "You don't know what we are."

"I just said —" He stopped. She could hear the beat of his heart. He was very afraid.

"We're not werewolves." She hesitated. Should she drop the Masquerade? Wolfpack had repudiated all the other laws of the Camarilla. They despised the aimless evil of the Damned — the Get of the Wyrm, as the blessed Garou called them. And they had turned against their own prince and tried to kill him.

She remembered it even now: the dissolute young man, so pale and handsome, lounging in a dark room filled with incense, upon pillows of silk. Women were draped all around him, wearing dresses of Chinese silk — peony, jade, crimson. They were smoking something in little pipes — opium, she later discovered. At the time she was Shiloh Marie, the sweet little schoolmarm in the nearby town Littleton; her brother, the blacksmith.

The young man was a prince of the Blood, and he was amused by this novelty, the American West. Against her will he Changed her as the women held her, and then Lance. Then the prince revealed to them how hated he was, and how many enemies he had, and made brother and sister join his other childer and kill for him. Every slight against him, every wrong, no matter how insignificant, was another death. Shiloh was too enthralled to refuse, and after a while, she found she did not mind the killing so much. Amused, the prince nicknamed her Vengeance, and called her the perfect instrument of his wishes.

Though not content, she was not yet miserable and wretched and filled with hatred.

Then she met the Garou, and saw how beautifully they lived and hunted. She came upon them during one of their festivals; she sensed they meant for her to see. She was too ashamed to join them, though she Changed in the darkness and bayed softly, wishing with all her heart that she was one of them, and not what she was.

She told the other childer; they followed her and watched. They were overcome.

Then the prince said, "There are diseased animals in the forest who mean to infect me. Kill them." She knew whom he meant, and she knew she would never do it.

They warned the Garou — the ultimate disobedience — and ran.

"We're not werewolves," she said again, stirring herself.

"But you...I saw you change," the man murmured.

Her mind was racing, trying to make sense of everything. Their Blood Bound ghouls must have betrayed them to the humans. Their blood was weak, because the sire of their sire — the prince — was weak. Shiloh and Cutter had Bound the ghouls, and clearly the tie was easy for them to break. When those who were now Wolfpack had struggled against the prince, they had been glad he was weak. It had made it easier to lose their awe and fear of him, although many of them were his own childer.

Outlaws among outlaws. If they could have become true werewolves, they would have done anything.

Anything.

"I can't let you go," she said. He was silent. His heart was pounding, and yet he showed no outward sign of fear. She respected that. She wanted to honor that.

She didn't want to lose him.

"I can't let you go," she whispered.

"It doesn't matter. You'll never beat us," he flung at her.

Wounded by the hatred in his voice, she dropped to her knees, straddling him, and touched his face. His neck. His skin was slick with sweat. His pupils dilated. Perhaps he knew now. Perhaps he turned his head, just the merest bit, offered her his neck....

No, not him. Not a man like him.

She took him. His legs kicked. He bucked. She drained him of all his sweet, brave life. Into her body he came, invading her, taking possession, giving no quarter. It was sweet and bitter and terrible and a dream. She thought she would go mad, or find Golconda...if such a paradise truly existed for misbegotten creatures such as she.

Too soon he struggled, panting, on the verge of death.

"You're starving," she whispered. "Drink from me. Come with me." She placed her neck against his cold, pale lips.

"Nnnnnn." He clenched his mouth shut. Yet she could feel him shaking with need.

"Please, please," she begged, pushing her neck against him. He cried out in agony, refusing her. Desperately she laid her wrist over his mouth. "Please, I — I love you."

"Ahhhhh," he moaned, but he would not bite.

"Please!" She forced open his mouth with her fingers. "Drink of me!"

His eyes opened. And stared. The blue shone like the sky that she had not seen for a hundred years.

She threw back her head and assumed her Gangrel vampire form. Her howls of grief reverberated to the stars; they seemed to shatter and rain down on the earth in megaton fury.

He was gone. The buzzards would come, and the drying sun. In days he would be bones.

"No!" She raged, almost until dawn, until the sun began to boil her weak blood. He was dead, True Dead. He had gone somewhere she would never, ever go.

Blood tears welled and glistened. Feeling nothing solid, drifting and numb, the girl, Shiloh, mounted her bike, kicked off the stand, and started the motor. She rode.

As far away from Wolfpack as she could. Her mind began to thaw. This was Cutter's fault. Cutter had set it all up so she would have to kill the humans. He knew there'd been no danger. Silver could do nothing to Gangrel vampires, even when they appeared in their wolf forms.

"Damn you!" she bayed. And the blood tears whipped from her eyes, smearing against her white-streaked mane. She thought of her poor brother, Lance. Trying so hard to become human once more, he had betrayed them all: They who had betrayed a prince of the Blood by abandoning him to his enemies, who had not prevailed over him. Now the prince searched for Wolfpack everywhere. "Damn you!"

With coyotes howling around her — howling the name of the man, which she had never learned — she kept riding. The waning rays of the sinking moon glowed on her pale skin, her endless eyes. Her mind careened with images of him as he had died.

Though the sun was near to rising from its grave, she rode.

Away, away, she had to get away.

But she would be back.

She would take them all, everyone who had plotted against her. Cutter would die horribly. They all would.

Oh, yes.

The blood tears of the vampire flowed.

The sun began to rise.

She was not afraid. She would survive. And she would go back. She would send their souls to hell, and then she would cleanse the earth of all vampires, everywhere. She would join the final battles. She would make the earth shriek with the dying of the undead.

And then she would fight for the Garou, if they would have her.

Shiloh Marie, outlaw among outlaws, nineteen forever, whose other name was Vengeance.

The leader of the pack.

Nancy Holder's horror novels include *Making Love* and *Witchcraft*, collaborations with Melanie Tem, and *Dead in the Water*, her first solo horror novel. She has also written over fifteen romance and mainstream novels, forty short stories, and has received the Bram Stoker Award in 1992 for Best Short Fiction. Nancy's credits also include game fiction and comic books.

Tool of Enslavement

by Rick R. Reed

> oth life and death arise from the mind and exist within the
> mind. Hence, when the mind that concerns itself with
> life and death passes on, the world of life and death
> passes with it.
>
> — The Dharma of Buddha

PART ONE: NIGHT

I

A merry band of three. Evening light creeps in through leaded glass windows revealing: Terence, broad shoulders cloaked in Armani raw silk (gray) jacket, jeans, white T-shirt and biker boots. Blond hair cut short except for the thin braid that hangs, black, to his waist. Glint of silver on both ears, studs moving like iridescent slugs upward. Black mustache, goatee. Cohort Edward at his side, musculature in miniature, stubbled face and a shaved pate. Leather vest, black cargo pants tucked into construction-worker boots, no jewelry save for the inverted cross glinting gold between shaved and defined pecs. On his bicep, a tattooed band: marijuana leaves repeated over and over, rimmed with a thick black line. And last comes Maria, on silent cat feet, moving down the stairs. A whisper of satin, the color of coagulating blood: rust and dying roses, corseted at the waist with black leather. Black hair falls to her shoulders, straight, each strand perfect, sometimes flickering red from the candles' luminance. Dark eyes and crimson lips, full. Maria stands over six feet and her body, even beneath the dress, is a study in strength: muscles taut, defined, like a man save for the fact that the muscles speak an almost feminine language: sinew locked with flesh in elegance and grace.

She pauses, turning slowly in front of the men, *her* men, waiting for an appraisal.

Terence, first: "What will we lure tonight?"

II

Elise Groneman stares out the window, stomach roiling. Before her, the denizens of Greenview Street stroll the night. Hot, moist air presses in, smothering. Unconcerned: boom boxes blaring (Public Enemy, Dr. Dre), the flare of a match, arguments and professions of love shouted with equal force. East of her the cold waters of Lake Michigan, south of her Howard Street, purveyor of pawn shops and prostitution.

Her destination.

Elise turns to survey her cramped apartment. Near the

ceiling, paint (industrial green) peels from the walls to reveal other coats of grimy paint no color describes. Metal frame twin bed, sheets twisted and gray, damp from sweat and humidity. Next to that the Salvation Army-issue scarred oak table, small enough for two, with the remains of this night's meal: apple peelings, a knife, a glass half filled with pale tea, darkening in the dying light.

The remainder of the space is occupied by huge canvasses mounted on easels, bits of heavy paper taped to her drawing board. All splattered (*drawn? created?*) with various shades of gray, black.

Where is all the color? Elise herself wonders as she dresses for the evening.

Short black skirt bisected by a wide zipper ending in a big silver loop. White T balled and tied above her waist. Dark seamed stockings, spike heels. Tools of the trade as much as the brushes, sticks of charcoal and pencils littering her space.

In the mirror: lining her lips with crimson, green eyes cheapened by heavy black mascara, competing. Elise pulls whiskey-colored hair back, away from her damp neck, and up, pinning it all together with a silver barrette adorned with the smiling face of a skull. Pentagram earrings. Tonight a witch, creature of the night.

Turning, hand on doorknob. The night awaits: exhaust fumes, traffic, the chirping of cicadas.

III

Terence, Maria and Edward sit in a circle, facing one another on a floor of polished oak. There is no furniture in the room. What there is, is this: a fireplace fashioned from fieldstone, topped with a black granite mantel, tall as a man. The hearth cold, yawning open, inviting darkness and embracing it. Atop the mantel, an army of candles, blood red

— pillars, votives, tapers — flickering, banishing the shadows to the corners, and barely succeeding. Paintings of every description compete for wall space: an original etching by Van Gogh hung next to a portrait of Terence done by a bag lady in Lincoln Park. Picasso (in his blue period) contrasts with a drawing of a scream, giant, done in shades of magenta, black and yellow...a siren. More art, sculpture choke the room, making of it a gallery, a warehouse, anything but what it is supposed to be: a *living* room.

Terence holds a glass cylinder, topped with a glass bowl. His long, flat palm covers the cylinder's opening at one end as he brings it to his lips. A flame shoots up from a sterling silver lighter and Terence ignites the bowl of marijuana. Smoke rolls into the cylinder, pipe bowl glowing amber. Terence removes his hand from the end of the cylinder and his mouth becomes a vacuum; the smoke disappears.

He passes it to Maria. "To the Toreador! To hedonism! To art!"

Where his mouth and his hand have been are cold, the glass ice.

IV

Elise paces Howard Street. Her face, lit by sodium vapor lamps from the parking lot across the street, reveals apprehension and longing in yellow. She toys with an earring. Behind her a 7-11 and an adult bookstore compete for not-so-conspicuous consumption.

Elise leans against the brick facade of the 7-11. Cars cruise by. Which will slow to look? And then: eyes will meet and the deal, before any words are spoken, will be struck. Elise's slow walk to the idling car, the negotiations: nothing more than busy work, after-the-fact necessities.

Elise smoothes her skirt, stiffening as a gang of Hispanic boys charge up the street. There are at least eight of them, their youth raucous and threatening.

And she is a woman alone. No matter that she is plying a trade almost as old as mankind itself. Never mind that she is a criminal in this commerce.

These boys could take what she seeks to sell.

Take and destroy.

Elise prays they will surmise she has a pimp; leave her alone. Running in these heels is a fantasy and a gang bang was not what she had in mind for tonight.

The boys press closer and Elise strains to understand the quick, staccato rhythm of the Spanish. But only the most basic words filter to Elise, not enough to make sense. Their laughter is evil, predatory.

The boys surge close — their heat and aggression a warning scent. Elise moves on.

V

Maria sets the glass cylinder on the floor. Without exhaling, she grunts, "cashed." The two men nod and Edward rises and moves to the rheostat on the wall.

Recessed lighting disperses the room's shadows and brings the paintings on the wall to brilliant life. Sculptures, formed from granite, marble and metal, move in the sudden light. The three's eyes glaze at the drama the paintings and sculpture present: the liquid flow of color, images conflicting, jumping from canvas and paper, rock or metal becoming bone, flesh.

There is mockery in this art. Love, too…sex, death and betrayal. Violence. Serenity.

They see it all. And, as the Toreador they are, their sensitivity to the creativity surrounding them approaches empathy.

Maria takes Edward's hand in her right and Terence's in her left and squeezes. No need for words.

This is an old ritual, one that has gone on for hundreds of years.

It attunes them to the night…and the hunt.

VI

Elise has found solace under the Howard Street el tracks, under a streetlamp's pool of light. The light obliterates her features.

She has become nameless, a utilitarian tool.

An el train rumbles by above her, the brakes squealing as the muffled voice of a conductor announces: "Howard Street, change here for Evanston/Wilmette trains. Howard Street."

A rush of people behind her as passengers descend the stairs from the platform. Stares...in an instant, contempt, desire and indifference.

"Excuse me, miss."

A wheedling voice. Elise tries not to jump. Before her a man, shifting his weight from one foot to the other. Seersucker suit, frayed around the edges, dirty, colorless hair hanging limp across a creased forehead. Black plastic frame glasses... the glare on the lenses makes it impossible for Elise to discern color or intention in the eyes beneath.

"What?"

The man slides his hand around in the sweat on his forehead. Thin, pale lips like worms break into a grin. "You sellin' it?"

What is this? Elise wonders. Chicago vice? He's got quite a disguise. The nerd routine, perhaps it's worked before....

"Well?" The man moves even more restlessly, toying with buttons, mopping sweat, popping up in frantic beads, from his forehead.

"I don't know what you mean."

"You know," he says like a whining child. "Come on."

Elise shakes her head. One of his shoes, a scuffed Hush Puppy, has a hole in it. His baby toe, pink and crowned with a dirty nail, pokes out.

Is this character for real?

"I can't help you, sir," — Elise puts mocking emphasis on this last word— "unless I know what it is that you want."

"You," he stammers, "I want you."

"Well, you can't have me." There's something too odd about this one, something too bizarre. Besides, if he can't afford even a pair of shoes, how could he afford her?

"Even if I pay?" Words tremble. His shirt collar darkens with perspiration.

Something better will come along. Elise's stomach churns at the thought of this man above her. Still, the rent will be due in a few days.

No. "Get lost," she whispers to the guy. "You repulse me."

Even though nothing has blocked the glow from the streetlight, a shadow darkens the man's face before he turns and hurries away.

VII

The night is alive. Humidity and heat press in, bringing out the smells and feel of living, breathing flesh.

Hunger.

They have moved north, to Rogers Park. Here Terence, Maria and Edward can mingle with the detritus Lake Michigan and the city have washed up: the homeless, the runaways, those addicted to drugs of many sorts and those who seek to addict others. Prostitutes.

The ones no one asks questions about. The ones few notice missing and fewer still care about.

In their clothing, their looks, the images they have chosen to project, the three are all bait. Lures. The twinkling of an eye, a smile, an outstretched hand: all are nothing more than razor-sharp steel, ready to hook the unwary.

Maria sees her first: a whore. Ash-blond hair and tight clothes. Stiletto heels and black rubber bracelets climbing up one arm. Maria moves back into the shadows, pulling her companions with her.

"Look," she whispers. All three pairs of eyes train on the woman before them. Unaware, the whore scans the traffic for potential johns. At once, each of the three are aware of more of the woman than she could ever realize. Even from their vantage point across the street, they feel the heat emanating from her body: animal, drifting over to them in shimmering waves. Her scent, sour body odor not masked at all by cheap cologne, rides the heat like a magic carpet. The blood pulsing in the whore's veins reveals itself, almost audible, its pulse from her racing heart pounding out a beat.

Blood and warmth cause the three to become aroused. Maria turns to Terence and wraps her arms around him, her mouth devouring his, tongue exploring the dryness within, sliding over his teeth. Edward presses himself into Maria from behind and she is sandwiched between the two men. Cold flesh touches cold flesh. Eyes close. Each whisper and moan is a proclamation of lust and desire. Edward nuzzles the icy skin just below Maria's hairline in back, biting, biting harder until the skin breaks. Edward explores the small barren openings his teeth have made with his tongue. Maria arches her back and stops.

"Now. We should go to her now." Maria pulls away from the panting men… lust and want brightening their eyes, even here in the shadows. "Terence, you approach her."

Breaking away, Terence waits for the passing cars and crosses the street. He knows exactly how he looks: the blond hair shining in the artificial neon brightness of the night, the high cheekbones and full lips. A whore's dream: money and beauty, too.

The whore is about to light a cigarette. An opportunity. Terence brings out his silver lighter, hurrying to her, flame erect, before she can raise the cheap plastic disposable in her hand. He meets her eyes as the flame transfers some of its glow to the tip of her cigarette.

"Thanks." Their eyes meet. She is appraising him, wondering perhaps what someone like him is doing in her part of town. She draws in hard on the cigarette, cheeks collapsing. Thin tusks of blue-gray smoke rise.

Conversation, then. Cheap words mouthed to get to the real purpose.

"What do you want?" Her eyes flicker, moving down Terence's body like liquid. Her voice has a broad, Midwestern twang: flat a's, sharp and nasal.

"There are three of us."

"Group scene." The whore nods. "Been there."

"So that's all right with you?"

"Anything's all right, so long as it's worth my while." She takes one more drag off the cigarette, drops it to the pavement and grinds it under her toe.

"We have a car nearby. Come with us?"

"What kinda car?"

"A black Mercedes."

"Let's go."

Back at their house, a turn-of-the-century graystone, the three introduce themselves. Terence, purveyor, sits next to her in a bedroom done entirely in red: red satin settees, heavy red drapery, blood red and velvet, flocked wallpaper.

Terence strokes the woman, cupping and holding her breasts while the other two, silent, watch.

She giggles. "Your hand's so cold."

"Warm it." Terence's hand dives between the whore's thighs and she gasps. "I don't understand...." Whimpering. Maria, attuned to the fear in her eyes, rises and moves to a Walnut armoire. She extracts several hundred-dollar bills and scatters them over the whore.

"Warmer?" Maria's voice is throaty and scarred. Deep as a man's, yet in no way masculine.

"Yes-s-s," the whore hisses, staring at all the money. She

spreads her legs to give Terence better access. Maria kneels at the whore's feet and removes a stiletto heel. She takes the whore's great toe in her mouth and sucks it. The whore closes her eyes as Terence moves to kiss her.

At the touch of his lips, the woman stiffens. She sits up abruptly, pulling her foot away from Maria. "Why are you all so cold? I don't get it."

And Edward is there to calm her. "Have some of this." He hands her a lighter and the glass cylinder, its bowl filled with a fat bud of marijuana glistening with resin.

The whore's chest heaves. All three sense her dichotomy: dread and desire wrapped into one conflicting package, each emotion pulling with its own force.

The whore takes the pipe and fires up the bowl. The cylinder fills with smoke, becoming opaque. Clarity returns in seconds as the woman sucks down the smoke. "Damn," she whispers. "Where'd you find shit like this?"

No reply. Terence takes the woman's hand and forces her to put the pipe back to her mouth. She giggles. "Okay, okay."

After three hits, the woman has forgotten her fear, has stopped wondering why her three companions for the evening have such cold flesh and empty eyes, pale skin cold and smooth like polished stone. She clumsily stands and steps out of her tight clothing. Standing naked, the whore surrenders to the trio's touch: all over, hands moving faster and faster, exploring. She closes her eyes, no longer aware who is twisting her nipples to an area where pain and pleasure mesh, no longer aware whose fingers are exploring her sex, her ass. The pot has filled her with a warm stupidity. She can think of only one thing at a time and that is how good these three pairs of hands feel on a body that is growing hotter and hotter with their chilled caresses. Juices run down her thighs, viscous, fragrant. Three tongues lapping make it almost impossible for the whore to stand. Dragging the three with her like sucking leeches the whore moves to the fireplace and lies on the red-and-black-patterned rug before it. She spreads her legs wide, pushing at them to enter her more deeply, to continue to bring out this wondrous pleasure she has never felt before.

And then, the whore is sitting astride Terence, cock like an icicle buried deep. Edward squats behind and above her, pelvis arched out to thrust more deeply into her ass, while Maria presses the whore's face into her own cold but yielding sex-lips.

The whore sees this tableau in her mind's eye, almost as if she is at once removed from it and deep within it, the center. She cries out, not knowing how she can stay conscious under the weight of such pleasure.

And then they are biting. And at first, it's all right. The tiny nips and nibbles are nothing more than an extension of their lust, making it better and better.

But then the bites become harder and harder and the whore awakens from the haze of the marijuana as the teeth, suddenly razorlike and distinctly not human, pierce her skin. The whore lies trembling, realizing she cannot move as the bites penetrate deeper into her flesh, ripping and shredding, faster and faster, on her breasts, her stomach, her thighs, her ass, all the tender areas. Piercing and penetrating. Sucking sounds filtering up to her dull hearing.

She sees one thing before everything goes dark: Terence and Edward biting down into her breasts, their mouths ringed with blood, ripping her nipples away from her body.

The whore closes her eyes, surrendering, and does not wonder why the cold bodies have suddenly become hot.

VIII

Darkness clouds the eyes of the stranger. The face above Elise's is little more than a mask, white shapes in all the right places, backlit by the streetlight filtering in through the van's windows.

The man pants, squeezing her breast with one hand as he thrusts within her. Elise lies with her arms at her sides. Immobile, she tries to discern the color of the shag carpeting that covers the interior of the van, making it cave-like and muffling the man's grunts.

He stops and stiffens. Elise bites her lips, tasting blood, as he comes.

In an instant, he has pulled out of her. Digging in his pants that lie in a corner, returning to her.

"Here." Two twenties thrown on her chest. He leans back and lights a cigarette, the acrid burn of the match filling the air. He settles against the carpeted wall, panting still.

The act has taken no more than ten minutes, yet the man glistens with sweat, fat hairy belly covered with slick. Elise feels soiled, but scoops up the damp money from her breasts and sits.

She struggles into her clothes; zippers catch, nylons run…her shirt gets stuck as she pulls it over her head. Sheepishly, she grins at the man, her lover, her partner in sin and crime.

He glares at her.

"That was nice," she says with little emotion and even less veracity.

"Just get the fuck out."

Elise scrambles backward, like an animal out of a hole, from the van. The night surrounds her. Cold. Forty bucks.

PART TWO: MESH
IX

Each line has to be perfect. Elise steps back, the drawing before her, parchment paper that she has stained darker with coffee, taped to a board on an easel. There he is, the man from the night before, the one in the van. He had been middle-aged, overweight, pale featureless face, doughy. But Elise has transformed him with charcoal. Dark squiggly lines have made of him an insect: the eyes black orbs, blind, a cavity for a nose, black pincers almost mobile at the corner of thin lips. Delicate wings sprout from his back, segmented, bifurcated, transparent. Elise has made her perspective from below, so the man/creature looms above, menacing yet distant.

Elise picks up a tube of black acrylic paint. She creates a border, thick like piping, around her drawing. And then, sobbing, smears the ink, obliterating, erasing what has taken her all day to create.

It was too good. Too good for him.

The sky outside glows purple. Night awaits and with it will come the night creatures, the ones Elise must feed from to continue to make her art, to create… and destroy.

X

The three do not always travel together. This night, Terence heads north on his Harley. Wind slithers through his short hair. Lake Michigan glistens in the light of a full moon at his right, the waves' caps silver. The glow of the moon makes his skin bleached bone, marble, alabaster.

His destination: Howard Street. Perhaps he will strike gold again. As he rounds the corner from Lake Shore Drive onto Hollywood, he remembers the whore from last night… the heat of her blood as it pumped into his mouth like a copper ejaculation, the flavor of her flesh as he ripped it away. Terence's cock squirms inside tight jeans. Heading north once again, now up Sheridan Road, Terence feels anticipation: an electric current, pulsing.

There will be another perfect one, waiting once more. Waiting for a fall.

Terence twists the throttle, revving the engine and swerving left to claim the open space in the lane.

XI

Elise pulls the door closed, not bothering to lock it. After all, what is there to take? Her art? Who among these filthy minions would appreciate it? Where could it be fenced? Her other belongings? They could be found anywhere, discarded with the trash.

And what if someone is lying in wait when she comes home...ready to slit her throat? Elise shakes her head. She could never be so fortunate.

Howard Street swarms with people. Friday night: the cars rows of insects, headlights glowing like hundreds of pairs of eyes. Exhaust fumes perfume the air. Profanity and greetings compete with car horns and mufflers.

Elise takes her place near the 7-11, hoping she won't be chased away tonight by marauding youths or vice cops.

Only moments pass until the rumble of a motorcycle.

The engine cuts and for just a second, it's as if all the sound in the street cuts as well. Elise turns.

A man, impossibly beautiful, is astride the motorcycle. Leather and chains, boots, tight jeans.

He must fancy himself quite the prize. Cheekbones sharp and defined, skin almost too smooth to be real, white in the light from the moon. *Poseur.*

Elise turns away... not the sort of trade she deals in.

A gloved hand, fingers cut off, caresses her shoulder. Elise shrugs the hand away and appraises the stranger. He grins. Warily, she smiles back.

"I'm not certain you're in the right part of town," Elise says.

"I am." A voice, deep, resonating, distinguishes itself from the sounds of urban night. "How much?"

Elise shakes her head: laughter mocking, derisive.

"How much?"

Elise pulls hair from her neck, where it's stuck with the glue of her sweat. Vice? Just get it over with. She's been run in before. An inconvenience. They stop no one. In her desire to hasten the bust, Elise blurts, "Fifty dollars for a blow job, a hundred and up for more."

He doesn't blink. Reaching into the pocket of his motorcycle jacket, he pulls out a wad of bills. Elise recognizes a hundred on the outside of the roll. He tucks it into her cleavage. "Got someplace we can go?"

The money between her breasts is enough to free her for several nights. She takes the man's hand. "This way." She leads him east, toward Greenview and the place she calls home.

"My name's Terence," His grip on her hand is firm and cool.

"Mine's Midnight," Elise murmurs, glancing at him out of the corner of her eye. *Will this be the one who brings death?*

She does not want to turn on lights once they are back in her studio. Does not want to share her created world with a trick, with anyone, really. Not yet.

Moonlight streams in. Easels, drawing board and furniture nothing more than dark shapes in the silvery darkness. She drops her clothes as she leads Terence to her single bed. Then drops his hand when she reaches the bed. Lying down, she parts her legs, moistens her lips, waits.

"What about light?" Terence stands above her and suddenly fear grips Elise. The dark shape of him, the smell of the leather, the chain around his neck, the thicker one around his waist.

Her lackadaisical attitude about life crumbles as her heartbeat picks up, thudding, uncomfortable. A line of sweat forms at her hairline and her muscles flex, tauten.

"You don't need any light." Her voice comes out, hoarse from fear, a croak.

"I think we do. And I'm paying. I call the shots."

Elise sits. "This is my place. I —" Before she has a chance to say anything further, he is moving toward the door, where the switch for the overhead light is.

"No!" Elise shrieks and runs toward him. "No." She takes his arm and pulls it back. "I've got to have the darkness. Please."

He reaches out and Elise tries not to flinch at the coldness when he caresses her face, long fingernails sliding across her cheek like the tender touch of a switchblade applied lovingly.

"All right. If it's so important to you."

When Terence reaches into his pocket, Elise expects a gun or knife, but all he has withdrawn is a small wooden pipe.

It's been years since she's gotten high, partying days left behind her long ago. College, art school, memories of another life. But the idea doesn't seem so bad…perhaps the smoke will obscure the experience, cloud and befuddle her brain, allow her to get through this, anesthetized.

"Go ahead." Terence hands her the pipe and a silver lighter.

Elise fires up the bowl. In the flame, the hunger in Terence's eyes is startling…more than lust, it encompasses and embodies him. Elise draws the smoke into her lungs quickly, holding it as she returns the pipe.

What has it been? Minutes? Hours? Elise has no idea. She feels numb, bordering on paralysis. Her legs feel weighted, glued to the floor as the chill of his lips and tongue move up and down her thighs. Her hands have somehow become buried in his thick blond hair as he kneels before her, supplicant and messenger of a pleasure so intense Elise cannot consciously describe it.

His tongue moves up and inside her and for now, nothing else exists. Elise closes her eyes, panting as shudders and waves of pleasure claim intellect and body.

Suddenly, he withdraws and she can only cry out, synapses tingling, craving, yearning. Mute, she watches as he undresses, the leather and denim falling to her filthy floor in a heap, a burrowing animal in the shadows. The naked body reminds her of Michelangelo's David, and she knows at once what the sculptor was saying with his creation. Elise reaches out, fingertips tingling, wanting to cry out, "Come to me," but unable to form words with her thick tongue.

And then he is moving across the room.

And then the room is flooded with yellow light.

Elise closes her eyes, something from underneath a rock exposed suddenly, cruelly. All her work. "No," she whimpers.

Jealous. His lover's gaze no longer on her, but on her creations, boring into them, penetrating them instead of her.

She watches, mute and paralyzed…as he takes in her drawings and paintings, one by one, opening them with his eyes, seeing everything Elise has said in the last few years with her dark vision.

His cock is stiff, jerking as he absorbs the art. Elise crumples to the floor. What he has paid her is not enough.

"You're a genius," the words filter down as if played at slow speed, heard through a tunnel. What need has she for praise? Angrily, she watches him devour her art, stealing it.

And then he is gone, leaving Elise, naked and betrayed on the floor, where a cockroach, sensing her heat, skitters across her thigh.

XII

Terence blazes through the night, Harley roaring between his legs, wind whipping his hair behind him. His teeth are clenched as he tries to sort out the emotions caroming through him, crashing like cymbals. Is it rage he feels? He grips the throttle so tightly it's as if his knuckles will burst through the skin. The world whizzing by is a blur, incomprehensible.

All he can see is Midnight's art. He remembers leaning against her peeling colorless walls, finishing the pipe, letting the THC do its work: sharpening his focus, bringing her art to life. What horrifying vision. Terence swears the art has let him see the woman's soul, dark, her own, no way to possess it. The bleak drawings, black and gray, layers of shadows, spoke of the void in which she lived: the animal lusts, the chains that held her earthbound…the need for survival. The woman spoke with a knowledge he thought no human possessed.

And the woman herself: reddish-brown hair, fright in her eyes as he stood above her, blood heat pulsing through her veins. He could see it all, even in the lightless void that was her apartment. The temptation to devour was almost unbearable, filling every fiber of his being with need so intense it virtually erased his reality.

But he stopped.

He could not destroy her, not the vision she had splattered or had drawn with precise detail on paper, on canvas.

And yet the red aura surrounding her called to him with the voice of a siren. Called still.

The flames were a peripheral orange blur, caught by dangling threads of consciousness.

Terence stopped the bike, looked back.

The answer to his needs.

Smoke rose from a black metal trash can, its sides rusted. Back from it, in the entryway of a warehouse, silent this late at night, slept a man. Black, nappy hair poking out of a coat wrapped around him like a cocoon.

Why so cold on this hot night of summer?

Terence can bring a chill this slumbering man has never dreamed of. Moving quick, he descends like a shadow, gliding, so quiet the man does not murmur or awaken as Terence feeds.

When he roars off on his Harley, there is nothing left of the homeless black man but a pile of ragged clothing, bones, hair and pieces of flesh too tough for Terence to digest.

PART THREE: LOVE
XIII

Elise has been alone so long the sound of a knock at her door is startling, frightening. She puts down the charcoal pencil and goes to quiet the pounding.

The pounding grows louder as she skirts easels, a drawing board, her meager furniture. "All right, all right."

The door opens, memory rushes in: images forming and dispersing with the rapidity of montage. Terence. Gone are the chains and leather. Tonight, nothing more than jeans and a Notre Dame sweatshirt. The clothes should bring to him normalcy, but do the opposite, emphasizing ashen pallor and gray-eyed intensity, pale and liquid.

"What do you want?"

A smile. His teeth are tiny, baby like, pearls between thin pink lips. "I wanted to see you."

"Didn't you see everything you wanted when you were here last time?"

Terence laughs, his deep voice dead, an echo. "Yes, as a matter of fact I did. I saw probably more than you realize."

Empty words. Did he mean to praise her? "You've seen me. I'm busy, so please…could you go now?" Elise begins to close the door.

Terence puts up a hand that Elise could not fight. The door stays open. She stares at him, waiting.

"I want you to come with me, meet my friends."

Elise cannot imagine these people. "That's impossible. I don't have time."

"It might help your art."

"In what way?"

"Experience. Isn't that what you feed from? Isn't that what inspires all artists?"

Oh stop, Elise thinks.

"Please come with me." Terence takes out a wad of green and presses it into Elise's palm. For a moment, she is tempted to slam the door in his face, leaning against it and counting the money. Instead, she looks down and counts five hundred dollars.

"All right, I'll come with you, but for just a little while."

Elise wanders through the large room, heels of her boots clicking on the wooden floor, polished to such a high gloss it's easy to see her reflection.

She is enchanted, swept away by magic. She has never before seen such an eclectic collection: paintings, drawings, etchings, sculpture… all in a pastiche of style and color.

All of it good, better than anything she has seen at a show or even a gallery. Almost every inch of wall space is covered; the floor is crowded with pottery and sculpture.

Terence left her moments ago, telling her to wait. Elise doesn't care how long he keeps her. For the first time in months, she feels alive as she drinks in the genius of the work. She hadn't realized she was starving.

And then Terence is back. Too soon. Elise pulls herself away from the figure of a woman, welded from metal, her mouth open in torment or orgasm.

"These are my friends, the ones I told you about." Two people emerge out of the shadows. "This is Edward." First comes a man, much shorter than Terence, but muscular, strength bound into a compact frame. He gives a lopsided grin to Elise, not showing teeth. He takes her hand and kisses it. The gesture would seem affected were it not for the earnestness in the man's brown eyes. It's almost as if he comes from a time when making such gestures was natural. Elise smiles as the man stands, still feeling the cold impression of his lips.

"And this," Terence pauses, "is Maria."

Gazes lock. The art in the room, the highly polished floor,

the huge fireplace vanish as Elise drinks in the woman: exquisite, bone white, smooth. Dark curls frame a face of Botticelli beauty. Elise is swallowed up by dark eyes that bore into hers with knowledge and certainty.

Elise bows her head, suddenly feeling a loss of words, a loss of self. What to say to this creature who is so stunning she is almost monstrous?

Maria embraces her. Elise's heart pounds so hard the blood rushes in her ears. Maria's embrace is ice, but Elise doesn't recoil. She pulls the woman closer, wanting to warm her, to share her heat.

Maria finally breaks the embrace. "Terence tells us you're an artist."

And Elise looks to Terence, who stares away, into the shadows. Edward is grinning.

XIV

Elise peers into the mirror. "What have you gotten yourself into?" Her reflection stares back, a stranger. She has pulled her auburn hair away from her face, done her makeup subtly (not a whore tonight) to bring out the definition of her cheekbones, the fullness of her lips, the oval shape of her face...a little mascara highlights the green of her eyes. She wears a long green silk dress, with the imprint of oak leaves in the fabric. "Looking your best tonight," she whispers to her reflection.

All day she has cleaned: scrubbed Linoleum, dusted what little furniture she has, changed sheets and moved her works in progress to a corner, secreted behind a bookcase. Her best she has put on display.

The bass note of a motorcycle engine trumpets Maria's arrival. Outside, Maria straddles the Harley, dark hair windblown. The bike's chrome glints yellow in the streetlight. Maria dismounts, shakes her black hair. Elise cannot see what she is wearing:

darkness shrouds her.

For the first time, Elise shows her work. For the first time, Elise cares whether someone else will understand, appreciate what she has done with her pencils and paints. For once, Elise wants someone to understand.

When Maria comes in, she is cloaked in leather: tight leather pants, a zippered shirt of thin, pliable hide, dark leather boots. She smells animal and the black offers a bizarre contrast to her skin. Elise swears her heart stops beating.

Maria brushes her lips, cool, across Elise's and greets her. "I brought you some wine." Maria sets a bottle of cabernet on the kitchen counter. "And this," she holds up a carved wooden pipe.

Elise shakes her head. "Is that the same stuff Terence had? I don't know if I can handle it. Where do you get it, anyway?"

"We grow it ourselves." Maria grins. "Ancient Chinese secret."

"It wipes me out."

"It attunes me." Maria fires up the bowl and inhales. She passes Elise the pipe and Elise, not wanting to disappoint, draws in a lungful of smoke, knowing that it will numb her almost beyond reason. She wonders if the pot is cut with something more powerful.

The women pass the pipe back and forth: three hits each.

Maria, whose gaze has been on Elise since she entered, turns finally. "Your art. Terence tells me you're a genius. I want to see." Maria's voice comes to Elise through a tunnel and in response, she gestures to the work hung on the wall that afternoon.

It seems as if hours pass as Maria stops before each piece, saying nothing, black eyes intent, drinking it in. It's as if she's devouring the art, much the same way Terence did. There is a difference though: this time it is not a violation, not a rape; Elise wants to give, to open herself and her creations up to Maria.

To commune.

After a while, the walls melt and Elise sees only Maria, standing in a dark void, her work suspended before her, work that has slouched toward life: three-dimensional, breaking chains of paper and canvas.

Finally, Maria turns to her and Elise tumbles into the blackness of her gaze. Maria nods. She understands.

Dreamlike, time rushes forward and Elise finds herself in Maria's arms. Maria's eyes suck in the darkness, capturing and holding it. Elise fears being swept into those eyes, losing herself, no way to come back.

Lips merge: cold meets heat; tongues intertwine, dueling. Now, even the backdrop of her apartment falls away and Elise is alone with blood rushing through her veins, heat of her skin against the cold fire of Maria's flesh, wet between her legs, dripping down her thighs.

They writhe on the sheets, bodies grinding.

Maria's tongue nuzzles her thighs, drinking her in. Her tongue surrounds her clitoris, teasing, toying, then entering. Elise grabs a handful of hair and pulls hard, hard enough to hurt.

Maria is above her, hair swinging into her face, her mouth.

Sliding down: Maria is at her breast, sucking, licking. Biting.

A gasp as the tender skin of her areola is broken by tiny, razor teeth. Spots of bright red blood rise against salmon skin. Elise's command of language is gone and she whimpers as Maria's tongue, rough and cold, a cat's, laps away the blood.

"Just a taste," Maria's voice floats above her. "I must have a taste. But that is all. That is all. I would never harm you...my love."

Elise surrenders to the darkness of her pleasure.

XV

Day's harsh light arrives like an unexpected visitor. Elise stirs, turning over, pulling the sheet over her head. How can it be morning already? Elise whips the sheet away from her as the heat from her body fills the enclosed space, suffocating. Squinting at the sunlight, she wonders where the darkness and the cool cover of night have gone. Already it's hot, air hanging palpable and dead. Elise sits. Where has Maria gone?

Memories, like dream images, rush back, knowing no chronology or order. Sensations: Maria's hair on her stomach, cool caresses, icy roughness of Maria's tongue, probing. Embraces. Whispers. Sighs.

Why did she leave her asleep and alone?

Elise puts her feet on the floor and rubs her eyes. Today she cannot paint or draw. Everything is crowded out with thoughts of Maria.

She must see her.

Elise takes the el and then a bus to reach the graystone she remembers. One street in from Lake Michigan, Elise hears the angry roar of the waves. She pauses in front of the building where she met Maria, wondering if she is inside. Outside, the house is unkempt. Weeds choke the sidewalk; discarded cans, flyers and other detritus mingle with the grass and weeds in the front yard. Paint flakes away from the concrete front porch.

The place looks abandoned, darkened, empty. Fear grips her as she wonders if these people who came so mysteriously into her life will leave just as mysteriously.

As she approaches the front door, she wonders if she will find the place empty...all the art gone. Perhaps it was never there in first place. Perhaps Maria and her friends are nothing more than phantoms, dream images made flesh.

Knocking, her signal sounds hollow, reverberating inside. After her knuckles have become reddened and sore, Elise gives up and turns away. *While I'm here...* Elise turns back and tries the doorknob. To her surprise, the door opens.

"Maria? Terence? Edward?" Her voice echoes. Dust motes play in sunlight streaming in through leaded glass.

The art is still here.

No one responds and Elise makes her way through the gallery that makes up most of the first floor. She steps into the kitchen and finds it empty. The refrigerator is unplugged; no humming. Elise opens it and finds nothing more than a bunch of withered roses. Where is the food?

There is a back staircase here in the kitchen and Elise, her heart pounding, mounts it. Fear has gripped her all at once and along with the fear another image from last night flickers back: Maria biting her breast hard enough to bring blood. Part of Elise wants to turn and hurry back down the stairs and out of here. The sweat at her brow and the queasiness tell her to go. But she remembers how complete she felt with Maria. How could anything associated with Maria be harmful to her?

A large, dark-stained mahogany door is on her right when she reaches the upper floor. Elise pauses to listen: stillness. No breathing, no sighs of slumber. Elise opens the door and draws in a quick breath.

It takes minutes for Elise's eyes to adjust. All three are there, lying next to one another on a huge canopy bed. A red velvet coverlet conceals much of their sleeping forms. Red velvet curtains, heavy, are drawn at the window.

Elise waits a little longer, until the light in the room becomes gray and she can see well enough to approach the bed. She wants just one more look at Maria, just to see her again will be enough. Elise moves closer to the bed and stops.

Something is wrong. It takes her a second to figure out why this tableau is so disturbing: these people don't appear to sleep. There is no rise and fall of chests, no sounds, no drowsy slow movements.

They lie still as corpses.

Suddenly, the darkened room seems oppressive, the flocked wallpaper closing in. Elise moves nearer, noticing Maria's face looks different. All of their faces, in fact, look scarred; darkened areas rim their mouths. Elise brings her face close to Maria. Crusty dried blood covers Maria's face in patches. Elise finds she cannot swallow when she sees tiny flecks of skin in the corners of Maria's lips.

Elise's stomach roils and churns. Covering her mouth, she turns to run from the room.

Just as she approaches the door, Maria's voice stops her.

"Wait. Elise? Please come back."

Maria is sitting up in bed. The red blankets have fallen away; her breasts are ghostly white in the darkness. "There's so much I have to tell you." She smiles and displays not teeth but rows of tiny fangs.

The room blurs, then darkens completely as Elise collapses.

When she awakens, Elise focuses on Maria above her. Maria has donned a wine-colored robe and she's holding a cool cloth to Elise's forehead. Elise gets up on one elbow. She's lying on a red velvet settee near the fireplace. Terence and Edward still sleep in the huge canopy bed, bodies intertwined.

"Better?" Maria whispers. Gone are the rows of tiny fangs Elise thought (?) she saw before. Her face is clean: smooth and white as a marble tombstone. Only the fire in her dark eyes breathes life into her countenance.

"Yes." Elise's tongue is thick in her mouth, a speech impediment. "Could I have some water?"

Maria doesn't move, yet suddenly she holds a cut crystal tumbler of water. Elise gulps it. "What's going on, Maria?" All sorts of absurd notions run through her mind, involving the supernatural or insanity (hers or theirs, she's not sure). None of these notions seem plausible, yet how does one explain?

Maria smoothes Elise's hair back away from her face and presses her gently back on the couch. Elise allows herself to recline, accepts the kiss, cold, from Maria's lips. "I'm going to tell you the truth now. But you won't believe it. Not at first, anyway.

"I know this idea has come to you and that you have probably rejected it. I can't blame you. Most of you with your modern ideas and technology have no concept of things lying beneath the surface of palpable reality. Gone are the notions of romance...of the inexplicable. But you, my love, are an artist. And artists are the only ones that understand things not explained by science or numbers. I hope you understand us, because it's rare I find a mortal who does."

"A mortal? What are you talking about?" The room closes in on Elise again, panic rising, firing synapses, making her tremble, run hot and cold all at once.

Maria smiles. "We are vampires."

She pauses. And the words hang in the air like dust in sunlight. Elise wants to laugh, but there is no humor in her desire. It is the giddy laugh of hysteria, just before a shriek. "Please don't do this, Maria. It's been so long since I've had anyone in my life. Please don't turn out to be insane; don't turn yourself into some Anne Rice heroine."

Maria laughs. "I do love you." She grows serious again. "It's true, Elise. I know you saw the blood. I know you saw our faces, my fangs...efficient tools." She takes Elise's hand in hers, squeezes. "Feel that? Feel the cold? No warmth runs through my veins. Surely, you've noticed."

Elise pulls her hand away, recoiling at the dry iciness of Maria's skin. Maria takes Elise's hand back, pressing it to her breast. "There? Feel anything?"

No heartbeat. Elise pulls away, hiding her face in the velvet of the settee. "No."

Muffled, Maria's voice comes to her. "Elise, there's nothing to fear. All of us, I especially, admire you. We care about you, your art. You're brilliant... brilliance we don't often see. Especially as time passes. We would never harm you."

Elise turns back. The beauty of Maria's face, her body, the shine in her eyes...the most beautiful woman she's ever seen. And even though her body is cold, she radiates warmth and intelligence...and understanding, understanding Elise has not yet encountered in anyone else.

"Terence, Edward and I have been together for over three hundred years," Maria begins. Elise tries to relax, closing her eyes as Maria spins her tale. And what a tale! Spanning continents and centuries, she tells of their nocturnal existence, their pursuit of blood, flesh and art. Their wealth and how easy it has been to accrue through the centuries and finally, their kin.

"Elise...please understand what we are." Maria takes Elise's hand in her own, almost as if to warm it. "There are seven principal clans that we have formed over the centuries, clans that each of us plays a special part in."

Elise's confusion mounts. When will Maria's face break into laughter? When will she tell her this is all a joke?

"Although Terence, Edward and I do not mingle freely with others of our clan, preferring instead a life of quiet solitude, where we obtain our gratification for the closeness of others through only ourselves, we belong to the clan of Toreador."

Elise swallows. There is no moisture left in her mouth.

"Toreador are the only vampires who could ever appreciate you for what you are...an artist. A true artist. And true artists, my dear, are rarer than vampires."

Lovingly, Maria strokes the whitening skin of Elise's face, her long, blood-red nails gently passing over milky warmth.

"There are very few of us. Forget the lore you read in pulp novels. We do not form a new vampire each time we kill. The process is complicated, involving ritual and faith, two concepts you moderns seem to have lost stock in. Those of us who have survived are spread throughout the world: feeding quietly on society's outcasts, of which there are many. All told, there are no more than a few hundred of us and we've had hundreds of years to perfect our techniques of hiding, our techniques of killing.

"I don't know all the history or even why we exist. I do know that our roots are in China. It is there we began, in fertile valleys, a cradle.

"Our biggest influence on the world, the one most noticeable anyway, is in something you might find bizarre, or even silly." Maria stops and brings out a bowl filled with dried marijuana, leaves, buds, stems and seeds mingled, all redolent of resin, glistening in the dim light. "This is part of our ritual, developed over thousands of years. We used it at first to stun and pacify our victims while on our systems it had the opposite effect. It awakens our senses, attuning them to your thoughts, your auras, your health, everything about you, before we kill."

Elise stares down at the marijuana, afraid she will be sick.

"It's pure, this. Mortals have taken it upon themselves to trade and grow their own, but what they grow is polluted, impure...hardly the same thing. But I suppose if you're looking for some huge sign of our existence it would be this, and that we introduced it to the world." Maria's hand rolls the marijuana into a slim cigarette, expertly; the joint is perfect. "Let's smoke this now."

"No!" Elise gets up from the settee and runs from the room, from the house. All of this is too strange. What can she do to forget?

PART FOUR: BLOOD HUNT
XVII

Elise stares at the wall, tracing a crack in the plasterboard up, noticing how the line flows: a river.

"Hey babe, thanks," the man's voice comes to her from a distance, although he sits next to her, dressing, on the bed.

Elise doesn't reply. Reaching out, she traces the crack's progress.

"That was some hot time." He laughs, unaware of her ignorance. "You around on Howard Street a lot?"

What had this one looked like? Middle-aged? Young? Potbellied? Balding? Elise wouldn't have been able to say and she hadn't the energy or the strength to turn over and look at her trick: the fifth of this day. They all blurred into one and what did it matter, anyway?

"Hey." The man touches her shoulder and Elise recoils. "I asked you a question."

"Yeah, you can find me there just about anytime."

Elise curls her legs up close to her chest.

Later, after Elise has showered the man away, she sits at her drawing table. The psychology of what she has drawn is not lost on her: she has coated the heavy paper taped to the board with black crayon, until the surface of the paper is nothing more than a dark, waxy surface. And then, with an X-Acto knife: she has drawn Maria. Not the Maria she fell in love with, but a grotesque: a monster. Present are the black eyes, the waving hair, the long, delicate neck. Gone is the beauty. Elise has drawn in a gaping mouth, filled with tiny, pointed teeth, each perfect in its detail. She has managed to capture an expression of both hunger and ferocity: it is distorted almost beyond recognition: desire out of control.

And so it has been with Elise these last several weeks: since she had rushed, with a silent scream, from Maria's home…and her news. That day, Elise felt as if her skin had been peeled away, left raw to experience everything with painful sensitivity.

Since that time, Elise has done everything she can to blot out the reality of that day, to forget. Drowning herself in tricks, Elise found herself on her knees or on her back, open to strange men as much as six or seven times a day. What remaining time she has not used for sleep, she has used for art. And all of it the same:

dark landscapes or portraits, horror-drenched, full of perverse longing. Fangs, blood, bodies torn apart, cannibalized.

And none of it has worked. It is as if Maria, with her face of fragile beauty, calls to her. Even while on her knees in some alley, a dark figure spouting his seed on her face, Elise recalls Maria: the face floating to her dreamlike, smiling, hands outstretched to touch. Silence…only the sound of her beating heart to accompany her.

And now Elise replaces the X-Acto to its ledge as she feels herself growing drowsy. She moves to the bed, where she sits, cross-legged, her back against the wall.

"The one thing in the lives of you mortals that you can never change, no matter how hard you try to deny it, is your desire for love." It is as if Maria is there with her, kneeling by the bed, stroking her calf. Feel: the brush of her hair across Elise's leg. Listen: the whisper of satin as Maria shifts in her gown. "And I love you, Elise. Won't you come back?"

A montage of images: Maria's breasts, her thighs, the feel of her tongue at Elise's ear. Elise touches herself, lying back, remembering.

XVIII

Maria's head pounds: the calling to Elise, the concentration, has made her temples throb. She massages her forehead, squeezing her eyelids tight, to send one more image.

There is Elise beneath her, lying on the rumpled sheets of her twin bed. Her auburn hair fans out across gray pillows. Maria stares into her eyes, locking with them, drowning in the green irises. Maria holds Elise with her eyes, minds meeting and merging, desire kindled between them like a flame. Maria lowers herself, supporting herself with the warm satin of Elise's body. Maria dips her mouth to Elise's, biting gently, pulling Elise's tongue into her mouth with her teeth. Sliding her hands beneath Elise's back, Maria holds her close, tight, attempting to make their bodies one. She imagines music: Philip Glass's "Facades," soft in the background.

Tongue in ear, then a whisper: "Come back."

Maria opens her eyes: communion has left her drained. Gradually the room filters in: plank flooring, oak pedestal table and chairs, with their straw seats, gathered round it. A meal, service for one, chills on the table. Chicken bones, a baked potato skin, congealing grease. The room is redolent with the odor of the meal; it makes Maria nauseous.

She looks down at the boy who had devoured the meal while she watched, less than two hours ago. Reaching down, she tousles blond hair: varying shades of yellow, white and soft brown mingle in the dim light. She remembers his face: freckles and a gap between his front teeth, blue eyes...trusting. The lithe form of his body: white and graceful, legs long and lean, muscles not yet stretched to manhood. The pale swatch of pubic hair above his sex.

Maria reaches out with her tongue and snares a piece of flesh from the corner of her mouth. Flecks of blood that Maria missed dot the floor around the boy. His stomach is ripped open, exposing entrails. Little is left of the face of boyish innocence: red tissue beneath where his skin was, tissue that speaks of musculature that once made the face frown, smile, cry and laugh. Pieces of flesh are ripped from his limbs in jagged, reddened lines.

Maria wishes for just one moment that she could take what she needed from the boy and then return him to the way he was.

The food rumbles in her stomach, mocking.

"We have to find her. We can't leave her out there." Terence. Maria jumps at the sound of his voice, having had no warning of his arrival. He stands before her, almost as if he has materialized there, brushing his blond spikes back. His stance and sneer makes her wish she could think him away. "You're aware of the First Tradition, aren't you?"

Maria's laugh is bitter. "I taught you and Edward the Traditions. Don't insult me."

Terence's eyes bore into hers. "Then you know you've already broken it. Our first law, Maria, and you've ground it under your heel as if it didn't matter." Terence takes a deep breath. "Thou shalt not reveal thy true nature to those not of the blood. Doing such shall renounce thy claims of blood."

"You don't need to quote for me, insolent bastard. I know. We've had this talk before. Over and over."

"Yes. And it doesn't seem to make any difference."

"I told you: I'm trying to bring her back. She'll come."

"And how many nights now have you sat in darkness, broadcasting to no avail?" Terence is very good at sneering. Over the centuries, he has perfected the scowl and frown.

"Who says it's to no avail?"

"She isn't here, is she?"

"No, but she'll be here. I promise."

"I wish I could trust you." Terence paces, the floorboards making no sound beneath his weight. Feline grace.

"I wish you could, too. Why are you so eager?"

Their eyes meet, flashing: competitors. Yet Maria can treat him with the condescension of victory: Elise could never be his.

Terence says, "We've made it our work to collect the creativity of the mortal." He frowns. "It's the only thing they can hold over us, so we worship. We always have. I don't want anything more from her other than some of her art." He smiles, a death rictus. "That's all."

Maria shoves the corpse of the blond boy away and stands, bringing her face close to Terence. She can smell a mixture of cannabis and blood on him: he too has fed recently. "Well, it's not all I want." Maria stops, uncertain if she should go on, wondering how her desire will be taken by Terence, or even the agreeable Edward, with whom she has spanned countless years.

"What are you talking about?"

Maria realizes she need really say no more. Terence knows. The knowledge glints in his eyes. But words tumble out of her in a rush, anyway. "I want her to become one of us." Maria searches Terence's face for signs of insubordination, waiting for him to rile against her. "Another Tradition," Maria whispers, "the Progeny. We *can* make others, Terence. Where do you think you emerged from?"

Terence laughs until he is gripping his sides. Laughs until there is no longer any humor, until it becomes painful. Abruptly, he stops. "You can't be serious. And besides, you're not the only one who knows the Traditions backward and forward."

Maria casts her eyes down; she knows what's coming.

"The Tradition of the Progeny is very clear: Thou shall only sire another with the permission of thine elder. If thou createst another without thine elder's leave, both thou and thy progeny shall be slain."

"And I suppose you'll make certain that Elise and I reap fitting punishment for flouting Tradition."

Terence shakes his head. "Of course not."

"She's all I think about."

"I thought it would always be just the three of us."

"You should know: always is a very long time." Maria smiles. "We need a change. Elise can bring that."

"You're a fool." Terence turns away. "A selfish fool."

"Damn you. Why can't I have her? Why can't I have someone who loves only me?"

"Love? What a concept."

"Just because you don't understand —"

Terence cuts her off. "I understand love. It's what I feel for you, for Edward. It's not what you feel for Elise. If you truly loved her, you'd want to take nothing more than some examples of her art."

"That's shit."

"No, it isn't and you know it. And you know why."

This stops Maria and she lowers her head in shame. "Isn't it time for you to go somewhere?"

"Don't avoid the issue, Maria. If you bring Elise over to us and make her one of us, you know what it will do to her."

"What it will do is make her happy! At one with the person she loves most!" Maria cries.

Terence hisses. "What it will do is take from her her art...the one thing that *can* grant her a sort of immortality. One that at least has more meaning than anything you can give her."

The pain in her head comes back, stabbing. She doesn't want to hear this. In fact, she wants to claw Terence's face, make him hurt. "We don't know that. Just because she'll have a different perspective from one of us doesn't necessarily mean that perspective will impede her artistic sensitivity. It could, in fact, do the opposite. Look at all the other Toreador artists — the blood heightening their vision! And anyway: the trade would be worth it, Terence. Eternal life."

"You're pathetic. How can you say you love her and yet want to expose her to such risk?" Terence turns to leave the room.

"She's coming back to us...soon."

"Good," Terence shouts over his shoulder. "Maybe then we can get what we really should have from her, for our collection, and we can end this nonsense."

"How can we end it? She knows! She knows!"

Terence waves her words away with his hand. "Good-bye, Maria, poor thoughtless, love-struck Maria. It's almost quaint."

XIX

Elise stands at their front door, wondering why she has come. What's happened to her will, so defiant it caused her to cast away everything for the sake of art? How has she come to bend so easily to a pretty face, a graceful form, the promise of love?

The door, painted black, seems to have a life of its own…as if it moves imperceptibly, breathing, waiting: the watchful eye of a cat just before it pounces.

Behind her the sky is a mass of darkening purple clouds, as dusk winds down into night.

They're inside now, willing me to come in. They won't hurt me, but there is someone out there, a stranger, who will be hurt, who will sacrifice his blood to feed them. Part of Elise wants to run…the conscious part of her, the reasoning part telling her these people are insane or worse, are what they say. Logic tells her to stay away…the danger here is real. But her emotions, an artist's curse and blessing, cause her to place her hand on the doorknob and turn. What's inside? Forbidden fruit, all the more tempting because it is forbidden…and something as simple as the feel of a lover's arms.

Inside the foyer: quiet. Elise moves silently across the marble-tiled floor, heading for the gallery.

A hundred…no, a thousand candles glimmer in the room, casting flickering illumination on the sculpture, painting and drawings. And there, in a corner, warmed by the light of the flames, is Maria. She wears a flowing dress of white lace, no shoes. Her hair is brushed away from her face and her dark eyes drink in the light, sending it back: jewels.

There are no words as the two women come together. The embrace embodies weeks spent apart and the merging of thought that continued in their absence. Elise no longer cares about the iciness of Maria's touch; she wants to devour her. Her mouth finds the silk of Maria's body, sinking teeth and tongue into yielding flesh.

They pause, together on the floor, to share a pipe while staring wordlessly into each other's eyes, girlish smiles playing about the corners of their lips.

And when the marijuana overcomes, Elise feels once more the reality of everything around her melting until her world is consumed by the presence of Maria. And then their bodies truly merge and each of them is all that exists for the other. More than bodies come together: their intellects, their souls.

The communion leaves them exhausted, panting and sweating in a mass of clothes on the floor, lying in each other's arms.

After a while, Maria speaks. "I'm glad you came back. I didn't dare hope that you would."

"I don't know that I ever had a choice."

"There's always a choice." Maria brushes some of Elise's hair away from her face. "I think you know what I want."

Elise's heart begins to pound. She nods.

"I want you to be with me. To be one of us."

Elise turns away. "I don't know if I can."

"You can; the question is: will you? Will you, as Shakespeare said, 'live with me and be my love?'"

Elise laughs and bites her lips. "It would mean becoming one of you?"

"Yes...yes. And it's a gift, a gift we don't bestow very freely."

"Will it hurt?"

"Not at all. I'll lead you through it slowly, my love. The change will take some time, but you'll find it painless."

"And I'll have to do what you do to survive?"

Maria nods, stroking Elise's cheek. "Your perception of it is at odds with what you'll feel once you've crossed over. You'll come to see it as a beautiful thing, more satisfying than sex, more fulfilling than anything you've ever experienced; that much I can promise."

"The idea revolts me." Again, Elise's intellect and emotions war.

"It won't be that way. Nothing you've experienced in your life can compare to the joy and pleasure feeding brings."

Elise grimaces at the word 'feeding,' but in Maria's brown eyes, trust flowers. "I don't know," she whispers, but the phrase comes out more as an affirmation.

Maria surrounds her with her embrace. "It's going to be

wonderful, you'll see. And we can always be together."

Elise collapses into her arms, shutting out thought.

Terence watches from the shadows. Rage bubbles just beneath the marble-white exterior, for the line his sister is feeding Elise. How dare she! How dare she leave out the most important part of what Elise might lose should she become one of them!

He bites his lip, bites until the coppery taste of blood rises up through the broken skin…blood that is not his own, but that of a young girl he had fed on earlier in the evening. A young girl he had taken on her way home from school and kept prisoner since yesterday, feeding on her living flesh for two days. For two days watching her terror, watching her lose her mind with fear and revulsion as he ate her.

Their lives were not as wonderful and poetic as Maria wanted Elise to believe.

Terence leaves the room like a chill, hardly discernible. He knows one thing and this is what enrages him most: he wanted Elise for himself.

"So you'll come with me, then?" Maria searches Elise's eyes for the answer that will come before she opens her mouth.

Elise nods. "I think so. I think I would be happy."

Maria waits for a while, then says what she must. "There's one thing I haven't told you, and it wouldn't be fair if I didn't let you know."

"What?"

Maria lowers her eyes, for once her voice is devoid of promise or excitement. "Your art. Once you've become one of us, you might not feel or experience things in quite the same way."

"What do you mean?" Panic, a scaly creature scurrying along her spine, rises up.

"There are few vampire artists. Your perceptions will be more acute, I promise you, especially with the pot, but their expression will more likely be in the form of the hunt, rather than on paper or canvas."

Elise turns away, bile rising up. She pulls at her hair, hard enough to detach some of it, and cries out in a strangled wail. A vision comes to her with all the clarity of a movie: *Black night, deeper than any black on her palette. Alone, she wanders the streets south of the Art Institute, streets abandoned, punctuated only by the sounds of the wind and the occasional el train, rumbling. Her face is smeared with blood and she beats on the doors of the Art Institute, begging for admission. But no one hears, except the stone lions guarding the place and miraculously, they turn their leonine heads to mock her.*

Elise struggles to her feet and dashes from the house, salt tears stinging.

XX

On the night after Elise rushed, horrified, from the house, Maria sits, mute and numb, listening to Edward and Terence. They are trying to talk reason to her. Their voices filter in dimly, as if they are neighbors on another floor, overheard. She tries to conjure up erotic images to send to Elise, but all that happens when she tries is pornography, having nothing to do with either of them.

And the images go nowhere. It's as if Maria has cast a letter to the wind.

Maria closes her eyes, willing herself to slip away. Her attempts to communicate with Elise are pure despair, pathetic. Maria has never felt so weak. She hones in on Edward, who speaks.

"Maria? Maria, are you listening to us?" Edward's face is marked by concern: the way his head is cocked and his eyebrows come together demonstrate a regard for Maria that is absent from Terence, who is nothing more than a powerhouse of hatred and malice.

Maria nods.

"She knows too much. I don't know why either of you didn't think of that. I guess you both were too infatuated with this mortal that you were blind to what our Tradition is. To what our Tradition has always been...since the second cycle." Edward frowns, sorrowful. He hates to deliver the news they all know.

Maria feels numb. "I know, Edward, I know." And to prove her knowledge, Maria quotes the First Tradition, the Masquerade, and how revealing themselves to those not of the blood renounces their claims of blood.

"You know then that she has to be," Edward breathes in, waiting for a moment "Killed." He shakes his head. "There's no other way. We can't let her live, not with what she knows. It could jeopardize all of us."

"Edward's right." Terence's anger glints: flint.

Maria turns to Terence. Mocking: "'Edward's right!' How dare you."

Terence grabs her arms just before she's about to pummel his chest. "Don't take it out on me! All of us must live by the law...or we could all perish."

"I don't believe it! I don't believe it!" Maria wishes she were able to shed tears, but that release, like many others, left her when she crossed over, hundreds of years ago. Instead her sorrow and longing storm inside her, butterfly wings beating the walls of a sealed jar. "What would happen if we left her alone? Nothing! What if, just suppose, she did tell someone about us? For one, we could be gone from here in an instant. And maybe it's time for us to move on, anyway. So what if she told? Who would believe her? Vampires!" Maria laughs, but the laugh has no mirth, only bitterness. "Blood-sucking fiends responsible for bringing marijuana into the world! I'm sure the mortals would rush to demonstrate their alarm, their credulity."

Edward tries to put his arms around Maria. She pushes him

away. "Listen, Maria, you know we can't take a chance. We can't. It's always been the way."

"Damn 'it's always been the way!' Haven't we learned anything in all these centuries?"

"No!" Terence shouts. "There is no room for debate on this. We must get rid of her as soon as we can. Tonight."

Maria runs to the window. Outside, a breeze stirs the few leaves left on the trees. The withered leaves rustle, branches of an oak tree creak. Darkness envelopes everything. The first cool night of fall. Fog has moved in off Lake Michigan and the streetlights glow, cauled, in the dim gray light.

"Let's just be done with it, then."

A slow night. Elise leans against the brick facade of a Howard Street Mexican restaurant, long ago borne out of business by poor quality and the demands of city health inspectors. She wears jeans, a cropped rabbit-fur jacket and boots. She has pulled her hair up into a purple felt fedora.

She doesn't know if it's the fog or the chill that's keeping them away. She wishes a man would come by. A man with money, who would sweep her away, for however brief the moments are, from her thoughts of Maria and the horror and loss that combined in last night's revelations. She would gladly succumb to just about any trick's desires to be free of intellect and emotions for a half-hour.

The bass of the Harley's engine filters dimly to her. The revving engine is far off, but stands out as it grows closer. Suddenly, Elise is infused with energy. Her mouth grows dry as she wonders what to do with herself. *Is it her? Is it them? Should I run?*

What can I say?

Before she has a chance to decide, the gleaming black-and-chrome bike pulls up. The engine dies. Terence, astride the motorcycle, grins. His blond spikes are perfect. He is clothed, head to toe, in black leather, chains, handcuffs.

A slave's dream.

Maria swallows. What could he want from her now?

"One more time," he mouths, barely audible. "I'll make it worth your while."

Elise fidgets with the fur buttons on her jacket, trying to look away, wishing he weren't there, throwing her into turmoil. What should she do? Maria's disapproving face rises up before her: marred by jealousy and envy.

Elise approaches the bike, strokes Terence's thigh.

"Five hundred dollars. That's what it'll cost you. For anything . . ."

"Not a problem." Terence takes a wad of green from his jacket pocket and thrusts the cold money into her hand. "Hop on."

Elise climbs on, wrapping her arms around Terence's back, fitting her body close, breathing in the scent of the leather. The wind rushes by faster and faster.

Where is he taking her?

From the shadows, they watch. They had agreed earlier on this place, here on the south side of the city. The city's skyline with its lights festooned on towers, practically leans over them in the darkness, at once protective and menacing.

But here, the gleaming towers speaking of wealth, commerce and creativity present a bizarre contrast. Here, where they hide, waiting, watching, the towers are surreal, something out of fantasy. Edward and Maria lean close in a vestibule. At their feet: mashed carcasses of rusting tin cans, discarded rubbers, rat droppings and pieces of torn newspaper and advertising flyers, all begrimed with grit, smeared with mud. Behind them double doors, the glass long ago boarded up, passage in and out of them dim memory.

They wait in the yard of an abandoned factory. The place used to be a foundry, a place where bitter smoke and arcing sparks of lights once pervaded. Now, there is darkness so palpable it presses in, defying the moonlight and the lights of the city.

Surrounding the factory are housing projects, rising up, grim white bricks. The streets are quiet tonight, as Terence and Edward knew they would be when they convinced Maria earlier that this is where they should bring Elise.

Maria clutches at Edward, pulling him close to her as the quiet of the foundry yard is invaded by the roar of the Harley. Maria clutches handfuls of Edward's flesh in her hands as she sees Elise, behind Terence on the bike. Edward doesn't complain: he knows how hard this is. She buries her head in his chest, whimpering.

The ride had gone so fast. With the roaring of the engine and the rushing of the air, Elise could do nothing to stop him as he pointed the bike south and rode on and on, past Lake Michigan on their left, the towers of downtown on their right, the Museum of Natural History, Soldier Field, Shedd Aquarium, on and on until the city landmarks disappeared, replaced by hulking shadows of housing projects and dying industry.

As the bike slowed and pulled finally through a hole in a rusty chain-link fence, Elise wanted nothing more than the bike to stop, so she could get off and run.

But when the bike stops, she is seized with terror. What can she do? To her north is the skyline of the city, impossibly far away. All around her is abandonment and decay. What ghouls will find her should she run screaming for help? A woman and alone?

But what awaits her here with Terence?

"You looked petrified." Terence smiles, teeth glowing in the pitch. She can barely make out his features; how can he read her emotions so clearly?

"Why are we here?" Elise glances around, trying to steel her muscles so he won't see her trembling. "I thought we were just going to your house."

"To see Maria?" The smile disappears from Terence's face.

Elise shakes her head. "Nothing like that."

Terence reaches in his jacket pocket and brings out a small pipe: the bowl dark wood carved into the shape of a face. In the darkness, Elise can't make out the features.

"Smoke?"

The idea brings her to new heights of terror. She remembers what the pot does, how powerful it is, like another drug completely different from the stuff she used to smoke in college. "Let's do it straight tonight."

"Why?"

"Because I want to!"

Terence holds up his hands in supplication, bone-pale fingers pointing toward black sky. "Let's just make love, then."

"Where?"

"Over here."

Cold, bony fingers encircle her hand, impossibly huge and encompassing. He leads her into a vestibule. As she enters the shadows, she sees Maria and Edward, waiting: wraiths in a rectangle of black. Something is horribly wrong! Elise's throat constricts. Her heart stops beating for just a second and then begins to pound irregularly, thumping wildly. The panic of an animal courses through her, pumping up adrenaline, making her sweat.

Terence turns to her and smiles. The smile is cruel and Elise cries out. His teeth have become rows of tiny fangs, razor-sharp.

A flash to Maria: *how could you betray me like this?* And then Elise is turning and sprinting through broken glass and cinders, running heedlessly north, anywhere to get away. Even what might await her outside the chain-link fence would be preferable to what awaited her here.

At least what was out there was human.

"Let me do it!" Maria hisses and grabs Terence's arm. Both

Terence and Edward, who have started off after Elise, laughing, stop at the sound of Maria's voice. They look back at her, puzzled. Elise would be easy prey; they had yet to find a human who could outrun their fleet, silent speed.

"What are you talking about?" Terence's voice teeters on rage. He clenches and unclenches his fist, keeping an eye on the dwindling figure of Elise moving through the night.

"Please," Maria whispers frantically, "I need to do it. I need to be the one to bring her down." Her voice breaks and quivers. "It's my fault and...I love her. I need to do this. My way."

"No!" Terence shouts, "We all share. We always have."

Terence starts off after Elise when another firm grasp pulls him back. Edward's hand digs into the leather on Terence's arm. "Let Maria go. We can all feed after the kill." He turns to Maria. "Fair enough?"

"Yes, yes, anything!" The impatience chokes her. "Just let me go after her before she's gone!"

Maria disappears into the night.

It is only minutes before Elise stumbles and falls. Her hands burn as rough concrete rips skin away from her palms. Her lungs burn too, from the exertion of running.

As her breathing slows, she notices there are no sounds behind her, no following footsteps.

Perhaps she has eluded them. She rolls over on her side, where a painful stitch is screaming its red hurt into her ribs, and tries to sit. When she succeeds, she sees Maria just behind her.

"What do you want?" Elise whimpers, the fear being replaced by a low boiling anger. "Do you want to kill me? Is that it? If you can't have me no one will?"

Maria shakes her head. "I won't grace your remarks with a denial. Get up, please."

Elise manages to stand, holding her side. The pain there is

just beginning to ebb.

"Come with me." Maria begins to walk around the building, behind a low, crumbling brick wall.

Elise folds her arms across her chest, resolute. "No."

"Don't be stupid. Come. Do you really think I would hurt you?"

Elise doesn't know what she should think.

And then Maria's hand, soft as a whisper, is gripping Elise's and tugging. "Please do this for me."

And Elise follows her into the shadows.

Terence and Edward watch and wait, listening. The kill shouldn't take long. Within seconds, Maria should emerge from the wall she took Elise behind and signal them to come join her.

Their patience is interrupted by a scream. A shriek cuts through the dead night, piercing and laying it open.

Before they have a chance to think, Elise runs from behind the wall, purple hat askew, rabbit jacket unbuttoned.

Panic sets in. Has she wounded their Maria? The bitch!

The figure scrambles north again, at a much faster pace, hair dripping out from the hat and blowing back over her shoulders.

"Let's get her," Edward says.

And the two are upon the woman, covering the distance with feline speed. Rage constricts their throats as they rise up into the air and come down, knocking the woman, face first, into the ground.

Rage, white hot, immune to reason, blinds them.

They tear into her, ripping flesh from bones, biting, clawing and shredding in a fury of pink haze.

She doesn't make a sound.

And Terence at last, turns the body over and reaches inside her chest, breaking bone with powerful hands, and rips out her heart. Triumphant, he offers it up to the moon.

But the heart is cold. A fist closes inside him. He drops the heart and notices, for the first time, Edward sobbing.

There before them lies the ruined corpse of Maria.

Running. Gray light spills over the housing project as the first fingers of dawn creep over the lake to reveal the city.

And Elise runs, breathless, looking behind her, always looking behind her.

End

Rick R. Reed is the author of Obsessed and Penance, both in the Abyss horror line. Obsessed will appear in a German edition later this year, and both Penance and Obsessed have recently been sold for Russian publication. He is currently co-authoring Grandpa, an autobiographical novel, with Douglas P. Bell. Grandpa is scheduled for publication in 1994. Rick lives in Chicago.

To Dance

by Alexandra Elizabeth Honigsberg

To dance,
to fall into the arms of
the Beloved
and spiral inward,
to become
the music.

To dream,
the dream of making
where reality is fantasy
and fantasy is but a part
of Spirit.

To love,
    and dance into
        the circle
    bare, stripped of fear.

To become the Beloved
        and shine like
    the mirrors in
    one hundred thousand dreams.

To dance
    and be born anew.

Alexandra Elizabeth Honigsberg's short fiction has appeared in *Unique* and *Fresh Ink* magazines, as well as the *Angels of Darkness* anthology. This is her first appearance as a poet. Professionally, she is a counselor and scholar of comparative religions. Alexandra is also a concert violist/conductor and a song writer. She lives in New York City with her husband and two cats, in the land of the Unicorn Tapestries.

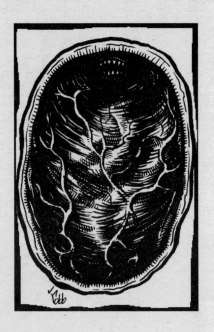

Small Brown Bags of Blood

by C. Dean Andersson

Here, in the whirlpool of European races, the Ugric tribe
bore down from Iceland the fighting spirit which Thor
and Wodin gave them, which their Berserkers
displayed to such fell intent on the seaboards of
Europe, ay, and Asia and Africa too, till the peoples
thought that the were-wolves themselves had come.

— Bram Stoker, *Dracula*

Yes, we became killers of Christ-Priests. Would you know
why, or no?

It is not a pretty truth. With your modern thoughts and well-
trained, sheep-like ways, you may prefer the lies you have been

told. Lies called history. Recorded by our enemies.

Yet, if there is iron in your soul…if you are more than most, more than mere chattel waiting complacently to be slain…

The first notice history took of my northern homeland's war against the Wyrm is dated the eighth day of the sixth month in the year Christ-Priests number 793. On that date was said to occur the first raid on the English coast by men from the Northlands, marking the beginning of the so-called Viking Age.

I do not dispute the date. But it was not a raid. It was survival.

I was there.

Would you know more, or no?

Yes, I was there, sixteen summers old.

Though later I took the name of Kveldulf, which means Evening Wolf, in those days I was named Egil, son of Olaf the Strong, who was the son of Kveldulf the Skald.

Grandfather Kveldulf was a staunch supporter of the God Odin. He became an honored vitki, a master of Odin's Holy Mysteries, the Runes, and a far-famed Skald, or Poet in your tongue, another endeavor over which Odin holds sway. But Grandfather earned the name Kveldulf for a different reason.

Odin is also the God of Berserkers.

Grandfather possessed the Berserker God's Gift of Fury. When the battle-rage was upon him, he could become a ravening wolf, a werewolf or Garou as some would say, lusting to kill the enemies of our folk.

The blood of a Berserker, passed down to me through my father, therefore flowed in my veins.

Father, though a renowned warrior, had neither the Gift nor any great feeling for Odin's ways. Such things often skip a generation. But I was drawn from an early age to Odin.

I dreamed often and well of running with Odin's wolves, Geri and Freki, said by some to be the first Get of Fenris from which all shapeshifters of the Northlands descended. And in my ninth year I experienced a vision of Ragnarok, the Apocalypse, in which the Wolf God Fenris did not fight against Odin as most tales have it, but with him against the brother of Fenris, Jormungandr, the World Serpent, also called the Wyrm, and against their father, Loki.

The sister of Fenris and Jormungandr, the Death Goddess, Hel, I also saw, though she did not take part in the fight, but greedily drew the dead of both sides into her icy realm beneath the Earth.

Then, in my vision Odin and Fenris became one being, a Man-Wolf that struggled without fear against prophecies of certain doom. And by the Man-Wolf's side fought the son born of Odin and our sacred Mother Earth, the strongest of the Northern Gods, Thor, wielding his War Hammer, Miolnir, the Crusher, from which came sizzling bolts of lightning.

My vision ended as I joined the fight, a Man-Wolf too, together with Geri and Freki and all the Get of Fenris, fighting on and on against the forces of the Wyrm.

When Grandfather Kveldulf heard of my vision, he solemnly took me aside and told me secret things I must never reveal to one who is not Garou. But even after having recurring dreams and the vision in my ninth year, until I was tested in battle no one knew for certain whether I would berserk, and if I did whether I would have the Gift.

My future was, therefore, an uncertain one. But whose future is not? Truly, beyond our next heartbeat, our next breath, the unknown awaits us all.

Would you know more, or no?

During the winter of 792 to 793, I helped Father and a crew of kinsmen build a sturdy new longship. Ships built by Olaf the Strong had become highly prized by those who could afford them, and Father's wealth had grown along with his fame. But this ship he built for himself, the first of its kind, having several innovations of Father's devising that we planned to put to the test come the spring.

The ability to design superb wave-steeds was a gift, Father believed, from the God Niord, the Vanir deity who ruled the Sea. Indeed, mother often said he loved building and sailing his ships more than he loved her, and she knew he loved her mightily.

Mother's name was Inga, daughter of Sunna, who was a daughter of Guthrun Freyadis, a far-seeing *volva* who, had she been yet alive before our fateful voyage, might well have warned us not to go. But most of us would have gone anyway. Only weak fools try to escape their *orlog*, their fate, woven by the Three Holy Norns whose power extends over even the Gods.

Would you know more, or no?

When the Goddess Freya saw fit to bring the spring thaw early that year, I sailed with Father and our crew of kinsmen to test his newly built ship.

He named the vessel *Swan-Pacer*, for it seemed that such a fine ship might ascend into the sky and follow the Swan's Road itself, as Northlanders from my region called the Milky Way.

Our first voyage passed without incident, and our second, but on the third a sudden storm struck before we could return to land.

We quickly drew up *Swan-Pacer's* great sail, hurried to lower the strong mast, and made certain the oars were lashed securely in their rack. Then, with Father at the side-mounted rudder, *Swan-Pacer* rode the storm-tossed waters, almost joyfully it seemed, leaping from wave to wave, tempering our anxiety with pride.

Now and then amidst the howling wind and crashing thunder I heard Father's laughter booming out as he steadfastly gripped the rudder, and once I heard him shout out, "Niord! What a ride! What a steed!"

Some in the longship shouted to other Gods, of course, for comfort and strength, most of them to Thor, a well-known friend of humankind. Around the necks of men who favored Thor hung amulets symbolizing Thor's Hammer.

I, however, called out to Odin. But Odin was not a comforting God, and I well knew that it might be his desire, for unknown purposes, that I drown in the storm. So I sought my comfort from the knowledge that Father designed sound ships, and that I had with my own hands helped build the wave-steed beneath me.

Carried westward by the violent weather, we endured the storm for two days and nights. Then the winds began to die and the churning skies to lift.

By mid-morning of the third day, sunlight warmed us.

To the west we saw land, foreign but not unknown. Trade between Northlanders and Englanders was not uncommon, and with land ever scarce in our mountainous homeland, some of our people had already begun a peaceful migration to the isles now called the Shetlands, Orkneys, and Hebrides.

Swan-Pacer had withstood the storm well, but Father judged she could benefit from a few minor repairs before we turned homeward. In addition, we were all rather hungry and thirsty, having finished on the second day the provisions we had brought along for what we had thought would be but a short voyage.

We therefore made our way to the mainland and dragged *Swan-Pacer* onto the beach.

Offshore was a small tidal island, but we had no need to visit it. All we needed to effect our repairs and fill our bellies was available closer at hand.

We found a flock of sheep grazing on long spring grass near the coast and bought two from the shepherd who tended them, paying him a more than fair number of links from the golden chain Father always wore around his neck when away from home, a convenient way to carry with him a portion of his wealth.

After we had eaten, we set to work on our repairs. But near

midday, Haakon the Hawk-Eyed, son of Kettil the Generous, called our attention to a small boat with five men in it, rowing from the island toward our position on the shore.

As the boat drew near, we noted that the men in it were apparently weaponless. They wore simple black robes. When they were closer still we saw they also wore unequal-limbed crosses around their necks.

Christ-Priests.

Seeing what they were, several of my kinsmen groaned.

Three years before, two Christ-Priests had visited our region. Using words badly spoken, what little they knew of our language badly accented by their foreign tongues, they struggled to tell us, though none of us had asked to hear, a story most strange. It was about their God, Whom they said was the only *true* God, and His only Son, the White Christ, Who was the only One Who could save our souls from eternal punishment for sins we had committed against their God before we even knew He existed!

The foreigners further told us that our own Gods and Goddesses were to be revered no more. They said our deities were Demons and Devils who had been deceiving us for centuries, which meant, they explained, when we asked, that the souls of all our ancestors, ignorant of the White Christ as they had been, were indeed suffering the torments of the damned. Even the souls of our greatest heroes and heroines were being punished in a place of eternal pain!

Always a people who appreciated an entertaining story and even more a good joke, though offended at having our ancient deities called Devils, we listened politely, at first, until we realized that the Christ-Priests were not joking and only knew the one story. They were *serious* about our worshipping their White Christ, a living corpse, according to their story, Whose Priests used sorcery to turn wine into His blood and bread into His flesh.

Blood and flesh His worshippers then ate!

And they wanted us to do other odd things, too. We were thereafter to strive to be meek and weak instead of strong. We were to admire sheep above wolves and not fight back if attacked! And, most importantly, we were to worship their God on *our knees!*

After only two days, we politely asked the Christ-Priests to leave. They had entertained us but slightly in return for the food and hospitality we had freely given to them. In truth, everyone agreed that our two unwelcome visitors were without doubt the most rude and boring people any one of us had ever had the misfortune to meet.

But, proving how rude they truly were, after we asked them to leave, they refused!

The next morning, we found them in our sacred grove, destroying carven images of our deities and chopping at the Holy Trees.

We would have been within our rights to have killed them, of course. But they were foreigners in our land and, quite obviously, not entirely sane. So we gave them a small boat and forced them to use it.

Many were the cheers and sighs of relief when they vanished around a bend in the fjord! Now, however, five such men were approaching. The groans of my kinsmen were therefore understandable. I groaned a little myself. Our only hope was that not all Christ-Priests were like the two who had visited our homeland, and we soon discovered that at least their leader was not.

The leader, climbing from the boat first, surprised us by speaking our language reasonably well. He had, he explained, spent time with people from our homeland who had immigrated to his country's northern islands. He identified himself as Bishop Eadfrith and the island as the Holy Island of Lindisfarne.

Another surprise came when Eadfrith said they had brought to us a gift. Each of the four men accompanying Eadfrith carried a full wineskin, which they gave to us.

The skins did not contain as heady a brew as the mead and ale to which we were accustomed, but we thanked them most graciously and passed the crimson wine around, each of us in his turn taking several appreciative swallows.

Some of our kinsmen, remembering the other Christ-Priests' claim that our Gods were Devils, used the occasion to raise a wineskin to the sky and pronounce the name of their favorite deity before taking a drink. But others of us, my father and I included, thought this a rude way to treat givers of gifts, even Christ-Priests.

The cross-wearers reacted by making the sign of the cross at the sound of our deities' names. It was amusing to note, however, that their sign of the cross was extremely similar to the sign used by our people, the sign of Thor's Hammer, with which we blessed and hallowed our homes, marriages, children, and weapons.

But we should not have been so ready to accept their gift. It was more than wine we drank. Something had been mixed with it, something that made us fall asleep.

We awoke on the beach near our longship, tied securely, hand and foot, our weapons gone, and our clothing as well!

It was growing dark. The tide was coming in.

At first we thought they meant us to drown when the water reached us, but that was not to be our fate.

As the twilight sky slowly darkened and we struggled in vain to get free, we saw three distant lights in the direction of the island.

The lights drew nearer and revealed themselves to be torches carried in the bows of three small boats being rowed toward us by Christ-Priests. But this time the men who wore crosses did not ride in their boats alone.

When they reached the shore, the Christ-Priests, four to a

boat, climbed out, pulled the boats onto the beach, then knelt as the passenger in each boat stepped onto the sand.

Tall and thin those passengers were, dressed all in black like the priests but with long, distorted faces as pale as a winter moon and huge, elongated eyes that glowed as if they were not eyes at all but red-hot coals.

They moved unnaturally. Jerkily. Almost bird like.

We learned, then, what manner of monsters they were.

They knelt among us and began tearing open our throats with their pointed teeth, lapping up the crimson streams that flooded forth.

Frightened curses and entreaties to our Gods bellowed forth from all of us as we struggled to get free before our turn came to be slaughtered.

But for those of us who were not the first to be attacked, our turn never came. Something else came instead.

From the north arose a cold breeze that fast became a howling wind mixed with another sound that came out of the empty sky, a bestial bellowing that grew louder and louder, until suddenly it was gone. *Into me.*

My fear vanished. Rage took its place.

I opened my mouth and shouted, meaning to call on Odin. But instead a bestial bellow of rage exploded from my throat, and I saw, towering into the sky above me, the ghostly image of a Man-Wolf I recognized as the merged form of Odin and Fenris from my childhood vision.

Odin-Fenris looked down upon me, whispered Runes only I could hear, and I began to change.

Inhuman strength flowed through me as the Gift of Fury transformed my flesh. I broke my bonds and sprang to my feet, a Berserking Man-Wolf lusting for battle.

I slashed at the nearest blood-drinker and my claws all but decapitated it. Then, howling with fury, I attacked and destroyed a second of the monsters. But the third escaped into a boat and, protected by Christ-Priests who threw themselves in my path, it rowed itself into the water out of my reach before I disemboweled the last priest who stood in my way.

With no priests left to kill, my companions feared I would next begin killing them. Such a thing was not unknown for warriors who became Berserkers in battle. The Fury passed from me, however, and I returned to my own form, my muscles pained by the inhuman force that had flowed through them but my soul exalted by the fierce transcendence I had just experienced.

I freed Father from his bonds and then began working to free the man next to him while Father worked to free the next man in the line. But then, in the light of the two torches in the two boats left on the beach, I saw one of the slain blood-drinkers move, then the other. But no, they were not really moving. Only their skin was moving. Or, rather, something *beneath* their skin.

I remembered once finding a dead animal filled to the bursting with maggots whose crawling made its decomposing skin move exactly as the skin of the blood-drinkers was now moving. But it was not maggots inside the blood-drinkers.

Out of the two corpses burst a flood of dark and wriggling things that silently and swiftly covered the ground and attacked us, biting us, trying to burrow like blood-starved ticks into our flesh!

We fought them, desperately stamping them beneath our bare feet, breaking them open like pus-filled boils, the liquid within them stinking like the fluids that drip from rotting flesh and feeling like freezing drops of slime-slicked water from an icy stream.

I grabbed a torch from one of the boats and pushed the flames toward the icy-blooded things on the ground. They recoiled from the fire, bulged from the heat, then exploded, spraying me with their cold insides.

I shouted my success. Father grabbed the other torch and helped me fight them with fire. But there were too many for us to stop all of them, and two of our men, still bound, screamed with horror and agony as the remaining things, in spite of all our attempts to prevent it, burrowed inside their bodies and began devouring them from within.

The men's screams weakened as they grew thin, sucked dry of blood and fluids. Their skin became as white as a winter moon. Their faces distorted, elongated. Then both men stopped moving, and we knew them for dead. But suddenly they opened their eyes, eyes that now glowed as if made of hot coals.

Their ropes had loosened when their bodies grew thin. They began to wriggle free.

My father acted to stop them. He shouted that we must push the two men each into a boat and set the boats aflame.

We hurried to do just that, then stood and watched the boats burn on the beach, watched as the flesh of our two kinsmen blackened and blistered, listened to their mindless screams.

Torches in our hands, Father and I watched closely, the rest of our men behind us, to make certain none of the dark things escaped the flames.

The bodies of the burning men grew horribly bloated as the things within them expanded from the heat. Then, each in his turn, the blackened flesh of the doomed men burst apart in an icy blast of putrid spray.

No crawling shapes escaped the flames. But we knew the horror was far from over. It was only just beginning.

As one, we who had survived looked across the dark waters to the island. To Lindisfarne.

We made more torches. We found our clothing and weapons in the longship. We assumed the Christ-Priests had planned to sell the clothing, along with the ship, after we were dead.

We placed guards to watch for new attacks. Then the rest of us worked all night to hurry our longship's repairs.

At first light, on the eighth day of the sixth month in the

year the Christ-Priests number 793, we rowed *Swan-Pacer* to the island and attacked.

We killed all who stood in our way as we searched for the blood-drinker that had escaped us. But we did not find the monster. It had wisely moved elsewhere during the night.

We did find, however, where it and its companions had been, in the deep cellars below the buildings. We could tell by the stench.

We returned home, taking plunder from Lindisfarne with us, gold and silver, found inside the building where the Christ-Priests worshipped their living corpse of a God.

We told our story to our kinsmen and to others in our homeland. And we showed them examples of the plunder to be had, for we knew that many would accompany us on future raids more because they were interested in the wealth they could steal than because they truly wanted to help us find and destroy the monster that had escaped.

I do not know if we ever found that particular monster. But we did find many other blood-drinkers, though some proved to be a different type and did not have dark wrigglers inside.

We found them in cellars as on Lindisfarne, and as on Lindisfarne often protected by Christ-Priests, but protected by others as well and sometimes in places elsewhere than beneath the churches of the White Christ.

Wherever we found them, however, with fire we destroyed them and the dark things inside some, the wrigglers seeming little more than small brown bags of blood. Parasites. Evil manifestations of the Wyrm.

And we wondered from where they had come. From the south? Spreading northward and westward with the spread of the Christ-Priests over the centuries? Was it, perhaps, some unguessed-at power or trickery of the blood-drinkers that had allowed the White Christ's religion to conquer and displace the native religions of Europe? Was it the monsters' desires that caused the massive cathedrals to be built? So that they could rest securely beneath? Or was their association with Christ-Priests a more recent one, a convenient way to spread an evil far older than the religion itself?

But, ultimately, the blood-drinkers' origins and history were not the most important thing to us. What was most important was their destruction, to protect our northern homeland. Our folk. For our survival.

So, yes, we men from the North, called Vikings by others, became killers of Christ-Priests, first at Lindisfarne, then elsewhere, reaching Wales in 795, Scotland in 798, France the next year, then Ireland, Russia, the Ukraine, finding a dense infestation in the region of the Carpathian Mountains, then in Spain, Morocco, Greece, Italy, on and on, those of us who knew always looking for more monsters to kill, more of the dark things to destroy.

I and others of the Get of Fenris, Garou blood in our veins, who accompanied kinsmen on expeditions also met others with the Gift along the way, other warriors against the Wyrm, some of whom had been fighting the blood-drinkers far longer than we.

In Greece we encountered the Garou tribe known as Black Furies, warrior women all, staunch worshippers and protectors of the Wyld, their violence breathtaking to behold. A nomadic tribe called the Silent Striders we found in many places, while the Red Talons tribe, looking upon all of humankind as agents of the Wyrm, longed to cleanse Mother Earth entirely of Her human infestation.

And along the way, in addition to Garou warriors we found others who fought against the Wyrm, including, to our surprise, a few Christ-Priests who seemed not to have succumbed to the evil, though we remained wary of them always, cautious lest it be a trick.

Of course now, if you feel the truth in my tale, you must know that many are the lies told about us and our enemies in history recorded by cross-wearing servants of the Wyrm.

Do you still believe that blood-drinkers, called vampires by some, are *repelled* by the symbol of the cross? Indeed, we came to regard it as *their* symbol, and where better for them to hide than within holy structures the legends they invented about themselves say they are unable to enter! Certainly no Christian who endeavors to struggle against the Wyrm's evil would think to look for them there. *But we would.* And did. And still do, those of us and our descendants whom our Gods have gifted with immortality, even today.

Yes, today. For in the end, the monsters spread faster than we could kill them, and they are now everywhere in the world. No place exists where they do not lie waiting for sunset and then in darkness creep from their cellars and crypts, coming forth in the night to drink the blood of the living once more. But they thrive best in cities.

Some say the spread and growth of cities was in part their doing, for in cities their crimes, their kills, are easily disguised and rarely noticed, *except by us.* The Garou tribe called Glass Walkers has, however, followed them there and adapted to urban life with a vengeance.

And be assured that my tribe, the Get of Fenris, is ever vigilant still, Hammers of Thor around our necks, shouting to Odin and Fenris as we slay.

Hope, then, that we, whom history has named barbaric killers, may always exist, becoming beasts more monstrous than those we kill to defend our sacred Mother Earth and all Her children, including the likes of you.

Hail to Fenris! Odin! And Thor! Would you know more, *be more?* Or no?

He looked like a figure of Thor as his untrembling arm rose and fell, driving deeper and deeper the mercy-bearing stake, whilst the blood from the pierced heart welled and spurted up around it.

—Bram Stoker, *Dracula*

C. Dean Andersson is the author of the horror novels *Fiend, I Am Dracula, Buried Screams, Raw Pain Max,* and *Torture Tomb.* As Asa Drake, he has written five fantasy novels, including *Warrior Witch of Hel, Death Riders of Hel,* and *Werebeasts of Hel.* He lives in the Dallas / Fort Worth Metroplex. Dean's works in progress include *I Am Frankenstein* and *I Am the Mummy.*

The Love of Monsters

by Nancy A. Collins

embroke peered through the windshield, scowling at the rain pouring relentlessly from the sky. He could not help but feel that things were already going from bad to worse. As if navigating the narrow, two-lane Pennsylvania mountain road wasn't problem enough, Mother Nature had to pick this night to unleash a veritable flood. Sian grunted and shifted uncomfortably in her seat.

"Are you alright, honey?" he asked, nervously eyeing her swollen belly.

"I'm okay. They just kicked me, that's all."

They. Sian was carrying twins, of that there was no doubt. When she'd announced the fact to Pembroke, he didn't ask her if the doctor was sure. Not that she'd seen an obstetrician anytime during her pregnancy. She simply, instinctively *knew* what was inside her belly—much the same way she'd known of her condition the morning after she'd conceived. Sian was a natural woman. It was one of the things Pembroke loved about her.

He sneaked another look at her as he drove. He liked looking at her when she wasn't aware of being watched. Which was pretty rare, actually. Sian was alert, even in her sleep.

Her features were dramatically lit by the off-green glow from the car's instrument panel, making her appear even more striking than usual. Her cheekbones were high, framing almond-shaped eyes of luxuriant green. Her dark brown hair tumbled down past her shoulders, as soft and sleek to the touch as a rabbit's pelt. Her complexion was golden-brown, but without the leatheriness of a habitual sun worshipper. Pembroke vaguely remembered her saying something about American Indian blood in her family. He wondered whether their children would have their mother's coloration or be pale as himself.

Sian stiffened suddenly, leaning forward, her fingers digging into the dashboard. Her eyes seemed to grow larger in their orbits.

"Philip—do you see it?"

Indeed he did. The rain might have been heavy enough to obscure the deer when it first leapt onto the road, but there was no mistaking it—or the crumpled ruins of the vehicle that had smashed into it—on the road ahead.

There was barely a shoulder to pull onto, but somehow he managed. Pembroke put the car into park and engaged the emergency brake.

"I'm leaving the emergency flashers on to make sure some local yokel on his way home from the farmer's market doesn't slam into us from behind," he explained. "Sit tight—I'll only be a minute."

Sian smiled tightly and took his hand in hers, squeezing it. "Be careful, sweetheart."

"I will," he assured her, kissing her on the cheek for emphasis. He opened the car door and stepped out onto the road.

The rain was cold and heavy, soaking him to the skin within four quick strides. He hurried to the disabled vehicle—a '90 Toyota truck—which was turned sideways, blocking both the uphill and downhill lanes. The truck's front end was crumpled, the hood accordioned like tinfoil. Pembroke could hear the hiss of a damaged radiator beneath the persistent drumming of the rain. A greenish liquid dripped from underneath the car. The right headlight was still on, although its mate was nowhere to be seen. There was a shadowy shape slumped over the steering wheel, a fist-sized crack in the safety glass in front of the driver's seat.

As Pembroke opened the driver's side of the truck, he heard a car door slam behind him. He saw Sian, looking like a grossly deformed jogger, sprint in the direction of the mangled deer. Maybe she had to pee again. Ever since the pregnancy began to show, she'd turned into a regular fire hydrant. Then he saw her drop onto her haunches and tear at the deer's exposed viscera with her bare hands. No. The problem wasn't her bladder. It was another attack of mommy-to-be munchies.

The driver of the truck moaned, drawing Pembroke's attention from Sian's roadside snack. The driver was a man in his late thirties, wearing an oil-stained Pittsburgh Penguins cap—the kind they give away at sporting events—and a poorly maintained mustache that did nothing to hide or to help his weak chin. He smelled of cheap bourbon and cheaper beer. Pembroke glanced into the foot well on the passenger's side; sure enough, a bottle of Old Grandad and several cans of Schaeffers, empty and full, had been thrown under the dash during the collision.

The driver's forehead was bloody from bashing the windshield, his lower lip split from impacting against the steering wheel. Pembroke could tell by the way the unconscious man breathed that he had several broken ribs. The driver was lucky that the engine block hadn't ended up in the front seat with him, skewering him like a butterfly on a mounting board.

The driver's lids fluttered, revealing wildly rolling eyeballs. Major concussion. Possible brain damage. Pembroke leaned in and sank his fangs into the driver's exposed throat. His victim jerked once, crying out like a child caught in a bad dream. He smelled of equal parts alcohol, rancid body odor, and forty-weight, and his blood tasted of intoxicants. Pembroke felt his anxiety fade as the stolen blood washed into his system. Just what he needed—a little something to loosen him up. But he didn't need to be drunk. He pulled back from feeding, casually wiping a drop of blood from his lower lip with the back of his hand.

The driver of the truck was now white as a sheet of paper. Pembroke noted that the gash on his forehead and the cut on his lip were no longer bleeding.

He checked the truck's gearshift. The force of the impact had jarred the transmission into neutral. Pembroke pulled his head out of the cab, opening his senses to the night. Sian had been right; this particular stretch of road was indeed lonely after dark. The few local farmers who lived in the area made a point of avoiding it during nights such as this. There was little chance of anyone happening to drive by between now and dawn.

Gripping the steering wheel with his left hand and pushing forward with his shoulder, Pembroke maneuvered the damaged truck from the middle of the road, aiming it downhill. The driver muttered a woman's name—his mother? wife? daughter?—just as Pembroke gave the vehicle one last shove, sending it sailing over the wooden caution fence and into the darkness beyond.

Sian was back in the passenger seat by the time he returned to the car, worrying on a chunk of liver she'd torn from the deer carcass. Her clothes were sopping wet, her hair plastered to her skull. She smiled at him as he climbed in behind the wheel, her face smeared with gore. God, she was so beautiful it was almost impossible for him to feign anger at her.

"Sian—have you gone mad? What if someone had seen you out there, tearing away at that deer? I could have passed myself off as a Good Samaritan trying to help a fellow motorist. But how could I have possibly explained a pregnant woman scarfing down roadkill?"

"Sorry about that. I couldn't help myself. The moment I caught sight of the deer I suddenly had this craving for liver—want some?" She held out the bleeding organ to him.

Pembroke smiled and shook his head. "No thanks—I'm full. Besides, I never feed on animals unless it's unavoidable."

"You and your diet," Sian teased. She reached into the back seat and retrieved a towel, which she handed to Pembroke. "Here, you'd better dry yourself off. You'll catch your death of cold if you're not careful."

Pembroke laughed.

———

Two hours later they were even farther into the mountains and it had stopped raining. Sian dozed lightly in the back seat, whimpering every now and again like a dog chasing rabbits in its sleep. Pembroke wondered if they would be able to reach their destination before dawn. If not, he would have to hide in the trunk of the car. That would leave Sian on her own, and the thought of her going into heavy labor unprotected did not sit well with him.

Pembroke checked the rearview mirror. If they were being followed, it wasn't by car, that much was certain. It had been well over an hour since he'd last seen any headlights, either coming or going.

He frowned and drummed his fingers against the steering wheel. So much had changed in the last year and a half. For a creature prone to planning things over the course of decades, if not centuries, eighteen months was little more than the batting of an eye. He had not experienced such a radical change since the day he surrendered his mortality and became one of the Kindred.

Whenever he looked back on his life as a human, Pembroke could only shake his head in disbelief. To think that he could have ever been such a miserable specimen as Philip Herbert, the seventh Earl of Pembroke!

He had been born in 1653, the scion of one of England's greatest houses, only to go on to become one of the country's most notorious and reviled rakehells.

During his daytime slumber, where dreams and memories often mingled in a fantastic soup, he often saw himself as a suckling babe, wrapped in swaddling clothes so tightly he could scarcely breathe, and hung from a peg on the wall like a blancmange as his wet nurse busied herself with her kitchen chores. One thing he did remember from those dim and distant days. It was when, at the age of twenty months, he was taken away from his subsitute mother. He could recall very little in the way of detail about the event, save that he did not want to go and that he'd been very frightened.

Even when he was mortal, Pembroke's memories of his biological parents had been fuzzy and indistinct. The only emotion he could associate with his father was that of hatred and resentment. The fifth earl used constant and severe corporal punishment as a way of bending his children's will to his own, much the same way he would have broken in a dog or horse.

By the age of seven, Pembroke was no longer cute or small enough to be cuddled in his mother's lap like a pet, so he was sent away to school. He soon discovered it was better to be a bully than bullied and quickly developed a reputation for cruelty and an unpredictable temper. Once out of school and loosed on society at large, he became notorious for his drunken and violent habits, and people were openly afraid to sit near him at taverns.

In 1674, after his elder brother drank himself into an early grave, Pembroke found himself heir to the title at the tender age of twenty-one. He now had more money and power than he knew what to do with. What few restraints existed on his behavior suddenly evaporated, and he set forth on a desperate revel, determined to experience every pleasure that crossed his mind the moment it did so.

In 1677, while drinking at a public house, he insulted a commoner by the name of Vaughn, who took exception and challenged him to a duel. When Vaughn got the better of him, forcing him to the ground, Pembroke's footman came up from behind and cut Vaughn over the hand, disabling him. Pembroke then got to his feet and ran his opponent through the belly.

In 1678 he was placed in the Tower on orders from Charles II for daring to recite a bawdy version of the Lord's Supper in a local tavern, substituting piss for sacramental wine. He remained in the Tower for two weeks. The night he was released, he accosted a complete stranger who was leaving a friend's house at the exact moment Pembroke happened to be passing by. Pembroke struck the hapless man in the eye, nearly knocking it from its socket, and began kicking him as he lay in the street. Pembroke certainly would have killed the man had his friend not dragged him back into his house and bolted the door.

Later that same year, Pembroke was drinking with his entourage at a tavern in the Haymarket when he spied an old companion, Nathaniel Cony. Cony had a friend with him and Pembroke invited them both to drink with him. It wasn't long, however, before he and Cony's friend got into a drunken argument. Pembroke threw his wine into the other man's face and kicked him out of the tavern. When Cony went to see if his companion was all right, Pembroke set upon him without warning, hitting him over the head with a chair. He then began to jump up and down on Cony's back and stomach, kicking the poor bastard yellow. Cony lived for a week before finally expiring, and Pembroke found himself up on charges of willful murder.

However, he escaped justice by use of the Statute, a privilege that had been granted to peers in the reign of Edward VI, by which they might claim 'benefit of clergy' for manslaughter if it was a first offense. Thus the Lord High Steward, the Earl of Nottingham, had no choice but to release him. Pembroke used his freedom to arrange the murder of Sir Edmund Berry Godfrey, a friend of the late Cony, who had brought him to trial in the first place.

Two years later, Pembroke and six of his servants were returning from a dinner in London. As they crossed Turnham Green, they were stopped by the Chriswick watch. The constable asked who was in the coach and where it was bound, as was his duty. While the constable questioned the driver, Pembroke crept out and, without provocation, drew his sword and ran it to the hilt through the constable's stomach. The constable somehow managed to raise an alarm and felled Pembroke with his watch staff before collapsing.

This time a Middlesex jury found him guilty of murder, but being the brother-in-law of the King's French mistress did have its advantages. Shortly after receiving his Royal Pardon, Pembroke got into a knock-down brawl with Lord Dorset in a dispute over some land. Dorset filed a complaint against him in the House of Lords. Pembroke was persuaded to apologize publicly, if not sincerely, and he was released provided he remain on his estate at Wilton.

And, as far as the history books were concerned, that was the last to be heard of the mad and bad Lord Pembroke, who drank himself to death in 1683, not long after his thirtieth birthday. But that was only the beginning, really, not the end.

Used to the wild pleasures of London, Pembroke soon wearied of being confined to his country estate. He grew restless, but he feared that if he was found in London again there would be no escaping the Tower—or worse. During his unhappy exile, he was visited by a man he remembered, if only vaguely, from the gaming tables and taverns that catered exclusively to the gentry. He was a German nobleman who went by the name of Ruhl.

When Ruhl strode into his drawing room that fateful evening, Pembroke was impressed by his mastery of his surroundings and self. Pembroke had never seen its like, even in the king's court. Here was a man who feared nothing and no one. Pembroke, who, like all mortals, feared many things, was in awe of the stranger's presence.

Ruhl was fearless. And fearsome. And gifted when it came to manipulating the weaknesses of those surrounding him. He had carriages of rowdies and harlots brought up from London and staged orgies for his host's amusement. He had a bear brought in for Pembroke's hounds to bait. He orchestrated an obscene parody of the Lord's Supper in the family chapel, using a nude eleven-year-old girl as the altar. By the time Ruhl revealed his true nature, Pembroke was beyond fear or loathing. He begged to be made one of the Kindred as well.

And Ruhl obliged him.

When Pembroke awoke from his Embrace, it was as if his body had been hollowed out and a completely different person had been slipped beneath its skin. Gone were the hatred, unhappiness, and insane rage that had clouded his mind since earliest childhood. It was as if he had been in pain all his life and someone had finally made the hurt go away. Where his mortal life had been without focus, now he served his sire and the secret, world-spanning vampire sect that called itself the Camarilla.

Since Pembroke was known to be dead, they could not remain in England without arousing suspicion. Too many people in the society Ruhl traveled in knew what Pembroke looked like. The same held true for the Continent. So they went to the Colonies.

Ruhl found the Colonies' comparative youth a challenge. Granted, it was harder for the Kindred to work unnoticed in the newborn cities of New York, Philadelphia, Baltimore, and Boston, but the potential rewards were far greater than those that awaited those who remained in the Old World.

When the witch-hunt began in Salem, Ruhl was quick to defuse a potentially dangerous situation by diverting inquiry away from actual supernaturals and focusing it on outcast humans instead. Pembroke remembered how the witch-finder Cotton Mather had spoken earnestly about the need to ferret out Satan's own, all the while unaware he was breaking bread with a vampire prince.

Ruhl cultivated the friendship of Benjamin Franklin, whose scientific interests and rational mind were ideally suited to the needs of the Kindred. For, as Ruhl was quick to remind him over the years, only upon the death of superstition could their kind truly be safe. And as a high-ranking member of the Masons, Ruhl subtly shaped the coming Revolution.

Although he was initially dismissed by his fellow Kindred as deluded, Ruhl's interest in and development of the American colonies eventually paid off. Within a century of his arrival in Boston, Ruhl was the unchallenged Prince of the New World, his domain stretching from the Atlantic Ocean to the Mississippi River. And Pembroke had been there the whole while, helping his sire every step of the way, watching Ruhl, as aristocratic a creature as ever walked the earth, nurse democracy and egalitarianism as a means of screening the activities of vampires from the breathing world.

Ruhl was unusual as vampire lords went. He was not satisfied to simply stay in one place for the remainder of his days. He craved challenge. He was especially drawn to the chaos and energy of human strife. Perhaps humans' petty struggles for power and land amused him. It was hard to say. Even though Pembroke had been his constant companion for over a century, there was much he did not understand about his sire. In any case, when the Napoleonic Wars broke out, Ruhl was drawn to the Continent like a moth to the flame.

Although the elder vampire was the closest to a friend and father Pembroke had ever known, he was hesitant to leave his adopted homeland. He had come to appreciate, perhaps even to admire, the fledgling country's people, and he associated the crowded, narrow streets of the Old World with his unhappy mortal existence. Ruhl seemed to understand and granted Pembroke his freedom. Pembroke elected to remain in New York City, which by the early 1800s was already showing all the signs of a prime hunting territory.

The young metropolis was excellent cover for the likes of the Kindred. With its constant influx of immigrants, strangers were seldom commented upon—or their disappearances reported. The high incidence of disease brought on by crowded conditions and improper sanitation helped disguise deaths from decidedly unnatural causes. And the violence among the various ethnic bands that battled one another, as well as the police, for control of the city's criminal rackets provided a perfect screen for covert blood wars between rival clans.

And so Pembroke became, in his own right, the Prince of New York, ruling the city from the depths of Five Points, a district famed for its poverty and wretchedness of both body and soul.

He had been born to rule—although it had taken the transforming kiss of a vampire to draw his potential out. He was a wise and just prince, settling disagreements amongst the Kindred who dwelt in his realm. Although he was generous to those who had sworn blood fealty to him, he proved a vicious foe when crossed. For the better part of a century Pembroke reigned supreme as, time and again, the streets above his throne room filled with rioters armed with torches and cudgels. The sight of such rabble would have, at one time, filled a vampire's unbeating heart with dread. But instead of venting their hatred on the Kindred and other such creatures of the night, now the humans raged against such monsters as Abolitionists, English actors, the Draft, and Communists. Behind the chaos of burning buildings and looted storefronts, the Masquerade continued its slow and stately dance, unnoticed by those on whom it fed.

Respected by his allies, feared by his enemies, Pembroke could have remained the Prince of New York. But, like Ruhl before him, he began to grow bored.

So, on the first day of the first year of the twentieth century, he abdicated and left the New World for the Old. He would spend fifty years wandering England, Europe, and the Middle East in search of his missing master. Pembroke was certain his mentor was not truly dead—such news tended to travel quickly amongst the Kindred. No doubt the elder vampire—who once spoke of Charlemagne in the terms of a contemporary—had elected to go to ground, preferring suspended animation to the tedium of unlife.

Pembroke arrived back in America during the height of the paranoia generated by the House Un-American Committee investigations. During his absence his own progeny had flourished, some becoming as powerful and influential as he had once been. None were delighted to hear of his return, fearing he would try to reclaim his throne. Pembroke had lost interest in such trivial games of cat's-paw; however, he made it clear that he was far from weak. Those of the Kindred who were foolish enough to cross him soon discovered that Pembroke was not a force to be trifled with.

Shunning the endless infighting and bickering of the clan, Pembroke took on the identity of an expatriate British artist and moved into Greenwich Village. Over the next few decades Pembroke came to be recognized as an elder of wisdom and restraint—far removed from his reputation during his mortal span. Most of those who sought out his company were younger vampires, the ones the elders contemptuously referred to as "anarchs"— rebels who dared to question the purpose of the Masquerade and who often tried to talk him into helping them in their cause. But, despite his own dissatisfaction, Pembroke was far too loyal to ever go against the Camarilla, so his young visitors usually left unhappy, disgusted by his mossback conservatism.

Over the course of the last decade he had found himself succumbing more and more to the Ennui, a condition that haunts those vampire who begin to weary of the cycle of eternal unlife. Pembroke found himself growing more and more dissatisfied with Kindred society. Surely there had to be more to immortality than the petty acquisition of power and moving those weaker than yourself—human and otherwise—like pieces on a chessboard. No wonder many of the ancient ones, the Methuselahs, had removed themselves from the fray, placing themselves into suspended animation for decades at a time. He himself had toyed with the idea on more than one occasion.

And then Sian came along.

They met cute. Or what passes for cute amongst their kind.

It was eighteen months ago. Pembroke was out hunting, prowling the after-hours clubs on the Lower East Side. He'd spotted his victim for the night—a young man with a silk jacket on his back, gold chains around his neck and a crack pipe in his pocket, in town from Jersey City for a weekend of unsafe sex and even more dangerous drugs. The human was so trashed he didn't realize his traveling companions had ditched him at the last bar, and he was wandering the streets alone, looking confused. The idiot was giving off victim vibes like a wounded seal in great white territory. If Pembroke didn't take him down, one of the city's numerous human predators would surely do it.

Pembroke temporarily lost sight of his prey as the drunkard rounded a corner onto a side street. As Pembroke made the intersection the human suddenly reappeared, eyes wide with fear, and ran headlong into him. The vampire grabbed his prey as if pretending to steady himself.

"Mister—you gotta help me, mister!" gasped the human.

Pembroke smiled and the human's pleas for help trailed off. Pembroke snapped the hapless mortal's neck as if it were a dry twig. Stepping deep into the shadows, Pembroke held his kill close, so that anyone looking out their window onto the street would see what seemed to be two lovers enjoying a late-night rendezvous.

Then what had frightened his prey rounded the corner.

It stood at least seven feet tall, weighing in at close to three hundred pounds of solid bone and muscle. Although it had the head, fans and talons of a great wolf, it stood upright, flexing its long, apelike arms. Its fur shone dark brown in the glow from the streetlights, the eyes a lambent green.

Pembroke tensed at the sight of the werewolf. The Garou and the Kindred had a long, bloody history of enmity. The prospect of battling such a creature did not cheer him. In truth, he could not find it in him to summon up the hatred that was expected of him.

"I have no wish to fight you, Friend Garou," Pembroke announced. "The human is dead. His blood grows cold even as I speak. Allow me to take what I need—the rest is yours."

The werewolf growled and snuffled, its eyes narrowing, but it did not move to attack. Pembroke quickly drained what he needed from his kill, tossing the corpse at the werewolf's feet. The beast dropped to all fours and seized the dead man in its massive jaws, disappearing into the shadows from which it had come without another sound. No doubt it had retreated to some rooftop hideaway, where it would be free to feast to its heart's content without fear of discovery.

It was almost dawn before Pembroke returned to his own lair. As he surrendered himself to the death-sleep he could not shake the memory of the werewolf's eyes.

Two weeks later he found himself at a coffeehouse on St. Mark's Place, pretending to drink a double espresso as he watched the college students from nearby NYU and Pratt cruise the gypsy bookstalls and novelty T-shirt shops that lined the street. Mixed amongst the students were the usual hustlers, dope dealers, and panhandlers endemic to the city. These were the ones Pembroke culled as his victims, not the fresh-faced coeds. Coeds have family and friends in respectable society. Coeds are missed.

"Hi there, handsome. You come here often?"

Pembroke turned in the direction of the woman's voice, expecting its owner to be one of the thin-shanked whores that worked Second Avenue. To his surprise, he found himself staring into eyes the color of forest.

The werewolf smiled, tossing her mane of dark brown hair over her shoulder as she plopped down on the seat beside him. "Mind if I sit next to you?"

"N-no. Not at all."

They sat there for a long moment, side by side, staring out the window of the coffee shop at the human throngs idling on the street. Pembroke looked down at his coffee, grown cold between his bloodless hands, then back at her. Pembroke found himself unable to look away from her face. There were forests in her eyes. Forests full of dark and toothy things.

"I didn't realize you were female."

"Flatterer!" She laughed.

"So why are you here? Why have you sought me out?"

"Did I say I came here looking for you?" she sniffed, trying to look disdainful. "How do you know it's not a coincidence—like the last time?"

"I know your kind well enough to realize that such accidents occur only once. You got my scent that night and you tracked me to this place. Why?"

"You interest me. You could have challenged me over the kill. You could have—should have—battled me for right of possession. But you appealed to my reason instead. Why?"

Pembroke shifted uncomfortably. He was no longer used to being questioned in such a manner. "I have had my fill of needless violence. I kill what I must to survive, nothing more. I have seen enough of death and suffering for several lifetimes. To battle you would have served no purpose except that of ritual and pride. I have wearied of ritual, and pride is the downfall of fools."

"I respect your answer. I've really gotten tired of all the bluster and strutting I get from the males of my tribe. They're all full of macho bullshit, trying to prove they're 'warriors born.' It really gets tiring after a while." The werewolf leaned in close, the smell of female heavy on her skin. Pembroke could not remember the last time he noticed how good women smelled. "You are very old, are you not?"

"It depends on how one defines 'old.' In human terms—yes. By Kindred standards, I'm hardly middle-aged. But this is not the place to discuss such things—I'm afraid I don't recall your name?"

"Sian."

"I am Pembroke. Perhaps we could retire to a more appropriate place and continue our little talk—?"

They left St. Mark's Place and made their way to the waterfront, to a pier so treacherously decrepit even the male prostitutes and junkies skirted it, and talked long into the night. Sian was young by Garou standards and a bit of a rebel as far as her people were concerned. She had abandoned the forests and glens held sacred by her kin in favor of hunting in the urban sprawl. She was full of questions and doubts, and Pembroke found himself attracted to her youth and vitality. In many ways she reminded him of the young anarchs who had tried to talk him into rebellion. It was her suggestion that they hunt as a team. He told himself that she amused him. And that was how it began.

At first they only met to hunt together once or twice a month. Then it began to be once or twice a week. Finally they were hunting in tandem every night. After their kill—or kills, if they were really successful—they would retreat to some derelict spot, away from the outside world, and talk and joke the night away. Sian would tell of her life as a cub, how she'd learned the ways of the Garou at her mother's teat alongside her littermates. Pembroke would reminisce about his years spent as Ruhl's apprentice, learning the finer points of manipulating human greed, vanity, and fear for the betterment of his clan. Sometimes they would simply discuss literature or music or the latest movie.

One night, roughly nine months after their first meeting, Sian turned to Pembroke and said, "I love you." She sounded almost shy.

Pembroke sat there motionless, staring up at the night sky.

"Did you hear me? I said I love you, Pembroke."

"Yes. I heard you."

"Do you have anything to say?"

Pembroke turned to look at her. She resembled a forlorn puppy, uncertain whether her master would reward her with a kick or a pat on the head. Although she had metamorphosed from her half-wolf state to a more human phase, her eyes still gleamed in the dark like those of a beast.

"It makes me very happy to hear you say that."

"Does that mean you love me, too?"

Pembroke smiled. "Love is a strange and difficult thing for my kind. I'm not even sure I knew it when I was alive, much less undead."

"Does that mean no?"

He laughed and drew her to him. "I think it means you can call me Philip from now on."

As they lay there in each other's arms, he realized it was the first time in centuries that he'd held another being so close without intending to rob it of its life. Even as he held her, he could feel her blood pulsing under her skin, hear it calling to him from its hidden courseways inside her. But then she kissed him and all thoughts of bloodletting fled.

Pembroke had not performed the physical act of love since his Embrace, three hundred and twelve years ago. Since he'd recently fed, there was enough stolen blood in his system for him to achieve and maintain an erection. He felt horribly out of practice and clumsy, but if Sian noticed she did not comment on it. And, for a few brief moments, they were no longer creatures of the night that fed on the blood and flesh of living beings, but merely a man and a woman doing what comes naturally to those in love.

Since he was, for all practical purposes, one of the walking dead, it had never occurred to Pembroke that anything might result from their lovemaking. But the morning after they had consummated their love, Sian said that from the smell of her pee she could tell she had conceived.

They discussed what to do at great length. Both knew that their love was taboo, punishable by ostracism from their respective clans. They could only imagine what the penalty would be for bringing half-caste progeny into existence. The prudent thing would be to abort. Yet something inside Pembroke rebelled at the idea. Before Sian had come along he had felt hollow and without purpose. Sian had made him feel whole again, just like when he'd first awakened from his Embrace. He ached to belong to something beyond the sterile world of the living dead.

And so Pembroke and Sian set off on the bumpy road to parenthood. They still maintained their separate domiciles and continued to meet in secret during her pregnancy. All the while Pembroke was quietly arranging to relocate, as Kindred often do when they have stayed too long in one city, transferring his funds via a Swiss bank account and arranging for the necessary documentation for both himself and his family-to-be.

As Sian's time grew closer to hand, it was agreed they would simply disappear without a word to any of their acquaintances. Sian would birth her children in the wilderness of upstate Pennsylvania, where she knew the terrain. Then father, mother, and newborn babies would make their way to someplace like Peru, far from the normal haunts of Kindred and Garou.

They only had a couple more weeks to wait when Pembroke received a sudden visit from Tilton, one of Lord Peale's servants.

It was Lord Peale's duty, as appointed by the Camarilla, to decide the fate of any Kindred on the Eastern Seaboard discovered to have violated the laws of the clan. Tilton often served as Lord Peale's instrument of judgment in such matters.

The sight of Peale's hit man, pale and ruby-eyed, on his doorstep made Pembroke uneasy.

"Good evening, Pembroke."

Pembroke smiled and gestured for Tilton to enter his abode. He struggled to keep his ill ease from tinging his voice. "Good evening, cousin. You honor my house."

Tilton brushed past him without any pretense of pleasantness. Not that Pembroke was surprised; the vampire was famous for his brusqueness. He eyed Tilton's back apprehensively. He was impressively built, even for one of the Blood. His shoulders were wide and his chest densely muscled. Even before his Embrace he would have been someone Pembroke steered clear of.

"My lord sends me to you to ask your counsel. He wants to know if you have heard rumors of a Kindred running with a Garou bitch."

"Surely you jest!" Pembroke tried to laugh, as if the idea was too ludicrous for serious consideration. "But why come to me?"

"My Lord Peale thinks the Kindred responsible must be one of the younger bloods—no doubt one of the degenerate anarchs. He thought you might have heard something, seeing how they respect you and come to you for advice."

"I have heard no such rumor. Why, the idea of vampire and werewolf working together—it sounds like something a human would come up with! But why is Lord Peale so certain an anarch is involved?"

"That goes without saying, doesn't it?" Tilton's eyes, cold and sharp as ruby chips, narrowed as he spoke. "Surely no elder would be fool enough to commit such an act of treason?"

Pembroke met with Sian the night after Tilton's appearance. He told her of Lord Peale's suspicions. They decided to flee the city, then and there. And now, six hours later, they were hurtling down an isolated back road in the mountains of Pennsylvania as if all the hounds of hell were on their heels.

Pembroke turned off the asphalt onto an unmarked private road, cutting the headlights as he went. It wasn't like he'd needed them to see where he was going in the first place. The rental car jounced violently in the ruts left by larger, heavier vehicles. After about five minutes he came to a wooden gate that read POSTED: PRIVATE PROPERTY.

"Sian—? Honey? Wake up—"

Groaning, Sian sat upright. Even with puffy eyes and tousled hair she looked beautiful. "What is it? Are we there yet?"

"I'm not sure. You tell me."

Sian opened the door and stuck her head out, sniffing the air like a hound. She turned and gave him a big, toothy smile that would have sent Red Riding Hood running for the woodsman.

"We're there."

Pembroke climbed out of the car and withdrew a black leather satchel from under the front seat. In it was the necessary false identification they needed to leave the country, plus fifty krugerrands. Also inside was a semiautomatic pistol complete with two ammo clips. One clip held silver bullets, the other wooden ones. Although the bag was heavy enough to drag a drowning man to his doom, Pembroke shouldered it with ease.

Sian moved ahead of him, her head cast back as she sniffed the mountain air. It was crisp and cold, redolent of pine trees. She shivered in anticipation of rejoining the wild, like a hound eager to slip its leash.

"It's so—clean out here," she whispered. "I'd almost forgotten what real air smells like, away from the stink of man."

Pembroke looked around uneasily. He was a thing of urban sprawl, used to hunting his prey in the blighted heart of man's domain. Being outside the city made him feel vulnerable. "Is the place you were talking about near here?"

"Near enough." Sian produced a set of keys from the pocket of her coat and unlocked the gate. "The car won't be able to go much farther, but we're better off leaving it on the posted side of the property line. This land once belonged to a human ancestor of mine—one of the Quakers who first settled in Pennsylvania. It's been in the family for centuries."

"I didn't realize the Garou held private property. My impression is that they're nature worshippers that don't believe in dividing up the land."

"They don't. But my father was human. He left this to me when he died. It's where he first met my mother."

"You never told me you were half-human."

"It didn't seem important. Honey, could you hurry it up a bit? My water just broke."

———

After Pembroke covered the rental car with brush, Sian locked the gate behind them and they began to make their way into the deep woods. Pembroke had offered to carry her, but Sian refused.

"I'm in labor, damn it, not crippled! I'll be okay for a while—the contractions are still ten minutes apart." She winced. "Make that nine."

"Where are we going exactly?"

"There's a cabin a couple of miles from here. It opens onto a shallow cave in the mountain behind it. My father lived there after he came back from World War II. He'd seen a lot of shit over there—it did something to his head. He moved away from the city and became a recluse, living off the land. That's how he met my mother."

A half-hour later they found the cabin—or what was left of it. The crude structure that had once hidden the entrance to the cave had collapsed on itself. Sian shook her head sadly at the sight of the ruins. "I haven't been here in a long time. Not since my father died ten years ago."

They picked their way through the rotten lumber and into the cave. Pembroke wrinkled his nose. It smelled of fungus and bat shit. Sian quickly shed her clothes and human skin, turning around three times before lying down on the rocky floor.

"Guard the entrance," she panted, her tongue lolling from between her jaws.

Pembroke nodded his understanding and moved the semiautomatic to his coat pocket, along with its ammo clips. He squatted on his haunches in the shadows at the entrance to the cave, trying not to be distracted by his mate's growling and snarling as she went about the business of giving birth to their children. He hoped it would be a quick delivery—dawn was not too far away. Come sunrise he would have to retreat into the cavern's deepest recesses to sleep away the day. His only solace was knowing that if they were being followed, their pursuer would be forced to seek cover as well.

He found himself wondering if he had produced mortal heirs when alive. He honestly couldn't remember, which made him sad. He recalled having been married, but he did not remember much about her except that she had been French and didn't speak English terribly well. He thought he might have had a child with her, but wasn't sure. He'd spent so much of his mortal span drunk that a lot of what had transpired during those days was lost to him.

There was a sudden squealing noise, like that of a small animal in distress, followed by the cry of a human infant—then another tiny voice joined in. Pembroke abandoned his sentinel position and knelt beside Sian, stroking her fur. She sat with her back propped against the wall, looking exhausted but satisfied, licking the pink, wriggling newborns feeding at her teats.

"Aren't they the most beautiful things you've ever seen,

Philip?" she whispered.

Pembroke put the gun down and pulled one of the babies away from its mother's nipple. It whined and sniffed him like a puppy, its head wobbling blindly back and forth. It was a boy. A son. His son. While it had all the regulation number of fingers and toes, it also possessed pointed ears, claws, and a full head of silky dark hair that, once dry, would do a feather duster proud. Pembroke handed his son back to Sian in exchange for his twin—who shook its tiny fists and yelped in displeasure at having its feeding interrupted.

"It's a girl," Pembroke said, grinning like an idiot.

"Their eyes won't open for a couple of days yet," she explained. "We can't leave until then—it would be difficult to pass them off as normal at this stage."

Pembroke leaned forward and kissed Sian's shaggy brow. "Are you happy, sweetheart? Was it all worth it?"

"It was worth every damn contraction," she replied, nuzzling him. "We make quite a team, don't we?"

"How touching. And incriminating."

Pembroke spun around, reaching for the gun beside him, but it was too late. He knew it was too late the moment he heard Tilton's voice behind him, but he had to try. Tilton brought his boot heel down on Pembroke's right hand like he was grinding out a cigarette butt.

Tilton scooped up the semiautomatic and aimed it at Pembroke's head. There was no need to chamber a round— Pembroke had already done that for him. It didn't matter whether the bullets in the clip were silver, wooden, or simple lead. A point-blank head shot kills everything, living or not.

Pembroke cradled his ruined hand against his chest. Although the pain had quickly disappeared, it would take hours for his system to regenerate the bone and nerve tissue necessary for it to function. And he knew he didn't have that long.

"Pembroke of the Clan Ventrue, avowed servant of the

Camarilla, you have been judged and found guilty of high treason against the Kindred. The sentence is death everlasting."

"Treason?" Pembroke's eyes flashed crimson. "It is treason for me to love? To find happiness with one not of my kind?"

Tilton shrugged his indifference. "The decision was not mine to make. I am merely the hand of just retribution."

The shadows behind Tilton began to twist and bend, as if they had suddenly taken on solid substance. Two gaunt, bone-white faces emerged from the darkness. Pembroke recognized the pinched and powdered visage of Lord Peale, still wearing his periwig from his days as Lord High Magistrate to George I. It wasn't until he spoke that Pembroke recognized Peale's companion.

"So it *was* you, after all. I did not want to believe it."

"Ruhl?"

The last century and a half had worked considerable changes on his mentor. Although he looked no older than the day Pembroke first met him, over three centuries ago, a feeling of great age clung to him like a mist. There was a weariness and a sadness in his eyes that Pembroke knew all too well.

"Ruhl—my friend, my sire—let me explain."

"The time for explanations is past. Lord Peale summoned me from my sleeping place in Macedonia so that I might defend my progeny to the Inner Circle, as is expected of a sire. But as much as I love you, Philip, I can not find it in me to do so. You have committed abomination."

"I only wanted to know happiness—to know what it was like to love without killing—to create without destroying—"

Ruhl shook his head, his eyes even sadder than before. "In life you were a monster. In death you became more than a man. You had the seed of greatness in you, but you turned your back on it yet again. You should have followed my example, old friend, and gone to ground and slept until the Ennui subsided in you. But you allowed yourself to be seduced by the living world. That, above all else, is folly for our kind.

"When you became one with the Kindred, you were forever freed from the miseries of mortal existence. And its joys. For our kind there is no death. And no life."

"Enough jabbering!" snapped Lord Peale. "You are guilty of treason, Pembroke! And the sentence is death to you and your progeny!"

"Why do you have to kill them? They have done the Kindred no harm! They're just—"

"Babies. Yes, I know that!" Lord Peale shook his head in disgust. "What makes you think their infancy renders them incapable of harm? Your children are harbingers of doom! The Kindred and Garou are the most skilled predators on the face of the earth! The offspring of two such superior hunters would be unstoppable! Within a century and a half your children's children's children would make their ancestors extinct!"

"You don't know that!" Sian snarled, hugging the twins tight, her ears laid back and her fangs bared.

Lord Peale turned his cold stare in her direction. "Sometimes it is better not to know the exact outcome of an event than to regret knowledge. As for you: while it is not within my power to condemn you, your fate is sealed as surely as your lover's! While the Kindred and the Garou have worked at cross-purposes for millennia, we maintain channels of communication with one another in case of an emergency. Your perfidy has been relayed to your elders—"

There came from outside the cave the howls of approaching wolves.

Peale smiled. "Ah, it seems that the Garou contingent has arrived."

The smell of animal filled the cave. Sian shivered and lowered her eyes.

Tilton and Ruhl moved aside to allow entrance to what looked to be a monstrous wolf. The wolf stood up on its hind legs, becoming a woman in her middle years, naked except for body paint and a necklace made of polished stones and a belt of knotted leather, from which hung a silver knife.

"So, daughter, I should have known you would come to no good in the world of man. It is a corrupting place."

Sian struggled to stand on her hind legs, clutching her children to her breasts. "Mother—Shadowfang—I beg of you, do what you must to me—but spare my cubs, your grandchildren."

Shadowfang's face, so much like Sian's, twisted in such disgust it seemed as if she was about to turn back into a wolf. "You expect me to accept the get of a vampire as my own? Man's world has indeed driven you mad, child—as it did your father before you!"

"Mother—please—"

Shadowfang removed the silver knife, the klaive used by werewolves in ritual battle, from her belt. "You have sinned against your people, Sian! And as I was the one who brought you into this world, it is my duty to see that you leave it as well."

Sian leapt forward, bowling past Tilton. Pembroke used the confusion to tackle the elder werewolf, knocking her to the ground.

"Run, Sian! Run!" he yelled.

Ruhl grabbed Pembroke by the nape of the neck, yanking him free of Shadowfang and slamming him against the wall. "Fool! Where can she run that her people cannot find her? You're only making it worse for all concerned!"

The sound of gunfire filled the cave. Tilton stood at the entrance, firing after the fleeing werewolf. The silver-jacketed bullets tore into her back, stitching a line from her buttocks to her shoulders. She crumpled to the ground, falling atop her children.

Pembroke tried to break free of Ruhl's grip and go to his lover, but the elder vampire was too strong for him. He trembled like a man in the grip of palsy, his eyes feeling as if someone had filled them with broken glass and steel wool. He realized suddenly that he was crying.

"The kill was mine by right, dead man!" Shadowfang growled as she pushed past Tilton.

"Then you shouldn't have let her get away," he replied.

One of the babies was crying. Pembroke couldn't tell if it was his son or his daughter. Shadowfang knelt beside Sian's bullet-riddled corpse, checking it for signs of life. There were none. She rolled her daughter's body over, exposing the children she had died trying to protect.

The fist holding the silver dagger rose and fell twice. The crying stopped.

Shadowfang stood over her dead daughter and grandchildren, staring for a long moment at the blood seeping into the ground, then tossed back her head and gave voice to a howl of mourning. A chorus answered her from inside the surrounding forest. Turning to face the vampires who watched her from the cave, the werewolf elder hurled the knife point-first into the dirt.

"I'll never forgive the Kindred for what they made me do this night," she snarled. And with those words she dropped onto all fours and slunk off into the woods to rejoin her pack.

"Master, the sun approaches," Tilton announced, gesturing with the gun muzzle to the lightening sky.

"So it does," Lord Peale muttered. "So it does. Shoot the bastard, Tilton, and get this mess over with."

Screaming in wordless rage, Pembroke tore himself free of Ruhl's grip and launched himself at Tilton. Pembroke slammed into the bigger vampire before he had a chance to fire, gouging the hooked fingers of his good hand into Tilton's eyes. It was an old dirty fighting trick he'd learned back in his roistering days. Tilton screamed and dropped the gun, clawing at his face.

"Stop him, Ruhl! Stop him!" screeched Peale, sounding more like an indignant fishwife than a member of the ruling class.

Pembroke ran from the cave into the clearing where Sian and

his children lay. Ruhl moved to follow him, but stopped short of leaving the cave. The sun was up.

Pembroke's skin prickled and itched as if he were covered in ants. Then it began to burn. The pain was so intense it made him stumble and fall. He had never known such agony in all the decades of his undeath. He lay panting on the ground, his eyes filling with tears and blood as the fluids inside him began to boil. The vampire part of his brain was babbling frantically, insisting that he crawl back into the cave. But he didn't want to die alone, shot like a rabid dog. He wanted to be with her. With his family.

His flesh was blistering like bacon in the pan. He could smell himself cooking. There was a low, dull cough and his hair caught fire, burning down to his skull. The skin on his face bubbled and sloughed away like wax. His eyes became dull white, like those of a baked fish, as they were boiled in their own ocular fluid.

Pembroke groped blindly with his fleshless hand. Although he no longer possessed a sense of touch, he knew he must be close. He tried to tell her he was sorry it had come to this, but his tongue was a piece of blackened leather. He wanted to kiss his children one last time, but he had no lips. There was so much he wanted to do. Wished he could do. Needed to do. And now, after more than three centuries, the unimaginable had finally come to pass.

There was no.

More.

Time.

Ruhl found them lying side by side, Pembroke's hand in Sian's cold paw. The sunlight had reduced Pembroke to a skeleton surrounded by the fine ash that had once been his flesh. The others—Tilton especially—wanted to hack the bodies to pieces and scatter them to every point of the compass, but Ruhl would not allow it. Although Lord Peale, theoretically, held more power in the matter, Ruhl was very old. And very powerful.

A cairn of stone was placed over the graves of the fallen lovers. Whether it was intended as a memorial or a warning is unclear. Perhaps Ruhl would have been able to clarify the situation, had he not disappeared again. The cairn can be seen there to this day, if one knows where to look. It is rumored by some that roses and wild wolfsbane grow, intertwined, from among the stones. But it is not deemed wise to go looking for such things, for on nights when the moon is full strange things have been seen lurking in the shadows between the trees on the edge of the clearing. Things as pale as vampires and as hairy as werewolves. And as small as children.

Nancy A. Collins is the author of the contemporary horror novels *Wild Blood*, *Tempter*, and *Sunglasses After Dark*. A special omnibus edition of the Sonja Blue cycle is forthcoming from White Wolf. She has worked extensively in comics, predominantly for DC/ Vertigo with *Swamp Thing* (1991-1993) and *Wick* (1994). She is a winner of the Bram Stoker and British Fantasy Awards for short fiction and has appeared in such venues as *Year's Best Fantasy and Horror* and *Best New Horror*. Born in rural Arkansas, she now lives in New York City with her husband, underground filmmaker and anti-artiste, Joe Christ.

Go Hungry

by Wayne Allen Sallee

S *ee—one kind of my face is gentle and kind, incapable of anything but love of my fellow man. The other side, the other profile, is cruel and predatory and evil, incapable of anything but the lusts and dark passions. It all depends on which side faces the moon at the ebb of the tide.*
—Lionel Atwill, 1944

I. BREAKFAST MASKS

In only his worst nightmares did he kill the innocent. And for Michael Napier, fifth in line of the Severn clan to be chosen as crip-gnawer, the innocent meant the healthy. The strong. Those who walked upright, ironically, like man.

The remainder of the clan had moved on to molest and ravage the Midwest from Racine to Louisville, and Napier had chosen to stay in Chicago for a time, until his brother passed on the title of the next killer of cripples. The sacred caern he chose to live in was an area on the Near South Side known as Back of the Yards, and it was here, late at night when the autumn moon was small and bone-white, the sky a monstrous vein, that Napier would walk and listen to the spirits of the cattle butchered a century before, when the Union Stockyards still existed.

The thirty-five-year-old man would cock his head and be angered over the spirits' wretched keening, knowing the helplessness that his grandfather must have felt at how the humans had begun to enjoy the bloodlust too much. How the entropy of the Wyrm was infecting the race. Killing each and every animal, hammer to the head, repeat action, hammer to the head, swing high and wide. Repeat action.

Homids killing indiscriminately, killing all, out of greed. There was no worry for their survival. Chicago at the turn of the century was no longer the awkward town that had welcomed a World's Fair with open and spastic arms; the motto of "I Will" was already evolving into "Where's Mine," and the butchers of the abattoirs from Exchange through the 45th Street Viaduct couldn't care less if the cattle were diseased with cholera or blood anemic. The meat would still be sold to their gullible kind. The homids could care less about the cleansing of the line, even now in this early October night in 1994, the stockyards a memory even for Sinatra, the butchers moving on to other uniforms of the day, other masks to wear and breakfast, lunch, and dinner, as they kill each other for lust or rape the farms and the forests for fuel to burn away the very air his nostrils flared in.

We should have allowed the whole city to burn, Granddaddy Grover had often said with disgust when talking about the conflagration of 1871. They had wanted bodies to feed on and there were plenty of strong ones then, before the greed and the blood simplicity of the Stockyards and Industry had set fully in. Napier visited his granddaddy every summer at his home in Dry Ridge, Kentucky, and the husky, bald man would still pinch his wire-frame glasses and say how if the Severns and their gallains, the Harrods and Fassls, had helped the great fire continue after the southerly winds had turned it back toward the lake at Cermak, just twenty blocks away, the city might have been crippled with the loss even now.

Another mistake regretted was the fact that Rory Harrod's father had been in the garage the day of the St. Valentine's Day Massacre. The tribe could have contained a second, human conflagration right then and there. Capone ended up keeping Chicago on the map as a sin capital as much as the rabid rebuilding after the slabs of downtown burned around the water tower, to be replaced by brothel after brothel and those damnable slaughterhouses.

Napier suspected it was Grover Severn's memories that kept him settled in the area while his kinain Danny and Rory and Brent ran with the wind in places with no sodium arc lights to make the freshets of blood pump a sickly purple. The displaced werewolf would listen and walk hangdog these bawns around the yards, killing the street hustlers of Canaryville and Englewood with subtle abandon. For the monte players and the moxie dealers represented the Wyrm; they were emotional cripples, fueled not so much by the greed of their forefathers, but by greed borne of stupidity and slothfulness. It was easier to sell drugs and live on welfare than to find a factory job or simply be content to do unskilled labor at McDonald's.

So until it was time for Napier to take over the mantle of crip-gnawer, he would continue preying on these secondary cripples. Doing his part to keep the line of future Garou as clean as possible. It was always the decision of the predecessor, unless he was incapacitated. Gaia help him then, the crippled wolf would be taken out to a field by his brothers and left to go hungry. Death was often swift, as it was not uncommon for the brothers to play with their wounded kin the same way they might play with the crippled and feeble townspeople before ripping out their quivering, turkeylike throats. Yet there was a story once of one of the Loudon clan hanging on for weeks with two missing limbs in the dead of winter, hence becoming a southern Illinois 'haint.

He would hunt and kill, then go home and sleep the morning away. The job Napier held in his human guise was perfect for his comings and goings. He had been working five years in the downtown subway system; afternoon and early evening shifts would leave him time in the shadows of metal thunder to shapeshift and gnaw on strays (never the diseased rats) and still give him plenty of time to run with the CNW trains and ponder the keenings of the cattle spirits before the false dawn.

He would walk up the four flights to his Hermitage Avenue apartment with all the world-weariness of his neighbors with the families and mortgages, shower, shave, and shit like those same humans, and try and sleep a sleep of reason.

And in only the worst of nightmares would he hunt and kill the truly innocent. In his best dreams, guilty as they might be, he would be coupling with desirable women he sometimes spoke with in the subway or saw on the cable news station from Oak Brook.

During the dreams he would stay in human form, but would masturbate, salivate, and eventually slobber and growl. But should he be heard by the neighbor in the next apartment over, that man might easily assume that Napier simply had problems with flatulence and bad table manners. He knew where Napier worked, and suspected the stomach growlings and bad hygiene to be products of both eating in the Loop's abundance of greasy spoons and getting paid to sit on his fat ass all day. The neighbor's name was Valton Tiche, displaced from Czechoslovakia after the recent wars, and he would often voice his opinions on Napier to his pit bull, Thor.

In the dream, Napier was a young pup running with Danny, Rory, and Brent in the winter snows of Lake Geneva, Wisconsin. In disjointed images that blended smoothly, Napier recalled the fact that the boys were just nineteen and making the tavern rounds for the first time in their adult life. The Playboy Club was still there and disco was not yet dead, although it was breathing irregularly. He was so young and strong in those days, not yet having resigned himself to staying with the attendant ghosts of the Stockyards, and they drank large shots of Kentucky Gentleman, flexed their muscles for the ladies at the bar, and danced to K.C. and the Sunshine Band.

The clarity of the dream was always overwhelming. The boys sniffed out fresh female meat on the ski slopes behind the club, and Danny was the first to hunker down and shapeshift into a brilliant auburn creature of the night. Napier was the largest of the four, and poor Brent and Rory were already losing their hair. It was Danny that always led, though. His looks in human form were mesmerizing even to lesbians.

They all bled just the same. The girls barely thrashed and the wine they had drunk to kill the cold served well to augment the meal Napier and his brothers had that night. "Beast of Burden" could be heard from the discotheque down the slopes, lights blinking red then blue then red within frosted windows.

The blood was black then maroon then black again, shining like oil as it spurted over the wolves, and the only sound besides their snuffling was the crinkling of the dead girls' ski garments.

Crinkling, mewling, wetness…

Napier awoke, the clock at the bedside reading 2:00 P.M.

Wetness. He had pissed himself. The sheets were stiff, not from ejaculate, but from urine.

And this had not been the first time such a thing had occurred.

His heart was beating hard, his pulse in his ears the way it should rightly be when he was out for the kill. In the past few months, though, he had started waking up scared.

Tremors and weaknesses in the extremities, thankfully only in his human form. But when the chest pains of anxiety started, and wasn't *that* such an amusing concept for a lycanthrope who had no fears or worries in the world, then the nerves in his neck would begin twitching like guitar strings.

Napier pushed the covers back, had to massage his right knee to bring the feeling back. Slowly shifted his weight to his other side as he tentatively stood up. Out the window, he saw the Congress & Northwestern tracks in the dying green grasses and immediately thought of the sutures on Frankenstein's Monster.

What he did not see was the bloodstain near the bottom of the bed.

Napier stared at the hand in front of his face: his hand, his calluses and scars. When he tried to flex, it was like clutching at an invisible ball. He stumbled to the dresser and dry-swallowed two aspirin.

He sat back at the edge of the bed, unsure of himself. He had been dreaming of his first days on the hunt increasingly over the weeks now, yet always awoke with the feeling that he had something to be guilty about. That the tribe had wanted to ostracize him even then. But that was crazy. The mental ravings of a lunatic.

He could still run with the best of them.

II. THE NIGHT OF THE FOLLOWING WEEK

The killing had gone bad enough, but it was Napier's return to human form that was worse. The dead man deserved to be dead, no matter how much the werewolf's disturbing spasticity made a clean kill into an awkward thing.

Madison Gallows liked to carjack vans and jeeps out of the gas stations along Halsted Street, and if the driver of the car happened to be female, then he would make a point of raping her repeatedly and, more often than not, dumping the body into the trash in an alleyway. He had been skulking around a Shell station at Forty-Third when Napier spotted him. The werewolf had no intention of killing him, wouldn't even know who the man was until his remains were found and his crimes were written up in the *Tribune* in the following days.

He had not intended to kill, having sated himself on a rare steak dinner at Berghoff's, in private celebration of a pay raise and extended dental benefits. Walking back to the old stockyards, he had the first seizure.

Napier felt light-headed and, at first, thought it was from the meat. When he started to change into wolf form, his face and arms twitching, seven in the evening on a nearly deserted main thoroughfare, he started to sweat.

And when the soon-to-be-departed Madison Gallows saw him, Napier started to snarl defensively, against his better reasoning. The carjacker never had a chance, his gun was out, the bullets usually reserved for the brain pan of a twenty-year-old never left the chamber. Napier himself was disoriented, his sense of smell off horribly. Off balance from a garbage scent, he swung with wild impatience, tearing away Gallows's left hand, the one holding the gun, and a chunk of flesh below the rib cage.

He blinked repeatedly, his victim beyond such matters as the ravages worsened. Through it all, Napier had difficulty remembering such a simple thing as how to turn back into human form.

That was the last he recalled. When Napier was next lucid, he was awake in his bed. Face down, smelling of shit, and dry-belching blood. He had no idea where his work clothes were; later, having calmed down, he would realize that if the change was that sudden, any evidence of his gray Chicago Transit Authority coveralls would have been shredded.

The *Tribune* ran first-page coverage below the lead story of the latest political upheavals in Eastern Europe, Napier's homeland four generations removed. Madison Gallows, last known address a gangbanger pad in the Harold Ickes Homes, was indeed the suspect in eight murders and twice as many carjackings. Area 2 Homicide Detective Shane Doolittle was quoted as saying that the state of the deceased was "a piece of work," and the last time a body had been ravaged with such disregard for the possibility of being caught in the act was when The Painkiller was working the Loop four years previous.

Napier clutched his sides and shivered like a dog left out in the cold rain. Next door, Valton Tiche was severely reprimanding his pit bull, Thor, for leaving a trail of shitty footprints up the hall carpeting.

Napier continued reading; the detective quoted commented on how he hoped the severity of Madison Gallows's killing would be an isolated thing, something perhaps related to drugs or similar retaliation.

Looking down at the tremors in his hands, how his vision would blur and he could almost see hair sprouting on his knuckles against his will, Napier wanted to believe that it would not happen again.

He sat the rest of the morning in the pose of someone nursing a hangover, although he had no such headaches or nausea of any sort. He drank chilled milk from a cocktail glass, part of a set he had purchased on a whim at the Maxwell Street Market several years before. Each glass read Name Your Poison. The other three were labeled Strychnine, Hemlock, and Arsenic.

The one Napier had in front of him at the moment, nursing his milk, read Belladonna.

An obsolete form of wolfsbane.

III. THE EVERLEIGH CLUB

That night, Napier found himself working overtime; both out of last-minute requests from City Hall regarding a visiting governor from out east and of necessity on Napier's own part. A need to push himself into his work and forget what had happened the previous day.

He was aboveground this night, helping remove the detritus of Block 37 to a spot on Lower Wacker Drive, closer to the lakefront. It was through this action that he came in contact with one of his past lives.

The leftover rubble and trash of Block 37: an eyesore for the city after demolition, the grand designs for a huge, eighty-six-story green glass tower to rival the Hancock center were still unbuilt, the firms who owned the land still looking for backers to complete the project past the blueprint stages. Since the mid-eighties, there had been several skeletons of buildings halted for weeks until the cash flow continued, and other sites, like where the old Montogomery Ward headquarters stood on Adams, were still vacant squares of blight and weeds.

Napier was here to clean up after a scavenging company drove off with various pieces of scrap metal. Until 1990, Randolph Street between State and Dearborn—Block 37—housed a Burger King, a video arcade, and a home for the disabled. Several tenants at the Rainey Marclinn Home were killed by a mysterious nighttime slayer. The press called him The Painkiller, some referred to him as a kind of holy terror, and Napier himself speculated that a cadaver had throated the wheelchair-bound victims.

The scavengers would lift the guts of a pinball machine from within the walled-in block, and Napier would sweep a little bit more. Beneath the wires and cables, the private workers unearthed a wrought iron sculpture in red and black, and Napier started drifting back to a time in the previous century.

The sculpture had stood over the entrance to the home for the handicapped as a kind of ironic balcony: the three Fates—Clotho, Atropo, and Lachesis. Napier recalled in a kind of dreamlike state that he had stood upon this very balcony, that he had spoken with someone else, in one of his past lives, about the Fates and the cruelties and frailties that were represented within the old crones' stares.

The Everleigh Club, a brothel on Chicago's Near South Side. August, 1898. Napier closed his eyes and swayed slightly. Three scavengers saw him and exchanged glances, one of them turning to adjust the radio station better. Nighttime interference with the wind off the lake, and all.

When Napier opened his eyes, they had taken on the lighter hue of his ancestor. Were one to know of the subtle change, one might liken it to the new tinting contact lenses offered. But no advancements toward personal enhancement could achieve the same effect as that the Garou now possessed.

Or was possessed of.

His name was Norma Travis and he was a whore. At least, it was one of the things (s)he passed him(her)self off as. The balcony felt cold against her bare feet, her toenails were lacquered blood red. She sat to the right of the doorway, braced by the first Fate, Clotho at her wheel, weaving destinies.

The whorehouse stood the full block of Dearborn between Twenty-First and Twenty-Second in the heart of the Levee red-light district. Norma was naked from the waist up, a plush green robe pooled around her ample thighs. Dangling one foot through the balcony balusters, she would gently tap the bowler hats of passersby, enticing them away from Sappho's or Polack Ben's, steering them with a flash of secret creamy thigh through the doors to be greeted by Minnie and Ada Everleigh.

An easy job it was, as she sat here in summer sunlight and across from the esteemed Tarrant "Eddie" Neal, a short, black, and beefy gadfly who also happened to know that Travis was a werewolf. It was not lost upon her that their talk was of another's weaving of destinies, a human, not a myth, not a statue that cared nothing for the battered souls that passed beneath her.

"So why are you working the district, after what you just said?" Neal scratched at the base of his skull, working the starched white collar of his shirt. Travis had just told him about her kinain and the battle against the Wyrm.

"You mean, why am I a...whorehound?" She arched her thick, brown eyebrows wickedly. Even Neal found desire in that, knowing exactly how far she could ravage him with her passions.

"I mean no disrespect, ma'am." The doors opened below and piano music floated out into the August air.

"Let me tell you, Tarrant," Travis spoke matter-of-factly. "This kind of blight around us here"—she waved a creamy hand at all of Dearborn, the Saratoga, French Em's, and Madame Leo's—"is all right for now, for right here."

They were silent for a moment; a streetcar pulled out of the car barn on Cullerton. One could see it all happen when one was leaning against the Fates.

"But I'm here in Chicago for a reason. There's human decay here, Tarrant. Not a vampire, but an actual flesh-and-blood human killer."

Neal gave her a look that would seem stereotypical in later years.

"You mean that you have trouble with the concept of the walking undead even after you've witnessed my change with the full moon?"

Neal had finally conceded that he believed just about anything Miz Travis told him. She explained about the search those like her had made for Herman Mudgett, the monster of the '93 Exposition, and of Dr. Neill Cream after him, and of the one she currently wanted to lead to her own special lair.

No, these men—and women, like Lizzie Crawford, in a few cases—were not cadavers. Humans had reason to be scared of those creatures. Travis's kinain, the Severns and the Napiers, were predatory for noble reasons; the populace of Chicago would only think of such lycanthopic sightings as that of a man wearing a wolf's suit. Whether this was a technique borne of hypnosis or something more supernatural, Travis did not know.

She did know that the biggest fear was vampires and…

"…you have nothing to fear from me, Eddie," Napier finished saying. He blinked at the onrush of the downtown pollution, and his vision cleared that he might see the faces of the scavengers in front of him. They looked back at him suspiciously.

"Whatever you say, boss," one of the two said.

"Sorry." Napier flushed. "I—I'm not myself."

"Whatever you say, boss," the same man said.

His partner turned the country station louder. Laurie Morgan started singing "My Night To Howl."

IV. ST. VITUS DANCING IN THE MOONLIGHT

The following is excerpted from THE PHANTOM NURSE OF WAVERLY HILLS and other Kentucky legends, by Thom Swortz, Oldham Press, 1994.

While much of the lore of our fine Kentucky bluegrass hills are rife with sightings of Civil War ghosts, newer stories have been cropping up that have borrowed from the northern states' so-called "urban legends." The most familiar of these would be the Case of the Choking Doberman, in which (to be as brief as possible) a family pet is found to have several severed fingers in its mouth, digits which just so happen to belong to a burglar who is passed out from blood loss just beyond the family's sight. Such cautionary tales are invariably told with the viewpoints and attendant embellishments as passed down from a friend to a friend of a friend, so that there is no possible way to distinguish a single morsel of meaty fact.

Another quick example is the man who takes a woman he met in a bar abed and wakens in the morning to find her gone, a note the only thing to mark her passing. The note reads *Welcome to the World of AIDS.* (It is common for females to be the catalysts in such tall tales, and this theme strikes common chords in so-called horror fiction in which a man would meet the same woman in the same bar, only this time she mysteriously casts no reflection in the mirror, nor does she drink...cocktails.)

And so our culture has changed that: instead of a stretch of land that is visited by the Confederate 'haints from the Perryville Battlefield, we have modern ghosts such as the hitchhiker with the clawlike hand or the crazy old recluse.

I would take this moment to relate a story such as my latter reference. Coincidentally, the tale, which is about a farm woman who claimed that her husband was a werewolf, also hailed from the family who originally ran the Waverly Hills Sanitarium, long the home of the title phantom of my book.

———

The story first came to my attention from a diminutive young woman named Millie who lives in Waddee. As a child, she had spent long summers at her grandmother's farm in Jefferson County, near Anchorage, and while there she had reason to encounter said woman whose marriage claim was of much disbelief.

The woman in question was a gray-haired woman whose name was Louisa Napier, who passed away during the early 1980s. Her husband, Ethan, hailed from an industrial city to the north, possibly Chicago or Kenosha, although other claims are that he was a troublemaker and an ex-convict from southeastern Kentucky. Not much is known of this man directly, although it is also assumed he is dead. Whereabouts of any children are unknown.

Millie Robeson of Waddee provided me with directions to the old Napier farm but declined to accompanying me, citing certain religious beliefs. I should be disinclined to think that she might believe I was writing this passage to discredit or ridicule the dead, for this is not the case.

The Napier farm is to be found on a certain dirt road off U.S. 60. The old Flat Rock Cemetery is a nearby backdrop for proper atmosphere, as is a small parcel of land where can be found the graves of the colored slaves of the eighteenth century.

I was able to glean much information from a "Mamaw" Nickels, who owns the adjoining tract of land. Louisa Napier was seldom seen by the Nickel clan, as she often worked forty or more hours a week at the Waverly Hills Sanitarium. But still, there were times in which several members of the Nickels family would hear Louisa talk of either her husband's turning into a hairy, nocturnal monster, or of her having some horrid curse that she would pass on to her only son.

It is said that she met her husband at Waverly Hills, nestled high on a ridge off Dixie Highway and East Pages Lane, which makes Ethan Napier's background even more suspect. After the Sanitarium closed its doors in 1961 (having served as housing for mentally ill patients the final decade), Louisa Napier retired to the confines of their 88-acre land, neither venturing out to the nearby grocery store in Eastwood nor giving so much as a simple hello to her neighbors. Without her husband to be seen, one must imagine that he was again incarcerated (as many of the townspeople leaned toward the acceptance of his being one of shady character).

Louisa Napier would have her neighbors believe otherwise, as it was she who said that Ethan was a monster, a creature of the night. He would change into a manner of wolf, and others of his ilk—she often spoke of a strange family named Severn—would run through the rolling bluegrass hills of the Commonwealth.

Mamaw Nickels was riveting in her recollection of nights alone on the farm, the trees barren beneath a full autumn moon, and being transfixed by "a keening and a howling and a general carrying-on" in the Napier back forty. Her youngest two would dare each other to jaunt past the Napier place on school nights. There were always tales of partially eaten fowl, and once an old sheepdog didn't return home.

Yet, as intriguing as this hairy 'haint that prowled the woods of Flat Rock Road might be, there is a simple truth to it all. The facts are to be found in the patient registry of Kings Daughter hospital in Shelbyville. Louisa Napier suffered from dementia, perhaps a disease as debilitating as Huntington's chorea. In any event, one can easily blame her condition on the daily hardships in a tuberculosis and mental sanitarium.

There was never any "werewolf." It was Louisa Napier who was spastically carousing in the autumn moonlight, while having a fit. It was Louisa Napier who would howl from her window and eventually her deathbed, alone and angry at her lot.

After the madwoman's death, the Napier farm was a spot of minor notoriety when a young artist from Nashville, Alan Matusak, derived a series of paintings from brambles behind the farm house, allowing them such intriguing titles as *Half-Scairt* and *Hairy Fossils*.

In the end, the entire story is yet another example of what could be one of those urban legends up in the Yankee states.

Louisa Napier was not an animal.

V. I'LL WATCH THE PAST

That's what he had told the others. "I'll watch the past." Napier, alone with his eyes closed, shutting out the tremors and the pain. He was in the Washington Street terminal and it was the fifteenth of October and his bones felt hollow, his veins caffeine-laden. An "A"-train roared by; in his darkness he could hear the approach building to a crescendo, the rustle of unseen newsprint blowing by around him, the smell of everything from piss to lake water in his nostrils. He was sick and knew not what to do. He was afraid that his fellow employees, the el train commuters, anyone he came in contact with would be thinking he had AIDS or some other communicable disease. Could entropy actually be upon him?

His knuckles were like gnarled nubs on branches. He could barely hold the sweeper; spasms in his wrists often caused the metal container to slap repeatedly against the cement platform, the rapid-fire shot skittering down the tunnel into darkness and startling the rush-hour rail riders. More than once he found himself with his head dipped down, his chin hunkered in like a turtle's. Unconsciously chewing and sucking on the collar of his T-shirt, pulled past his buttoned-up city-issued gray shirt.

Yes, this was Napier at his job in the subway, thinking. About the last time he had spoken with his kinain cousins. Danny, Rory, and Brent. They were curious as to why Napier was content with the brugh, the cave of the subway to play in, Danny tilting his red, hairy head like a big, furry dog with a human face and recent dental work.

It had been two years back, and they had been feasting where the old coal tunnels came aboveground at Stolen Street. The small tract of yet-to-be-incorporated land south of the Loop and just before Chinatown was actually called Stowell. Stolen Street's nickname was derived from the fact that few city maps still listed it, though it was right there at Seventeenth and Wentworth. It was on Stolen Street, a desolate area that matched his soul of late, a mile from where Napier stood as a silent monitor in the subway, thinking his long thoughts on the blight of the human form.

The four had eaten well, sating themselves on the dozens of fresh animal corpses that had floated up in the wake of the Loop Flood. On a Monday in April, construction workers had pushed a stone piling off center, flooding thousands of gallons of the Chicago River first into the turn-of-the-century coal tunnels, then the subways and basements of the State Street department stores. There were plenty of small rodents to be had. Brent thought it would be a decent story to tell Granddaddy Grover, how he was there for the fire and the boys were there for the flood.

But then it had gotten serious all of a sudden, the talk turning to the legacy of the crip-gnawer, the mantle Napier wanted nothing to do with. The idea of the pack continuing on as they had in decades previous was ridiculous, anyway. The packs were all splintering; the cousins slobbering here in front of him were an example. There was no need for someone to take away the most aged or infirm of a town. Not anymore. The wolves did their killing at random, though with considerable more cunning than their distant brethren, the vampires.

Napier's daddy, Ethan, had been a crip-gnawer. The Ohio Valley was his playground, the tuberculosis epidemic of 1948 his downfall, of a sort. Ethan Napier had been indirectly responsible for staving off what could have been tantamount to a plague in the Midwest during those postwar years. The junior Napier knew there was a journal kept back home, perhaps at the caern near Mount Endore.

From Little Egypt to the border towns of Indiana, Ethan Napier had fulfilled his duties in keeping entropy at bay, the Wyrm in the guise of a horrid, wasting disease of the body and soul. During one of the hunts he had fallen, the tuberculosis infecting him in wolf form, making him revert. Before the elders could tend to him, he was discovered by county officials who had Napier shipped by horsecar to Waverley Hills, a sanitarium for TB victims. Those who eventually died were tossed into a deep shaft, there to be incinerated and their ashes dumped onto the banks of the Ohio River.

Only Napier did not die, and it was assumed that he only showed the symptoms of tuberculosis but never carried the disease. It took him weeks to fully recover, though. Weeks spent in the fourth-floor solarium, sleeping days, staying up nights and listening for his brethren.

Nights when he was visited by a young nurse named Louisa Amanda Samples, and they made love beneath the pale blue veins of the moon, and she eventually married this man and bore a child of him in 1959, on her thirtieth birthday. For the two of them had been so young when they had met, when love had called.

Rory had been saying something, and it brought Napier from his reverie.

"Go hungry."

"What was that?" Napier asked.

"That's what they called it," Rory said again, grinning. "When one of the wolves got sick with a crip disease. Way your daddy did, only he got lucky. Normally they just let the wolf go hungry and die."

"Granddaddy told me another story once," Brent drawled quietly. "He told me how the Severns and the Harrods had matched up once during this big flu epidemic in 1918. There were people dying in the hundreds, all through the Ohio Valley and down in Tennessee. Called it a 'pandemic' because it was so bad. Killed more troops than got shot up in the last year of World War I."

"I recall reading about that recently," Rory surprised them all by saying. He normally looked at skin magazines. "Had an article in a newspaper, comparing those days with the Beijing flu or whatever you call it."

He must have seen the apparent shock in their faces, including Napier's, because he added: "Well, I was in a bathroom and there wasn't even a sports section to be read."

The cousins had planned to go prowling a new set of strip bars in Stafford, Indiana. Napier had no quarrel with the fact that his cousins would *date* rather than *hunt* their prey. Growing up in this city for so long now, he couldn't differentiate the brutality of the werewolf clan any more than he could someone like Madison Gallows, who would rape and kill a woman more for the sale value of her car than for her sexuality. In the 1990s, everybody had their needs.

And the ghosts in the stockyards weren't going anywhere. They understood the entropy long before those running the packs today did.

When he closed his eyes, Napier envisioned the hammers coming down.

The cattle's eyes open and all too aware.

Napier stared at his cousins without blinking, pausing as Danny brushed flecks of rat muscle from his beard.

Then telling them why he stayed where he did and how he had inherited the spirits of the past.

Knowing full well that they would never understand it.

———

He wasn't certain how many trains had passed, but a southbound was approaching. The rush-hour crowds were gone, and in their wake were left the street musicians that came down into the subways to practice or to play for themselves, not to perform for tokens or change. At times, there might be a crowd. Usually, backup rhythm was provided by the steady *shummp shummp shummp* of the Randolph Street escalator, and the instrument of choice was saxophone in winter, guitar in summer.

Napier did not leave the darkness to run the railroad tracks to his caern that night. He sat on a bench and later could not even recall what instrument was being played by the man who situated himself three pillars away. The man could have been playing harmonica and Napier would not have remembered this. He simply sat there the whole night long, his shirt stiff and pointed from where he had sucked on it.

Stared past the musician dressed in his glad rags, stared at the tunnel, the third rail, the blue steel wall curved with advertisements and movie posters. A PeTA ad against fur: Slip into Something Dead. Teasers for movies about clients and disclosure, seasonal films about the curse of the wolf and yet another sorority-row strangler. And an advertisement as heart rending as the one with the PeTA fox staring at the camera with the same awareness of the abattoir cattle.

A young girl staring at a vacant wheelchair, the one her grandmother died in, according to the text. The advertisement was to make people aware of the Huntington's Disease Foundation. The legend above the photo read: Let's Deprive Her of Her Inheritance.

Napier, never reading the words.

Napier, never realizing he had vacated his bowels, the musician not even making a face or missing a note.

VI. I WAS A MIDDLE-AGED WEREWOLF

Halloween is when it ended. The lycanthropy gene had accelerated the human disease that Napier never truly understood he carried. His own body filled with blight, an irony forever lost of genetic curses both scientific and supernatural. He was afraid to be checked out by the city doctors because he felt there was some chance that the nature of his shapeshifting be discovered.

Such a human fear.

He stared into the mirror with disbelief that afternoon, upon waking for work. His cheeks were sunken and sallow; he looked as if he hadn't slept in days.

He looked haunted. Thirty-five years old going on fifty.

And then all reason left him.

Napier never went to work that last day of his life.

He stood there, looking in the mirror as he shapeshifted, his jaw growing slack, a small pond of drool filling his lower lip at the gum line. The change complete, his eyes vacant, his mouth bubbling with foam like bad special effects in a fifties black-and-white horror flick.

Staggering backwards out of the bathroom, falling to the floor.

A knock, sounding far away. Neighbor kids, trick-or-treating at Valton Tiche's apartment across the hall. Napier lucid in these final moments, thinking about monsters of legend and those born of genetics; would the children outside be dressed like his kinain or like the psychopathic slashers of today's films, wearing hockey masks, spiked gloves, or evil clown makeup?

Oh, if his Granddaddy or brothers could see him now.

In his skull, the sounds of the stockyard hammers were stilled, the cattle raising their thick heads in defiance.

Convulsing on the floor, one clawed hand caught in a purple throw rug by the door. The doorbell ringing. Napier making pathetic mewling sounds, unable to free his hand. The doorbell ringing with hardly a break.

He wanted to snarl at the unrelenting sound.

In the hallway, a small goblin stood alone, demanding candy.

This story is for Tracy Albert Knight.

Wayne Allen Sallee
CHICAGO: 7 April 1994

Wayne Allen Sallee was born 9/9/59 and has been writing professionally since 1985. He's worked as a skip-tracer for a large law firm in the Loop, a PR man for an Elvis impersonator and as an unwitting Mafia dupe: the place he washed dishes for was the front for a chop shop. His novels are *The Holy Terror*, *Girl With the Concrete Hands* and *Marnie's Near Morning*. Wayne's chapbooks include *For You*, *The Living*, *Pain Grin*, *Insanitized Streets*, and *Untold Stories of Scarlett Sponge*. His stories have been selected for the *Year's Best Horror* for the past nine years.

Winter Queen

by Rick Hautala

BANGOR DAILY NEWS Wednesday, January 17.

MUSICIAN'S JET MISSING AND FEARED DOWNED.

Bangor, Maine. (UPI) Aviation officials in Bangor confirmed this morning that rock musician Alex VanLowe was one of six passengers on board a flight that is reported missing and presumed to have crashed.

Although there has been no official confirmation that the jet has been lost, air traffic controllers at Bangor International Airport state that at 11:34 P.M. EST, the pilot, Michael DeSalvo, reported navigational problems and requested an emergency landing at Bangor International. After giving the pilot approval, the tower lost contact with the jet.

The flight originated in Quebec, Canada, and was heading to Portland, Maine, when it flew into a severe blizzard which for the last twelve hours has been ravaging the entire northeast.

Search and rescue efforts will not be initiated until the storm diminishes, which is expected late tonight or early tomorrow morning.

Around the world, rock 'n' roll fans are anxiously following this story to hear if popular music has suffered yet another casualty, cut off in his prime. VanLowe, the lead singer for the rock group Phobia, was scheduled to perform at the Civic Center in Portland, Maine, tonight.

———

CLICK

The batteries in the Sony still seem to be good, so I'll make a tape of everything that's happened—you know, just in case I don't…well, I don't want to consider any of that right now, but it…Jesus! It sure don't look good.

It's so fucking cold!

I'm freezing my ass off!

I've gotta remember to keep an eye on the tape. Being cold like this can probably make it brittle, but it's relatively warm here inside the jet—or what's left of it. At least we're out of the wind. I should be able to keep recording—at least until the batteries run out. Don't know if there are any spares around. I'll have to check later.

I have no idea if it's day or night right now. My watch says it's quarter past six, but who the fuck knows?

Jesus, listen to that wind!

I knew we were in trouble long before Mike came on the intercom and told us all to buckle up, but after that, everything happened so fast, I'm not really sure I can keep it straight. I know I heard the jet engines start to whine, and the jet definitely felt like it was dropping. At some point I heard something hit against the outside of the jet—the side opposite from where me and Jodie were sitting. It sounded like we'd been hit by a big boulder or something, and then there was this big grinding sound, like metal ripping, and glass breaking. Then...

I don't know.

I must've hit my head or something and blacked out. I have no idea how long. I'm lucky I haven't frozen to death already!

I'm sure, once they find the wreckage, there are ways of determining exactly what went wrong with the plane. Whenever there's a news report about a plane going down, don't they always talk about trying to find the "little black box?"

I suppose this piece of junk must've had one of them, too, huh?

The only concern I have right now is, *when*...when will they find us and that little black box?

As far as I can tell, everyone on board is dead, except me and Jodie. Jeff and Johnny sure as hell aren't moving! Why me and Jodie didn't die is beyond me. Must've been just plain dumb luck—where we were sitting or something. We're doing the best we can, I guess. I was bleeding pretty bad from the cut on my head, but other than that and some pulled muscles in my neck and back, I guess I'm okay.

Jodie, though—God, she's a fucking basket case!

I can't really tell how bad off she is 'cause every time I even try to get close to her, she starts crying and pushing me away, screaming like she's fucking hysterical, man!

I keep telling her that she ain't got a prayer of making it if she loses it like this, but as far as I can see, she's way off the deep end.

She's sleeping right now.

I covered her up with whatever coats and blankets I could find by feeling around in the dark. The only way I know she's still alive is, every now and then, I hear her start whimpering and groaning in her sleep.

Shit, I wish I had a flashlight or something, but I can't even start looking around until this storm's over and it gets light.

Jesus, listen to that wind howl!

Sounds like a goddamned pack of wolves. Every now and then something bangs against the side of the plane. Probably a branch, or maybe something that was knocked loose from the plane. It's fucking weird how it sounds like there's someone's outside, knocking on the plane....

Trying to get in.

No! I've gotta stop thinking like that!

I know I shouldn't say this, but Jodie's not going to be any help in this situation. I wish to hell Mike and Denny hadn't been killed. They were both up front in the cockpit, so they hit the ground first and hardest. As soon as I could move, I crawled up there and saw all I needed to see. But shit! They were the technical people. They probably would've been able to rig up something with the radio or something so we could get help out here. I don't know jack shit about how to do something like that.

And I don't even have a fucking clue where we are, not that I think they'll be sending out any search parties until the storm's over.

And I don't know if I'll be able to hang on till then.

That's the biggie, as far as I can see.

No one knows where the hell I am!

For all I know, they might not even realize I'm missing yet.

Food's going to be another big problem. I found a couple of prepackaged meals, TV dinners, in the kitchen area, but they're frozen solid, just like everything else. I can't start a fire—not with the wind and snow blowing like it is, and the microwave oven sure as shit ain't gonna work without power. I suppose there's an emergency backup system, but damned if I know where it is!

Christ, I'm hungry.

I...I guess I'll try to get some sleep now, but...oh, Jesus, what a fucking mess!

CLICK

Eyes that glowed with a deep, vibrant green stared from the surrounding darkness of the forest at the hull of the jet. Thin, panting streamers of frosted breath were quickly whipped away by the swirling winds. The wolf watched, waiting with the vibrating patience of the wild. It could smell the warmth of living flesh that was inside the metal hull, and the smell filled it with a wild, primitive urge to rip open the human's belly and, for the first time in its life, feast upon steaming, human entrails—the *true* meal of its kind.

But as the creature crouched in the whistling storm and watched, another figure, smaller and more graceful, its dark fur highlighted with a pattern of white swirls, moved silently out of the deepest shadows and came to stop at the beast's side.

You know you can't do it, she said.

The communication happened without sound, even without eye contact—a mind link between the two creatures.

But can't you smell it?

Of course I can smell it, and it fills me with disgust.

Not me. Just smell it! Let yourself feel what it stirs deep inside you. Do you mean to tell me that it doesn't excite you? Have you ever tasted human flesh?

No! the she-wolf said, and her body stiffened as she snarled aloud and glared at the wolf beside her.

You know the Decree, she said, *and you must obey it. Come with me now. The pack is waiting to hunt.*

CLICK

Seven-forty-five. Morning. Must be Thursday, the eighteenth.

I spent last night shivering my ass off underneath a pile of coats and clothes that once belonged to friends of mine.

Very good friends.

Even Johnny, the fucking asshole. I'm sorry he's dead. But they're all dead, and there's nothing I can do about it. It isn't my fault they're dead. I have to keep telling myself that.

It isn't my fault!

I didn't sleep very much—if at all. I just lay there, watching until—eventually—a thin, gray wash of daylight brightened the porthole windows of the jet.

By the sounds of things, the storm's pretty much over, but last night... man, the things I heard. I—I don't even want to think about it!

My first impulse was to wake up Jodie, but I decided to let her sleep. She wasn't going to be any help to me, anyway. I've got to check out this situation. See what's up.

CLICK

Nine-eighteen. Same day. The eighteenth.

Well, the first thing I did was go back into the cockpit. I

didn't want to, but I figured any emergency stuff would be up there. The place was a mess—stuff all over the place, but I found a medicine chest, a flashlight, and a flare gun. There are only six flares, so I'll have to use them wisely. I figure I'll wait until it's dark before shooting off a few. I also found Mike's butane lighter in his jacket pocket—Jesus, it was tough, just bringing myself to touch him, but I got it, so I'll be able to get a fire going later, after I dig out of here. Probably a good thing he never listened to me when I was hounding him about quitting smoking.

Jesus, I wish I could forget what I saw in there.

The front of the jet must've hit into the trees head-on. I saw...Jesus! The blood was...

No!

I'm not going to talk about it, or even think about it! Let them rest in peace.

CLICK

Ten-fifteen.

It's taken me the better part of half an hour to get the side door open. Snow had drifted up pretty much over the hull, and I had to dig my way out like some goddamned animal. Mostly, though, I'm just really tired from not sleeping well. Don't know what the temperature is, but it feels like fucking fifty below.

CLICK

One-thirty-five. Still the eighteenth.

The sun's out, and it actually feels relatively warm. I even worked up a bit of a sweat, collecting a bunch of dry wood for a fire. I'm not used to working like this.

I got a fire going just outside the jet, by the open door.

Hopefully the smoke won't drift in and fill up the cabin. Kinda funny, but I started the fire with the first thing I found—the lyric sheet I was working out a new song on when we went down.

The working title?

"Gonna Be a Big One."

Huh!

I guess to fuck it was!

Jodie's been awake for a while, but she isn't moving much. From the smell of it, I'd say she must've crapped herself during the night.

Can't say as I blame her.

I tried cooking up some of those frozen dinners from the kitchenette, but they ended up pretty much black. I gave one to Jodie—chicken and rice, I think the package said, but she didn't touch it, didn't even look at it.

I ate what I could of mine and threw the rest outside. As soon as I did, some crows swooped down out of the pine trees and finished it off. Nothing goes to waste out here, I guess. I wonder...if I die, will the crows fly down and eat my...

No, damnit!

I can't think like that! I gotta stay focused and—and positive.

Next time, I'll try to cook the meals more slowly. I don't want to waste what little we've got here. There's only three more of those dinners. As long as we stay warm and have something to eat, I figure it's just a matter of time before they find us, isn't it?

Well, isn't it?

CLICK

⸺

"It's been almost twenty-four hours since the private plane carrying rock star Alex VanLowe disappeared somewhere between Quebec and Portland. Fans of the missing singer are maintaining a candlelight vigil here outside the Portland Civic Center.

"There's been little word from the Aviation Administration as to how search-and-rescue operations are going, but with each passing hour, as these candles burn in the blustery gusts of winter, hope, too, seems to be fading.

"We're going to switch back to the studio where David Gurney, lead guitarist for Phobia, is standing by for an interview.

"This is NewsCenter 13's Doug Moody, reporting to you live from in front of the Civic Center in downtown Portland.

"Back to you, Elizabeth."

———

CLICK

Eleven o'clock. Second night. Almost Friday the nineteenth.

I guess I should have collected more firewood. This stuff's burning up faster than I expected. I suppose I could use a branch for a torch and go off into the woods and look for some more, but I...I don't know.

As soon as it gets dark, the forest starts to seem really...I don't know... really weird, man. I don't want to say it, but it's kinda scary.

The wind's died down, and it doesn't seem as cold, but still, far off in the distance, I can hear this—I don't know what it is. It's like this howling. I suppose there are wolves or coyotes or something out here. Must be.

Shit, I hope they want to avoid me just as much as I want to avoid them.

Jodie's no better off than she was. All day, she just sat there in the back of the wreckage, staring off into space. I don't think she even knows where she is or what's happened. I moved all the bodies outside. Four of them. Mike, Denny, Jeff, and Johnny. I figured it'd be better if we didn't have to look at them. Especially when we're trying to sleep. Jodie still hasn't eaten anything. I can't even get her to drink water from the snow I've melted. I just don't see how she's going to make it.

I tried my hand at cooking again and got a half-decent meal this time. It's kind of funny, I guess, to think if this had been room service, I would have thrown the tray on the floor and ranked out the bellhop who'd brought it. I didn't cook one for Jodie. I figured, if she isn't going to eat anything, I might as well save what's left for me, for later.

Earlier today, I inspected the damage to the plane. A tree took the left wing clean off when we were coming down. I think I remember feeling the plane kind of spin around just before we hit. After we were on the ground, the plane skidded a few hundred feet in under the trees. I can't see very far in any direction. There's just woods all around me. So I don't think anybody's gonna be able to see us from the air. Not too easily, anyway.

Just after the sun set, I shot off two of the flares, but other than the stars, I haven't seen or heard a goddamned thing. An awful lot of stars up there, though. I've never seen so many. It kinda makes you realize how insignificant we all are, really.

God, it's so lonely and quiet out here. I'm gonna lose my mind if I have to stay here much longer. So alone. It's hard to imagine there's anyone alive anywhere on earth. It's like being crash-landed on another planet.

Well, I guess I should try to get some sleep. I'm gonna need all my strength in the morning.

CLICK

The flickering firelight stung the wolf's night-sensitive eyes as he crawled slowly forward toward the wreckage. His chest, dragging in the snow, left a deep furrow. The scent of dead meat was heavy in the air, in spite of the cold night wind that was blowing down from the north.

Prey was always hard to find when the snowfall was as heavy as it had been this winter. A cold, deep hunger growled in the creature's belly. It had been three nights since he had last eaten, ever since the last Turning, when the moon was full. The smell of human flesh—even the rancid stench of the four dead humans that had been lined up outside the plane—drew the creature forward.

A low whimper escaped the wolf's throat when he reached the bodies and stood up to paw and sniff at the frozen corpses.

The creature was no scavenger.

He was proud, a predator used to the exhilaration of the hunt. He didn't eat carrion.

But this was no ordinary carrion.

This was flesh! Human flesh!

The creature licked at the hot saliva dripping from his jaws as he took hold of one of the dead man's legs and pulled back, hoping to drag the carcass off into the woods, where he would—finally—be able to indulge his burning desire to taste human flesh.

But the wolf had dragged the body no more than ten feet when a commanding female voice spoke inside his head.

How dare you violate the Decree?

The creature whined pitifully as he let go of the man's leg, letting it drop stiffly to the ground. The stinging taste of anticipation turned sour in the wolf's mouth as he turned and looked at the she-wolf standing at the edge of the forest. Reflecting the dying firelight, her eyes glowed a vibrant green.

But this one is already dead. The Decree was made to stop the killing of humans, not the eating of them. What harm is there in eating what is already dead?

In answer, the she-wolf snarled.

You bring shame to our tribe. Already your breath reeks of the stench of rotting meat. Have you no pride? Perhaps you wish to change tribe and become a Red Talon.

The wolf shifted his gaze back to the human corpse, licked his chops, then looked back at the she-wolf.

Come now, said the she-wolf. *The moon is past full. Come and hunt with the pack.*

With that, she turned and ran into the night-stained forest.

The young male wolf had no choice. His desire to taste human flesh became a hard, sour burning in his stomach, but he knew he couldn't defy her. Not tonight, anyway, so he turned and followed her into the forest.

The pack hunted all that night but found nothing, not even a squirrel or raccoon. As dawn streaked the eastern sky, they made their way back to their den.

As they slept, their bellies growled and churned with tight knots of hunger; but for the male wolf who had held, if only for a moment, the frozen flesh of a human in its mouth, the pain was worse.

———

CLICK

Six-thirty in the morning. Second day, so I'm guessing it's Friday, January nineteenth. Yeah. gotta be that. Funny, though, how time seems to stretch out and not make much sense.

As if it matters!

I think our way of keeping track of time doesn't mean a goddamned thing out here. I can feel—there's a sense of a natural rhythm, a way things move here in the forest that has absolutely nothing to do with us humans.

Anyway, I have to record what happened last night before I forget it.

It was late. I guess I must've drifted off to sleep, but I'm not really sure. I don't feel all that rested. Anyway, something moving around outside the plane woke me up. I could hear whatever it was pawing around in the snow, but as much as I wanted to, I didn't dare go out and take a look. Maybe—if I had a gun, I would've gone outside, but I stayed inside the plane, more than half expecting whatever it was to come charging in and attack me.

As soon as the sun was up, I went out and saw what had happened.

Something—a very large and powerful something, judging by the tracks in the snow—had tried to drag Jeff's body into the woods. It was probably one of those wolves or coyotes I heard the first night. Jeff's pant legs were all ripped up, and I could see some pretty deep teeth marks on his legs. It was weird how there wasn't any blood, though, and it...

No. I can't think like that! I've got to handle this. First thing is to do something to stop whatever's out here from getting at the bodies.

These are my friends, for Christ's sake! I can't let them just...just...

CLICK

———

"Authorities at the Civil Air Patrol and the State Forestry Services told News Center Six today that they are expanding their search for rock star Alex VanLowe's missing jet to include large portions of western Maine and the White Mountains of New Hampshire.

"Plummeting temperatures and another blizzard that is moving into the area tomorrow are narrowing hopes that any of the passengers could have survived.

"At the Portland Civic Center, a few dozen die hard fans are still maintaining an around-the-clock candlelight vigil in hopes of hearing news that their rock idol is alive and safe; and while it's too early to give up all hope, time does seem to be running out.

"In other news today, in Lewiston, Marilyn Scoville, the woman who's been accused of keeping her baby daughter locked up in a…"

———

CLICK

Three-forty-five in the afternoon. Same day. The nineteenth, yeah, the nineteenth.

I'm exhausted after spending most of the day piling snow up over the… the bodies of my dead friends.

The best thing I could find for a shovel was one of the lunch trays that I broke off the back of one of the chairs in the plane. I piled the snow up as high as I could and then smoothed it all over, flattening it as much as I could. I don't think whatever was out here last night will know anything's under there.

I hope not, anyway.

Food's my only real problem now.

There's nothing left of those crappy TV dinners. I finished the last one earlier today, and already my stomach is feeling hollow. There's not much to those meals in the first place.

I try not to think too much about what I'm gonna do next, but I have no idea what.

I can't just wait here and starve to death!

Then—Jesus! I start thinking about that soccer team that crashed in the Andes or something, and in order to survive, some of them ate the flesh of the ones that had died in the crash.

Is that what I'm going to be driven to?

God, the thought makes me sick!

I could *never* do that!

I'd rather die!

I'm not a fucking cannibal!

I don't see any change in Jodie, except for the worse. She might just as well be dead, as far as I can see. She just sits there, staring up at the ceiling and groaning as she rocks back and forth. If I had the balls, I'd kill her myself, put her out of her goddamned misery.

Yeah, that's it.

And then I'd eat her.

Jesus, I can't believe I just said that!

Sorry. I shouldn't laugh about it, but it's kind of funny how I—I just pictured me as sort of like a character in one of those cartoons—you know, a stranded miner or something who's looking across a bare table at his partner and seeing him as a stuffed, steaming turkey on a platter.

But no!

Not Jodie!

Hell, she's too skinny, anyway. Wouldn't be good eating. Too bony.

God, I can't believe I'm talking like this. I must really be losing it.

It's got to be exhaustion, that's all.

Exhaustion and hunger.

How long has it been, now?

Two days or three?

Christ, what's it matter? It feels like weeks!

You'd think I could last a little longer than that, wouldn't you?

But the cold!

It's *so* fucking cold! No matter how much firewood I collect or how high I build the fire, I just can't get warm enough. The fire's blazing away. Just listen to it crackle. And then I think how

I wasted most of the day, and all that energy covering up those bodies with snow when I could have been collecting more firewood. Maybe enough to make a big enough blaze so someone would see it.

No, I know what I should have done. I should have cut off some of the best chunks of meat off those guys and fried it up. Lord knows Johnny's ass is big enough.

Jesus! Stop thinking like that!

And now night's coming.

As soon as it starts getting dark, the wind starts to howl and moan. Sometimes, I swear to God it sounds like there's someone out there in the woods, dying.

Hey, maybe that's it.

It's me.

There's a thought!

What if I go out there and find someone facedown in the snow. After I cut off a big chuck of meat to cook up, I roll him over and see that it's me!

No, no, I gotta keep it together better than this if I'm gonna make it. I ain't doing this for Jodie anymore. Hell, I don't know if she's still alive or not.

Who the fuck cares?

I'm gonna try to sleep now, and if I die in my sleep, who the fuck cares?

Huh?

I asked you, who the fuck cares?

CLICK

The firelight pushed back the darkness, making thick shadows waver and dance across the orange-tinged snow. Knots in the wood heated up and exploded, sending sizzling showers of sparks corkscrewing up into the sky where they dissolved into the stars.

At the edge of the forest, five pairs of eyes glowed green in the night. Five pairs of eyes, but one pair was narrowed to mere slits of evil and hunger as they stared at the wreckage of the plane.

I still have the right to disagree with the Council, do I not? the young male wolf said.

There was a brief silence filled only with the low hissing of the wind in the trees, the distant crackle of the fire, and the soft thump of snow falling from heavy-laden branches.

At last the she-wolf spoke.

Yes, you have the right to disagree, but you do not have the right to act contrary to a decision handed down by the Council. And you can never defy the Decree and still remain within the tribe. However, if you choose to become a Silent Strider....

No. I never said I wanted to do that!

The one pair of green eyes stared at the female and narrowed all the more with a deep, burning hatred.

But what if the Council is wrong? What if their decision is foolish?

The she-wolf turned and glared at the young male wolf, making him cringe.

The Council thinks it will not prove so, the she-wolf replied coolly.

But the Council doesn't know everything. Perhaps the Council should reconsider. Saving the life of this human could prove harmful to the tribe. We have worked for generations to keep this forest wild. We certainly do not want to help the humans!

Then one of the other wolves, the largest of the five, stepped between the two.

There will be no more discussion, this wolf said. *We are here to make contact with this human, and there will be no harm done to him.*

CLICK

I know I'm losing it…after what I saw…or think I saw!

What time is it? Let's see. Okay. A little after two o'clock and still dark, so it must be two in the morning. That makes it—what? Saturday? Saturday or Sunday? I don't know for sure. Jesus, I can't think straight anymore!

I couldn't sleep at all last night. My stomach's a knot of pain, and it's so cold… so fucking cold! I don't think I'll ever be warm again!

Okay. Okay. Focus. Concentrate. This is what happened.

I don't know how I knew they were out there, all right? But something, some primitive sense or something made me look outside…I guess I wanted to make sure nothing was—you know, out there getting after the bodies.

I had really stoked up the fire earlier, and it was still blazing high when I peeked out around the edge of the plane's door and saw them.

At first I wasn't sure how many there were.

Five, maybe six.

They kept moving in and out of the shadows, their eyes glowing green in the firelight. It took me long enough to believe there was anything there, that I wasn't imagining the whole thing. I didn't even believe they were real when I watched one of them start toward me.

It was a beautiful animal. Not large, really. Not as large as I'd think a wolf should be. It had a thick, dark fur that was streaked with lighter markings. Some—I know this sounds crazy, but some of the markings looked like lightning bolts!

That's when I was pretty sure I was imagining the whole thing.

The whole time, this wolf kept staring at me, not even blinking. I felt like I was under—I don't know, some kind of mind control or spell or something. It wasn't until it was more than halfway to me that I realized it really was a wolf.

There was a whole fucking wolf pack out there!

And I knew what they wanted.

They wanted me.

They wanted to kill and eat me.

I knew I had to do something to defend myself, but I was too scared to move. It was like the eyes of this one animal had a hold on me, had hypnotized me, and wouldn't let go. I just stood there, staring like a damned fool at this... this thing until it began to...to, I don't know—like, shimmer and glow in the firelight.

And then—and I know this is gonna sound completely crazy— but while I was watching it, another one of the wolves came up next to it. This wolf had something in its mouth. It took me a second or two to realize it was a rabbit.

Anyway, this one wolf drops the rabbit down in front of the other wolf. In an instant, before the rabbit could get its bearings and hop away, the other wolf snapped it up into its mouth and bit it almost in half. Blood squirted like black ink all over the snow. The rabbit kicked for a second or two, and then lay still.

And then—oh, boy! Now I don't even believe this myself, but then something *really* weird happened.

I was still watching this whole thing from inside the doorway of the plane when this one wolf started to... to change.

The first thing I thought was that my eyesight was going bad, or that I was hallucinating or something from being so cold and hungry and lonely. Maybe the whole fucking thing was a dream I was having before I died. But after a while, the—this wolf shape sort of transformed into a woman.

I couldn't believe what I was seeing!

One minute there's this wolf, standing there, glaring at me like it wants to fucking eat me, and then the next minute there's this gorgeous, naked woman standing there. If she'd just disappeared then, I'd have chalked it all up to a dream or hallucination, but then she smiled at me. Looking me straight in the eyes, she raised both arms to me and said, "We want to help you. We want you to join us."

It was real!

I swear to Christ, she was real!

She was standing there...naked...unbelievably gorgeous, and not even shivering while snow was blowing and swirling all around her.

And her voice!

Her voice!

It's still echoing in my memory like it's become a part of me or something.

We want to help you. We want you to join us.

She just stood there, holding her arms out to me, and then she started to come closer.

I tried to say something but couldn't.

I knew her for what she was.

She was Death!

She was hunger!

She was cold!

She was the Winter Queen, and her embrace and kiss would mean death.

I dropped to my hands and knees and felt around until I found what I was looking for.

The flare gun.

I cocked it, making sure it was loaded, and then wheeled around quickly and shot.

The night exploded into red. The light from the flare dazzled my eyes, making it impossible for me to see anything except for the brilliant zigzags of blue afterimages. I think I heard a loud howl of pain, but I'm really not sure. It might have been me screaming. I was so overcome that I must have collapsed right there in the doorway. I didn't wake up until much later. I was shivering my ass off because the fire had burned down.

I know this all sounds absolutely crazy, but in the morning, once it's daylight, I'm going to have to check around in the snow for footprints…and blood. There must have been blood, at least from the rabbit she killed, right?

I really can't talk about it anymore.

I need some rest…and some food. I need some goddamned food!

CLICK

———

"This is Spotter Four calling Sky Chief One. Spotter Four to Sky Chief One. Do you read me? Over."

"Roger that, Spotter Four. I read you loud and clear. What've you got? Over."

"I just saw something that might have been a flare off my left wing. It was pretty far away and awfully low to the ground, but I'd swear it was an emergency flare. Over."

"I didn't see anything over this way. Make sure you mark your heading and report back to headquarters. Over."

"Roger. I'm going to take a quick flyby first. Over."

"If I was you, Spotter Four, I'd hustle my hinder back to the airport. This storm that's coming up is supposed to be a real whopper. Over."

"Roger that, Sky Chief One. Over and out. Spotter Four to base. This is Spotter Four calling base. Do you read me? Over."

———

CLICK

Eight-oh-five A.M. I'm pretty sure it's Sunday, so that makes it the twenty-first.

It's starting again. Another storm. I thought I could feel something coming. All night, there was this... this feeling in the air.

I thought maybe it was just me—you know, imagining things again... especially after what happened last night. And then finding Jodie.

She died last night.

Probably a blessing, really.

She wasn't going to make it, anyway.

Neither am I.

Not if this is a real blizzard coming. It'll bury me and the plane and everything else. Some hikers are gonna find the wreck this summer or in a couple of years, but by then, my bones will have been picked clean by those crows...

Or the wolves!

Sometime around six o'clock this morning, the wind started picking up, and it started to snow. I thought about going out and trying to get enough firewood to last me through the day, but I sure as hell am not going out into those woods in the dark—not with those hungry wolves around. Maybe I scared them off for a while, but if they're hungry enough, I'll bet they didn't go very far.

They'll be back.

I didn't go out and check the snow for footprints or blood or anything, either. What I saw last night seemed so unreal, but I know I didn't imagine it. Besides, any tracks would be covered up already. I'll probably never know what really happened last night.

Maybe it's just as well.

I can hear the snow blowing against the side of the plane. It sounds like it's almost ice, rattling like we're being sprayed by thousands of rock pellets or something.

Wait a second. Why'd I say *we*?

There's no *we* anymore.

There's just me and my dead girlfriend, and four other dead friends I've got stacked up outside the plane like fucking firewood. I want to stay focused, stay positive, but I don't see how I'm going to make it more than another day or two. My stomach's a constant knot of pain. I haven't even dared take Jodie outside yet. I'm not sure I can bring myself to touch her.

The others—sure it was hard, but I hadn't slept with them—or made love to them. Huh! Except for my manager, Denny. I guess you could say he fucked me over a few times over the years.

That's not funny!

But with Jodie, though…I can't stop wondering if I'd be able to stop myself if I was going to—

To…

Jesus, no! I can't think about it. I'm not going to—I *couldn't* cut her up and eat her, even if it means I have to die out here!

Oh, yeah—sure, right now I'm hungry; it hurts, but I'm not crazy with hunger.

Not yet.

But what if I'm snowed in here for a day or two before I can even dig my way out?

What if I'm too weak to dig myself out this time?

What then?

I won't be able to keep the fire going. And how hungry will I get before I finally lose it?

Hungry enough to start thinking about it even more?

Hungry enough maybe to *want* to do something about it?

Maybe that's why I haven't taken her outside yet. I want her here in case I *need* her.

How hard could it be, anyway?

I'd just have to take one of the steak knives from the kitchenette and cut into her, right?

What part, I wonder.

Probably the leg.

Yeah, the upper leg. That'd be the meatiest part.

So what would be the problem?

I'd treat it like any other piece of meat, wouldn't I? Just like a steak. I'm no fucking vegetarian!

What's the big deal?

I can almost kid myself that it's what Jodie would say she wanted me to do, if she could talk. She'd say—"Come on, Alex. Do it. Let me give you the ultimate gift…of life. Eat me, baby. Eat me!"

Christ, I've done that plenty of times before…in a manner of speaking.

So how big a step could it really be?

A couple of slices, stick a slab of juicy, red meat into the flames, and let it cook.

God knows, if I'm not hungry enough to do it right now, I'm gonna be soon enough, so maybe I damned well better start getting ready for it.

If I'm gonna survive this, I'm gonna have to do *something* desperate…

And soon!

CLICK

———

"So tell us what's up with the weather, Dave."

"Well, it sure looks like we're in for another big one, Kimberly. That low-pressure area that's been sweeping up the coast is getting into position for another classic nor'easter just like the one we had last week. We could see as much as a foot of snow along the coast and, of course, much higher accumulations farther inland. Maybe even two to three feet. I'll have all the details for you when Six Alive continues its morning report."

———

The tribe was sleeping in the den. Three of them, besides the she-wolf, had made a kill during the night and, thus, had resumed their human forms. But even as the storm raged outside the mouth of the den, Lyssa, for that was her name, couldn't stop thinking about the man at the plane wreck. She had spoken to him, had invited him to join them, had offered him life—a *real* life of running with the pack, not living in the sterile, choking confines of civilization.

And what had he done?

He had shot a bolt of red flame at her.

For several seconds after the flame had whisked past her head, Lyssa had stood there, dazed and frozen in her tracks. From the time when she was young and had lived closer to humans, she had known about fire and had learned to fear it. Her ancestors, when she contacted them in her ancestral memory, told her that control of fire by humans was what had first begun the corruption of Gaia. But she had lost her instinctive reaction of fleeing from fire and had stood there in the snow, amazed.

Then, as though through a mist, she had become aware of what the rest of the pack was doing. Realizing that the human may be reloading his gun, she quickly turned and ran into the forest. Naked and shivering, it was only by traveling among the furry bodies of her friends that she arrived at the den alive.

But now she couldn't stop thinking about the man and how much she wanted to save him. She had reached out to him, had touched his mind, and had felt that he was close to her in spirit.

She and the other members of her small tribe were different from the rest of their kind. Even more so than most members of the Uktena, they were considered outcasts by most Garou and had been for centuries. But long ago, back when the Europeans had first arrived in their land, these few members of the Uktena had chosen to live in the Wyld, which they cherished and hoped to defend. A few of them—most importantly one of Lyssa's ancestors—had been sickened by the memory of the slaughter of both the natives and the newly arrived Europeans. More than two hundred years ago, they had adopted the Decree, which forbade them from ever taking human life.

Or of eating human flesh.

Over the course of time, this decision—and their dedication to it—had caused inexplicable changes in their essential nature. They found that, once again, as in ancient times, they were subject to the Curse of the Full Moon and were unable to control their Change as others of their kind could. Whenever the moon was full, against their will, they would change into wolf form, and they discovered that, in order to resume human form, they had to kill… they had to drink hot, living blood.

This curse alone would have been easy enough for the tribe to accept—it was a small price to pay for the freedom they sought and found, living away from society both human and Garou; but there was one other development for which they couldn't account. While in wolf form, they discovered that they aged faster than they did in human form. They soon learned that, while in wolf form, they aged as does a wolf or dog—seven years for every one year.

So with the Change that came with the Full Moon, their need and motivation to kill became stronger than ever, but they clung to the Decree and refused to kill humans, as was the custom with most of the rest of their kind, especially the Ahroun.

Lyssa arose and hurriedly dressed, putting on her warmest fur cloak, and left the den. The sentinel at the mouth of the den asked her where she was going, but she told him nothing as she strode out into the storm.

CLICK

"...and you don't mind that I'm recording what you said?"

"Oh, no. Not at all."

"I mean—tomorrow morning, or sometime later, I'm going to have to listen to this all over again."

"It will help you understand it all on a deeper level."

"Shit, I'll need to hear it just to help me convince myself that I'm not—you know, that I haven't completely lost my mind."

"You haven't lost your mind, far from it, but you *are* in danger of losing your life. That's why I've come here. To save you."

"What do you mean? You're, like, a—an angel or something?"

"No....I'm probably the furthest thing from an angel."

"Who are you, then."

"I told you. My name is Lyssa."

"Lyssa who?"

"I have no need of a last name."

"So what are you? The Queen of Snow? The Winter Queen? Is that it?

"No, I'm not that, either. Look, we don't have much time."

"What the — Oh, my God! What the hell are you doing?"

"This will save your life."

"But you just—oh, Jesus! You just cut your arm wide open. Look. It's bleeding!"

"Here. Take this."

"Are you crazy? Now I know I'm insane! This can't be happening! There's no way! No way I'm going to eat that!"

"But you have to. It will give you strength."

"No...I...that's a piece of your arm, for Christ's sake! I can't just...just..."

"I'm doing this willingly, Alex, to save your life."

"But I can't eat…that's your…that's human flesh."

"It will make you become as I am."

"But what if I don't want to become like you are? What if I'd just as soon die here rather than…than eat your flesh?"

"It's the first and only time you'll ever have to do it, Alex. After today, the Decree will forbid you to eat human flesh. But right now, you must."

"No…I can't…"

"Please. Take it and eat. Eat it and live."

CLICK

He ran, and the deep snow tugged at his legs, tripping him up.

He ran until he thought his chest would burst, until his lungs felt like they were on fire.

He ran, and the sour, coppery taste of blood, the rank taste of flesh filled his mouth, gagging him. When he clamped his teeth together, they met a rubbery, fatty resistance, and the thought of what was in his mouth made him want to spit it out.

But he didn't.

He swallowed, straining to force the lump of cold flesh down his gullet. Hot vomit churned deep inside his gut.

And still he ran.

He ran until he fell.

The impact wasn't hard in the soft snow. Cold and cushiony, it reached up to embrace him, but he enjoyed its comfort for only a few seconds.

Then something else started to happen.

He felt his bones begin to shift and crackle like crumpled paper inside his body. Nerves and blood vessels roared with pain and new life as the Change came over him for the first time. He was terrified. He felt his face compress, and then it began to extend outward. His spine curled up and around like it was forming the shape of a question mark. Some of his bones lengthened; others shortened. All crackled like a raging fire beneath his skin. Muscles and tendons twanged like taut elastics connecting new and unusual angles of bone. Something tugged back at his face, and he felt his ears slide up to the top of his head and flatten. His eyes shifted to the sides of his head, and as they did, his vision gradually sharpened. He began to see the world in a unique way.

Sights became sounds.

Sounds were tastes.

And all around him, the world exploded with new, deep, and vibrant scents and sensations he hadn't even imagined were possible.

He wanted to cry out in his misery and joy, but the pain of the Transformation began to blend into something else…into a fierce strength and a dizzying, almost terrifying sense of power.

He tilted his head back, filled his lungs with cold air, and let loose a rising, keening howl that echoed throughout the snow-laden forest.

And then he ran, but now he ran on four feet and with a new sense of strength and purpose.

"You're looking at the scene earlier this morning when a National Forest Service ground rescue team finally arrived at the crash site of the private jet which had been carrying Alex VanLowe and some of his entourage to a concert in Portland, Maine, when it disappeared last week.

"For four days now, the search for the missing plane had expanded until last Saturday night, when a Civil Air Patrol pilot reported seeing an emergency flare here in the National Forest northwest of Mount Washington. Because of the blizzard conditions that swept through the area, rescuers weren't able to get to the downed plane until this morning, just after dawn, but the plane has been positively identified as that of the missing rock star. How it came to be so far off course is still a matter of speculation, but authorities report that the pilot of the jet, Michael DeSalvo, had reported navigational problems. Obviously, they were way off course.

"And when the rescue team parachuted down this morning, what a grim sight they found!

"The bodies of four dead passengers, identified as the pilot, Michael DeSalvo, Mr. VanLowe's manager, Dennis Cody, and two members of the road crew, Jeff Connors and Johnny Rice, were found buried beneath a mound of snow. A fifth body, that of Jodie McDaniels, Alex VanLowe's girlfriend, was found inside the plane. As of right now, the rescue team has not found any trace of Mr. VanLowe.

"Fans around the world are hoping and praying that the rock star will be found alive, but rescuers are holding out little hope. Tracks which the rescue team thinks may have been made by Mr. VanLowe were found leading off into the woods. After following them for nearly a mile, the team lost them in the dense woods and decided to return to the crash site until a larger search party could be formed.

"We'll keep you updated as these events unfold, but for now, it looks rather doubtful that Alex VanLowe will be found alive.

"In other news today, the trial in Augusta of the man arrested for shooting his neighbor's cat…"

Rick Hautala is the author of eleven novels, including *Twilight Time*, *Ghost Light*, *Cold Whisper*, and *Winter Wake*. He has had more than thirty stories published in such anthologies as *Stalkers*, *Shock Rock 2*, *Narrow Houses*, *The Ultimate Zombie*, and *Night Visions* 9. He lives in southern Maine with his wife and three children.

Lone Wolf

by Edo Van Belkom

Val Kodlack had feasted.

Wet threads of blood and flesh hung loosely from his muzzle, glimmering in the moonlight as he crouched over the human's still-warm body. His growl was a low and contented sound deep within his throat. The kill had been a good one, something to be savored. The memory of her terror — as sweet to his senses as her flesh had been to his palate — would give him pleasure for days to come.

He turned the body over and examined it, checking for areas he might have missed in the rush to slake his hunger. He saw her face then, and took a close look at its features. She'd been a young woman, probably still in her teens. Her eyes, still open and wide with fear, were the pale blue color of the sky. Her long blond hair almost matched the yellow of the corn growing in the field around them. Her clothes were a mixture of pine and leafy greens, and her skin was a deep tan color, as dark and rich as Gaia herself.

Attractive, thought Kodlack, by human standards, perhaps even by those of the Garou.

No matter.

Attractive or not. Young or old. Male or female. She was human. And like all humans, she had to die.

It was his curse.

He found a spot of virgin flesh on the upper part of her left arm. He lifted the body off the ground by the shoulder and clamped his teeth down on the meat. Two violent sideways shakes of his head, and the flesh tore free. Then he raised his blood-reddened muzzle toward the moon, snapped his maw at the air, and slid the steaming gobbet of meat down his gullet.

He remained motionless a moment, listening to the wind whisper through the corn stalks, basking in the waning light of the moon.

His hunger slaked, and his rage having run its course, he felt his corded muscles beginning to slacken beneath his fur, and the fur itself retreating beneath his flesh as if cowering from the approaching dawn. His fangs began to dull, his snout to shrink.

He let the body fall heavily to the ground, leaving it for scavengers to pick clean…and for Gaia to reclaim. The humans would no doubt find her remains come harvest time, but that did not concern him. By then, she'd be just another runaway found dead by the roadside, one of countless thousands. An unfortunate statistic.

And while they searched for a killer, he'd be hundreds of miles away, stalking the Blight for another victim.

It was his curse.

Kodlack reared up on his hind legs, his head just clearing the top of the corn. In the distance he could see his rig waiting by the roadside, its orange-and-red running lights shining like colorful pinprick stars against the still, blue-black backdrop of night.

He moved toward it, slipping silently among the neat rows of corn. His gait was slow, giving the sun the chance to erase the moon and his body the chance to reclaim the Beast.

At last, as dawn's light peeked over the eastern edge of the world, Kodlack reached his truck.

Although he was naked and still in Glabro form, he strode easily toward the cab of his sleek, black semi. He put a bare foot onto the step above the gas tank, and his hand arced past the spot where the words *Lone Wolf* were inscribed in fancy silver letters on the side of the door. Then he took hold of the gleaming chrome door handle, opened the door and pulled himself inside.

The interior of the truck was as warm and comforting as a den full of his fostern. He was torpid from his feeding, but he fought off the urge to sleep and quickly put on some clothes.

There'll be time to sleep later, he thought, turning over the key in the ignition. *Now, I need to put some kilometers between myself and the carcass. If I make Winnipeg by midafternoon, I'll be able to catch of a few hours sleep before nightfall....*

And the rise of another moon.

The big diesel engine rattled to life, permeating the air with the stench of the machine's acrid black exhaust. Without giving the engine time to warm up, he shifted the rig into gear, eased it back onto the highway, and headed west.

Kodlack made his formal challenge for the leadership of the pack and waited for the battle to begin.

He was more than ready. He had no intention of losing this fight and had prepared accordingly. He had made contact with an ancestor — not just any ancestor, but Man-Eater, the most powerful and sadistic chieftain the pack had ever known.

Now Kodlack's body seethed with rage as Man-Eater, a Garou many claimed had been a slave to the Wyrm, usurped his body for the duration of the battle.

Springing Elk, a large and strong leader, but one whose best years were behind him, entered the clearing ready to defend against the challenge.

The battle was over almost as soon as it began; Springing Elk proved no match for the combination of Kodlack's strong young body and Man-Eater's vicious, battle-hungry spirit.

Springing Elk soon lay dead, and Kodlack was leader of the pack.

His first official task would have been to give Springing Elk a burial befitting that of a fallen chieftain, but the ghost of Man-Eater would not allow it. Instead of leaving Kodlack's body after the battle, Man-Eater's ghost lingered.

And instead of burying Springing Elk with dignity, Man-Eater's ghost forced Kodlack to tear out the dead chieftain's heart and devour it in front of the pack, sending a clear message that they would now be ruled by violence and intimidation — just as the pack had been ruled by Man-Eater so many years ago.

It was the beginning of Kodlack's curse.

By two o'clock, Kodlack had placed a distant second in his westward race with the sun. It hung in the sky before him like a naked bulb, burning bright, blindingly white. He found it difficult to keep his eyes open, even through the dark lenses of his sunglasses. He decided to pull off to the side of the road, curl up in the sleeper behind him and wait for nightfall.

It was always difficult to put kilometers behind him when the ghost of Man-Eater raged. Fortunately, Kodlack's cargo wasn't due in Vancouver for several days. He'd be able to make up for lost time in a day or two by driving straight through the night under the darkness of the new moon.

It wasn't anything he hadn't done before.

Kodlack lived his life in the guise of a long-haul trucker. Such an occupation wasn't exactly in keeping with his totem, but living among humans, as one himself, gave Man-Eater's ghost fewer chances to rage. Last night's rage had been the first one in a month. Although the transition from pack-dwelling Garou to his current status as a lone wolf had been necessary for Kodlack, it had also been difficult. Many nights he'd longed for the company of his kin, to run and hunt with the pack, or to feel the brush of fur against his own. After a while, however, he managed to adjust.

He scanned the road ahead for a suitable spot to park his truck. There was a bridge about a kilometer away. On the other side of the bridge would be a widened stretch of gravel shoulder. He eased his foot off the accelerator, and the truck began to slow.

Kodlack was a Garou of the Wendigo, a tribe that laired in the deep Canadian taiga while struggling to win back the lands that had once been its. He had been leader of the Kapus Pack, a closely knit group settled in the part of Gaia the humans called Muskoka. But along with the position came privilege, and with privilege came those who would want it for their own.

Like most leaders, Kodlack had expected challenges to his leadership, and from time to time even welcomed them, but each one evoked the ghost of Man-Eater, bloodthirsty and fresh, hungry for flesh. The challenges soon became too much for even Kodlack's stout heart to bear. In time he came to dread them because he knew what force they would unleash within him.

There was another problem as well. Each challenge he successfully put down resulted in the death of another strong-willed, fierce-fighting member of his pack. What would be left to lead if the strongest Garou were left dead by his own hand? The more powerful he became, the more time he spent warding off challengers. Somewhere along the line, he and the rest of the pack had lost sight of their most important tasks: eradicating the Wyrm, getting rid of the planet's corruption, and reclaiming Gaia as their own. In these times, the only thing anyone seemed to want was the leadership of the pack.

Kodlack had considered abdicating many times, but he knew Man-Eater's ghost would never be at peace in the body of anyone but a leader.

The matter was settled for Kodlack once and for all the night he killed one of his own sons in a challenge.

Before dawn of the next day he'd packed a few belongings and a change of clothes, and walked away from the pack.

Toward the Blight.

For the good of the pack.

It was his curse.

Kodlack eased the truck onto the shoulder. After making sure everything was secure, he crawled into the sleeper compartment behind the cab. Once there, he curled himself up into a tight little ball and immediately became warmed by the heat of his own body. He let out a long, tired sigh, and in seconds his breathing fell into a deep and regular rhythm.

———

Kodlack dreamed.

Man-Eater stood at the edge of the clearing, prepared to defend his leadership against a young firebrand of a Garou named Phelan Hayes, more popularly known among the pack as Throat Ripper.

He was just another in a long line of challengers, but this time Man-Eater genuinely feared for his life. He was getting old, not so quick as he once was. It was said that age and treachery always won over youth and skill, but Man-Eater had relied on the adage once too often and knew his end was near. Whatever the outcome, he vowed not to go out without a fight.

The battle began and soon turned bloody. Throat Ripper tore open Man-Eater's belly; gore and entrails spilled out onto the ground.

Still he fought on....

Throat Ripper laughed. "You fight like an ape," he cried, howling an extended Song of Mockery.

Man-Eater, resisting the urge to release his rage, continued to fight a tactical battle, postponing the inevitable for a few moments longer. Finally, Throat Ripper pinned Man-Eater to the ground. Throat Ripper raised an arm and brought it down hard, digging his claws into Man-Eater's throat.

Kodlack cried out, feeling a searing pain in his neck.

It was his curse.

———

Kodlack was awakened, hours later, by the rising of the moon. Although Man-Eater had yet to rage within him, he could feel the ghost's encroachment upon his body. His bones had become soft, his joints loose. His body hair itched, and his skin tingled, as if circulation to it had been cut off for hours. A dull ache suffused his body, and his throat was as dry as parchment.

He stretched his arms and legs as best he could in the tight confines of the sleeper, then wiped the sleep from his eyes. He crawled back behind the wheel and cranked the engine into life. He switched on his running lights, then the headlights. As he pulled onto the highway, he could just make out the pale disc of the moon rising over the horizon.

A few miles down the road, he came upon a truck stop. Although he rarely ate human food when the moon was full, he decided he could do with something to drink. Besides, the fuel gauge was creeping dangerously close to Empty.

He pulled in to the right of the gas pumps and walked over to the coffee shop while an attendant set about filling his tanks.

The coffee shop was filled with a low hum of voices. It smelled of old coffee, stale cigarettes and foods refried in fat. He walked over to the counter, picked up a large bottle of Evian water from the cooler and approached the cash register.

In front of him stood a young woman. She wore heavy boots, thick denim pants and an overstuffed winter coat. A large green backpack hung down from her right shoulder. She had a can of Coke in her hand.

Kodlack had seen plenty like her on the road. Young women — girls really — running away from something that wasn't nearly as bad as where they were headed. Funny, thought Kodlack, how they thought life in one Blight could be better than another. When would they learn that Gaia was the one true way of life?

Probably never.

"That stuff isn't very good for you," he said, gesturing at the can of soda in her hand. "It's full of all kinds of chemicals your body was never meant to deal with." He held up his bottle of water. "Straight from the earth. Nothing finer."

She looked up at him, her eyes widening in something like recognition. Then she raised the can and smiled shyly. "It's all I can afford."

Kodlack returned her smile, careful not to expose too many teeth. "You can have some of mine."

She put down the can. "All right."

He paid for the water and walked over to a nearby table. She followed close behind and took the seat across from him. He opened the bottle and poured her a cup. "Where you headed?" he asked.

She took a sip, then said, "West."

He was silent a moment. It all seemed so easy. Too easy. But why fight it? His lips pulled back in a tight little grin.

"That's just where I'm headed."

"How 'bout a ride?"

"You got it, darlin'."

"Well, all r-right."

They drank, then got up from the table. At the door he turned to her. "Are you hungry? Would you like something to eat…for the road?"

She shook her head.

It was odd that a runaway would refuse food, especially one who couldn't afford more than a soda. But, he'd seen all kinds in his years on the road and knew enough not to ask too many questions. Although they were desperate, runaways were seldom careless. The less he said, the better.

The attendant was waiting for him when he returned. He paid the grimy little man, then opened the cab door for his new passenger. She gracefully climbed inside.

Minutes later he was behind the wheel and pulling out of the truck stop. The sun had finally set, but the sky hadn't faded completely to black. The moon was big and bright over the western horizon, but still an hour or so from full luminance.

He drove in silence, something unsettling gnawing at the back of his brain. Something about this girl was strange. He glanced at her several times, but it wasn't her appearance that bothered him. She was actually quite attractive. He took a deep breath and suddenly realized what was bothering him.

Perfume.

The girl smelled heavily of man-made scents and oils. It wasn't like runaways to have a pleasant smell about them — at least what passed for pleasant with humans. They were supposed to have a strong body odor from days on the road and weeks in the same set of clothes.

At last Kodlack spoke. "Been on the road long?"

"Ten days or so."

He considered this. Ten days was a long time for a runaway to travel and still be on the road — certainly more than enough time to reach any destination, even the west coast. "Spend all that time on the road, did you?"

"Mostly."

Kodlack didn't answer, and for a moment the cab was silent except for the ever-present thrum of the engine.

Just then, a semi passed them on the left, roaring loudly as it inched by. Kodlack kept his speed constant. When it was safe for the passing driver to pull into the lane in front of him, he flashed his headlights to signal all-clear. The rig eased right, then thanked Kodlack with two blinks of his red rear lights.

Kodlack opened his mouth to speak, but hesitated, leaving his mouth open and his lower jaw slack. He felt the Change approaching, and it grew harder and harder to speak. Still, there were too many unanswered questions.

"What are you running from?"

"A lot of things."

"What are you hoping to find when you get to where you're going?"

"Something better."

Kodlack's senses were growing keener and sharper. There was nothing particularly wrong with what the girl was saying; there just wasn't anything about it that was *right*. As his feral instincts became sharper, something told him to be wary of the woman.

"You're not running away from anything, are you?" he said, checking the highway, then turning to face her.

She looked back at him and for the first time he saw that her face had changed. In the dim glow of light shining up from the dashboard, he saw that her mouth and nose had become more prominent, elongating into something like a muzzle.

She looked to be...in Glabro form.

The sight of her sounded an alarm inside him. He could feel his bones and muscles growing, his skin stretching, and the hair slithering up from his pores. And deep inside he could feel the ghost of Man-Eater beginning to stir.

He had to get off the road.

With a series of smooth and precise movements, he slowed the truck and guided it onto the side of the road.

"What are you doing?" she asked.

He did not answer.

When the truck had come to a stop, it was a hairy, clawed hand that let go of the steering wheel and engaged the parking brake. The engine settled into a rough, clanging idle. An air-pressure release valve let out a long, exhausted sigh.

"You're not human!" he said at last, his voice midway between normal speech and an angry growl.

"No, Kodlack. I am not."

The mention of his name caught him off guard. For a moment, he backed off, realizing he might be at a disadvantage. "How do you know my name?"

"What member of the Kapus doesn't know the name Val Kodlack, one of the most powerful leaders the pack has ever known?"

Kodlack remained silent, choosing instead to look the woman over. Her eyes had grown dark and had recessed deep in their sockets. Fine hair had appeared on her face, soft rather than bristly, like the pelt of a small animal.

She was Garou, shifting slowly from Glabro to Crinos form. He was changing as well, his muscles rippling under the confinements of his human trappings. He clawed at them unconsciously, easily tearing the fabric with the sharpened talons that tipped his fingers.

"So, you know my name and have tracked me down. What is it that you want?"

"The leadership of the pack."

He shook his head. "It's been years since I've run with Garou, even longer since I've led them. I live alone now. As far as the pack is concerned, I do not exist."

"Oh, but you do, Kodlack. You are a legend. Why, your name alone strikes fear into the hearts of young and old."

"Perhaps, but how can I possibly give you the leadership of the pack? If it's what you truly desire, you can make a challenge for it like everyone else."

"Of course I could challenge and possibly defeat the current leader, but that would provide me with little more than a temporary hold on the leadership. There would soon be challengers conspiring against me, ready to challenge the moment I became vulnerable."

Kodlack listened closely, watching her. She was small for a Garou, but what she gave up in size and strength she probably more than made up for in cunning.

"But," she said, her hands digging for something in the bottom of her bag, "if I could bring back your head as a symbol of my strength and power, Garou everywhere would fear me. I could become the one true and permanent leader of the Kapus Pack. After all, with your head mounted on a staff like a scepter, who would dare challenge me?"

"Believe me, I speak from experience — intimidation is hardly the mark of a great leader," Kodlack rebutted.

"Perhaps not, but it is the tool of a strong one."

She was out of her mind. Kodlack lifted his snout to the moon and was about to laugh when he saw a glint of light out of the corner of his eye.

He looked over.

Just in time to see five silver blades heading straight for his heart.

He jumped aside in time to see the blades slash the fabric of the seat behind him.

As she prepared for another attack, he opened the door and scrambled onto the highway.

He took a moment to recall what he had seen. Knife blades instead of fingers, stretching out from a glove encasing her right hand.

She had cunning, but obviously no respect for the Ways. What Garou would use a human device to kill one of their own? The answer was obvious — a very, very dangerous one.

"I warn you — you can't possibly defeat me," he said. "Man-Eater's ghost will not allow it."

"Do you think you are the only Garou who can call up the ghost of an ancestor?" she asked, her voice changing slightly, as if in the process of being taken over by another entity. "I have defeated you before, Man-Eater. I shall do so again."

"Throat Ripper!" said Man-Eater's ghost, called to the forefront of Kodlack's mind by the sound of a familiar voice.

Kodlack's heart pounded wildly in his chest as he moved cautiously around the truck. An open stretch of field by the side of the road led to a deep, dark forest. If he could reach the forest, Gaia would help him battle this insane young Garou and the powerful spirit possessing her body. He padded around the front of the truck, feeling the heat from the roughly idling engine. As he peered around the right front fender, he heard a sound above him.

He jumped back without looking up, then wheeled around. She was there, holding the glove before her as if ready to strike.

Kodlack wanted no part of this fight, but Man-Eater had a different opinion of the matter. "End this now," said Kodlack, pushing aside Man-Eater long enough to get the words out, "and I will forget it ever happened."

"Do you think I've come this far, Kodlack, simply to give up?" It was the voice of the female.

"If you stop now, I will let you live."

The basso voice of Throat Ripper snickered from somewhere deep inside her. "This is a fight to the death. Unfortunately, Man-Eater, the death will again be yours." She lunged at him, silvery blades extended.

Kodlack jumped back, but not far enough. The tips of three of the blades grazed his chest, breaking the skin.

He let out a yelp. All at once his flesh felt aflame as blood bubbled up from the three lines across his chest. The pain seared him.

But before she could manage another attack, he had regained his composure and was bounding away across the open field. In seconds he was in the woods. The touch of leaves against his wounds was like salve.

He ran downwind, concealed himself in deep brush, then turned to watch her approach. The knife-tipped glove must have been heavy, for it slowed her and made her movements awkward and ungainly.

Her apparent edge had turned out to be a hindrance.

She entered the woods.

Kodlack's ears pricked up.

Time for reason and reflection was over.

Now was time for the kill.

——

Throat Ripper stood over Man-Eater, laughing — savoring his victory over the great chieftain and his imminent crowning as the new leader of the pack.

"You are old and weak," he snarled. "Perhaps it's best you were pushed aside in favor of…younger blood."

Throat Ripper laughed again, a long, mocking howl designed to humiliate Man-Eater in the eyes of the pack before he died.

Again, Throat Ripper raised his arm and brought it down hard, digging his claws into Man-Eater's throat….

No! cried Man-Eater's ghost.

My body is not old now. This one is still young and strong, and can fight long, hard and well.

This time it is I who will win….

Kodlack followed her for a few minutes until she came upon a large, oval clearing — a clearing very much like the one in which their ghosts had fought. The light of the moon pooled in its center, while moonbeams bathed the surrounding trees in pale white light. She hesitated at the edge of the clearing as if she had lost her bearings, then slowly moved across it.

Kodlack felt pity for her, and for a moment thought about turning around, heading back to the highway and leaving her there in the forest. But Man-Eater's ghost reminded him of the sharp pain in his chest where she had touched him with her abomination. She had to die.

The sooner the better.

He grabbed a length of dead wood and flung it across the clearing. As it crashed through the trees on the other side, her ears became erect and the hair along the back of her neck stood on end.

Kodlack sprung from the edge of the clearing, closing the gap between them in great leaps and bounds.

As she turned, she raised the glove to meet him, all five blades glinting in the moonlight.

This time Kodlack was expecting the weapon. He made a final

leap, traveling the last few meters through the air. With a hard swing of his left arm he swatted the glove aside. A moment later his entire body plowed into her chest, knocking her heavily to the ground.

Before she could recover, his powerful jaws had clamped onto the meaty part of her right arm, midway between the elbow and the glove. She howled in pain and beat weakly at his head and body with her free left hand.

He strengthened his hold on her arm, and began swinging his locked muzzle from side to side in a series of violent jerks. After several pulls on the arm, he pinned her elbow to the ground with his hands, and yanked at it with a savage, unrelenting pull of his jaw.

The arm broke, then slowly tore free from the elbow, tendons and ligaments snapping like kindling.

He spat the gloved hand and forearm out of his mouth, then looked down at the body of his vanquished challenger.

"You cannot best me in a fair fight, Throat Ripper," said the ghost of Man-Eater through Kodlack. "Without the advantage of youth against an old Garou, the element of surprise, or the treachery of a man-made weapon, you are nothing!"

The Garou's eyes were slowly closing into narrow slits, and her breath was quick and shallow. Blood spurted freely from her wet, red stump.

"This is the waste of Garou life I left the pack to avoid," said Kodlack. "For the sake of your kin I hope you informed someone of your intentions. At least then your disappearance will send a message to the rest of them that Val Kodlack is a Garou best left alone."

She howled mutely, overcome by the pain.

Again Kodlack considered getting up and leaving her there in the clearing, but knew that if she recovered from her wounds, she might return to the pack and recall the ghost of Throat

Ripper in a challenge against its present leader. He couldn't let that happen.

The pack had been better off without Man-Eater's ghost. And the pack would be better off without Throat Ripper's as well.

Spurred on by Man-Eater's ghost, Kodlack picked up the severed arm by the wrist, held the glove firmly in his hands, and brought the blades down into the middle of her throat.

The knives easily pierced her flesh and embedded in the hard ground beneath her.

She let out a howling yelp of pain. It soared up toward the bright disc of the moon, then died somewhere in her throat, little more than a gurgle.

Moments later, her body was still. Wisps of steam rose up from her wounds like smoke. He climbed off the dead Garou and walked away without looking back.

The fight had taken a lot out of him, not only physically but emotionally as well. The bloodthirsty ghost of Man-Eater had been sated...for now.

Kodlack thought about what had happened and shook his head. He found it hard to believe that even this far removed from the pack, he'd had to dispatch another of his kin in a challenge.

A challenge for what?

He wasn't even leader anymore, hadn't been for years. It had been nothing more than a desperate, senseless grasp at power.

It was the thing he'd left the pack to avoid.

He let out an anguished sigh. It was more obvious to him now than when he'd left. They'd become blinded by the Blight, infected by the corruption. Gaia and the pack's totem had been forgotten, possibly forever. It was power they craved now. Leadership over all else...at any cost. He'd had a taste of that power and knew it to be meaningless. For what was it to have power over a pack that was powerless against the Blight? It was as senseless as humans fighting the right to rule over some

Third World nation while their countrymen died of starvation in the crossfire.

What would there be to rule over in the end?

He shook his head in a mixture of disgust, contempt and anger.

By the time he reached the truck he had slipped into Glabro form. He climbed behind the wheel and saw the lights of the Blight called Winnipeg up ahead. They looked like a blanket of stars, unnaturally covering the ground instead of the sky. Absolute corruption.

Kodlack's anger flared at the sight of it.

And Man-Eater stirred within him.

They both began to rage.

And Kodlack lost all control over his form.

The change into Crinos form came harder and faster than ever before. His body was racked by an intense kind of rage that could only be quelled by one thing.

Human flesh and blood.

He sat there, seething with anger until he was a hulking mass of muscle and fur, claws and fangs.

He took hold of the steering wheel, slammed the truck into gear and headed for the Blight.

Tonight, they vowed, the humans, the apes, the monkeys, were going to pay.

Edo Van Belkom has sold over 60 other stories of science fiction, fantasy, and horror and is currently at work on a novel set in the world of **Werewolf: The Apocalypse** which will be published by HarperCollins SF in 1995. Edo became a full-time freelance writer in 1992 and is currently a contributing editor to SFWA Bulletin and the HWA's Canadian membership representative. He also writes a column on Canadian horror for *Horror!* magazine.

Night Games

by Richard Lee Byers

I.

As history tells, when Constantine marched on Italy, he dreamt of a blazing cross. Some weeks later, so did I. Red as blood, the symbol burned amid thunderheads, its radiance staining the gray cloudstuff crimson. Beneath it, my comrades and I refought the Battle of Milvian Bridge. As before, I bore a mace, the weapon of choice against Maxentius' *cataphractarii*, soldiers in mail riding armored horses. The clangor of arms and the screams of the dying all but deafened me. Sweat stung my eyes.

In waking reality, the tyrant's forces had met disaster routing over the narrow stone bridge. But in the dream, they'd managed to cross in good order, and now we were fighting our way over it to engage them anew. As more and more men crowded onto the span behind me, the press became deadly. When anyone fell, he was trampled. Javelins plummeted into our ranks like hail.

Suddenly the bridge groaned and shuddered, and I realized it was going to collapse. I cried that we had to fall back, but in the cacophony, no one heard. Wedged among my fellows, I couldn't even save myself.

With a roar, the bridge disintegrated. I plunged toward the bloody surface of the Tiber, jagged stones and armored men falling around me. Then a hand gripped my shoulder and shook me. A deep voice said, "Wake up."

I jolted up in bed. "Dress," said the voice. "Hurry. I need you."

Befuddled, still half mired in the nightmare, I looked up. The speaker was Ragnachar, Constantine's Frankish magician, a rangy man of indeterminate age. Despite his years in the Augustus' service, he still affected barbarian garb — breeches and a checkered cloak pinned at the shoulder with a brooch — still sported a bushy mustache and a shaggy mane bleached with lime. However, upon meeting him, what one noticed first were his cold green eyes. There was something uncanny about them, something that made people shun him, and now they seemed to virtually shine in the gloom.

I tried to swallow my distaste. It didn't matter that Ragnachar made me edgy. He was one of Constantine's lieutenants, and I owed him respect. "What is it?" I asked. "What's amiss?"

"Not here," he said. "Someone may be listening."

I threw off my quilts, and winced at the November chill. Though ordinarily grimly self-possessed, Ragnachar fidgeted as I put on my boots, cuirass, cloak, and helmet. When I was ready, he led me across the palace, out of the section where we soldiers and servants bunked, through vaulted corridors and enormous halls of state, and into Constantine's private quarters. Our footsteps clicked on the marble floors.

We passed two pairs of living sentries, then came to a dead one. Throat torn open, he lay in a pool of blood. Behind him gaped the doorway to Constantine's bedchamber. Voices murmured within.

I snatched for my sword. It cleared its scabbard with a hiss. The wizard said, "Too late for that. They're long gone. Just come inside."

Feeling sheepish, I sheathed my weapon, then followed him through the door. The room beyond was far grander than a common person's sleeping chamber. A bronze statue of Venus stood in an alcove, and frescoes of farm life and hunting scenes adorned the walls. Somewhat to my surprise, there was no sign of Constantine's assassinated corpse, nor, alas, of his live self either. The voices I'd heard belonged to three of his ministers: Ossius the Christian priest, Crocus the Alemannic chieftain, and the poet Optatianus Porphyrius. From their tousled hair and rumpled clothes, it was plain that, like me, they'd come here in haste. Their faces were drawn and tense in the oil lamps' glow.

"This is the man," said Ragnachar, and the others turned to stare at me. For a moment, stupidly, I thought he was accusing me of abducting the emperor myself.

Optatianus peered down his long, thin nose. "Absurd," he said, though I fancied I looked as able, as soldierly, as the next centurion. "I still say, call out every man. Search every house."

The sorcerer sneered. "As I keep trying to beat into your thick skull, there are at least two reasons we can't do that. First, foully as Maxentius abused Rome, there are some here who mourn him. Indeed, the remains of the Praetorian Guard are still lurking about. A mass search would inevitably reveal that Constantine is missing, and then our foes might rise against us."

"I agree," said Crocus. He was a burly, red-faced man whose appearance was a mix of Roman and barbarian. Except for gilded highlights, his armor looked like mine, but he had a drooping, crumb-speckled mustache like Ragnachar's, and carried a broad-bladed battle lance. "And the troops are still licking their wounds from the fight by the river. They're in no shape to put down a revolt."

Even though the Alemanni had supported him, Ragnachar was scowling at the interruption. "Second," he continued, "I'm sure that at the moment, the Augustus is alive. If the kidnappers wanted him otherwise, why not simply butcher him in his bed? But I daresay they'd rather see him dead than rescued, so if they notice search parties combing every street, drawing inexorably closer, they're likely to stick a knife in him after all.

"Thus, the best plan is for two inconspicuous searchers, Titus here and myself" — no doubt I goggled in amazement — "to look for Constantine discreetly, while the three of you conceal his absence."

Bald, stoop-shouldered Ossius stepped closer to me. "Are you a Christian?" he asked.

"No, sir," I said. In fact, I was a Hidden One, a second-degree initiate of Mithras.

Ossius turned to Ragnachar. "Then he won't do," he said. "For that matter, neither will you. If we're forced to pin our hopes on only two men, I won't rely on pagans. When the Lord spoke to the Princeps, He told him that only under His sign can we conquer."

A maelstrom of emotions churned inside me. Resentment at the implication that religious differences or anything else could make me betray my commander. Frustration that the bigoted priest wouldn't allow me to seize the career-making chance of a lifetime. And, simultaneously, guilty relief at being passed over, because it would be a catastrophe to fail.

As it turned out, these feelings were beside the point. Ragnachar wanted me, and no one was going to thwart him. "You know I pray to Jesus," he said, "for all that you deny me communion. *I'll* bear His standard in this effort."

"How dare you claim that," Ossius said. "You, a filthy sorcerer."

The Frankish wizard glared. His jade eyes blazed. "Have it your way, then. Send your own picked men to search for Constantine, without the aid of my wicked conjurations. *If* you're willing to risk losing him. To see one of his rivals, Licinius or Maximin Daia, seize all we've won, resume the persecutions, and condemn your folk to slavery and death."

I felt a power throbbing in the wizard's stare and voice, something beyond both anger and the force of his ideas. Ossius tried and failed to hold his gaze, began to tremble.

"You mean," growled Crocus, "that if we don't do it your way, your way exactly, you won't lift a finger to help us?"

The Frank shrugged. "Either you trust me or you don't. If the latter, why would you even want my aid?"

"And I confess, I do trust you," said Ossius grudgingly. It was as if the force of Ragnachar's will had ground his obduracy into dust. "Despite your sins, you've always been loyal. What's more, any means, even your satanic arts, are justified to recover Constantine unharmed."

The sorcerer looked at Crocus and Optatianus. "Do you concur?" The Alemanni nodded grimly. For a moment, the poet seemed inclined to balk, but finally grimaced and shrugged. "Then leave us. I need privacy to work." The three ministers filed out like schoolboys dismissed by their *grammaticus*.

With their departure, the shadows in the room seemed to deepen, and I smelled the coppery scent of the dead guard's blood. The essential mystery of what had happened struck me anew. A chill oozed up my spine.

"Do you understand this?" I asked. "Who could spirit the Augustus out of the palace without being seen? There are sentries everywhere." Of course, one obvious possibility was that he'd been betrayed by some of his own troops, but I couldn't believe it. Why would men who'd fought faithfully sell out their commander now that the prize was won and everyone had been richly rewarded for his efforts?

"I *think* I know," said Ragnachar. "Now that those fools are gone, perhaps we can find out for certain. You be quiet." Breathing deeply, he stared into space.

I'd watched other magicians at work. All of them chanted incantations, brandished wands and amulets, or inscribed magic circles on the ground. Here there was none of that, just concentration. It was as if Ragnachar's powers were less a matter of lore and craft than of innate facility, a fundamental part of what he was.

My skin tingled and my ears ached, as though I were deep under water. A musky scent pervaded the air; if I hadn't known better, I might have imagined that some great beast had stalked into the room. Then a crouched, inhuman figure flickered into view atop the bed.

Like everyone else, I knew that men share the earth with all manner of strange beings: ghosts, naiads, satyrs, and the like. But it's one thing to understand that such things exist, and quite another to actually see one. I gasped; it took an effort not to recoil.

The creature was somewhat manlike, but with its shiny brown shell, eyestalks, and mandibles, it resembled a crab or an insect as well. It stood motionless for a moment, then sprang at Ragnachar.

I frantically reached for my sword, but there was no need. Ragnachar shouted, a ghastly sound like a tiger's cough, and the cry knocked the spirit down. It started to scramble up; the wizard drew another breath and it froze. "Free me," it said. "Free me or die."

"I'll free you after you do my bidding," Ragnachar replied.

"Who took the Augustus?"

"How would I know?" the creature said.

"You see everything that happens here. Tell, or I'll bind you into my boot and trample you with every step I take."

"Very well," said the spirit. "Behold." The lamps went out, plunging the room into darkness. Just enough light remained for me to see the man-crab fade, and the massive, bull-necked form of the sleeping Constantine appear in its place.

After an instant's bewilderment, I understood. It was a vision. Rather than describe what had happened, the spirit was showing us.

Three gaunt, pale men slipped out of nowhere, as if there were a portal hidden somewhere in the gloom. One stared through the doorway at the oblivious bodyguard, who fainted, his armor clanking as he hit the floor. The other two intruders seized the Princeps. He thrashed until one of them, a handsome fellow with curled hair, an ornately embroidered tunic, and several rings, caressed his brow with spidery fingers; then he lolled motionless again.

The first kidnapper moved to join his fellows, then whirled and dove on top of the guard instead. His snarl bared glistening fangs. His accomplices glowered impatiently while he ripped the sentry's neck and guzzled the spurting blood.

When he'd drunk his fill, he and his comrades picked up the Augustus as easily as they might have lifted a child, then vanished. A moment later, the lamps resumed shining. The man-crab reappeared.

"Who are they?" Ragnachar asked. "I know you know that too."

"Find out for yourself," the spirit said. "I obeyed you once, and now I'm leaving."

Ragnachar barked the magic word, if word it was, a second time, but to no avail. The creature seemed to twist out of sight, as if squirming into a hole in the air.

I had so many questions, I scarcely knew where to begin. "What *was* that thing?" I asked.

"A *lar*," said Ragnachar. "The spirit that dwells in this part of the palace."

"You're joking," I said, shocked. *Lares* were supposed to be kindly minor gods, genial household spirits who brought luck to the mortals living beside them. They were nothing like the hideous, hostile thing we'd just encountered.

Ragnachar sneered. "By no means. This is what you've bred and built a home for."

I didn't understand what he meant, but I supposed it didn't matter. There were more important things to think about. "And the kidnappers were" — I hesitated — "vampires?"

Ragnachar nodded. "What do you know about them?"

I shrugged. "They're dead. They subsist on blood. They sleep in their tombs by day—"

"Wrong. You Romans nurture them in your bosom, too. A number of them, ancillae and elders of the Ventrue, Lasombra, and Toreador clans, live in mansions, rich, powerful, shaping your Empire to suit themselves, revered even though some of their fellow aristocrats understand what manner of fiend they truly are."

I felt as if I were mad, dreaming, or the butt of an elaborate jest. But by conjuring the *lar*, Ragnachar had proved he truly did possess arcane wisdom. If *he* claimed that some of the Roman nobles were vampires, then I supposed it must be so. "Why would they abduct the Augustus? Were they on Maxentius's side?"

The wizard grimaced. "No. They aren't on any mortal's side. Ordinarily, I doubt they'd care who wore the purple, as long as they were confident they could have his ear at need. I think this concerns religion; Ossius, in his idiot way, is right about that much. Specifically, Constantine's refusal to sacrifice to Jupiter."

I frowned, trying to grasp the point. "I know he broke with

custom, but where was the harm?"

"The old faiths have no profound quarrel with inhuman beings, be they lamias, genii, centaurs, or whatever. Indeed, the vampires *preside* over certain cults; it's one of the sources of their influence. Christianity, on the other hand, abominates all such creatures as demons, and would gladly exterminate them if it could. And so, when the Augustus gave the leeches cause to fear that he intends to declare it the state religion, they moved against him. I was afraid something like this might happen, but I hoped that, surrounded by his followers, he'd be safe. Curse it!" He kicked a trunk, smashing in the front panel.

"Are you saying that you anticipated this threat, but didn't see fit to warn the rest of us?"

"We who penetrate the clandestine order of existence pay a heavy price. No one else, not even the lords to whom we swear allegiance, has a right to share our secrets, nor would most men wish to. The knowledge would disturb their slumber."

That answer didn't satisfy me, but I supposed that at this point, the reason for his reticence wasn't important either. "What will the vampires do with Constantine?"

"They'd relish torturing and killing a Princeps, but I suspect they have a subtler end in mind. With their powers, perhaps by forcing him to drink repeated draughts of their blood, they can enslave him, then release him to reign as their puppet. We have to free him before that happens.

"I'm a son of the western forests. There, I could track them easily, but my magic is weak among all these wretched walls. You saw how the *lar* defied me. And so I need you, to help me search by mundane methods."

At last I understood why I'd been chosen. I'd imagined that some occult sign had led Ragnachar to me, but it wasn't that at all. Rather, he was aware that, unlike the provincials and barbarians who made up the bulk of Constantine's retainers, I'd grown up in Rome. I was supposed to know my way around, even though, prior to the Augustus' triumphant entry, I hadn't laid eyes on the place in fifteen years.

Feigning a confidence I didn't feel, I said, "I'll do my best, sir. Let's consider how to proceed . . . ."

II.

We left the palace at first light. In place of my familiar *gladius*, I wore a longer, unpointed barbarian sword. According to Ragnachar, it was enchanted, and would slay creatures somewhat resistant to ordinary arms.

Perhaps I should have been daunted by the notion that I might require such a weapon, but I wasn't, much, not yet. I was still too busy worrying that I *wouldn't* need it, that our search would come to nothing.

Certainly, magnificent as it was, the view from the Palatine Hill did nothing to reassure me. Before me, still half shrouded in gloom, stood temples with brightly painted entablatures. The great bowls of the Circus Maximus, the Flavian Amphitheater, and lesser stadia. Domed baths. Theaters. Basilicae. Fora. Aqueducts snaking their way over gilded and red-tiled roofs. Block after block of houses, shops, and apartments. Provincial prejudice held that no lazy Roman would work when he could subsist on the dole, but still, I sensed movement in the streets, a horde of laborers pouring out of their homes to set about the business of the day.

How were two strangers — and I was little better than a stranger, whatever Ragnachar thought — supposed to locate a single captive in such a colossal, teeming maze? We'd be lucky to find our way back to the palace.

I tried to hearten myself with the reflection that matters could have been even worse. If I'd kidnapped Constantine, I might have taken him away from Rome, thus making it *absolutely* impossible for anyone to find him. But Ragnachar was certain the vampires hadn't. Apparently they only felt secure in cities. So at least we had a chance, however slim.

It would be tedious to recount every step of the search. For the initial hours, a summary will suffice:

Reasoning that some priest might know of a rival cult ruled by vampires, we spoke to servants of Jupiter Best and Greatest, Mars the Avenger, Bellona, Christ, Isis, Cybele, and Dionysus. None could help us. Before long I realized that the countless barbarians and provincials who'd relocated here had imported such a plethora of religions that no one could keep track of them all.

It was customary for nobles to receive their clients first thing in the morning, so we sought out the names of those who habitually delegated this chore to a subordinate. Alas, we soon had more than two men could investigate in a week. Evidently the late-night debauches of Rome were too enticing for any spirited gentleman to resist.

And, we asked policemen if they knew of a part of town where vampiric attacks occurred. None did, which actually came as no surprise. Why would a vampire bother to stalk strangers when he could take blood from a slave or a willing disciple?

Periodically, as we trudged from place to place, Ragnachar paused to interrogate the spirit lurking in a fountain, promenade, or wall. Sometimes I saw the ugly things, sometimes I only heard their hissing voices, and occasionally I couldn't sense them at all, which suited me fine. None disclosed any useful information.

With each failed inquiry, mundane or supernatural, Ragnachar grew surlier. His face reddened, and his jaw clenched. I was frustrated myself, but the rage I sensed building in him made my response seem puny.

And finally, as I'd begun to fear, he lost control.

We were pushing our way down a narrow, crowded street.

Several of the shopkeepers, a barber and a coppersmith among them, had expanded their operations into the thoroughfare, rendering it even more impassable. Indeed, the press was so tight that it reminded me of my nightmare, as did the unrelenting din. Beggars wailed, cataloging their misfortunes, and peddlers extolled their wares. A carpenter sawed and a stonecutter chiseled. Despite the congestion, the air seemed cold, for the towering tenements blocked the sun.

Because Ragnachar was a pace ahead of me, I saw what happened. A slave carrying a ten-gallon jug pivoted abruptly, rapping the back of the mage's skull with his burden. Ragnachar stumbled against the barber's chair. The razor nicked the customer's cheek, and he yelped. The barber, a fat man with hairy arms and a squint, cried, "Stupid barbarian!" and pushed the sorcerer away.

Ragnachar stood rigid, trembling, plainly trying to contain himself. An apple core, tossed from some upper-story window, dropped on his head.

The wizard seemed to swell. His strange eyes blazed. With a sweep of his arm, he tumbled the chair and customer into the mud, then grabbed the front of the barber's tunic and hoisted him into the air.

I was afraid he was going to kill him. I lunged forward, struggling through the frightened souls scurrying in the opposite direction. Grabbing Ragnachar's arm, I said, "Is this your idea of searching inconspicuously? Put him down."

He turned his head. For a moment, his expression remained so fierce that I thought he didn't recognize me. But then some of the wild light faded from his eyes. He threw the barber against a wall. I drew him on up the street, the wide-eyed, tight-packed throng somehow parting before us.

Turning a corner, I found a spacious plaza. It seemed as good a place as any for us to pause and collect ourselves. "Are you all right now?" I asked.

"Yes," he growled, but he still seemed half drunk on fury. "It's this place. You people live like a clot of maggots writhing inside a corpse."

I hadn't expected him to say that. I'd thought that, like me, he was simply vexed by our lack of progress. "Are you serious? I admit, I don't like the stink, the noise, or the crowding either. But still, this is the greatest city there's ever been. The model for every settlement in the Empire."

He spat. "More's the pity."

I realized it was a waste of time to sing the glories of Rome to him if he couldn't discern them for himself. His opinion didn't matter anyway, except insofar as it hindered our mission. "All right. You hate it here. I'm sure that once we recover the Princeps, he'll send you back to the frontier with a barrel of gold. But you have to control yourself till then."

"Yes. You're right. I didn't bring him this far —" The cool wind shifted, and a drumbeat of sound throbbed through the air. Ragnachar stood up straight. The glaze melted from his eyes. "What's that?"

At first, I didn't know, but when the noise recurred, I recognized it. "Spectators cheering in one of the arenas."

Ragnachar inhaled, his nostrils flaring. "So much blood."

"I suppose," I said. "People say the games we had in Gaul are nothing compared to the ones here."

"And if that's so, how could vampires resist them? It's the kind of entertainment they relish most."

"Except that the games are given during the day," I said, then grasped that that was the point. "We could look for nobles who hire fighters for private, nighttime affairs."

"Yes. Where do we begin?"

"Well, obviously, a number of the gladiatorial schools are represented at the games we're hearing. So let's start there." We strode up the street, following the noise.

It led us to the Flavian Amphitheater, a huge gray cylinder covered by a flapping wool awning. Up close, the clamor was constant. Even when the spectators weren't cheering, one heard a murmur like the hiss of surf, the trumpeting of elephants, the roars and howls of other beasts. Beneath the tiers of seats, vendors hawked sausages and skins of wine, Moorish women danced to the music of drums, cymbals, and castanets, and plump, painted boys minced about with buttocks bared. The air reeked of sweat, dung, leather, garlic, perfume, and the blood that Ragnachar had scented from afar.

As we entered the stadium, the crowd started laughing and jeering. Down in the ring, convicts wearing helmets with no eye slits were reeling about, slipping in the blood-spattered sand, and slashing wildly with their swords. I'd never been able to see the humor in such antics; I went to the games for displays of martial skill. Apparently Ragnachar shared my feelings, for his mouth twisted in disdain.

We descended a ramp into a warren of subterranean chambers. Here all was furious activity, everyone working frantically to make sure the action overhead never faltered. Animal handlers rolled a cage of jackals into an elevator. Stagehands hauled scenery. One fretful fellow chivvied a band of lanky Ethiopian spearmen along, his manner making it clear that he didn't speak their language, or they, his.

As was only to be expected, none of these busy people wanted to pause to answer questions. But even though Ragnachar and I couldn't reveal the urgency of our errand, we were imperial officers, and they had to accede to our authority.

Soon we came to a hulking, scar-faced Retiarius. He was stretching, breathing deeply, and glaring into space, preparing physically and mentally for the match to come. His net and trident lay on the bench beside him.

"We need a word with you," I said.

"Later."

"You might not be alive later," Ragnachar said. "And this is state business."

The gladiator's eyes flicked to his weapons. I tensed, because I'd seen soldiers work themselves into a similar state before a battle. He'd pumped himself full of belligerence, and it was quite possible that he'd direct it at us.

But he didn't. Ragnachar leered at him, and he almost seemed to flinch. "All right," he growled. "But make it fast. I'm on any second."

"We're looking for a noble who hosts private games," I said. "Invariably at night."

The Retiarius snorted. "Did you march in with Constantine? I can tell you're new in town. *Most* of the gentry hire gladiators any time they throw a supper party."

My heart sank. It seemed likely that Ragnachar and I had gone down another blind alley. Still, I persevered. "I don't mean on a small scale. Our man buys spectacles nearly as lavish as the ones here."

The Retiarius frowned. "You know, I think I did hear about something really fancy."

My pulse quickened. "Where?"

"At Quintus Marius' place. He's in the trade himself, runs a school for *bestiarii*. He used his own people for the animal acts, hired fighters from other promoters for the rest."

"Thank you," I said. "You'll be rewarded. Good luck today." Ragnachar and I rushed for the exit.

When we got outside the amphitheater, my elation died abruptly, because I saw that we'd been searching all day, and now the sun was going down. We couldn't allow the Augustus to languish in captivity a minute longer than necessary, not with his free will in jeopardy, so we'd have to investigate the school tonight, when our undead foes would be awake.

III.

Quintus' establishment stood atop a hill on the outskirts of the city. The school proper was a rectangular two-story building. Like the labyrinth beneath the amphitheater, it smelled of caged animals. The owner's spacious house was only a few yards away. One hoped it was generally upwind.

Surveying the scene from the cover of a copse of oaks, I shivered, and not solely because of the evening chill. If I hadn't felt particularly frightened of vampires that morning, I seemed to be making up for lost time now.

I wished that Ragnachar and I could have brought my century of stalwart *hastati* along. But we still didn't know if we were on the right track; our suspicion of Quintus was really only a guess. Until we discovered considerably more, we'd continue to work alone.

The wizard sniffed the air. "Do you see anyone?" he whispered.

"No."

"Nor do I. Come on." We rose and skulked toward the school. Such facilities routinely incorporated a prison, to discipline unruly gladiators and prevent the escape of slaves used to teach beasts to attack human beings. It seemed likely that if Constantine was here at all, his captors would hold him there.

Something rustled.

Ragnachar and I froze, peered about. I didn't spot anything threatening, and could tell he hadn't either.

I looked at him inquiringly. He nodded, and we moved on.

The sound repeated. I looked around again. I *still* didn't see anything, but I no longer doubted we were being stalked. The hairs on the back of my neck stood on end.

Despite my wariness, I barely glimpsed what happened next. A squat, long-armed shape hurtled out of the branches overhead. It landed on Ragnachar's shoulders, tumbling him to the ground.

I drew my barbarian sword. The way the thrashing combatants

were intertwined, I was afraid that any attack of mine would strike the wizard. But he seemed to be getting the worst of the fray, so I had to try. I thrust, and hit the creature — a malformed, black-furred dwarf or a manlike beast, in the dark I couldn't tell which — in the back.

Unfortunately, in my excitement I'd forgotten my new weapon lacked a point. But I'd drawn the little horror's attention. It sprang at me, knocked me down, and grappled me.

Though the size of a child, the creature was stronger than I, and it seemed that some lunatic had taught it to wrestle. In short order, it began to throttle me. Since the sword was useless in such close quarters, I fumbled for my *pugio*, the dagger sheathed at my side, but for some reason my groping hand couldn't find it.

Then something tore the monster off me. My vision blurry for want of air, I watched Ragnachar maul the brute about. It gibbered, bit, pummeled, then collapsed.

His back to me, the Frank stood gazing down at the creature for a moment. Making sure it was dead, I assumed. Then he came and squatted beside me. "Are you all right?" he asked.

"I think so," I wheezed. "Thanks to you. What was that thing? Another spirit?"

"No, a chimpanzee. An ape that lives in the jungles south of Egypt." It seemed odd that a barbarian from the West would know that. But apparently he knew all manner of things, including how to draw his sword, cut a foe to ribbons, and return it to its scabbard with such celerity that my pain-fogged eyes had never glimpsed the blade, and I supposed I ought to be glad he did. "But I think it was something more, too — a ghoul, a watch-beast nurtured on vampire blood — because it was too hard to kill."

Excitement washed away the worst of my pain. "Then we were right."

"To a point. We've uncovered a leech. We don't know that we've found the Princeps."

I sat up, listened. "I don't hear anyone coming, do you? Maybe no one inside heard the fight."

"Or ignored the sound if he did. They may be used to animals screeching."

I rose. "In that case, let's go on." I suppose that if I'd had good sense, the ghoul's attack would have made me even more apprehensive, but actually, the reverse was true. The same thing had happened to me in war. A skirmish with the enemy got my blood up, and then I was eager to fight in earnest.

Skirting the school graveyard, we made our way to a window, on the hunch that the shutters might be easier to force than one of the doors. Ragnachar worked his knife into the crack, then pried at the latch. After a second, it popped open.

I pulled the panels ajar and peeked through the gap. Inside was a dormitory where half a dozen slaves lay sleeping. We climbed in, then tiptoed past their pallets to the door.

The school was built around a courtyard containing a miniature arena. Seeking the prison, we skulked down a covered walkway, past the kitchen, the armory, and the cells of some of the *bestiarii*. I kept expecting someone to spot us. My mouth was dry.

In one sense, we were lucky: no one cried the alarm. But when we finally found the prison, nobody was there. Ragnachar glared at the shackles hanging empty, the door to the cramped solitary confinement cell standing open, then snatched a whip off a table. Straining, he snapped the wooden stock in two. I winced at the crack, but no one came to investigate.

"What now?" the sorcerer whispered when his spasm of anger had passed. "Search the rest of the place? I suppose they *could* be keeping him someplace else."

Somewhere outside the prison, a soft voice whimpered. "To Hades with this groping around," I said. "Let's persuade someone to direct us."

We crept out of the room and on to the next doorway.

Beyond it stood a stocky man with a twisted leg. From the quality of his crimson tunic, I inferred he was not only an ex-*bestiarius* but the school overseer. He held a long goad, and was teaching a leopard to rape a human female. The bony, grizzled object of the cat's attentions was wrapped in pungent, bloody rags. At a word from the trainer, she wriggled, feigning resistance, or perhaps, given the terror in her tear-streaked face, not feigning. The beast dug its dew claws into her shoulders and seized her neck in its jaws, immobilizing her.

"On my signal, take the man," Ragnachar said. "I'll handle the rest." He stared at the leopard. Suddenly it bit down and shook the woman, breaking her neck. Raked her with its hind paws. Blood flew. Cursing, the overseer lunged toward the animal, goad upraised. Ragnachar pointed.

I rather wished that he'd thought of a way to divert the trainer's attention without killing an innocent slave, but it was too late to fret about it now. We burst into the room. By the time the lame man realized what was happening, I had my *pugio* at his throat. "Shout and you're dead," I said.

Snarling, the leopard rounded on me. Ragnachar gazed into its amber eyes. Abandoning its aggressive posture, the cat dragged the woman's corpse into the corner and began to eat it. Bone crunched.

"What do you want?" stammered the overseer.

"Information about your bloodsucking master." His eyes widened in shock that I knew Quintus was a vampire. "In addition to his other peculiarities, he's a traitor. Where is he? Where's his prisoner?"

"I don't know!"

I dug the point of the dagger into the underside of his jaw. He rose on tiptoe in a futile attempt to escape the pain. "Evidently you're a traitor, too. I trust you're ready to pay the price."

"Please! Quintus disappeared last night, without telling anyone here where he was going. Two of the other vampires did the same; I know because their servants contacted us to ask if we knew anything about it. And that's *all* I know!"

I felt a sinking in the pit of my stomach. I rammed him headfirst into the wall. He fell in a heap.

Ragnachar gaped at me. "You *imbecile*! Why did you do that?"

"You don't want him telling anyone about our visit, do you?" I answered wearily. The lame man wouldn't wake for a long time, if, in fact, his broken skull and the leopard permitted him to wake at all.

"But we weren't done with him! Couldn't you tell he was lying?"

"I could tell he wasn't. What he said made too much sense. Think about it: if you were going to commit treason, would you want *anyone*, even your minions and slaves, to watch? Mightn't you and your fellow conspirators repair to some secret den removed from your usual haunts? You know, this is maddening. Against all likelihood, we discover who the enemy is, yet we're no farther ahead than we were before."

"We have to work out where they'd go to ground."

"Of course," I said sardonically. "And how do you propose — wait a minute."

"What? What have you thought of?"

"If they left their households and friends behind, they abandoned their usual blood supply. Wouldn't they need to get it somewhere else?"

"No. They can go a night or two without it."

"Even if they're bleeding themselves to drug the Augustus? Are you sure? And even assuming they can, *would* they? You saw how the one delayed their escape to feed on the guard. It didn't look as if they're much inclined to deny their cravings."

Ragnachar's luminous eyes narrowed thoughtfully. "You may be right. Perhaps they'll stalk prey in the streets tonight."

"I'd guess that even for vampires, hunting men can be a chancy, lengthy business. Would any of them care to risk absenting himself from the Augustus for hours at a time? Mightn't that hinder their work?"

The sorcerer grimaced. "First you say they'll hunt, now you say they won't."

"What I'm suggesting," I said, "is that they'd hunt in a secluded place where they could count on finding utterly helpless victims."

"Do you know of one?"

I smiled.

IV.

Since Rome was the greatest metropolis in the world, I supposed it stood to reason that it would have the biggest city dump, a vast field buried in rustling, rat-infested mounds of garbage. Ragnachar and I were hiding behind one such. No doubt the place had been picked over by slave takers earlier in the day, but even so, the wails of abandoned infants filled the air. Luckily, their parents tended to expose them in one particular section. Otherwise we couldn't have kept track of them all.

The sorcerer gripped my forearm. "The Toreador," he breathed.

Squinting against the darkness, I peered about. Finally I spotted a shadow gliding along. When it stepped into a patch of moonlight, I saw that it was the dandified vampire, the one with the exquisite tunic and the ringlets. He picked up a squalling baby and stroked its face. The child fell silent. The vampire stuffed it in a sack, then reached for another.

He gathered half a dozen in all. The sides of the bag rippled. Softly crooning a lullaby, he threw it over his shoulder, then turned and vanished back the way he'd come.

Fearful that he'd get away, I almost leapt up and went after him at once. But the idea was to let him lead us to the Princeps, and if we followed too close, he was likely to sense us.

I waited until his sweet song ended, then set out, Ragnachar skulking at my heels. Despite all efforts to move silently, trash rattled and crunched beneath my feet. Fortunately, even if the vampire heard, the noise didn't alarm him. Perhaps he thought it was the rats.

After what seemed a long time, he exited the dump and headed up a tenement-lined alley. I'd hoped that at this point the pursuit would get easier, since we'd no longer have to worry about losing him when he slipped behind a heap of refuse. But I soon realized that the way the passage twisted, we needed to stay as near as before, and without any towers of trash concealing us. I thanked Mithras that the way was inky dark.

Once, the vampire halted abruptly. Certain we'd been detected, I flattened myself against a wall, while Ragnachar jumped into a doorway. Then a yowl split the air. The monster opened his bag, reached inside, stroked the crying infant back into quiescence, then stalked on.

Another few steps and he rounded a corner. Ragnachar and I quickened our pace. By the time we peeked around the turn, the vampire was picking his way through the scree of rubble sloughed by a partially collapsed apartment house. He glanced warily about, then slipped through the entrance in the cracked brick wall.

Due to shoddy construction, such ruins were common in Rome. They were notorious death traps; people said even mice wouldn't venture inside. A good place to hide a prisoner, provided one was willing to run the risk of the rest of the structure falling on top of him.

I relaxed slightly. Even though I had yet to come face-to-face with a vampire, I felt that the worst was over, because Ragnachar and I had done as much as we meant to alone. Now he'd keep watch here while I fetched my men. Then we'd raid the place in force.

The wizard cursed.

Prompted by instinct, I raised my eyes. A white face shone in one of the tenement's upper-story windows. Despite distance and the gloom, I could feel that it was staring directly at us.

No time to go for reinforcements now. Ragnachar charged. Praying his magic was potent, I drew my sword and dashed after him. As we ran, his shoulders seemed to broaden, his limbs, to lengthen. I supposed it was only a trick of the shadows.

We plunged through the entry into a foyer. It wasn't *entirely* dark; the chinks and gaps produced by the ongoing deterioration admitted a hint of starlight. At the far end, rickety stairs ran up and down, while doors lined the walls on either side. Suddenly three of them flew open, and the enemy lunged out at us.

I should have stood fast, made sure I stayed close to my comrade, but, startled, I flinched. My heel caught on something and my backward step became a stumble. My shoulders slammed into a door. It fell off its hinges, dumping me inside an apartment.

A vampire dove at me. I rolled out from under him, scrambled up, swung my sword. Too slow. He tumbled out of its path and onto his feet.

If I'd been fighting a human, I would have killed him in the next few seconds. I had a blade and armor; my foe, his teeth and nails. I was dressed for battle, while he was encumbered with a toga. But I'd never seen anything so agile. Time and again, he slipped in close, nearly managing to kick my legs out from under me or fling his arms around me before I drove him back. And if I met his gaze, it made me dizzy.

Even more alarming than his prowess was his manifest monstrosity. This close, even in the dimness I could see more than pallor, gauntness, and fangs. I noticed a deeply cleft chin, ears that stuck out a bit, the mole on his cheek. It should have made him seem more of a man and less of a demon, but it didn't. No one beholding the quicksilver way he struck and dodged could have mistaken him for a mortal.

The tenement groaned as if our stamping about was going to shake it down. Somewhere, something began to snarl. I surmised that either one of the other vampires was doing it, or they'd unleashed some allied horror, another ghoul perhaps, on Ragnachar. Whichever, the ambient sounds were far from reassuring.

I tried to stave off panic with the grim reflection that at least this time I was remembering to cut, not stab. And eventually it did me some good.

Fast and vicious as my adversary was, he wasn't a trained fighter. He only had a few moves, and before long I learned them all. The next time he faked left, I met his spin in the opposite direction with a solid stroke to the ribs.

In other circumstances, his reaction would have been comical. Clearly believing the sword could do him little harm, he began to sneer. Then his mouth fell open, and his knees buckled.

I tore the weapon free and hacked at his head. He ducked, but I still sheared off an ear. The next blow maimed his shoulder.

He wheeled, raced out of the apartment, across the hall, and through a door on the other side. I pounded after him.

The foyer was empty. Ragnachar's half of the battle had moved elsewhere, though it was still audible, growls and all. Hoping he was winning, I scrambled on.

The door slammed in my face, knocking me on my ass. I jumped up and kicked it open.

Beyond was a larger apartment, a suite of rooms. The sack of infants lay discarded on the floor. The vampire was nowhere in sight.

I cursed. A mortal wounded as grievously as the bloodsucker would be incapacitated for weeks if he lived at all. But according to Ragnachar, the undead healed with unnatural speed. If I didn't want the fiend creeping up behind me, hale as if I'd never touched him, I'd have to find him and finish him off.

Senses straining, I stalked deeper into the apartment. A faint sheen of lamplight tinged the gloom ahead. Holding my breath, I crept toward it.

Stepping through an arch, I found myself in a spacious chamber where black cloths shrouded the windows. There were four beds, one occupied. The Augustus slept, no doubt entranced, but they'd bound and gagged him, too. A bloodstained lancet and chalice sat on the table by his head.

I stared stupidly, awed by the simple fact that I'd actually found him, and at that instant the vampire hurtled out of a shadowy alcove.

My luck held. I glimpsed movement from the corner of my eye, and reflex took over. I pivoted, slashed, and my sword bit deep. Blood drummed on the floor. Clutching his belly, the creature staggered back, and I went after him.

To my amazement, he evaded my next few strikes, circling around furniture to keep me away. But it didn't matter. He was slowing down, getting less steady on his feet, and couldn't release his stomach to attack lest his guts spill out. Perhaps even that terrible wound could have healed in time, for his other cuts had already begun to close, but not when he was exerting himself. As long as I kept him from reaching and threatening the Princeps, his destruction was assured.

"Please, stop!" he gasped. "You don't understand. What we've done is for the sake of *all* Rome, not merely ourselves."

Of course it is, I thought ironically. I cut at him. He twisted aside, a shade too slowly. The sword gashed his arm.

"It's true," he said. "We don't want to *harm* Constantine; he could be the strong, sane ruler the Empire desperately needs. But only if purged of his Christian predilections. Otherwise he'll complete the ruin his predecessors began."

I realized I was getting winded, and, if worst came to worst, might still have two more vampires to fight. Perhaps if I pretended I was willing to parley, my present opponent would relax his guard, giving me a chance to land a mortal blow. "What are you talking about?" I asked.

"The worship of the emperor is the cord that binds the state together. Abolish it, and the social order will fall apart. What's more, the Christians are fanatics. If granted ascendancy, they'll try to force their faith on everyone. The result will be *further* civil war, in an empire too debilitated to bear the strain. And after we've squandered what's left of our strength fighting one another, the barbarians will sweep across the borders and slaughter us all."

I was sorry I'd let him speak, because he was making a disquieting amount of sense. After all, thanks to Ossius, I'd tasted Christian intolerance myself, that very morning. And hadn't my dream seemed to link the religion with disaster? Perhaps some god had sent it as a warning. Trying my best to ignore my sudden misgivings, I struck at the vampire's head.

He jumped back. The sword missed the tip of his nose by an inch. "What's the matter with you?" he cried. "Are you blind, that you can't comprehend?"

"It's not my job to decide how the Empire should be governed," I said, pursuing him. I realized he'd disturbed me pretty badly; otherwise I wouldn't be wasting any more breath explaining myself. "It is my duty to keep anyone from turning the Princeps into a puppet."

The vampire dodged behind a lamp stand, then kicked it at me. I sidestepped. Crockery smashed, and burning oil splashed across the floor. "At least we want to make him a puppet for the right side. Where were you when your friend Ragnachar put that miserable vision of the cross in his head?"

The air seemed to turn colder. "I don't believe you. Why would he do that?"

"Because *he* knows Christianity can destroy Rome, and that's what he wants!" The vampire staggered. He momentarily lost his grip on his stomach, and a loop of intestine bulged out. "He hates us for our conquests and commerce, our cities and roads. If he could, he'd turn the earth back into primordial wilderness, with no hut standing, no field cleared, no beast tamed or fire burning anywhere."

I sprang, striking at the juncture of neck and shoulder. This time, he couldn't slip out of the way. The blow thudded home, and he went down.

"You're a glib liar," I said, raising my sword for a final stroke, "but ultimately, not convincing enough. No man, not even the rudest savage, would want to live in a world like that."

The vampire laughed, and choked on the gore welling up in his throat. "You're right," he croaked. "No *man* would. However, behold." Behind me, footsteps thumped, and something snarled. I pivoted, then froze.

The battle I'd been hearing had reeled through the door. The other two vampires, the Toreador and a tall, hook-nosed one, were fighting a creature so dreadful that it almost made them seem innocuous by comparison. Nine feet tall, it stood on two legs, but had a lupine head. Disdaining the sword at its side, it struck with foaming jaws and bloody claws, to such good effect that it was holding its own, which is to say that each side was inflicting terrible wounds on the other. Its green eyes blazed, the tattered remains of a checked cloak swirled about it, and the fur between its pointed ears was white with lime.

I knew what it was. I'd listened to campfire tales of such horrors in Britain and Gaul. Ragnachar was no sorcerer, or at least, not merely a sorcerer. He was a werewolf.

It looked as if my intervention could decide the melee, but I held back, not from terror now, though my bowels squirmed with it, but from confusion. If *everybody* was a demon intent on bewitching Constantine, then whom was I supposed to side with?

I might have hovered forever if something hadn't touched my

heel. My heart slamming in my breast, I whirled, but the fallen vampire wasn't attacking me. He simply wanted my attention. Looking up at me with a strange sympathy, he said, "Just choose. I know it's hard, but you have to do *something*."

"You're right," I said. I cut his head off, then attacked his fellows.

They were so busy with Ragnachar that they didn't see me coming, and together we made fairly short work of them. When they lay in pieces, the werewolf shrank back into human guise, or rather, most of him did. I noticed he kept the talons. "Thank you," he said. "Though I must say, you took your time jumping in."

"I had things to think about," I said. "My vampire claimed you'd enchanted the Augustus yourself, so you could make him destroy the Empire."

Ragnachar clasped a bite wound in his shoulder, trying to stanch the flow of blood. "I'm glad you didn't believe it."

"But I did. I've heard stories of werewolves fighting against the Legions, but never for them. What's more, I was there when your mask slipped, remember? I heard what you think of the world my people built."

The sorcerer smiled unpleasantly. "So you did. Why, then, did you help me?"

I shrugged. "Perhaps because you saved me from the chimpanzee, and we were comrades when we charged in here. Or because putting a dream in a man's head seems a gentler violation than snuffing out his will. Or maybe I thought it would be safer to wind up treating with one demon rather than three. By the Bull, I don't know myself. In the end, I acted on impulse. But it doesn't matter. The important thing was to free Constantine from all inhuman influences, and I've done that. You're leaving court."

Ragnachar lifted an eyebrow. "Indeed? Remember, my friend, only you know I'm a 'demon.' And even if there's only one of me, I daresay I could keep you from sharing the secret." In the gloom,

I couldn't be sure, but he seemed to be growing taller, his shadow lengthening on the wall.

I struggled to hide my fear. "Don't count on it," I said. "I imagine that, ordinarily, you're more than a match for any lone man. But now you're wounded, and I'm not. Besides which, I still have this excellent sword." I came on guard.

Ragnachar glared, trying to stare the backbone out of me. But, having seen him play the trick on others, somehow I managed to resist. At last he grinned. "Very well, have it your way. After all, *my* work is done, too. A Christian reigns, secure for the moment, in Rome. Constantine was drawn to the faith before I ever met him, and his partisanship will wax ever more blatant even after I'm gone. Ossius and his ilk will see to that. Why, then, should I fight you? So I can linger in this cesspit? Ha!" Casting off his shredded garments, dropping to all fours, he changed once more. In seconds, he'd become a huge gray wolf, which wheeled and trotted out the door.

Now that the struggle was over, I supposed I ought to feel jubilant. But I couldn't. Perhaps, by opposing the vampires, I truly had doomed the Empire. And even if I hadn't, the "clandestine order" I'd glimpsed, where monsters not only dwelt unsuspected in the heart of humanity but manipulated our monarchs and kingdoms like tokens on a game board, was so ghastly that I feared what I'd learned would haunt me forever.

Then my gaze fell on one of the vampire corpses, decaying already and raising a noxious stench, and my spirits began to lift.

Because it occurred to me that despite the demons' formidable powers, things hadn't worked out as they'd planned. Instead, the undead had perished, and Ragnachar had been driven out of Rome. Clearly, it wasn't easy for their kind to direct the course of human affairs. With knowledgeable mortals scheming against them, it might become impossible.

Mortals like me, for example. Surely, now that I'd rescued

the Princeps, I could prevail on him to make me an adviser. Then I'd help him steer the Empire in the right direction. If Christianity was the faith that vowed war on the likes of Ragnachar and Quintus, then it *should* be promoted. Hades, I'd embrace it myself. But Constantine mustn't foster it as past Augusti had supported the old religions. Whatever zealots urged, there'd be no vengeful persecution of pagans, and thus, with luck, we'd avoid unrest.

As I shook the Princeps awake, one of the newborns started to cry. Thus reminded of their presence, I resolved to make sure that some slave trader took them in. They were, after all, human beings, and in my present humor, that sufficed to make their survival seem important.

Richard Lee Byers is the author of the dark fantasy novels *Deathward*, *Fright Line*, *The Vampire's Apprentice*, *Dead Time*, and *Dark Fortune*, as well as the Young Adult horror books *Joy Ride*, *Warlock Games*, and *Party Till You Drop*. His short fiction has appeared in numerous magazines and anthologies. He lives in the Tampa Bay area, the setting for many of his stories, where he teaches Fiction Writing at Hillsborough Community College.

Touch The Flame

by K. Ken Johnston

Sometimes, it's frightening.
Sometimes the darkness is so strong
that you can feel it.
Power lying in a semi-dormant state,
hovering just out of reach —
in wait for one who can harness and wield it.
Power so tempting…
like the fire that calls out to the child to
touch its beautiful flame.

At the edges of my consciousness,
I see darkness, night, damp fog,
I see twisted trees...
they appear, to me, to be the skeletons of the dead
in a somber march.

I can feel the chill of the air,
and the anticipation —
the night drawing closer — whispering, commanding.
All the strength of evil and darkness,
all the fear...all the horror...
all the unspoken acts of unholiness, all beckon.

I tremble — power surging; pure energy —
still held within.

There is the unholy lust for blood,
and the drive of lust itself.
There is every dark design that has ever been,
time out of mind.

I am on the brink of final knowledge,
and then...
And then there is the light.
The light which binds the pagan.
The light which shackles the beast
and purges the soul.
The light, making all clean and pure,
burning through dark desires and lust,
burning the hand that dares to reach
for the reins that are the mastery of
the beast within
burning the thin filaments that bind the soul

to desire and its perversions.

I wonder at myself
I see my weakness, and wonder that I do not
plunge headlong into the depths of the abyss —
soul burning and bursting;
burning for a single, intense moment —
like the fire which draws the child to touch
its beautiful flame.

K. Ken Johnston is a member of Atlanta's sub-cultural elite, earning a living (yeah, right) as a performer, writer, musician, and director. He has appeared in low-budget horror films, improv comedy, Shakespeare productions, TV commercials and movies (gag), children's theatre, full-contact jousts, rock 'n' roll clubs, numerous SF conventions.

One of the Secret Masters

by Darrell Schweitzer

When we were both freshmen in high school, Frank Bellini had all the answers, and I believed everything he said. Einstein was wrong, and you really could go faster than light. Frank said so. Time machines were possible too. "Because time is relative!" he shouted again and again in the long and roundabout schoolyard argument we had over that one, the both of us equally passionate and equally ignorant of what such terms actually meant. But he won that one too, because he was Frank.

Later, when he was old enough to drive, it was the magic carburetor treatment that could give you two hundred miles to the gallon, and, of course, the gas pill, both of which had been suppressed (and here the dark theme entered our discourse) by the oil companies and the government. Frank was on to the extracurricular activities of the CIA. Once I asked him why they didn't silence him, if he knew so much, but he just hit me and wouldn't talk to me for a week.

He commanded authority. At fourteen he was already over six feet tall, all arms and legs but somehow massive, with a dark face like the business end of a hatchet and bushy eyebrows over dark, penetrating eyes. But it was more than sheer I-can-beat-you-up size. He was smart, articulate, forceful, imposing.

By the time we got to college, the relative sizes had evened out a little bit, I had acquired what I thought was an intellectual swagger of my own, and doubt began to creep in. My friends and I baited him, demanding news of the Conspiracy of the Week.

"It's the right-wing Texas oil billionaires. We're in Vietnam because they *own* Lyndon Johnson."

"And the Trilateral Commission?"

"Them too."

"Kennedys and Rockefellers?"

"They decide who gets to be a Kennedy or Rockefeller. It's all genetic engineering."

"They?"

Nonplussed, he produced his secret-identity card, showing him to be a high-ranking operative of the Technological Hierarchy to Enslave Mankind, otherwise known as T.H.E.M. "Whenever you hear that 'They' are behind something, that's because they are." And he smiled slyly, hinting at unfathomable depths of conspiracies within conspiracies, and no one could answer him back.

That was what made him so fascinating. He was always in *control*, either toying with you ("The Bavarian Illuminati killed JFK, you know....") or just peeling you off from reality like a stamp from an envelope.

Once he led me into the cavernous cellars below Mendel Hall, the main science building on the Villanova campus. Where he went, I followed, even as we passed old radiation-warning signs ("There used to be an atomic pile down here during the Fifties....") and went through several doors marked RESTRICTED AREA and DO NOT ENTER. Somehow, Frank's presence overruled all restrictions.

We hid behind a pile of boxes as a security guard went by, then descended a long, spiral staircase. A trapdoor led to a metal ladder. Down we climbed in almost total darkness, and groped our way along a dusty tunnel amid what felt like old electrical equipment until we emerged onto a metal catwalk overlooking a vast, underground chamber the likes of which you only see in movies about mad scientists. Television monitor screens flickered. Banks of lights blinked off and on in some arcane sequence, while computer-tape reels turned slowly, something bubbled and smoked in a vat, and electricity arced up a Jacob's Ladder for no discernible purpose.

"This is one of their installations," he whispered.

"Whose?"

He gagged me with his hand. "Quiet! You want to get us killed? *Theirs*. The Owners. The Secret Masters. They control everything from places like this."

I wriggled free, then watched in silence for several minutes. No one was there. Once or twice I thought I saw something move, but it was a trick of the light. The machinery ran itself. Things flicked on and off. A TV screen showed sweeping views of the campus overhead.

"So where *are* they?" I said as faintly as I could.

He pointed. "Invisible. The men in black you hear about covering up UFO evidence. The same ones. But invisible."

At that very moment, he had me so convinced that it didn't occur to me to ask how he could know they wore black if they were invisible. Instead, I meekly followed him back up to the "real" world, where the ROTC squad drilled on the lawn in front of Mendel Hall and other students sunbathed on the slopes around the edge of the field. I wasn't sure what I had seen, if anything. I wondered if Frank had slipped LSD into my lunch. No, more likely he was experimenting with mind-control.

"You seem like someone I can trust, Tom," he said at last. "So I'm going to confide something very important to you, something I've learned, that *They* don't want anyone to know. The more people who know it, the safer we are. It's the password."

"Huh?"

"Not '*huh*,' but *leotfatu*. It's Old English for 'light-bearer.' Remember that. It may save your life someday."

"What?"

He merely walked away, leaving me scratching my head and blinking in the bright sunlight.

———

Twenty years later, all this stopped being a joke. I had a writing teacher once who said that a story really begins when the protagonist gets hit in the head with a brick. The rest is prologue.

So, end of prologue. Enter the sudden brick.

I was sitting at home, watching, of all things, *The Simpsons*, when the phone rang.

"You'd better get that," my wife Marjorie called from the sewing room. "It's undoubtedly for you."

I hit the 'mute' button on the TV's remote and picked up the phone.

"Leotfatu," said the voice on the other end.

"Excuse me?"

The voice cleared its throat and spoke again, very precisely. "Leotfatu, the bearer of light."

I almost, repeat *almost*, hung up right there. It was a true turning point in my life, when what I did would determine all that followed after, although of course I couldn't know that at the time.

"Who is this?" I said.

"Tom? Tom Satterfield? It *has* to be the same one. I looked you up in the phone book. It's your old pal, Frank Bellini. I've got to talk with you. In private. There are some things you can't say over the phone, if you get my meaning."

I felt a certain irritation. Who the hell was he to barge into my hitherto placid life like this on a moment's notice, spinning webs of God only knew what sort of weirdness? I had hardly seen him since college. I remembered him as an amusing character and had told perhaps a few too many hilarious stories about him at parties, but he was no more my 'old pal' than I was the gullible disciple I had once been.

"Okay, Frank. Maybe we can get together for lunch over the weekend."

"No. This is *serious*. Right now. Tonight."

"Daddy?" came a new voice from the top of the stairs. I glanced up. There was Jane, my daughter, thumb in her mouth, teddy bear under one arm.

"What if I *can't?*" I whispered angrily into the phone.

"It's life and death. Yours and mine both, my friend."

I sighed. It was still impossible to contradict Frank Bellini. "Can you at least wait until ten, when everybody's in bed? My wife has to get up and teach tomorrow."

"All right. Ten. *I know where you are.*"

"You make that sound like a threat, Frank. I'm in the phone book, remember?"

"Leotfatu." He hung up.

My head was left spinning with the impact of that particular circumstantial brick, but duty called. I flicked off the TV, leaving Homer Simpson on his way to India on a quest for the meaning of life. If he achieved enlightenment, I was sure, he could explain it to me someday.

But now it was time to go upstairs, pull Jane's thumb out of her mouth and scold her for sucking it ("You wanna grow up to look like a walrus?"), then tuck her in and tell her a bedtime story, the kind I write for a living. ("Arnold!" "Okay, an adventure of Arnold the Vacuum Cleaner. What if he takes up bodybuilding? We'll call it *Sucking Iron!*")

Once I got her to sleep and checked on baby Charlie, then explained to Marjorie that an old school friend was stopping by ("He must be *quite* some friend if you let him come over at this time of night just because he calls you up."), it was surprisingly close to ten o'clock. All I could do was sit down in front of the silent TV and wait.

The doorbell rang at precisely ten.

Frank Bellini, when I admitted him, was not his old self. He looked like he needed a shave and a bath, and seemed...I grasp for the right word... shrunken: tall as ever, but stooped over, skeletally thin, his hairline back past his ears, his face beginning to sag. I kid myself that my own preternaturally adolescent appearance gives me the excuse to go on thinking in terms of *What am I going to be when I grow up?* instead of *What have I become?* But Frank had become a scarecrow left too long out in the wind and rain. There was no room for kidding around. He looked terrible.

"Leotfatu," he said softly.

"Hello, Frank. Come in."

It took a while to get him settled. He wandered aimlessly around the living room. I had to ask him several times before he handed me his hat and coat. When I came back from hanging them in the closet, he was still standing, paging through a copy of *Arnold on the Moon.* He held it up quizzically.

"Yep, my latest masterpiece. I'm afraid I've become disconcertingly normal over the years. I write kiddie books for a living."

When I finally got him settled into a chair, awkwardly, his knees and elbows jutting hugely, brought him coffee (into which he added something from a silver flask when he thought I wasn't looking), and pleasantly began the conversation by telling him a little about what I'd done with my life since college, it took only a couple of minutes for him to convince me that my old classmate was now hopelessly and totally insane.

He launched into a raging, literally frothing tirade about the CIA, the KGB, something called Tristero, men in black, deros from the Earth's core, mages, the blood-drinking Verbena, the Technocracy, the Cult of Ecstasy, Great Old Ones from Yuggoth, the Virtual Adepts, not to mention the assassinations of everybody from Abel onward. It was all part of a secret war going on all around us for awesomely high stakes, everything devolving into one grand Conspiracy whereby the entire history of the human race had been shaped and manipulated by forces we cannot control toward ends we cannot imagine.

"Have you ever heard of the *Nephandi?*" That name seemed to mean something special to him, beyond all the rest. He spoke it with obvious dread and something resembling reverence.

"Uh, no."

"'Uh, no.' Of course not. They're very good at concealing their existence. But they do exist. Make no mistake about it. They are agents of corruption and despair, servants of the Wyrm...about which, even now, I don't dare tell you more."

Several minutes of silence followed. I swallowed hard, unable to find something to reply.

"You know," he said finally, with a sigh, "a skeptic once argued that if you substitute Divine Providence for the Conspiracy and God for the Owners, it works out pretty much the same. I suppose it does. They've been around nearly as long."

It seemed that he'd embarked on a writing career of his own

after getting out of school, but with far less success than mine: a book linking the Kennedy Assassination with the Jupiter Effect; another about Lemurian adepts living secretly among us, working for good; several more exposing the "dirty secrets" of the Owners, how they had crippled FDR and finally killed him with an electronic beam, and later framed Nixon with Watergate when he caught on to their scheming. But Frank's *magnum opus* was something called *The New Liberty*, which actually contained a plan for freeing mankind. ("I wrote it when I discovered that the Libertarians had sold out, like everybody else.") None of these efforts had ever found a publisher. ("Suppressed, of course, by agents of the Conspiracy.") Somehow he'd scraped together enough to print a few hundred copies of *The New Liberty* himself, then hoofed to every bookstore in the Philadelphia area, more often laughed at than selling copies. But, still, the Conspiracy had been quick to act. The public storage facility where he kept the remaining copies promptly burned down.

"That's why I came to you, Tom," he said, for the first time in all the years I'd known him, *pleading*. For once, he wasn't in *control*, but still I could only listen.

"Tom, I came to you in desperation, because I may not have a lot of time. *I can see them now.*"

"Wait," I said, waving my hand in the air, plunging into the mirrored funhouse of amateur psychology, subsection Dealing With Lunatics. "Let me get this straight. You're seeing invisible men? Doesn't that make them, ah, not invisible anymore?"

"God damn you!" he screamed, pounding on the arm of his chair. "Don't make fun of me!"

Marjorie called down from the top of the stairs. I went halfway up and assured her that everything was all right.

"You sure?" she said.

"Yeah. Maybe we'll go out for a little while."

Frank had already retrieved his hat and coat from the closet.

"Good idea. I can't stay here very long. It wouldn't be safe for your wife or kids. I've been on the run for days. I've been sleeping out like a bum. I can't go to a hotel or even a bank machine—those cameras, you know."

I got my own coat. "How about I treat you to a late supper at Denny's?"

"No time. We have to go to my apartment. I want to see if you can find it. I *can't* anymore."

I let that pass until we were in the car. He hunched down in the seat. In the closed-in space of the car I could tell that he did indeed need a bath.

I drove for several minutes in silence before it occurred to me that I didn't know where we were going.

"You can't *find* it? You mean you've forgotten where you live?" I was beginning to feel a certain compassion for the man, but the sort that would make me drop him off at the nearest mental hospital.

"Sure, I know the *address*." He gave it to me. Somehow it didn't surprise me that I'd already been driving in precisely the right direction. "They've made my apartment *invisible*. To me at least. Some kind of force field that tunes me out. But maybe you can get in. Reality, as you know, is relative. It's like a stage set to them. They can take away pieces any time they want."

We came to a less-than-prosperous neighborhood. "But they—the little men—have become visible in the meantime."

"They're of quite normal stature. Otherwise you're right. The night of the fire, I happened to be pulling into the public storage lot just then. I don't know if it was a trick of the sodium-vapor lights on my windshield or what... maybe they want me to see them now. I can, anywhere. No, it can't be the windshield, because I still see them, and the car disappeared almost as soon as I got out of it that night. They're *everywhere*. And they really do wear black jumpsuits, and goggles of some kind, which let them see while they're invisible. Otherwise they'd be blind. The light would pass right through their retinas without reflecting."

I just let the tide of words wash over me, interrupting only for directions as I wove the car between derelict hulks, down an unlighted alley, all the while increasingly convinced that this *hadn't* been such a good idea after all.

But somehow Frank rallied some of the old magic. He commanded. I obeyed.

When we parked and got out, he stood up straight, holding his hand up for silence as he listened to something I couldn't hear. It was almost like old times. He led me into the darkness, then began to talk again. "The other day President Clinton was on TV, and there were no fewer than *five* guys in black suits with goggles standing behind him, mixed in with the Secret Service agents, which only figures, I guess. But *I got a picture of that*. I've been working on a new photographic technique for a long time. I can't explain now. Rays beyond the spectrum. It's got 'em really rattled. I can photograph them, even off the television. I've got *proof*. I can bring down the *entire* stinking operation by letting the world know what they are and where they are and how they may be destroyed. Their struggle with their enemies is reaching a climax, now. What they call the Great Crisis will soon be upon them —"

Just then something scurried across our path. Metal clanged. My heart jumped. I thought back to what I'd seen under Mendel Hall. What, if anything?

This time it was only a cat knocking over a trash can.

He paused at the base of a fire escape.

"Not very luxurious accommodations, I'm afraid. The only way you can get in this time of night is go up to the top and in through the outside door. Here's the key." He pressed it into my hand.

I peered up at the dark windows.

"So, what's the problem?"

"For you, I hope, nothing. But every time I try to go up, everything starts to twist around and I end up on the ground again. Like a Möbius strip. But if you can get the door open, that might stabilize the place long enough for me to get in and retrieve things I need, or at least for you to get the microfilm."

"What microfilm?" I put one foot on the bottom step.

"The pictures. Like I told you. If something happens to me, I need you to send copies of those photos to every newspaper in the world. It's the only protection I have now. Because of the crisis, they're vulnerable. They know it. I know it. They know I know it."

And he told me where to find the strip of microfilm.

"Right." I started up the fire escape, then turned back to him suddenly. "Is this dangerous? Aren't they up there searching your apartment *right now?*"

"I don't know. I don't think you'll be able to see them. So you should be okay. I *need* you to do this for me, Tom. Please?"

At that moment I felt as if I'd stepped through the Looking Glass with Frank Bellini as a kid, spent some years in Ga-Ga Land, then emerged into Reality after graduation, lived my life, begun a family and a career, only to discover now that *I was still inside the Looking Glass*, or had maybe even stepped through a second one. But I couldn't refuse. Not now. Not after we had come so far.

I climbed the stairs slowly, glancing down at Frank once or twice. He eagerly nodded, and motioned me on. I passed one dark, probably empty apartment, then another. On the third-floor landing, the fire escape seemed to shift and wobble a bit, and for one terrifying instant I almost lost Frank's key. It slipped from my hand and rattled on the grating. Somehow I was certain that if it fell through, I'd be caught in the Möebius strip too, and never find my way back.

Very carefully, I picked up the key, slipped it into the lock, and entered Frank Bellini's apartment.

I flicked on the light.

The place was a mess, much as I'd expected: heaps of newspapers, books, and dirty laundry everywhere, a half-eaten meal grown bearded with mold on the table. The most prominent decorations in what must have once been the living room were two posters thumbtacked to the walls, promos for books or movies, one with flying saucers descending over the Capitol in Washington, and lurid lettering: THEY ARE ALREADY HERE. The second poster showed the planet Earth in the crosshairs of a rifle sight: THE ULTIMATE ASSASSINATION.

The bookshelves were stuffed with paperbacks on conspiracies, ancient mysteries, flying saucers, witchcraft, and the like. Incongruously, among the paperbacks, exactly where Frank had described it, was a much older, fat book in crumbling leather. I opened it. Black-letter text, in Latin, something translated from the Arabic. I turned to page 725, as he'd told me, and right there, in the middle of a diagram for something called the Dhole Liturgy, was a tiny waxed-paper envelope with an even tinier black strip inside.

Something stirred in the kitchen. Quickly I snapped the book shut and dropped it on the junk-strewn couch. I slipped the envelope with the film into my coat pocket.

A cupboard door had come open in the kitchen. A dish lay broken on the floor.

Behind me, footsteps pattered across the living room. "Hey! Who's there? Frank, is that you?" It occurred to me that the footsteps had been entirely too light and nimble to be Frank's, and I had no business trying to confront burglars.

I made my way gingerly to the door, placing my hand stealthily on the doorknob. Just then the entire apartment shifted, jerking to one side in the periphery of my vision, the way the room starts to spin when you get suddenly and overwhelmingly drunk. But I wasn't drunk, and I saw clearly, distinctly, that the outlines of walls and ceiling, the doorway between the kitchen and the living room, were all twisting as if they were made out of rubber.

Then the lights went out.

"Daddy!" It was my daughter's voice, Jane, screaming. "Help me! Daddy!"

But she was safe at home, a good ten miles away.

"Daddy!"

I blundered into the darkened living room, crashing into and upsetting I didn't know or care what. Things fell, broke. "Let her go! Leave her out of this, for God's sake!"

Once again, footsteps pattered in the dark, a lot of them.

And someone grabbed me by my coat collar and whirled me around, and many hands shoved me out onto the landing, slamming the door behind me. I nearly tumbled over the railing, and hung there, gasping for breath, gazing down at the alley and my parked car.

There was no sign of Frank.

I pounded on the door. "Hey!"

But I couldn't get back in. I had no idea what had become of the key. The apartment remained dark and silent. I stood there for several minutes, helplessly, until all I could do was go meekly down the fire escape and get into the car. I found my way out onto Roosevelt Boulevard and just drove, trying to think, trying to convince myself that the easiest, safest explanation of all was that I was the one who was mad, that the return of Frank Bellini had occurred only in my own mind.

But by the time I got home, the police were already there. Marjorie rushed into my arms and explained, barely able to hold back tears, that Jane had been kidnapped. She'd called out once to me in the night, but by the time Marjorie had gotten into the kids' bedroom, Jane was gone, the window open, curtains billowing in the breeze.

I went upstairs like a man going to his own execution, defeated and resigned.

The bedroom was swarming with chattering cops, their radios squawking. Charlie, the baby, lay safe in his crib, screaming at the intruders. Marjorie hurried in and picked him up, but that didn't quiet him.

The police had a lot of questions, which resolved nothing. The best we could hope for was that my daughter would turn up somewhere, abandoned but unhurt, which sometimes happens, particularly with smaller children, if the kidnapper loses his nerve. Otherwise, we'd wait for a ransom demand.

I wanted to tell them what I thought. Morons. Imbeciles. But I held my peace, and it only figured that I discovered, as soon as they finally left, that they'd managed to overlook the most obvious clue of all.

On my daughter's night stand was a copy of *Arnold and the Crocodile*, a mutilated shell of a book, all the pages cut out, leaving only margins. Inside was Frank Bellini's apartment key, and drawn on the back board was the symbol of a lantern.

Light-bearer. Leotfatu.

———

Now this is the part of the story where the protagonist returns the brick to sender.

Let me tell you how it ends:

Marjorie wept in my arms for the longest time. She was afraid to go back upstairs, and eventually, fitfully, went to sleep in the chair in front of the TV downstairs, her hand resting on the baby's crib at her side.

The phone rang, once. I grabbed it before it could wake her and whispered.

"Frank." Not a question. I knew it would be he.

"Tom? What happened?"

"You mean you don't *know?*"

"No, I don't."

I had already thought long and hard about where I stood in all this, what was real, what was important, and what wasn't. Frank had a lot of nerve barging into my life like this, imposing such terror. If I accepted his paranoid world on its own terms, there was one and only one course left open to me.

I got out the microfilm and held it up to the light.

"I've figured it all out, Frank. Everything is going to be fine."

"Just like that?"

"No, *not just like that.* There are…certain things…that have to be done yet. Things I can't explain over the phone, if you catch my meaning. Look, I want you to come to your apartment this morning at five-thirty. You'll be able to get in. The door will be unlocked and I'll be waiting. We can beat this thing together, you and I."

"Oh Tom, that is *wonderful!* I knew I could rely on you."

"Just be there. Okay?"

It was now a little after three. I had enough time. I put the microfilm carefully into my wallet where I wouldn't lose it, turned out the lights, and kissed Marjorie gently on the cheek. She stirred and mumbled something in her sleep, but did not wake.

Outside, a cop sat in a patrol car. For an instant, I thought I saw someone in there with him, but when I looked again, he was alone. He made no move to stop me as I got into my own car and drove away. I don't think I was followed, not by the police anyway.

Once more, at the top of those rickety metal stairs, I slid the key into the apartment door.

They were waiting for me, inside, in the dark, as I knew they would be.

"Leotfatu," I said.

"Bearer of the eternal light," they all whispered back, in unison.

Then I sat as directed in the chair by Frank's kitchen table, while the men in black placed some kind of helmet all the way over my head. I remained motionless in the darkness for a long time, while electricity hummed and pins pricked my scalp. Slowly, waking dreams came to me, memories of lives not my own, of other times and places, from the collective consciousness of the Enlightened Ones. Revealed to me were the Mysteries of the Wyrm, the doings of the Hollow Ones, the menace of the insane Marauders, and the tenacity of our foes within the Technocracy. I knew so many things Frank had only dared speculate about. I understood how petty—though still dangerous—his lifetime of research and investigation had been, and why, at the advent of the Great Crisis, such meddling could not be tolerated, for all he somewhat exaggerated his ability to "bring down" our entire operation. It was all clear to me: the rise and fall of nations, the deaths of kings, why knowledge suddenly appeared when the time seemed right and was ruthlessly suppressed otherwise. I understood, too, how potential initiates to the Brotherhood slept among mankind, unaware of their nature and destiny, directed and manipulated as I had been ever since I was fourteen years old and met Frank Bellini for the first time. My life was a script, written by others wiser than I, acted, directed, and produced until I came to this ultimate test, which would lead either to death or to true awakening. Nothing had been left to chance. To everything, a purpose under heaven.

When the helmet was removed, I awoke. I gave my brethren the microfilm.

And in the first gray of morning twilight, at precisely five-thirty, I heard Frank Bellini climb up the fire escape to the landing outside. He hesitated for several minutes, touching and turning the doorknob, unable to believe that the apartment was solid and visible to him again.

He called out my name. I did not answer him.

When he entered and flicked on the light, he saw me seated on his living-room couch with my daughter Jane asleep on pillows by my side. I wore my regulation black jumpsuit, but with my goggles up on the top of my head, because I was not invisible.

"Tom?"

I raised my silencer-equipped pistol.

"It's all true, Frank."

The look on his face was indescribable. I think it was a kind of joy.

The instant before I killed him, he must have known that all the ambiguity had ended, that this was no longer a matter of shadows and fleetingly glimpsed figures. He had come, at the very last, in the clear light, face-to-face with one of the Secret Masters.

Darrell Schweitzer is forty-one and the editor of *Weird Tales* (which changes its name to *Worlds of Fantasy & Horror* next issue), for which he and George Scithers shared a World Fantasy Award in 1992. He has published about 200 stories, three story collections and two novels, *The White Isle* and *The Shattered Goddess*. Darrell has also written a lot of non-fiction, reviews, criticism, interviews and columns. His most recent work is pure scholarship: *H.P. Lovecraft: A Bibliography*, in collaboration with S.T. Joshi.

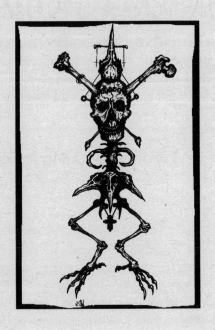

The Bone Woman

by Brian Herbert and Marie Landis

At midnight someone knocked on the Bone Woman's door. She pressed her shapely body into a shadowed corner of her house and didn't answer.

Too early for the delivery.

Still, she trembled with anticipation.

Was it one of the neighbors? They never spoke to her, but the night winds carried their voices. The voices said they didn't like her weather-beaten beach shack. It reduced the property values of their expensive homes. And her appearance was questionable—hair too long, too black, and her dark skin obviously not a hard-earned tan, but more the sort caused by genetic insufficiency.

"Whatever she is, she's not one of us," they whispered.

Sometimes the Bone Woman wished her hearing was not so acute, that she could drown their words in the roar of the surf. Sometimes she wished she was more human.

Sand drifted in and out beneath the bottom edge of the Bone Woman's front door and piled in the corners of her living room. Strange sculptures rose from these small sand dunes: animal bones and human bones fused into unusual animal shapes and coated with plaster and white resin. Her creations. Some were horned and winged and poised to take flight while others crouched deep in their beds of sand as though recently hatched from an alien egg.

A tall sculpture stood among them, created from the bones of a man named Michael, her last lover. The one she'd loved best. But he was long dead, and now she had neither lover nor friend. What kind of life was this? She smiled ruefully at her choice of words.

She, who was not quite alive.

The knocking persisted. She ignored it and spoke to the sculpture.

"Michael, do you know how difficult it was waiting until your flesh decomposed and your bones were ready to be sculpted? I took your pieces from the grave and bathed them and tried to recreate you."

A deep wail escaped her lips. "My grandmother, a mage, taught me how to alter reality. I am a Dreamspeaker, a shaman of great potency. I can divine the secrets of the spirit but cannot give you life. Shall I tell you again why I failed you, how I became what I am?"

As always, the bones did not answer.

Tabitta closed her eyes, reversed time, and forced her past to live again.

She stood within a grove of vines that coiled above her head like a roof of green serpents. Moisture dripped from their tendrils, fell on the dark skin of her shoulders and trickled across her full breasts.

A few feet away a man smiled at her from beneath the overhang of a wide-brimmed hat. The features she could see were handsome but twisted, his skin moon-white.

"Go with him," her parents ordered. "We owe him money."

"You will call me Colbert," the pale man said to Tabitta. "I am childe of Baron Dieudonne, who is descendant of Louis XIV. It is an honor to live in his house. How old are you, girl?"

"Fifteen," her father answered. "A good age."

"No!" pleaded Tabitta.

But Colbert's hands gripped her arms tightly, and she felt their strength and cruelty as he pulled her away from her parents forever.

Daily, Colbert fed her small or large doses of affection and cruelty. He seduced her with words spoken in a voice as soft as velvet and filled with promises. When finally he placed his lips against her throat and raked his teeth across its smooth dark surface, she no longer feared him but drowned in the sharp pain-pleasure of his bite.

"I want to be part of your flesh," she whispered as she sank into the oblivion they shared.

"You shall," said Colbert. He cut a small slit on his wrist and held it to her mouth. She drank until life flooded her body again. And then she slept.

Upon awakening in that long-ago time, she stared into the face of a stranger. A man with elegant clothes and eyes as cold and hard as black ice. Baron Dieudonne?

"I warned you, Colbert," shouted the stranger. "No vampire shall sire another without permission of his elder."

Colbert leaped from the bed. "Forgive me, sire. The girl is a witch and made me forget our traditions."

The Baron signaled two shadowy figures. "Kindred! Take them to the forest."

Shivering with cold and fear, Tabitta watched as the Kindred stuffed wood around Colbert's bound body and struck the match that would set him afire.

"One of the few ways to kill a vampire," said the Baron. He held Tabitta in a hard embrace, allowing her no choice but to stare in the direction of that frightful bonfire.

"Keep your eyes open," he warned, "or I'll make your death more painful than his."

She listened to Colbert's agony slash the air, his screams an endless cacophony until he was no more than a blackened lump of charcoal sizzling on the ground.

"Beast!" she screamed.

"Beast I am," the Baron laughed, "of the vampire clan Nosferatu. Nosferatu take only the most depraved for our progeny. Colbert is my progeny, and now you are his!"

Tabitta's anger rose bitter as bile and she concentrated, as her grandmother had taught her, stirring the ashes with her rage. They swirled upward, enveloping the Kindred in a noxious gray cloud. Those who had participated in the burning writhed on the ground with pain.

"Release them, witch!" shouted the Baron. "And I'll let you go."

"I hate you...." Tabitta cried as she ran from the Baron and the smoldering obscenity that had been her lover.

She returned her spirit to present time, her voice still echoing the words she'd spoken over two hundred years before. "I hate you, Baron. I'll always hate you."

Knocking...persistent knocking. She closed her ears to the sound.

"I am part Nosferatu," she said to the sculpture that was Michael. "As much a beast as Colbert and the Baron. Humans are so fragile, their circulatory systems ineffectively pumping blood through a maze of clogged arteries. It almost seems criminal to siphon off any of their juices. Yet the Hunger can be overwhelming."

Drowning in loneliness, she howled her grief. "I need flesh and blood, not bones and memories!"

Again she became conscious of the knocking at her door. Perhaps it was the blood delivery. But so early?

She took a chance and opened the door. Her eyes glittered red in the darkness like an animal's, and her senses were alert to each detail of the being in front of her. The creature on her doorstep was a heavyset, bleary-eyed human. She could smell his cruelty and something else. A sickness inside. Heart? Yes. It was pumping with difficulty. The sound of his moving blood was almost more than she could bear.

With a foolish grin, he extended a wine bottle.

"What do you want?" she asked.

"I'm your neighbor." His voice was well modulated but insincere. "Thought we should get acquainted. Good wine, two hundred bucks a bottle."

"You've wasted your time and money."

He swayed on uncertain legs, his face twisted into a scowl. "Look. I came to tell you something for your own good." He held the bottle in a gesture of salute. "You're a fine-looking woman. Some men don't like dark skin, but I prefer it."

"How nice for you," she purred, "deciding which slice of the bird you'd like to eat."

"No need to get snarly. I came in a friendly way. You've got some enemies you ought to know about. I've watched you walking the beach swinging those long legs. A woman like you needs protection." Forcing himself through the door, he put an arm around her waist. "It's about your house."

He ran fingers along her spine.

I could snap his neck with one hand, thought Tabitta, but she wanted to listen to his blood pumping. And his story might be important.

The delivery, where was the blood delivery? The Hunger came

over her suddenly, welling up unbidden and voracious. She fought it back. "What do they call you?" she asked softly.

"Ted."

"Who are my enemies?"

He smirked. "Be nice to me, and I'll tell you."

He pressed his heavy body against hers, placed a large hand inside the neckline of her silk dress. She removed his hand gently.

"First, tell me about the neighbors," she said.

"They plan to condemn your property...get the zoning people after you. Lawyers will take care of the rest. That's enough conversation." He tore her dress, pushed her toward the floor.

Tabitta stopped time.

A few moments was all she could manage. But any kind of dominance over the physical world was important to a mage, and it was enough time for her to turn her bone sculptures into flying, pouncing, nasty little beasts. She activated Michael, so thin and white, clattering around the room with threatening motions, placing his long, bony hands on her assailant's throat, raking his nails lightly across the jugular.

It was amusing to watch the man thrashing about the room clutching his chest, gasping for air and finally collapsing to the floor.

She bent to examine him. Stupid human, did he think the information he'd furnished meant she was bought and paid for? She'd spun a little magic, only intending to frighten him. But now he was breathing with difficulty.

"I didn't mean this to happen," she said. "But you were not a gentleman. Not at all."

She stared into his glazed eyes and saw his thoughts as clearly as if she were watching a stage play. His lust had turned to fear. Heart fibrillation!

She touched the side of his throat, detected no pulse. Dead now, but still slightly warm to the touch. Tabitta leaned over and bit his carotid artery, sucking hard to bring the congealing blood into her mouth. Already the elixir was losing its freshness but was still delicious, and she groaned with pleasure.

Two hours later she pressed her fists hard against his body, kneaded back and forth like a baker making pie crust. When she felt his ribs crack, she manipulated them into a flattened position. Then she folded him up neatly, carried him upstairs to her workshop and placed him inside a large, metal drawer beside other bones she'd collected. The bones of dead lovers.

Satiated, she tore off her ripped and bloody dress, walked naked outside, into the darkness. The beast within had spoken, but she'd only given in to the frenzy after the human died. Was it so wrong to take a dead man's blood, when one was hungry and the blood delivery was late?

Only humans would criticize her, like the neighbors who wanted to condemn her house.

It's not the house they want, she thought. It's my existence. I belong nowhere. Not with humans, not with mages, not with vampires.

She turned and looked back at her home teetering on the edge of the Pacific Ocean like upended debris washed ashore by the tides. The glass was missing from an upstairs window frame, which made the house appear to be staring at the world with a Cyclopean eye. A dead eye. As dead as I am, she thought.

The pulse of the ocean increased, grew louder. Waves crashed and churned into a white froth against the sand. Ahead, Tabitta saw a small figure, a female shape moving with a severe limp. What was she doing? Wading in the ocean? Should she warn the woman that the ocean was dangerous at night? On the other hand, what did she owe humans?

Still, she couldn't stand by and watch someone drown. After all, she wasn't a total beast, despite certain necessary acts. Remnants of her original humanity remained.

She increased her pace and began to run. Wet sand splattered across her legs, and she took a giant leap, sailed with the ocean wind and landed close to the place she'd seen the figure.

The female stood with her back to the shoreline, her dress trailing through the foaming water, her blond hair tangled like seaweed and her arms hanging limply at her sides in a gesture of apathy. She seemed unaware, detached. When she moved forward into deeper waters, the wind tore at her hair and the waves shook her thin body, as if she were a rag doll.

"Come back!" Tabitta screamed. "You'll drown!"

A great wave curled over the figure's head and broke into a rain of white foam. Tabitta dived into the breaking water, pushing against its force with her own. Struggling with the ocean for possession of their mutual prize, she was finally able to seize the female around the waist.

When she carried the limp body onto the beach and out of the ocean's grasp, she saw that this was a young girl, maybe sixteen or seventeen. Her eyes were closed as though in sleep, and her body was cold as the sea. Something odd. Body too thin? Heartbeat…couldn't detect it yet.

Tabitta carried the girl to the beach shack and placed her in the dark, soft cocoon that served as Tabitta's own bed.

The girl's eyes remained shut, but she sighed. "Where am I?"

"In my house, in my bed. What were you trying to do, drown yourself?"

"I can't drown," whispered the girl. "But I can sink. I can sink until I reach the bottom of the ocean and the fishes eat me."

She opened her eyes.

"You're a vampire," said Tabitta, staring at the red glow in the girl's pupils.

"And so are you," answered the girl. "I've been one since a month ago. My lover's sire didn't approve of me. I'm imperfect, crippled." She pulled up her wet dress. One leg was badly shriveled. It lay against the other like a small twisted branch.

"I've been running from the Kindred," the girl continued. "Hiding in public places. Taverns, all-night cafeterias."

"You're very pretty. I'm surprised some man didn't take advantage of you. What's your name? And where do you go during the daylight hours?"

"I'm Alicia. The street people let me crawl inside their cardboard boxes and under their blankets. They know what it means to be an outcast. But the Kindred will find me sooner or later. They'll kill me and anyone who tries to help me. I'm a monster. Look at me! A crippled monster."

"If you're a monster, so am I," said Tabitta. "There are many of us around. Who pursues you?"

"My lover's sire, Baron Dieudonne."

"I know him well," Tabitta said. "He's Nosferatu. Not as bad as the Sabbat Clan. But bad enough."

"I've put you in danger."

"Let me decide that," said Tabitta. "I think we can help each other. We are, in a manner of speaking, cousins. My sire was also the progeny of Dieudonne. Do you know much about the Baron?"

"Only what my lover told me."

"Dieudonne means 'God-given,' but God has little to do with the Baron. He is said to be the bastard of Louis XIV, a king who declared he was ordained by God, that he had absolute power and was free to do anything he desired. Dieudonne was the king's birth name."

"What does he have to do with the Baron?"

"Hear me before you ask. During his reign, Louis XIV decreed that all prostitutes should have their noses and ears cut off, if they cohabited with soldiers. What happened to those poor women? Disease, death? Males didn't fare much better. They were chained to galley boats, punished for crimes they hadn't committed. Homosexuals were put to death and peasants flogged for fun while Louis ruled.

"The illegitimate offspring of the king, our Baron, became a vampire while bedding one of the Kindred. It's no coincidence that the Baron possesses the disagreeable qualities of his birth father, Louis."

"Are we any better?" asked Alicia. "Am I destined to spend the rest of eternity killing, so that I may live?"

"We're no better or worse than humans. With the exception of Dieudonne."

"I've heard the Baron has developed a blood supply that carries no disease."

Tabitta nodded. "True. I buy it from him, or I was buying it from him. The blood doesn't satisfy the Hunger completely, but it works passably well. Have you fed since your escape?"

"Sucked on a few meat scraps."

In the small hours of the night, Tabitta lay beside Alicia. What to do with this girl? There were probably more like her out there, digging in the woods for mice or insects, trying to hang on to what little life they had. Had she, Tabitta, been so preoccupied with her own loneliness that she hadn't paid attention to anything else? Had she lost all her humanity?

The thick, stifling odor of smoke wakened her a short time later. The room was warm, too warm, and sound crackled and snapped in the lower half of the house. Tabitta crawled from bed and opened the door to the hallway. Flames and smoke greeted her. She slammed the door shut.

"Wake up!" she cried to the girl. "We've got to get out of here!"

From the beach, they watched fire consume the house, a great red demon swallowing walls and floors and ceilings and all that lay within.

She put an arm around Alicia's shoulder. "I have a motel room I keep for various purposes. We can go there. But first we'll steal something to wear. Before the sun rises, we'll visit the Baron. You need blood. He won't hurt you while I'm with you."

Miles away, in the quiet of a darkened industrial building, Baron Dieudonne flipped a switch. Along the conveyor belt empty plastic containers began to move, stopping and starting, stopping and starting like a line of dancers moving in rhythm to the whoosh and clatter of the machinery. The sounds brought Dieudonne deep satisfaction. During the day, the containers would be filled with milk and on their way to the packing and shipping room. At night his vampire crew filled similar containers with blood.

Located in Torrance, California, the bottling plant was one of the largest of its kind and head office for a worldwide organization of like facilities. Ownership had made the Baron acceptable in the human world.

At the rear of the building, in a small laboratory, a researcher tinkered with something other than milk. Blood! Blood from cows and humans in a marvelous genetic mixture that provided all that was needed by the Kindred. An endless supply of uncontaminated blood.

A human, Gene Spratt, was his scientific researcher, the genius who'd created the modern blood formula—far superior to the Baron's own early mixtures. Although he didn't understand the complexity of Spratt's discovery, he didn't worry. Spratt took care of such things. Spratt might not be a vampire, but in a sense he'd renounced his humanity in order to have the lab and the money to run it.

Out of necessity, since he relied on Spratt so much, the Baron never felt a strong desire to draw the human's blood. He had other sources. Maybe one day when the researcher was old and to the limit of human mortality, he would give Spratt the dark gift. But only after he, Dieudonne, understood all the details of the genetic technology.

Humans, if they'd known, might call Spratt a collaborator. Dieudonne didn't respect him any more than they might, but he was a pragmatist, understood it was necessary to pay for such people—necessary, if distasteful.

He'd understood this centuries before, and understood it now that he was a wealthy businessman applauded for his desire to benefit mankind. Television and tabloids wrote accolades about his financial contributions to various charities, about his humble nature that kept him from attending public functions honoring his generosity. How he donated free milk to underprivileged children.

Milk! His laughter carried across the plant, over the sounds of machinery. Milk made him money, and money paid for a huge cattle ranch near Santa Barbara that offered him the privacy he needed.

Bored momentarily with the equipment, he turned off the machinery and walked to the lab. The door was ajar. Spratt was working overtime tonight.

"Time for a talk," Dieudonne said.

The researcher, a gaunt young human with weak eyes, squinted at his employer. "Yes, sir, what do you need?"

"Don't you ever relax? Wouldn't you like to have some intelligent conversation?" the Baron asked.

"I'm not much of a talker."

"*I* intend to do the talking! In the old days, I was forced to roam the streets, searching for companionship, eternally in quest of fresh human blood. But now I have you to keep me company. And I have the blood." He pounded a tabletop. "The best there is. Still, despite all the progress I've made, there are a few vampires who don't like the taste of this processed blood. Not fresh enough, they claim. Too many additives. Anything we can do about that? Put on new labels that make them think they're getting something different? Go to work on it."

"That wouldn't be ethical."

"Ethical? You're working for me, don't forget that! Maybe

the blood doesn't taste as good as fresh-pumped, but we'll brainwash the Kindred."

"But…"

The Baron wagged a finger under Spratt's nose. "I've come a long way. The Kindred used to take advantage of young females because they were easy targets. Think about how many times you've read about young girls disappearing as a result of human assaults and kidnappings. Sometimes at the hands of boyfriends or husbands and sometimes by serial killers. Vampires don't do that anymore."

Dieudonne smiled inwardly. Of course, there were exceptions. Like himself. He was an elder and had the right to do as he pleased. Over the years, he'd invited many young females to his ranch, usually transients or hitchhikers on their way to nowhere. They came for entertainment and a good meal. A good meal. What a joke.

He felt no guilt. There were humans who did worse to their female companions.

No matter his public facade, the old ways were best!

Again, he turned his attention to Spratt. "This facility is based on an operation I set up over a century ago, the first vampire blood bank in London. It's still operating. Of course, in the old days we didn't have all your scientific know-how. The facility, ostensibly a brewery at the time, furnished dark green beer bottles filled with blood. We distributed them by beer trucks down alleys to decaying apartments where the Kindred lived. Ah, those were halcyon days. Now I prefer the pace of life in California, though I travel regularly to inspect my other facilities."

"You do a good job," said Spratt.

"Indeed I do. I developed the modern system of sustenance delivery out of necessity, to reduce the open conflict that for centuries threatened to break out between vampires and humans. The elders no longer have to add new members to Kindred society at the pace once thought necessary. Progeny can be added slowly and carefully, utilizing higher standards of selection. After all, the Kindred are an elite society. We, the undead, do our business best when humans don't expect us to be present, when humans are not thinking of vampires at all. I realize that legends of vampires remain in human society. But for the most part, we are shadowy figures, present but not present. Elusive targets. Only a handful of humans are aware of our presence, humans such as you. Trustworthy humans."

Spratt moved restlessly on his stool, began to remove his lab coat. "Sorry. I have to leave. Have to get up early."

The Baron examined his watch. "See that you're here on time. You have about four hours to sleep."

He bid Spratt goodnight and walked toward his office. Things were going smoothly, except for the witch, Tabitta. A burr in his side. And some of the elders...but he could handle them as well as he did ordinary Kindred. During the past two years he'd begun to furnish the elders with a special blood mixture. Richer and more rewarding than the one ordinary vampires received, he'd told them. Blood that would give them back their humanity within a hundred years. All vampires longed for their lost humanity. So he gave the elders, who missed most what they had lost, the special blood, and they rewarded him with favors.

Dieudonne opened the door to his office, sat at the computer and gave it instructions to continue reduction of blood deliveries to Tabitta. Not enough to send her into a feeding frenzy, just enough to let her know his displeasure.

He walked back into the bottling facility, and realized he had company.

The witch Tabitta stood before him. And next to her, the one he'd been searching for...the miserable outcast who'd escaped and never received proper punishment.

"Alicia," he said. "How pleasant to see you again! I've been looking for you." He extended his hand.

"Don't touch her," warned Tabitta. "She's under my care."

"And that's supposed to frighten me?"

"When I last saw you, I didn't understand the full extent of my powers. Now I do. I've come to demand justice for this poor girl. As vampires living in a civilized world, we shouldn't be killing ourselves off. There aren't enough of us to spare."

"She's not one of us. She wasn't invited."

"Your 'son' decided to convert her."

"That sounds familiar." The Baron's smile was sardonic. "Didn't something like that happen to you a couple of centuries back?"

"I didn't come here to discuss my history. I came to find out why I haven't been receiving the blood deliveries I've paid for. What are you up to? New ways to cheat us?"

"I perform a service for my kind. All Kindred know the sacrifices I've made in order to obtain fresh human blood for them. AIDS and hepatitis and other diseases have grown rampant. Humans aren't donating blood like they used to. I've overcome such obstacles! Made a breakthrough that benefits humans as well as vampires."

"You're a clever bastard," Tabitta answered. "I'll give you that much. But I ask again. What about this poor girl?"

Dieudonne glared. "Our Traditions must be obeyed."

"Our cruelties is what you mean."

"Cruelties? All over the world my political intervention has led to laws mandating that human adults give blood at regular intervals. To save them from killer diseases. For humanitarian purposes...for research. For all of us!"

"While you're blathering about your good deeds, I need blood for this girl. And don't forget I want the blood I've paid for."

"And what if I cut you off? Locally, I have twenty-two Kindred at my disposal. Shall I bring them forth? Care to test your feeble magic against our combined strength?"

Tabitta considered his words carefully. He looked as imposing as always, dressed in a black silk suit and red velvet vest, the picture of a ruler whose only ambition was the good of his subjects. A lie! As a mage, Tabitta understood better than he the true reality. Humans often deceived themselves, created their own reality so they could discount the truth. Dieudonne might be a vampire, but he was behaving like a human. He used blood as a weapon against both vampire and human.

"You manipulate humans and Kindred, as though they were dancing dogs."

"Watch your tongue!"

She knew he feared her, or he would have reacted immediately. Yet, were her powers strong enough to protect Alicia and fight Dieudonne and his followers at the same time? Her powers were untested in this arena. She'd always had only herself to consider. And as for his followers, it was obvious he'd already summoned some of them. There they stood, shadows within shadows at the rear of the building.

Despite their presence, it wasn't a good idea to back down or show uncertainty.

"Let's put each other to the test," she said, and drew an imaginary line with her mind, allowed it to circle her body and Alicia's. Then closed her eyes and pulled forth sparks from the fire that had destroyed her home. They flew to her like birds on the wind and she took them gently in the palm of her hand and scattered them on the circle. And lit them. Cold fire leaped upward.

The shadows in the background moved forward.

Tabitta could feel Alicia's fear scorching the air.

"Don't move," she warned the girl. She forced the flames upward and over their heads and shaped a protective dome of fire. Through the fire-tongues she saw the approaching shadows assume solid shapes. Three of them, vampire males moving slowly but with purpose, circling the fire like wolves. And urging them on, Baron Dieudonne. His eyes glittered in the semidarkness, and his descended canine teeth shone bone-white against lips turned black by lack of light.

Once again, Tabitta reached deep inside herself for the knowledge her grandmother had given her. "Turn your enemy's reality against him."

The fire that distracted the Baron's servants was cold and harmless, but the perception that it would blister their flesh restrained them. If necessary, Tabitta decided, she would blister their minds as well. Make them feel heat and pain where none existed.

The Baron was another matter. Not so easy to fool. Very powerful. His main weakness was his belief that he had absolute control over any situation or individual.

Louis XIV had kept his children...those of his mistresses as well as his wife... in his palace. Had Dieudonne been one of those privileged children, raised in an atmosphere of ostentation, influenced by the cruel philosophy of his father?

Whatever his background, she would have to divert him, stop time and disappear to some quiet place, to consider her solution. But what about the girl she was protecting? She couldn't leave Alicia behind.

Dieudonne spoke to his minions. "What you see is an illusion. Seize the females!"

The three vampires took tentative steps toward Tabitta's dome of flames and stopped at its edge.

"Cowards!" shouted Dieudonne. "I command you to destroy them!"

At that moment, Alicia screamed and plunged through the fire. As she passed through, the flames fluttered, as though a small wind had disturbed them.

The illusion died.

Tabitta leaped forward, seized Alicia's hand and clung to it tightly. "Don't do anything until I tell you."

Almost immediately, in one corner of the bottling facility, several dozen Kindred stepped forward.

"Why are you here?" asked the Baron. "I didn't call you. Identify yourselves!"

"Some of us belong to Clan Tremere, some to Clan Toreador, some to others," said a fair-haired man who appeared to be leader of the group. "Blood sources are scarce for all of us, and your blood is too expensive for us to purchase. You are starving us."

"We came to renegotiate!" cried another vampire,

"I charge what the market allows," said the Baron. "That's the price you must pay."

"Not a good answer. So, we'll take whatever blood you have on hand. Where is it?"

Dieudonne jerked a finger toward a large freezer. "Do you really believe you can steal from me and get away with it?"

The rebel didn't answer but proceeded to unload the freezer with the help of a companion.

Tabitta considered her situation, closed her eyes and floated out of her body. Now she was an unseen entity above the crowd, watching, listening, feeling. She turned her attention to the rebel leader. He's angry, she thought, but not poisonous. A young vampire. His beast does not control him. She touched his mind and found strength and charity. He had a cause but not exclusively for himself. She returned to her own body.

The Baron pointed a long finger at Tabitta. "Witch! I'll see you chained and spread-eagled in the desert under a noon sun. Your skin will shrivel and peel from your bones."

She ignored the threat, turned to the rebel leader and whispered, "This girl… the Baron means to kill her. Can you take her in?"

"We'll give her blood and sanctuary. But what about you? Come with us. It's nearly time for the sun to rise."

"The melanin in my skin protects me. I can endure the sun's

heat for periods of time. I won't leave yet. There's something I must do."

"Then, good luck!"

Tabitta smiled and slipped forward in time a few hours.

The day shift had arrived, and the music of machinery and humans clanged and clashed in an odd sort of harmony, as Tabitta moved invisible among them. Humans! Sweaty bodies and pungent odors. Different from vampiric bodies, which had a cool, dry texture and sweet scent.

She could hear myriad hearts beating, pumping blood, slowly and not so slowly. No two heartbeats were the same. Irresistible, overpowering sounds. She straightened her dress, shook her long black hair so that it floated around her shoulders, and walked barefoot toward the research lab at the rear of the facility. Upon reaching it, she became visible again and knocked. A gaunt young man in a white smock opened the door.

"Yes?" he said. His unlined face wore a puzzled expression.

"Gene Spratt?"

"That's who I am."

"I'd like to speak with you," said Tabitta. "I need some information. It shouldn't take long."

He hesitated, and she entered his mind and nudged him from indecision.

"Come in." He pulled something from one corner of the small room that served as a laboratory. "You can have my stool, and I'll stand." He stared at Tabitta's bare feet and legs.

She sat on the stool, pulled her loose-fitting red dress up to her thighs, and stretched a long brown leg in his direction.

He licked his lips with nervous excitement. "Who are you?"

She improvised. "My stage name is Michael." She heaved a small sigh. "I call myself that because the name comforts me, reminds me of a man I once loved."

"I had a girl," Spratt volunteered. "I wanted to marry her."

"And did you?"

"She ran off with someone else. So what is it you want?"

"I'm attending the University of California," she said. "Taking drama courses, trying to become an actress. I've been asked by a local theatrical group to play the role of a scientific researcher. I thought, if I could watch you at work, I'd have a better understanding of the part I'm to play."

"Who told you to come here?"

"Baron Dieudonne is an acquaintance. He speaks highly of you."

"He doesn't like us telling strangers about our activities. They're confidential."

She leaned toward the human, her eyes dark and soft staring into his weak, blue orbs. Her senses pulled forth information. His body pumped blood vigorously. Strong, healthy human, but colorblind! In dim light, he'd never notice the red glow of her eyes. She reached out and touched his hand and let her fingertips trail across each of his fingers.

"I'd never ask you to reveal business secrets. Just the day-to-day routines, without specifics." She paused. "This is a busy hour for you, so early in the morning, isn't it? Not a good place or time to talk. Could you meet me for lunch somewhere? Maybe at the motel where I'm staying?"

He hesitated. "Dieudonne doesn't like us to go out for lunch. We have a lunchroom here, though I usually brown-bag it."

"I think he'd forgive you this once. I could order us something nice, and we could eat it in the room and talk without interruption. Would you like that?" Once again she stared into his eyes, her own full of all the love she knew he'd been denied during his life. This human was too restrained to have known much affection. He desired it, but had no idea how to attain it. She planted a seed in his mind and repeated what she'd just said.

"Do you want to do that?"

"Yes," he said. "I'd love to. Where are you staying?"

"Driftwood Shores on Pacific Coast Highway near Torrance." She liked the place. The management asked no questions of its tenants. "Noon, Gene?" She could hear his heartbeat accelerate.

"I'll be there."

He arrived at exactly noon. The room was dark, the curtains drawn, the bed partially turned down. Soft music drifted from a radio, and there was food and drink on a coffee table by the couch. An inviting lair, she thought.

"I ordered sandwiches and coffee for you," she said. "Hope you like chicken."

"Anything's fine."

She saw that he was uncomfortable and gently tugged him toward the couch. "I feel so close to you, Gene, and I never feel that way about strangers. I want to know all about you."

And I want to listen to your heart beating and beating and beating, she thought. Most of all, I want to listen to that wonderful pounding music.

He chewed on his sandwich and swallowed a little coffee. She moved closer to him and pulled off his glasses. "You look uncomfortable. Why don't you take off your jacket and tie?"

He grinned.

An uncertain grin, she thought. He doesn't know I'm a predator, a vampire. Thinks I'm an aggressive human female.

"I'm not very good at conversation," he said.

"Would it be more comfortable to talk if you were lying down?" she asked. "We could lie together on the bed and turn the lights off, and you won't feel you're talking to anyone in particular. It's much easier to let feelings flow in the dark."

He followed her suggestion without argument. She turned up the music…a ballad…turned off the light and curled against him.

His skin was hot, damp with perspiration, and his heart jackhammered. A good strong heart. "Start at the beginning," she said, as if he was about to read her a child's fairy tale.

She stroked his forehead softly and undid his shirt as he spoke. Once unleashed, he expressed himself well.

"I've heard that Dieudonne is a wonderful employer," she said. "You must enjoy working with him."

"He's a bastard," Spratt replied. "You think you know him, but you don't. He lies. Makes promises he can't keep."

"To you?"

"Yes, and to the elders...I mean to the executives. Well, it's not something you'd be interested in."

"Oh, but I would," she said and pulled down the sleeve of her dress and placed one of his hands on her exposed breast. After a while, she let him make love to her in the human way.

When he lay back exhausted, she placed her mouth on his neck and bit deeply into his artery. Blood oozed and she sucked it and listened to his moan of pleasure and pain. The beautiful horror of it sent his body into spasms, as she drained him of life.

"I love you," she said. "Or I wouldn't do this for you. Can you hear me?"

Much later, she propped his limp body up and gave him a little of her own blood as required to complete his transition. "You're mine now," she said. "Not the Baron's but mine. Are you happy?"

"Very happy."

"And you'll tell me all your secrets?"

"All of them."

"You'll be with me forever, you understand. You'll be my companion."

He seized her. "I need you."

She placed her bloody lips against his. "I'll have to leave when night falls, but I'll return. I promise."

Baron Dieudonne was waiting for her in his office that night, his anger evident on his features. "Where is my researcher?" he asked. "What have you done with him, witch?"

"He's mine now," she said. "He won't share his secrets with you any longer. But he told me some of yours."

"I shall kill you," he said. "Slowly and with much pleasure!"

"Spratt said you deceive the other elders, sell them blood they believe will return them to a human state of being."

Dieudonne screamed, a piercing sound that reverberated from the walls. "You accuse *me*? You...you nothing! Your neighbors destroyed your house! It seems your power has limitations!"

"Thanks for your concern, but I have a great deal of insurance money coming. I can rebuild my house with fire retardant, space-age materials developed by NASA. I intend to establish a halfway house for outcast vampires."

Dieudonne snarled. "Do you know what we used to do to witches? We hung them by their thumbs, forced their mouths open and placed lighted candles inside. Then we flogged them to death. Those were my direct orders. Mine! The orders of King Louis XIV! History has hidden the truth for political reasons. The elders have concealed it for theirs. I'm not the bastard offspring of a king, I *am* a king! And I am Nosferatu as well. You will bow to me before I kill you!"

"I'll never bow."

The air crackled and cold light spilled into the room. Three elderly vampires emerged from the illumination.

"I'm sick of all these uninvited guests!" shouted the vampire, Louis XIV. Then he realized who his visitors were.

"We are the primogen," the three said in one voice. "Appointed by the most ancient among us. The elders are indebted to the mage, Tabitta, for revealing your lies to us. The consequences of your greed and deceit are upon you, Louis! Judgment is about to be passed. We will be taking over your bottling plants, all of them…in this country and other parts of the world. From this moment on we will make sure that the Kindred are well fed, that the Kindred survive! We share this world with humans, therefore we will share your scientific discoveries with them."

The primogen surrounded Louis XIV, containing him with their combined powers. The eyes of their prisoner reflected his fear and his voice wavered, yet his bravado continued. "I am a King!" he shouted. "And I will kill the witch who betrayed me!" The elders ignored him and turned to Tabitta. "Thank you for revealing the falsehood that has been inflicted upon us. You are dismissed now."

"No one dismisses me," answered Tabitta. "I leave because I wish to."

She soared upward into the night. Below, there was a great roar of sound. A hot wind licked her feet, and she rose higher to avoid the burning timbers that shot up like torches from hell. A scream tore through the flames, and she glanced down. The bottling plant was burning and Dieudonne's punishment had been delivered by the elders.

As she'd promised, Tabitta flew back to Gene Spratt.

Marie Landis has won numerous literary awards for her science fiction and dark fantasy stories, including the Amelia Award. Her writing background has been primarily in the news media as a reporter and columnist and in the literary short story field. She is the co-author of the science fiction novel, *Memorymakers*, a collaboration with her cousin, Brian Herbert.

Brian Herbert is best known for his science fiction novels, including *Sidney's Comet, The Garbage Chronicles, Sudanna, Sudanna, Man of Two Worlds* (co-written with his father, Frank Herbert), *Prisoners of Arionn*, and *The Race for God*. His most recent novel, *Memorymakers*, was written in collaboration with his cousin, Marie Landis. Brian has published two good humor books and edited three books. He has also appeared on a number of radio shows and panels to assist other writers.

Escobar Falls

by Stewart von Allmen

I t was already too late by the time she glanced at me. She didn't quite stare. A stare wouldn't have caused me so much concern. No, she looked at me as though very surprised — with delight, fear or simple astonishment, I didn't know — but then she tried to look away in a manner meant not to draw my attention to her. Of course, it did just the opposite. My schooling in people-watching helps me note such slightly conscious ploys, designed to divert someone's attention from your attention to him.

Because I interrupted her steady hustling along the crowded sidewalk, I felt as interested in her as she strangely was in me. I had just changed the course of the remainder of her life and, perhaps more profoundly, the lives of everyone she would ever encounter. That's why I was interested in her. I could not divine why she would react so to me. I purposefully dressed and appeared in a very normal, unobtrusive manner. I should have blended into the crowd, not drawn her attention from that even flow of sameness.

In any event, the responsibility for such an encounter is enormous, and all the weight of that responsibility was upon me.

When she turned away from me to disguise her interest, she faced a store window, where she pretended to inspect the contents of the display. I could see her pupil waver at the edge of her eye, though, as she sought to ascertain whether I realized that I drew her attention and what my reaction was if I was aware. I suppose she saw with surprise that I stood in the midst of chaotic foot traffic without being bowled over by the press of the crowd, which I was unconsciously diverting around myself.

Damnable magick! Even when I try not to use it, and it's a promise to myself that I will not, I unconsciously do to make the nature of reality surrounding me more secure. Magick puts the natural order out of order, and while my knowledge of magick tells me that the natural order is an immense fabrication and there's really nothing amazing about the seemingly impossible things I can do, there is no way to explain that to all the people around me. More specifically, to all the people who surround me. They were now a step behind for the remainder of the day and all because they took extra time to pass around me. Such a single step can become grossly exaggerated and make the likelihood of catastrophe ever greater. One step means missing a walk light at an intersection. Which means a missed train in the subway. And here they are mugged, raped, or killed, when otherwise they would have made the subway ride home.

Does this sound silly? Overwrought? It's not. There are serious repercussions for even the smallest chance event, like an extra step to pass around someone standing directly in your path, though to call them "chance" is an oversight, for that "chance" part is misunderstood and needs correcting. I've found that anything, absolutely everything, is one step removed from inevitable. And that "one step" is too often a chance event.

It's because my thinking was as involved as this that I remained motionless on the sidewalk. The woman apparently realized that something was wrong with me, and the wrong concerned her, so she made her move. It wasn't a sudden move, but it was a calculated one. Turning from the display window, she wove through the flow of people toward a pay phone near the curb.

As she moved, I did too, and I was sensible enough to push my way toward the storefronts and out of the press of the crowd that had been buffeting and crushing me since the moment I stopped redirecting people around me. From a position of relative safety at the entrance to a high-priced electronics store, I watched the woman closely. She was young, perhaps in her mid-twenties, and dressed very nicely. Her black slacks looked new and comfortable, and an attractive blue, black and white plaid vest partially covered her off-white blouse. It became a young professional's outfit with the small pager snapped to her belt.

She hurried a little too much at the last moment, though. Or maybe it was because she lost sight of me and craned her neck around to locate me again; and so the quarter her trembling fingers pulled from her small purse missed the coin slot and fell. It rattled once off the face of the phone and then disappeared.

I worried for just a second that I had unconsciously used magick again to keep the phone call from being placed, because her failure to insert the coin is just the simple kind of "chance" or coincidental way that mages like myself could alter the flow of reality. My control is better than that—this was a "real" coincidence. Strange that it fell in my favor. They never seem to.

Such events are dramatic temptations to me. It was obvious she wanted to make a call. A slight touch of magick, even a simple adjustment to true reality, that truth beyond where the woman operated, could have helped, but as I've said, I don't do that anymore. Besides, I was already the cause of too much disruption in her life this hot afternoon; I was not going to heap outright intervention atop my already chance encounter.

She was a little frantic now, though she calmed when she again saw me standing at the storefront. Our gazes briefly met, and when hers quizzically softened a bit, I became even more intrigued. I realized that she must be intent on her need or interest in me to withstand my intense look. My expression, even in repose, has always been very stern and uncompromising, so I think I would normally have seemed very threatening to her, though I'm sure there's nothing about my posture or size that would intimidate anyone.

After she pulled herself together, she turned to the phone again and hurriedly looked for the dropped quarter. It was no wonder she couldn't see it. The quarter was at the base of the pay phone between the pole and the cracked concrete, where it stood almost upright. She scanned the ground for a hint of reflection from the overhead sun, but caught none. So she looked around the phone itself — on the black lip that was the bottom of the open-faced black box enclosing the phone, and even in the coin return slot.

She tried the phone again in the vain hope that the quarter had fallen into the slot, and not out of it, as she thought. That was one way I could fix things, but I didn't. She slammed the headset onto the jack, presumably because she heard no dial tone. She closed her eyes, sighed and gripped her fists into tight, frustrated wads, but then she took a deep breath and slipped a now loose and seeking hand into her pocket for other change. She grimaced but pulled out the remaining coins anyway. I see a penny and a shiny nickel. So shiny I can see the year: 1986. I feel my mind wandering to that year, but I remain attentive to the present.

This jolt back to the present clears my thoughts and makes me wonder even more whom she's calling and why. Perhaps a man who resembles me has been haunting her dreams. Maybe she's an agent and I'm the perfect match for a part in the movie she's currently casting. Maybe she seeks her father, who orphaned her at birth after her mother died, and has mistaken me for him.

What is she putting into motion and how will it affect other people?

I can help her, but should I? Any number of innocuous-seeming coincidences could save the moment. I could simply give the quarter to her, but that would be just as immoral as working magick. It's changing reality without using magick, but conscious decision is still what shapes the future. Is there really a difference?

I catch myself absently rubbing my long, tangled hair as I consider this. I pretend there is a difference. I must or I would never even be able to walk the streets. I must make myself a part of reality, but I no longer allow myself to bend it to my will. That's going too far.

Maybe it's best that she didn't make the call anyway. I couldn't accept the responsibility of disastrous results if her future went awry because she used the phone. After all, she was calling on my account, and seeing this event curtailed probably suits me best in the long run, but it is her fate that fascinates me for the moment. I can see a number of possible futures unfold...

Perhaps if she lingers at the street-side pay phone, a car will swerve out of traffic as she speaks and crush her between its steely fender and the brick storefronts behind her. As I watch I can see this happen. She reaches down for the quarter I conveniently cause to roll to her feet with a soft clink so she'll look down again. A squeal of tires alarms her and causes her head to jerk up quickly as she begins to stand. A scream escapes her throat as an emerald-black G-20 sways across the center line, cruises unimpeded through a gap in the two lanes of oncoming traffic, and hurtles directly toward her. The car rebounds slightly off the phone pole but mostly slips past to strike the woman full on the chest. She's suspended in the air, seemingly attached to the car hood like a grotesque ornament, and ruptures when her flailing body impacts the brick wall.

Or maybe a gas main will burst in the ground beneath the pay phone and the region around the phone, and certainly the phone itself, will become a conflagration of fiery stonework, combusting flesh, and blazing metal. Am I to be accountable for delaying her here, to be swept into that inferno?

Conceivably, gunmen could drive by at this moment. While she dallies making her damnable phone call, juvenile gang members could turn onto this main thoroughfare and make her a random target for their puerile projectile playing.

She would be dead because of me, and I will not be the cause of such an event again!

Despite all of this danger, she negligently still wants to make her call. If she would just leave now then none of these things would happen to her. Doesn't she realize the danger she's in? I want to go warn her. To frighten her away. That too would be interfering, but what will she do now that she cannot call from the street?

Too many possibilities! Tragedy here is too probable. I need to escape her, but she's watching me intently. The foot traffic has died down a bit, so we once again have a good view of each other. She still holds the handful of change. She's counting it to be sure, but I can see from here that there is not enough silver to make up the twenty-five cents, even in smaller denominations.

She looks really heartbroken, and she seems to be on the verge of approaching me this very moment, so I decide it's time to act. I can't stand it any longer. I could walk away, but I know she'll follow. I'm going to have to use magick to escape. It will be best for everyone. My disappearance after her intense interest will send ripples through her life for some time to come, but I fear for anyone who associates with me for too long.

I worry that as a mage who has run afoul of Paradox, reality has somehow marked me and made me a locus for events that mundanes, people like her who are unaware of the magick around them, would regard as bizarre. In other words, long-term association with me can only result in exaggerated tragedies, much like how taking an extra step results in a subway mugging.

I concentrate for a moment to work magick. I need to disappear, but to do so literally means challenging the paradigm of reality that rules on this downtown street. So, I work harder and weave a more complicated effect that creates the same result. Through my Will I must thrust my knowledge of truer reality over the simple framework operating around me.

From the perspective of the victim of my magick, just the young woman in this case, I will appear to disappear a split-second from now. I have put the actual means of this occurrence into the hands of reality. I weave my desire into the fabric of reality by spinning the invisible threads that connect all things, and especially those that connect the woman to me, and now wait for it to unfold in a manner consistent with the laws of this location. The problem is, I don't know exactly how my magick will effectuate—that's up to reality.

If I cared to personify reality, I could do it, much as humans have done to Mother Nature or the Garou have with their many spirits. I see it as an uncaring, yet unmalevolent, force. Reality does what it must to maintain itself when a mage such as myself enforces his will upon it. It doesn't concern itself with what comes afterward, just as mages such as myself have done for millennia.

The means reality chooses is inevitably innocuous, for it chooses the smoothest means to the end a mage insists upon, but it seems to me that there is always the chance of catastrophe. Fortunately, this time it effectuates smoothly.

She's still stepping toward me when the phone behind her rings. She pauses, but only for an instant before turning to answer it. I guess she wants it too badly to pass up any chance to use it, and so reflex takes over. Before she can turn around again, I'll be gone.

I'll have disappeared.

As I carefully hurry down the street, I think how odd it is to be the one followed and not vice versa. Odd because I do not have my own life now. I only live the lives of other people now. Well, that and the permutations of their lives. I construct the paths of people's lives based on decisions they made or refused to make. Thanks to my intimate relationship with the temporal realities beyond this one, I have time enough for everyone.

The first few years following 1986 were different, though, because I became fixated with certain individuals. I am certain I once spent over a year following a garbage truck on its rounds. The immeasurable permutations of what could have happened in countless lives because of what people discarded were endlessly engrossing. I eventually got a hold of myself and nursed myself back to at least this state of health, such as it is.

I spoke of temptations earlier, and this woman is becoming one such as I have been able to avoid for many years now. I wonder what more harm I have done to her life. Who was on the phone she answered? I doubt it was anyone as harmless as a crank caller.

I do feel increasingly indebted to the woman. I worry so much about how I affect others that I forget that they can affect me as well. However, I know better than to attempt to repay that debt. The chaos I cause would only increase. I am not part of a system that tends toward order.

My mind is running too fast now. If I don't compose myself soon, then I will continue to make mistakes. Ahead I see a flashing neon display. It advertises a bar of some sort, but I require no further invitation. I enter.

I could, of course, simply create my own food with magick, but I don't consciously work magick anymore unless I feel absolutely pressed into it, as just now on the street. It's wrong. My past has made me a firm believer of this. Experts say there were forty-five flaws that could have caused the incident that makes me question my every move, but I know it was my fault.

It paralyzes me still and it sent me spinning into Quiet, this state of insanity and confusion to which only a mage, too long juggling the contradictory forces, laws and theories of the universe, can succumb. Quiet can be escaped, though I've failed thus far. The truth of an insanity, though, like the new paradigm any person presumed insane by his peers concocts for himself, becomes undeniable. The new paradigm, the one in which I currently exist, where I speculate my action or inaction is at the root of any misery I see, became so real that I cannot now escape it. This is despite my knowledge that this world view is as foolish and untenable as the fragile one most humans accept, only because it's what their five senses describe to them.

I try to rely mainly on those senses now myself. The bar is the typical sort I recall from a decade ago. Like everything else modern, though, it's sleeker, as if the design was actually a forethought, and not just a result of the owner filling a given space. Everything is in just the right place. There are a few wooden booths of the old sort, though the backs are not high enough to prevent viewing a neighbor in front of or behind you, but the tables are mostly new. The chairs surrounding them will require replacement in a few years.

Most of the patrons cluster around the bar, but I pay little attention to them. I sit in a booth and throw open the menu. Perhaps the waitresses will ignore me as long as the menu is open. I need another moment to calm down and gather my thoughts.

My previous avocation was the alteration of this reality they cherish so highly. I altered it toward the ends and with all the careful thoughtfulness my past acquaintances among the Progenitors, the Convention of mages to which I belonged, have for decades; but when the tragedy occurred, when my awful oversight opened my eyes to the misery I caused countless times, my Will fled me and with my Will so went my magick. My eyes also opened to the wrongs of the Technocracy, a larger organization which my Progenitors form along with four other groups—Iteration X, New World Order, Void Engineers and the Syndicate.

It's no wonder that Ascension, the quest to enlighten all humans to the nature of reality, continues to elude us. We so passionately pursue this end that we have little care for the smaller picture, the reality from which we all descend. Certainly there are mages who claim to watch this level of reality as well, but only I, I think, have found exactly how infinitesimal the picture truly is. To guard against degrading the good of the reality humanity has attained means more than avoiding vulgar magick, or magick that effectuates in the full and disbelieving view of the unenlightened. No, to guard against regression in the battle for Ascension means achieving a coincidental magickal effect—one that becomes hidden in events that seem natural—but then guaranteeing that the coincidental chain breaks. How to do that without working more magick baffles me.

This wouldn't be such a concern if the coincidental effect didn't spiral out of control to create events even grosser than the original. This, I expect, is why I succumbed to Quiet.

I imagine that a person so aware of his insanity should be able to awaken from it and return to a pattern of thought and action consistent with who he truly is and what he understands, but that's not the case. The severity of my error and the obvious nature of the events I should have altered so the tragedy could not occur continue to re-cycle through my thoughts.

Any more thoughts of self-reproach grind to a swift conclusion when the young woman from the pay phone suddenly walks into the establishment. She seems tired and thwarted, so I guess that she neither followed nor yet sees me.

I'm sure I would detect someone using magick against me, so I dismiss that as a possible explanation for the chance of the young woman entering here. I silently sit and watch as she goes to the bar counter and breathlessly asks for some change and the location of the pay phone. She must have been looking for me. The bartender drops four quarters into her palm, takes her bill, and points to the back of the building. I sit between that conversation and the back of the building.

A woman in the booth ahead of me sits looking in my direction as well. She's paused with a glass of water at her lips—I think my sudden animation startled her. I only watch her out of the corner of my eye, for I direct my attention squarely on the young woman at the bar counter, but the woman in the booth sets the glass down without taking a drink and part of my mind spins stories about her potential fate. Now she has less fluid in her body than if not for my interference. The results could be catastrophic. What if this is her last meal before tonight when, flying to a tropical destination, her plane goes down, and she's stranded on a deserted island in the midst of nowhere? Would that drink she had wanted translate into the few more drops of fluid in her body that would keep her alive, or at least not brain damaged, until rescuers found her?

I sit before a dead woman, but I maintain my attention on the young woman who seems to now be on my trail, for in her I am facing an unknown, a potentially lethal situation. She may be a Technomancer, a blind and artless pseudo-mage of the type I used to be, who seeks to consolidate reality to only an unchanging state where change, and hence the ultimate goal of the mages, Ascension, becomes by definition an impossibility.

When I worked magick on her earlier I noted nothing about her threads that would make me believe she is a mage, but some of the most effective servants of the Technocracy have disentangled themselves from the tapestry in many ways, which perhaps only validates my paranoid theory of her threat.

Maybe the Progenitors have finally solved the mystery of my disappearance from their labs eight years ago. I was able to cover my trail and intentions very well, but they still work magick, or their perverted brand of it anyway, and as I do not, that gives them a decided advantage over me. This woman could be a first contact, sent to warn me of my impending apprehension.

Such enforcers are not uncommon among the Technocracy, especially in the group known as the New World Order, with their so-called Men-in-Black, but the magickal tactic of the group is what galls me the most. Though they have only begun to popularize it now, some years ago a mage in the ranks of the Technocracy created the so-called Butterfly Effect to describe just what I encountered in 1986 for myself. The theory is a monstrous, and to my mind obvious, means of pinning down even this disastrous working of reality to their command.

Perhaps I should feel relieved that at least they are aware of it, but since the day I left the fold of the Technocracy, I could see from the outside how they limit the dynamic potential of Earth by claiming their woefully inadequate cosmology as truth. This is at the expense of the wealth of ideologies available from hundreds of other mages who live in dozens of different paradigms. I can only feel ill at the thought of their methods.

An intuitive feeling that this young woman is connected to my past leaves me completely cold. Intuition is a powerful thing for mages. She's followed me this far, so there is little need for continued subterfuge. She's probably come to punish me for my crime. My carelessness eight years ago put the Void Engineers' plans for the moon, and the subsequent domination of the fey folk there, in jeopardy. If there was any good in what happened then, it was the temporary dismantling of what those sell to the masses as the "space program."

I'll let her make her way toward me again. Her magick is working faultlessly, though I must say her act of surprise on the street earlier was a surprisingly low-tech ploy. If she's an enforcer then I would expect to see more technology, though she does have that beeper. On the other hand, she has successfully cornered me.

She turns and takes only one step toward the back of the bar before she sees me and pulls up short. She smiles and then continues to move in my direction. She hesitates as she nears me and I decide it's best to keep her as off-balance as possible. I spill the whole story.

"You too would wander insanely, Miss, if you considered for even a moment the eventual results of everything you ever do. I fled the Convention when my eyes opened to the witless carnage I was producing. It's so simple in hindsight, but believe me, it's taken years to piece everything together since I felt my threads tugging at me that fateful January morning. So many options. Each event spawned so many new ones, or slightly altered countless others, that it took years to follow all the leads and discover how my magick, and likewise the magick of many of my unknowing contemporaries, went amiss."

I continue the bombardment of explanation, "Pentex was going behind our backs by approaching Iteration X front organizations for a mechanical option to the biological solutions we presented. They did this despite our readiness to enter Replication Phase, with delivery of the first clones within a few months. I learned of the meeting independently and had to act without consultation to stymie the proceedings."

She loses her composure as she lowers herself to sit on the bench opposite mine in the large wooden booth. She succeeds in sitting only when it becomes reflex. She looks extremely perplexed. I press on, confident I can blurt this out in public because I know the beeper she wears is a conversation filtration instrument, a high-tech, or magickal if you will, device that will turn my words into ones more palatable for ears other than those of the speaker and anyone who wears a filter.

"It's because of the means I used to disrupt the meeting that the explosion occurred at all. More important than my initial decision to act and how to act, though, was my fundamental disregard for the long-term consequences of my methods. As I mentioned, one change that I orchestrated resulted in exaggerated effects as more time passed. It's much as how the delay of taking one step extra can result in a mugging or even death.

"The Pentex stooge had to run a gauntlet of office drones in order to gain access to the managers with any true connection to the mages of Iteration X. It's perhaps likely that the Pentex man didn't even realize what he would soon discover after news of his inquiries made it farther up the hierarchy of the company, but it would happen eventually. So it was here, early in the process, that I struck, for I knew it would be easier now then after an open dialogue had been established between Pentex and the mages.

"I was prepared to fight reality to make my magick work, but like a responsible member of the Conventions of the Technocracy, I worked harder to attain a coincidental effect. I was successful. The effect actuated as a broken alarm clock. There was one drone who was the point man for the deal. He was the only one prepared for the meeting, so consequently it was his alarm that didn't sound in the morning, and he woke only when a co-worker phoned in desperation. Over the phone the drone gave some garbled instructions on how to attempt to delay and/or entertain the Pentex businessman. In the end the businessman became frustrated and stormed out of the office before the meeting even took place.

"It all sounds okay so far, right? At first I was proud of my work, but how ingenuous I was, to think that any level of care practicing mages relied upon in working magick was enough! Frankly, I didn't consider the repercussions of my magick—of what else might happen because I intruded on the normal course of events. Well, that tugging of the threads told me something had gone awry.

"It was this: The drone still tried to reach the office in time, but that necessitated a high-speed race not safe for the best drivers, let alone a panicked fool about to lose what would have been the deal of a lifetime. Everyone died in the ensuing accident, including a NASA ground-crew technician's wife. From there it's straightforward. He received a call about the accident at just the wrong time and so set into motion the event that caused my flight from our less-than-noble ranks."

She barely manages a word, but mutters, "One extra step... death?"

She seems completely confused. She tries again, "What...?" but trails off into silence.

I realize that I have made an incredible error. She's no Technomancer with a conversation filter.

She laughs, "My oh my, Doctor! To think I thought my father was exaggerating about how strange you are! And a mind-reader on top of that! Surely you don't know me, but here you are explaining, I suppose, why you left the lab under such odd circumstances."

I can only sit dumbly. Fortunately she will think me simply insane, and it feels good to finally express so much of my recent past to someone else. Evidently, I need to share it badly. Despite my mistake, my debt to this woman is increasing.

She speaks again after a brief pause to collect herself. "I have so many questions to ask you, Doctor, but I must admit first that I wonder what exactly you're confessing to. Does it have something to do with why you disappeared from the lab? Was I correct in that regard, at least? Did that meeting have something to do with your research funding?" There is an excitement in her hazel eyes that I have never seen before. She is having fun! She seems keenly and authentically interested in what I have to say. She presses her elbows onto the table and leans forward conspiratorially.

In contrast, I am slouching in the booth. The innocence of her curiosity sets me at ease, though, and I sit up straighter to make myself more presentable. I can see she wants me to continue, but I recall something else. I can only croak it, "Doctor?"

She laughs. "Yes! I can't believe it's really you after all my father's said, but I'm sure it is or I'm making a bigger fool of myself than you are." Her smile after that remark is too friendly, too genuine to allow me to take offense.

She continues, "You are Dr. Hammelstein, right?"

The juxtaposition between my awful past and this unexpectedly cozy present makes me uncomfortable. As kind and apparently non-threatening as the young woman is, I can't keep my mind off 1986.

"Challenger exploded," I say flatly.

Her smile washes away. "What?"

I recite the next words like litany, so engraved are they in my mind from countless recitations to myself. "The accident was on January 19th, the day parts cannibalized from the Space Shuttle Columbia, shuttle mission 61-C, arrived at the Kennedy shuttle-landing facility. Technicians, among them the poor husband, were just setting to work and unfortunately, that's when the call from the hospital came in. Moments sooner and the technician wouldn't have been installing the external hatch handle, but chance saw fit to make things otherwise.

"In his hurry to leave, the technician applied the last of three external hatch fasteners without care and so stripped the threads. This handle allows access to the pressured cabin wherein the seven deathly-fated astronauts, or six plus one teacher, would twice recline later that month.

"Because the fastener was stripped, the launch on January 27th was delayed when the external handle did pop off easily after all seven passengers were in place inside the shuttle. This process took several hours instead of the split-moment it should have because of the stripped third fastener. And due to the several-hour delay, the launch window elapsed and the launch was re-scheduled for the next day.

"When the Space Shuttle Challenger launched as shuttle mission 51-L the next day, January 28, 1986, it exploded 73 seconds into flight. The entire crew, Christa McAuliffe, Greg Jarvis, Ron McNair, Ellison Onizuka, Judy Resnik, Dick Scobee and Mike Smith, vaporized."

Her smile is still missing and she seems concerned, but she

has the advantage of not believing the truth behind what I told her. "I guess you weren't talking about leaving the lab."

I say, "No." Then, "I suspect you are Harry Kimble's daughter."

The smile is back. "That's right! You're still in that garbled brain after all, Doctor."

"That's whom you were calling on the street?"

"Two for two. He's talked incessantly about you my entire life, so I knew it had to be you when I saw that white... well it's gray now, huh?... strip of hair over your left brow. Father always said you rubbed your hair along that stripe and that you'd worn the color right out, so it turned white. He also says you must be the most brilliant scientist who ever lived. I believe it now. You're as mad as any good scientist should be. From the stories I heard and from my few moments with you here, I'd bet Einstein didn't have any absent-mindedness zaniness on you."

It is nice to remember Harry, but her infectious smile is warming me the most; however, I have cold truth to reveal yet. I know she will get it out of me because I want to tell her. She is being so friendly and understanding, though not comprehending, which is another advantage.

Conveniently, she gives me the opening to continue, "So you think you caused the Challenger explosion because you messed up some guy's office appointment? I didn't follow the muddled details, but that's the gist of what I remember."

"Essentially, yes. Because of the stripped threads, the launch slipped to the next day when it was too cold for a safe launch. The cold caused a seal to crack and that crack became an explosion. The seal—."

"Thanks, but spare the technical details," she interrupts. "I think you'd lose me again. I really just want to ask you some questions. Father has been doing his best to duplicate the remarkable work you did when you worked in the lab next to him back in the seventies. I need to call him so I can find out what to ask. Or, maybe—"

"I won't speak with him myself, I'm afraid. However, I admit that speaking to you has been incredibly unburdening for me."

"I can tell. Your expression has gone from frightened to melancholy to now, when you actually have a bit of grin. It's a scary grin, though, because it makes you look as crazy as I think you are. It's too bad that you won't talk to Father."

"Sorry."

She speaks hesitatingly, as if saying it with much authority will mean she believes what I told her, "Well, you left for good reasons, I guess. Father knew something happened suddenly because you left all your journals and notebooks. When the company was cleaning your space after you'd been missing for a while, he took the journals. I don't remember much about them, but I do remember something about test-tube babies. You had a complete procedure you'd written sometime in the sixties, but no one else completed the procedure until like, 1978 or something. He built a lab in the basement of the house where I think he has been working independently to duplicate your work. I don't think he's been successful, and I think that upsets him, because he's always talking about how your experiments seem perfectly designed."

That's because he doesn't have an Avatar, the "soul" that would make him a mage, and I do, but I can't tell her that. Now I speak confidently, fondly remembering those early days before my formal induction into the ranks of the Progenitors, and feeling pride for the first time in eight years in the fact that I am still a mage, even though I made a terrible mistake, "I can make many unbelievable things happen." At least I learned from that mistake.

Her smile shows pretty teeth. "Yeah? Show me something."

I know I have to start slowly, so I scan the bar looking for something innocuous to affect. I find a suitable target on the wall behind the bar counter, where sturdy metal brackets hold a large color television. The incessant babble of sportscasters describes the action of a soccer game in progress. The people in the bar look reasonably interested, probably because the United States is playing at the moment.

With new-found confidence I say, "I guarantee that the U.S. team will score a goal within the next minute."

She is incredulous, "Score first in a game against Columbia? I doubt it. And what can you do from here anyway?"

"You asked for an example…" I trail off as I concentrate on my magick. I refuse to remain paralyzed any longer. Besides, the U.S. team is in scoring position. What harm could possibly come of an American scoring a goal right now?

"Just wait," I suggest.

The United States is pressing an attack. I can feel my magick lance out from my body, seeking shape within an appropriate form. It will not do for the ball to suddenly fly out of control, swirl through several loops and go bouncing of its own accord into the goal. If I am to work magick again, then I must be under control.

Suddenly there is an opening and an American player passes from the left across the front of the goal. The goalie is reacting in good time, though, to cover the best angle any attacking player will have, but I feel my magick suddenly crystallize, so I know a player will instantly make a spectacular shot.

That's not quite what happens. A Colombian defender shoots out a leg to intercept the cross, but his timing is off, or rather my magick makes it be off. Miss Kimble falls out of her seat in astonishment when Escobar, the defender, scores a goal for the U.S. team.

Stewart von Allmen got engaged to and then married a crazy but perfect woman, moved into a new house, published a short story which appears in White Wolf's *Tales of the White Wolf*, and wrote a first novel, *Conspicuous Consumption*, to be published by HarperPrism in August 1995. He hopes every year of his life is so harried and fruitful.

Poisoned Dreams

by Brad Linaweaver

We conclude with a field of unburied, dead children, pale and drained of blood, resembling ice-cold fish shining in the moonlight. But that is not where we begin....

The little, bald man was one of those people who can kill spontaneity in a roomful of people just by leaning forward and opening his mouth. Even if you've never met him before, you just know that he will bore you to death. And he'll have a joke, one of those laborious, long-winded affairs more likely to elicit a smile of relief when it is finally over than any genuine amusement at the punch line.

I braced myself the moment I saw him smile. But instead of

the dreaded funny story he surprised me by saying, "You're the only mage who can help me. I suppose your schedule must be very full with all the important people you handle, but I'm hoping you can squeeze me in."

Simply transcribed, the words don't convey the agony of listening to the man. He would pause between words as if they were sentences, and at odd places. I felt that even to respond would be rude, a possible interruption of one of his silences. Naturally I wanted to turn him down, but I couldn't.

The party at which he approached me was a private affair, courtesy of some of the highest practitioners among the Virtual Adepts. He stood out like a sore thumb among all the elegantly dressed gentlemen and ladies. But he couldn't possibly be there without a special invitation, which meant that he must be an initiate at some level, as hard as that might be to believe. To verify my suspicions, he added: "I come recommended." I told him a time he could see me at the start of the week.

Once our business was concluded, he didn't even stay behind for the ritual to Cerridwen. It was a delightful affair with the nine most beautiful women in the room dancing around a new piece of software dedicated to the goddess of wisdom. I'm glad I didn't miss the spectacle of the ornate roof opening to reveal the bone-white moon above. I still liked the sight of the moon then…before it took on a leering, uncouth grotesquerie more depressing than any of the gargoyles passing silent judgment on me every time I traveled the damned streets.

I was asked to recite a verse from Coleridge honoring the goddess: "Her lips were red, her looks were free; Her locks were yellow as gold. Her skin was white as leprosy. The Nightmare Life-in-Death was she, who thicks man's blood with cold."

The most beautiful of the nine stripped off her clothes as I spoke the words; then she sat at the console and typed in commands that turned my words into an interactive game. The computer-generated holograms danced among us and set my mind, if not my spirit, at peace for a short time.

I used to think that as one is initiated into higher orders of consciousness, a sense of well-being and purpose would increase. In my youth I'd been tempted by the pleasures of the Cult of Ecstasy. I'd felt cold shivers from the Euthanatos. I'd wondered if the answer to all problems might not be found in the Dreamspeakers. The point was that all my desires led in the direction of the Nine Traditions. Never in my studies or the dangerous games I played to collect information was I ever tempted by the true evils of the Technocracy, the Nephandi, or the Marauders. Or so I thought.

If not for the relativistic viewpoint inculcated by the Virtual Adepts, I would have gone crazy long ago. "All things are information quantified, and information wants to be free." And as I learned from the wise insights of the Prophet Wilson, one man's reality tunnel is another person's dead end! Or, as I like to say, one man's ascension is another's nosebleed.

I was smug in what little wisdom I had managed to obtain. I knew that the problem with the Technocracy and the Nephandi was their obsession that each had The One True Answer. In contrast, the Marauders had the virtue of individuality, but they would plunge the world into the dreary abyss of chaos. My old teacher used to tell me that ours was a high and lonely destiny, to steer a middle course, for the good of civilization, between Insane Order and Insane Chaos.

Of course I had hoped that I might play some role in determining the fate of mankind. Who wouldn't? But I never would have believed that a little, boring man met at a routine party would be my ticket to infamy.

The evening had begun with socializing and the proper wine, then concluded with an uplifting lecture, as usual. "Sexual madness is always the lot of the uninitiated," said our priestess. "Crime and violence always increase in times of repression. If this civilization is to survive the current crisis, we must increase the potency of our magick to compensate for the lack of wisdom in the people. A Gothic-Punk world needs guidance. Empty scientific materialism is not enough. Mindless instinct is not enough. We need the gnosis with the mostest! And I believe there is one among us tonight who will open the gate to True Wisdom."

At no point did I think she was talking about me. Now that I think about it, maybe she wasn't. She smiled, which was our cue to chuckle. The ape brain is so much a part of the human race that most people have never moved beyond their first encounter with abstract reasoning. They believe in a brute form of cause and effect, translating into blood sacrifice to get what they want. So it has always been. The great mages of the past who dared teach them something better have all too often met the same fate— one might say they've been crucified for their temerity. We are the wise ones who learned the obvious lesson.

It was a good party.

My mind full of vast historical vistas, I walked to work on a seemingly pedestrian Monday. I'd put on my Sunblock 1,000. I was wearing my trendiest sunglasses made out of the latest bioplastic, friendly to the earth but still capable of protecting the eyes from cataracts. My new Bogart hat felt good on my head, and I only had to step over six bodies on the way to work. I'd almost forgotten about the little, bald man.

On those occasions when a special patient requires special handling it behooves us to be prepared. My assistant at the office was Valerie, equally proficient at office work and performing the duties of a nurse. Whenever I beheld her lovely face under a halo of strawberry-blond hair I could only think that she would probably wind up with a higher position among the Adepts than I could ever hope to attain. She was doing a lot more than sleeping her way to the top; she was dreaming herself there.

Her lunch breaks were too long but she was worth it. Hell,

she often got the jump on problems and wrestled them to the ground before I knew of their existence. She was in fine form that Monday. With a minimum of fuss she hurried Mr. Bennett—did I mention that the man's name was Bennett?—into the preparation room. While she was washing his face I locked the door and made sure the blinds were pulled down at the window.

I went over to the safe hidden behind a picture of Apollo and Dionysus standing together, trying to outdo each other's grins. (To the uninitiated, they looked like two fishing buddies. I enjoyed imagining their having a lofty conservation about how "monotheism is the slippery slope to atheism.") Behind the picture was a device I could only use in special cases. Being ever so careful, I removed the equipment.

Then Valerie took over, attaching electrodes to the patient's forehead. At the other end of the wires was a crystal ball atop a red, silken pillow with a line of stitched, runic symbols taking the place of fancy embroidery. Blue-gray mists swirled at the center of the ball in anticipation of the ceremony.

"I've never seen a DreaMeter before," said the man.

"Just relax," answered Valerie in a voice as soothing as one of her back rubs. She didn't need magick to make a man cooperate. Before I could conjugate a Latin verb, the little guy was out like a light. Valerie works fast!

If you're not already asleep when you're hooked up to the meter, it puts you under immediately and, hesto presto, you're in dream-state. Whatever dreams you've been having recently leave a strong impression, and they are reexperienced, just like a summer rerun. Valerie and I had both been trained to separate public omens and symbols from the purely personal character of an individual's dreams. But neither of us was prepared for what was stirring around in the little man's head, just waiting to be projected in three-dimensional holographic images.

The dream began with Mr. Bennett's divorce from a woman

who disbelieved in all forms of magick. One is not required to marry a person who is aware, but one is expected to keep specific details secret from an unenlightened spouse. In this respect, Bennett had performed his duty. Suddenly I realized that his excruciatingly dull demeanor might prove advantageous for the keeping of secrets!

Valerie and I had been through this sort of thing before. We joined hands and did an incantation, tapping into the web of magick that was older than the earth. Of course, the Adepts kept up with the times when it came to style. Another three-dimensional image appeared, a bright red square floating right in front of us, part of the SPELLCHECK program. Reaching into a desk drawer, I picked up my wand and touched the square, which brought up a wall of shimmering lights. Next, I touched a yellow triangle the exact color of a fresh lemon, which conjured into the room the spirit force of MEMORY…a spirit that would keep a careful lookout for that moment when Bennett's dream departed from wish-tinged memory into the faery realms of pure invention!

We learned that his wife had been a plain and unassuming woman—almost as dull as he was. They'd both been teachers in the public school system, and were therefore acquainted with all varieties of evil. The only wonder was how they managed to hold the interest of their students! It might have gone on that way until they both reached retirement age and settled into a respectable dotage…except that Mrs. Bennett caught Mr. Bennett doing a bad thing. He strangled their cat.

At first she thought it was because they had been forced to spend so much money on Perseus, her name for the feline, when their pet came down with a serious urinary tract infection. But the cat had survived numerous trips to the vet, and there was no reason for Mr. Bennett to strangle the life out of the poor creature after they'd expended so much effort to save it.

The dream played on. Memory is pain. He'd apologized to his

wife for killing Perseus, more times than he could remember. He didn't know why he had done it. Wives don't like to hear that. And no amount of later goodwill dispelled her memory of the crumpled form of the dead cat or the thin, red scratches all over Mr. Bennett's wrists and hands.

He didn't really resent her for divorcing him. He took it as a sort of judgment. His feeling was that he should be punished for having married her in the first place, and the business of the cat justified her to act as his executioner. There was something of a self-esteem problem here.

So pathetic were these emotions that Valerie and I experienced a kind of culture shock when the images shifted from memory to dream. Suddenly we were plunged into vivid colors, and even the quality of the sound improved! Mr. Bennett, so slow and dull in real life, and not faring much better in his own memory, captured a splendid heroic quality when entering into the deep dream.

The SPELLCHECK was still functioning as MEMORY let us know its work was done. Lifting my wand again, I touched a purple circle and engaged the services of the Spirit of OMEN. The light flared bright, a sign that the dream was more than just a dream.

Now the little, bald man seemed taller, resplendent in golden robes, a jewel-encrusted scepter in his hand. Vague shapes swept past him, as if caught in a hurricane that left him untouched. His name was called out by high, piping voices; he was being honored by unclean things.

Then the picture changed. Now he wore red robes, with a curved dagger in his hand. Except that the robe wasn't really red—it was white underneath all the blood that had splashed on him from sacrificing hundreds of animals. They were all shapes and sizes, from a bull to a hen, from a snake to a sparrow, from a black goat to a pure white Alsatian dog. Surrounded by a sea of brown fur, bright feathers, shining scales, and pools of blood, he was fulfilled in this fantasy. Real life had left him empty of all meaning.

Suddenly Valerie whispered in my ear, which was not accepted procedure. She said, "The very best magick doesn't require blood sacrifice." Who did not know this elementary lesson, taught to members of the Adepts as a fundamental? But she had more to say: "Unfortunately, the old ways, bathed in blood, work!"

As if responding to her words, the dream became more unsavory. Bennett's lips were pulled back in a grimace that in no way could be confused with a smile. His eyes were glazed over and his heart beat like that of a trapped rodent waiting for its turn at the knife. Now there were thousands of animals lined up, all docile as if they had been selected for a hell-bound Noah's ark. Bennett started biting off bits and pieces of the hapless creatures with teeth that seemed sharper than those the little man actually had between his jaws. Gray, human figures appeared at the line of the horizon. They applauded the grotesque banquet.

When the three-dimensional figures faded away, the sounds of dying animals remained. They echoed within the walls of my office for a long time.

The session was over. "What does it mean?" asked our patient, waking up the moment the DreaMeter was removed. The meter was making a strange sputtering sound.

"Have you killed anything besides your cat?" I asked.

"No," he answered. "At least, I don't think so."

"When did the dream begin?" I continued.

"I'm pretty sure it was around the time I got rid of Perseus."

"I'm certain that's when you started having your problems," said Valerie, "and there's a cure for your condition."

I don't know what surprised me more: the fact that my assistant was preempting my authority or the cure she proceeded to administer. She produced a syringe—as if by magick?—and injected the patient before I could make a move to stop her.

"Valerie!" I shouted. "What the hell are you doing?"

"Don't worry," she replied as Mr. Bennett's eyes rolled up in his head and spittle appeared on his lips. With a gurgling sound, he collapsed on the floor. "He's dead," she went on, in that matter-of-fact tone of voice she used when going over accounts.

I'd heard of things like this. Not everyone can handle the pressure. On our backs rests what little civilization there is in the world. (Who am I to quarrel with the party line?) And attractive as Valerie's back appeared, especially when bare, I couldn't let something like this go unreported.

The only trouble was that even as I reached for that most mystical of all devices, a telephone, she intercepted me with a soft hand on my cheek. "Oh, my darling doctor," she cooed, "you don't realize how fortunate it is that I'm here to keep you on the one true path."

"Valerie!" I said her name as though it were an incantation. I wanted to touch her with my wand, the magickal one, as if by this action I could erase her crime. But she was one step ahead of me, as usual.

"Oh, my poor fool," she said, and at that moment I realized how much she must really love me. "There's no time for subtlety now. We won't let anyone sabotage our preparations for your future."

Our? What was this *our?* She didn't need occult powers to read the expression on my face. The day was not going well at all.

She sighed, a very pretty sigh. "You weren't supposed to be told until the end of the week, but you've been selected for the position of a High Mage."

"How would you know that?"

"I was assigned to you," she said quietly. Catching a glimpse of myself in the small mirror we kept by the vase of roses (a homey touch) did nothing to improve my mood. I'm sure that I'd never let a patient see such a face as I was currently wearing.

"But Xenton and Schulmann and Vanessa and the others wouldn't send you. This goes against the teaching of the Virtual

Adepts when you remember that…"

"Who said I was sent by them?" she announced with a grim smile. Funny how this woman I'd known for only a year suddenly seemed so different. "You've been searching all your life. Now the Truth has found you." She seemed to be the same woman I worked with every day—the same face, the same arched eyebrows, the same high cheekbones and full mouth. What had been alluring when she was only my assistant was now transformed into something Queenly—and untouchable.

I looked at the body of the little, bald man, who was somehow less boring in death. He made a perfectly adequate corpse. And I suddenly realized I wouldn't be subjected to any joke from the poor guy, unless his death counted as a punch line. "He'll be removed," she said, "and you won't have to bother with him. We've had dozens of others like him to deal with since I was assigned to you."

A therapist should be prepared for ambivalence. Part of me wanted to bow and worship her; but another part wanted to do to her what Mr. Bennett had done to his cat. After all, I still had my pride for a short time yet.

"Please tell me everything you can," I said.

She smiled her I'm-going-to-eat-you-up-but-you-won't-mind smile and did a terrible thing. She told me!

"You don't have bad dreams, do you, Paul?" I shook my head. She continued: "The True Ones don't. Now that the time of the great change is almost upon us, there are dozens of little false mages, such as Mr. Bennett, who don't even realize they are being summoned by gods of simple absolutism to lead us astray from the real gods of insight. At least the Adepts are right about relativity. When we find a narrow point of view, we remove it. We of the…" She smiled, aware that she had almost said who had sent her. "Nobody must be allowed to distract you from the important tasks that lie ahead; and especially not with the pathetic sacrifices they would offer."

"Excuse me," I said, tempted to raise my hand as if I were a pupil (which in a sense, I was). "What is this great change?"

She smiled with a touching degree of tolerance. "I have not been entrusted with information at that level. You know that all mages in all orders believe only themselves to be right and everyone else to be wrong. The Ascension War is in itself a contradiction—one does not rise by sinking to the lowest depths. The people have sunk so low that they must be reintroduced to more primitive forms of worship. And you, dear one, are to be the instrument of their salvation. No one must stand in your way."

If I'd been thinking clearly, I would have seen problems with her position from the start. The cold-blooded murder should have tipped me off. It was behavior worthy of the cold Technocracy or the malevolent Nephandi or the unpredictable Marauders. We who follow the Nine Traditions are supposed to know better. But the disagreements among the mages of the Nine Traditions had limited our effectiveness for so long that some of us could not help being optimistic. And Valerie knew me well enough to exploit that most dangerous parasite in my soul: hope for a united front against the darkness.

"You murdered for me today," I said in wonder.

"I would kill anyone for the man I love," she replied, further complicating the issue and leaning forward to kiss me with all the passion a man could desire. Under the circumstances, I could only behave as a proper gentleman and make love to her.

Naturally I was sorry about killing her later. She was my first sacrifice. Her masters were annoyed she had told me the good news before I was scheduled to be informed. Oh, well.

———

I still don't know who is behind this new world of mine. I only know it cannot be the Adepts. And there are times when I wonder if what has happened to me is real or if the DreaMeter broke and released nightmares into my head. Perhaps I died in my office that day and never had to kill all those children.

The world I knew had been a dark Gothic nightmare of neon sleaze. But now the public accepts things it never did before! Isolated critics aren't much of a problem, and the really bad ones can always be sacrificed. Fortunately, I have a lot of eager assistants in this work all over the world. It's a weird feeling giving approval for throwing maidens into a live volcano. It's not as hard as I thought it would be, and we have excellent television coverage. (When we sacrificed some young males, the ratings weren't as high.)

The only time I've been really uncomfortable, so far, was the mass sacrifice of children under the full moon. The ratings went through the roof. I know all the arguments. A few hundred slain before the eyes of the world means that thousands will not be raped, mutilated, and abused in secret by lone maniacs whose interest in the preservation of the social order is not very well developed. Civilization must have its little sacrifices now and then.

But I'm still uncomfortable. When I raise doubts that the forces we serve (or utilize) ever wanted human sacrifices, the Shadowy Ones I obey remind me that our civilization has sunk too low to worry over details. We have to work our way back up to where we may be worthy of moral distinctions. The only goal now is to keep Chaos in check by making sure that the oceans of blood the human race insists on spilling will be channeled productively. An ugly voice whispers in my ear with talk about building a dam, behind which all that blood will power the turbines of a renaissance.

Maybe so. Maybe those children had to die. Some of them agreed to the sacrifice, but you can talk a child into nearly anything. Unlike adults.

I'm an adult. I must be. Or they wouldn't trust me with this splendid, curved knife that is always at my side. Sometimes I think it looks just like the one in Mr. Bennett's dream.

I think about that dagger a lot. If the weapon was only in Bennett's dream, and now I seem to have the same cruel thorn in my blood-spattered hand, then maybe I am only dreaming. Maybe I haven't betrayed what I thought to be the human values of the Virtual Adepts. Maybe I haven't immersed my soul in a pool of red murder. What good is magick if it doesn't provide the opportunity of denying what your senses tell you?

Without denial, there are no gods. And lately I have the overwhelming desire to worship...something.

Brad Linaweaver is best known for his novel *Moon of Ice*, which won the Prometheus Award in 1989 and, as a novella, was a Nebula finalist. His second novel is *The Land Beyond Summer*. Brad is also writing, acting and doing interviews for *Horror House* and *Centauri Express*; and collaborating on a comic book with Brad Strickland. He is presently collaborating with Fred Olen Ray on film projects and a feature serial, *The Daughter of Dr. Moreau*, for *Argosy*.

Blood Magic

by Scott Ciencin

I

My lord first had use of me when I was fourteen and newly arrived at the castle. He was not gentle. I bled; it seemed to please him. Only later did I come to derive any brief glimmerings of pleasure from the act.

Much later.

II

You may ask how, in the year of our Lord, Fifteen Hundred and Thirty-Six, a woman of my station has come into possession of skills normally reserved for women of fine breeding. No other member of my lord's household staff can put her thoughts onto paper as I am doing now, or speak with any true eloquence.

My lord wished for me to be a whore to him in all respects. I was to entice not only his body, but his mind. England's finest tutors educated me in history and letters, while France's most inventive prostitutes taught me their secrets. There are few, I daresay, who might provide a more varied and complete night of entertainment than myself.

Do I seem proud? I have read that pride is not a virtue. In truth, I would not hesitate to return the gifts that have been bestowed upon me and pursue a quiet life in the country, perhaps as a teacher or governess.

You cannot hear my laughter at the sight of those words. It is, I believe, touched with madness.

III

I see that I did not mention children in my idyllic little daydream. I was with child once. The son of my lord grew within my belly. The day my lord learned of my condition, he worked upon me with his blade and his Art.

Children shall never again be a concern for me.

IV

I wish to tell you of my lord, and it seems impossible to speak of him without first mentioning Anne Boleyn. She is the reason for his existence, for she is the woman who cast a spell with her wit and guile that ensnared the heart of a true mage.

Some call Anne Boleyn the queen. Others refer to her as King Henry's whore. They say she has lovers. I know this for a fact. My lord is one of them. At times, I have also held that distinction.

The woman disgusts me.

My lord is sleek and elegant, a panther in human form. Boleyn is grotesque. My master will not see the woman for what she has become. He uses his infernal Art to cast illusions for his own benefit. I know this, because she was once young and beautiful. In the span of a few short years she has become a thin old woman. I bed her only when I must. My lord *lives* for the moments when she writhes beneath him, clawing at him like an animal. I do not see how any man alive could keep himself erect in the presence of such a withered husk without the use of dark sorceries.

I have no sympathy for her. I know the stresses that have been inflicted upon her by King Henry and his mad obsession for an heir. She knew them, too. My lord and Lady Anne — as he forces me to call her — concocted a plan years ago that would have given him vengeance while granting her ultimate power.

What I did not know until recently is the part I was meant to play in that plan.

V

I could tell you about myself — recount the brutal events that placed me in the tender care of my lord. But I am not important. I have never been, nor shall I ever be — except, perhaps, to those who read this account. I said that I wished to tell you of my lord, and so I shall.

My lord's name is Henry Weir. He is the first son born to the King of England. Only a handful of people know this. It seems there is no shortage of bastards sired by the king. The best known is that pompous little whip Henry Fitzroy, whom the king now labors to legitimize. Then, of course, there is the boy "Lady Anne's" sister Mary bore for the king.

The man who takes me to his bed each night, who vents his rage upon me and releases his seed within me, is one of the very few who has escaped notice by the tongue-waggers. His fondest wish is for that to change. He desires to reshape reality itself and mold it into a form that bears his image, that he will find pleasing.

God save me, I have helped him in this.

VI

I will not call her Lady Anne again. These are my private thoughts. My lord does not hold such sway over me that I cannot defy him in this secret place.

He does not.

He does *not*.

VII

Try as I might, I cannot banish a certain memory from my mind. Perhaps if I put it here, I can succeed in burning it from the recesses of my brain.

My lord and the king's whore had just finished rutting. She was sore. It had been their third time in as many hours. Anxious for some diversion, Anne shared with my lord a package of letters. Some were written by the king. Others quoted him.

"Look at this," the whore whispered. " 'A young lady who has the soul of an angel and a spirit worthy of a crown.' The fool said this of me to George Wyatt. I tell you, my love, this *will* work."

Smiling enigmatically, my lord rifled through the letters and found one that seemed to please him. " 'I now think the king so much in love that only God can get him out of this mess.' " He laughed. "It will take more than the hand of his pale God to extract the lout."

They called upon me, and I did everything within my power to make the whore ready for my lord's entry. Despite techniques I knew to be infallible, the woman stayed dry. My lord beat me to within an inch of my life, then smeared his lover's ugly little knot with my blood. Finally, she became aroused.

It wasn't until she had left that he healed me.

That is all.

VIII

My lord occasionally entertains. One morning, I overheard

him speaking to a guest and was shocked to note that I was the topic of conversation. My lord talked of me with genuine pride and called me his "acolyte."

The word is not unknown to me. Nevertheless, the manner in which he spoke the word caused me to imagine my lord and his visitor assigning the phrase an entirely different meaning, one of great importance. At the time, I thought it very odd.

I long for my lost innocence.

IX

The first time I became aware of my lord's calling as a mage is a happy memory for me. I know that must sound odd, considering all I have told you. Even so, it is true.

My only companion, my only friend through my ordeal, has been an unlikely one. A mouse. A small white mouse whose name I will not share. Very little in my life is private. After all that has transpired I am willing to reveal secrets that may sear a man's soul, but this I am determined to keep to myself.

The first time I saw the mouse, three and a half years ago, I was frightened. It ran over my foot as I was dressing for my lord, and I screamed so loudly that I sent the creature into a panic. The mouse raced from one end of the room to the other, desperately seeking the hole from which it had emerged. My terror was instantly abated as I saw the poor thing run into a wall with enough force to leave it dazed and vulnerable.

I heard footsteps from the hall — the distinctive heavy thump of my lord's boots — and I acted out of instinct, not reason. I snatched the mouse up and hid it under my pillow. My lord came in and was angered when I haltingly made up a tale of slipping into a nightmare and waking up with a scream. Taking him out of his foul mood was not especially difficult. I merely put my mouth to other uses.

That night, I saw the mouse again. I fed it. Over the next year, playing with the creature became my only release. I would not be surprised to discover that it was this enterprise alone that kept me sane. After all, the other women loathed me, and to my lord I was a vessel, a convenience, even an amusement — but never a person.

One afternoon, I returned to my room and found another of the servants within. I demanded an explanation for her presence. Her only response was a strangled cry of distaste before she ran past me.

I went inside and quickly pieced together all that had occurred. My little companion had become brazen. It had revealed itself to the woman who had entered my room. She had found a knife I used for whittling, another of my talents, and had plunged it into the body of the mouse.

I screamed until my lord arrived. He surprised me that day. Rather than treat me with his customary callousness, he brushed the hair from my face and asked what was wrong. The mouse was still clinging to life. He stroked its fur and asked me to get up and close the door. I did not think to question him. Perhaps I thought he would snap its neck. It was but a little thing after all.

As I sealed us inside my chamber, something I cannot fully explain occurred. Reality seemed to warp. My perceptions altered and for a moment I believed that I was looking into a vast pattern of pulsating light and shadow. In seconds, my vision cleared and the pattern reconciled itself to images that were far more acceptable.

My lord crouched over the mouse. The blade had been removed from the creature, and its wound had been healed. I opened my hands, and it raced toward me.

I was barely aware as my lord rose, all color drained from his face, and retreated from my chamber. I said nothing. The tears on my face, the happiness I displayed, seemed thanks enough.

Odd. As I think upon it now, that is, perhaps, my only happy memory involving my lord. Is it any wonder that it shines so brightly, a single lit torch in a cavern of endless darkness?

If only that brief moment of happiness could have been stretched over the course of a lifetime, I would not even contemplate the act I am soon to perform.

X

For months afterward, I treated my lord like a god, for so he seemed to me then. One day, he took me to the courtyard and pressed me against a great tree, one with endless clawing branches and a girth unmatched by any I have seen in my life.

I have witnessed my lord standing next to this towering oak many times, touching it, silently communing with it, or so it might seem. After these visits, the tree always appears different: at times healthier, more vital; at others, more skeletal and threatening. I have touched the tree myself and have wondered if it too is little more than a vessel for my lord, a repository for his unpredictable moods.

No answers were forthcoming that day. I waited for my lord's hands to work their will upon me. Strangely, he did not desire me in a carnal sense, though he was breathless and clearly aroused.

"I need you," he whispered. "Will you help me?"

This shocked me. My lord does not beg my leave in anything. After the miraculous events in my room that were not so distant, I readily agreed.

"Anything," I whispered.

Above, the sunlight waned and a steel-gray bank of clouds moved in, casting the courtyard in an odd, lifeless haze. My lord withdrew a scroll, which he stretched across my bosom and secured with daggers to the tree on either side of my shoulders. He instructed me not to move. The parchment was fragile and might tear at the slightest provocation.

My promise to remain still lay in my eyes, which, for the first time, were filled more with love for my lord than fear. He received my silent acquiescence and begged of me, "Close your eyes, sweet one. Think pleasant thoughts."

I heard the scrape of steel on steel and imagined a blade being drawn from a scabbard. My lord wears such a blade at all times. It is cruel-looking, with a hook at one end. I have seen it sparkling in the sunlight.

Suddenly, there was a hiss and a gentle breath of air. It felt so much like a feather being raked across my throat that I smiled and nearly laughed. When I tried to swallow and take a breath, I found that I could not. A weakness unlike any I have ever experienced threatened to overwhelm me.

"Steady," my lord commanded. "The slightest movement will be my undoing."

Panic seized me. I did not want to disappoint my lord, but my breath was an animal racing far beyond my grasp. A second odd sensation came to me. I felt moisture upon my skin. It was hot and thick. My eyes flashed open.

I found myself staring into the bloodstained face of my lord. Crimson liquid splattered upon his face, and I heard blood spraying onto the parchment. I tried to reach for my throat, which had surely been cut wide open.

"Damn you!" my lord screamed as he rushed forward and held me in place. His hand shot forward, covering my eyes, and all was darkness.

When I woke, I was well, but alone. There was no trace of the blood I had lost or the wound that had been opened upon my flesh.

There was no need for me to bear a physical scar.

The memory would suffice.

XI

As I returned to my room he accosted me in the hall. He grabbed me by the waist and spun me around. I was too weak to protest. He kissed me with his cold lips and said, "Blood is life. Without it, there is nothing. With it, all things are possible."

That day the woman who would become known as King Henry's whore made her first appearance.

A bloody scroll was clutched in her hand.

XII

Never have I cared for the way she looks at me. She sees me as something other than human. Even my lord treats me with the occasional common courtesy or some small kindness now and again. True, his actions might better befit a stray dog than a man's lover. Nevertheless, when tenderness is such a limited commodity, one does not question the level of its sincerity.

XIII

Often I am commanded to entice my lord's acquaintances to my bed. My lord is proud of his possessions and enjoys displaying them. My body, which I daresay is as close to perfect as any I have seen, is not the only possession of my lord I am charged with maintaining.

He keeps a collection of objects in one of his private rooms beneath the castle. I have heard him remark of his "talismans" when his odd guests are about. They speak of these objects in hushed voices filled with an odd gravity.

I am the one who cleans them each day. It has always been a point of personal satisfaction that my lord allows me alone access to his private rooms. Strange, is it not? To lead a life in which being charged with one form of drudgery over another is an honor.

Most of the objects seem unremarkable to me. In my lord's collection can be found a rather ordinary-looking blade, a hairpin, a splinter of wood, a ring with a glass stone, a dented goblet, and a butterfly broach. Only the last of these holds any interest for me. I have always been fascinated with butterflies. They begin life without beauty and end as its avatars.

When I hold the butterfly broach, I feel an odd tingling. A

giddiness overcomes me. I can almost believe that one day I will have my freedom, that one day I will know more than torture and rape.

I am holding it now. The pin used to fasten it to clothing pierces the flesh of my palm.

There is a good deal of blood,

XIV

Perhaps by now you are curious about my lord's plan. The roots of my lord's desire for vengeance stem from his lineage. As I have told you, his true name is Henry Weir. He is the firstborn son of King Henry. From an early age, he has cultivated an image of his future. He had planned to stand one day before our liege, his father, and be accepted as the rightful heir.

To this end, my lord spent his life studying the Arts. He used them to rise above his humble station and become a man of wealth and power. When the time came to seek an audience with the king, however, his way was barred. King Henry knew all too well the name Weir. The tryst with my lord's mother was now seen by the king as a nightmare he wished to forget.

XV

My lord's mother was also a mage. On the night she brought the young, handsome King Henry to her bed, she parted the veil and told him of the future that might be. The vision she planted in his mind of a healthy male heir would drive the king his entire life. He knew that sorcery was being worked on him and he was terrified.

"Our son," she whispered. "You see before you the product of our union."

"An unholy union," he roared. "Thou art a witch. A demon in a pleasing form. Approach me not or I will have you staked to the ground so that hungry ants can devour your black heart!"

Many years later, when my lord came to call, one of the king's advisors met with him. Henry Weir was told in no uncertain terms that his life had been a boon from a kind and generous master. If he attempted to spread his wild story of being the king's rightful successor, the full might of England would come crashing down upon him like an iron fist.

My lord left the palace and never looked back. He is a proud and dangerous man and he might have survived such a conflict; he may have triumphed. But such is not the way of the mage. He decided then and there that it is far better to conduct one's business from the shadows.

XVI

He learned of the king's designs on Anne Boleyn and summoned her through means I have already described. Falling in love was certainly not part of my lord's plan.

With the woman who would become the king's whore, my lord concocted a plan. To become the queen and maintain her husband's favor, Anne needed to bear sons. Boleyn's certainty that she would bear our liege a son was based on more than arrogance. My lord promised to help in means natural and otherwise. The son, of course, would be his. If he could not have the throne, his heir would rule in his stead, and with his strict instruction.

Something went wrong. The king's whore became pregnant three times. Elizabeth, the first child, was of the king's loins, not my master's. The next two children were sons, but they were stillborn.

XVII

King Henry has become convinced that he faces God's punishment. He rages like a lunatic and seeks the means to annul his marriage to Boleyn. I see this enterprise as doomed to failure. He petitioned the church to separate him from Catherine of Aragon not three years past. When his request was denied, he created a church of his own. What is he to do now? Create another religion and claim that he was mad then but sane now?

My master has been touched by a shade of the insanity that drives the king. His need for Boleyn to give our liege a son is perhaps even greater than King Henry's. Once, in trying to comfort him, I told him that he should be grateful for Boleyn's shortcomings; the king would never have been thrust so deeply into the arid lands of damnation and agony if Boleyn's first spawn had been male.

I will not tell you the means my lord used to punish me for my insolent remark. All I will say is that the blood running through my veins has many uses, and my lord seems intent on exploring each and every one. Over the last three years he has performed acts upon me I am loath to think about, let alone set down in writing.

Forgive me, I digress. The quill in my hand is a double-edged sword. With it I may make cuts into this tender parchment that reveal both love and hatred of my lord. He inspires both, but not in equal measure.

XVIII

While King Henry grew to hate Anne for her boisterous and unfulfilled assurances that she would give him a son, my lord treated her with increasing kindness. How difficult it has been to watch him fawn over her and comfort her when I knew he would later vent his rage upon me.

Still, I cannot help but wonder if his anger was entirely tempered by his love for the whore. I have described the odd effect my lord's touch has had on the tree in the courtyard. It has withered in the face of his rage many times. Gazing upon the countenance and body of the king's whore, who has gone from a beautiful young woman to a withered hag in less than three years, gives me reason to pause.

XIX

My companion, my confidant, is dead. I do not believe my lord killed him. The mouse was hardly fresh and new when I first made his acquaintance. Age takes its toll.

I want desperately to bring his body to my master and see if he can imbue it with some semblance of life, but the thought terrifies me. As I stare at the body of my only friend, I cannot help but ask: am I dead or alive?

I do not dream. That precious talent left me the day my master cut my throat. He used to ask about my dreams and delight in their tellings. Especially the nightmares. After that afternoon in the courtyard, he never asked again.

Did I die that day? Am I now his in body and soul?

Or has it always been that way?

XX

The drastic measures to which I must soon resort have their origins in two memorable days. The first occurred many years in the past, the second less than three weeks ago. I am grateful for each of these days.

I also curse them.

XXI

I have mentioned the butterfly broach and how taken I am with it. My lord has worn it only once in my presence. That was two years ago.

The day started out poorly. An important delivery was long overdue. My lord did not tell me the nature of the parcels he expected, and I knew enough not to inquire. When they did not arrive in the morning or afternoon, he grew furious and vented his anger upon me.

Moments before the dinner bells were rung, the parcels expected by my lord arrived. I was wholly unprepared for the entrance of two magnificent wild animals: a lion and a tiger. I assumed my lord meant to set them in a cage and allow them to fight to the death for his amusement. Such events are not uncommon here. Beggars from the street have engaged in similar contests for my lord's pleasure. Without exception, my lord slays the victor.

I watched with bated breath as my lord had the creatures chained in the receiving hall. He then dismissed the animal handlers and the rest of his servants. Only I was allowed to remain. He stepped between the creatures and laid his hands over the eyes of each animal. They seemed to go into a trance.

My heart thundered as my lord transformed each creature into the likeness of the other. The lion melted and became the tiger. The tiger shimmered and took on the appearance of the lion. Screaming with pleasure, my lord raced toward me, threw me down, and took me in the receiving hall of the chamber. The creatures roared behind us.

As my lord thrust his member into me with a frenzy I almost found arousing, I saw the butterfly broach pinned to the flesh of his breast.

The next morning, both animals were slaughtered.

XXII

Last week, I was called upon to join my lord and the king's whore in his chambers. They were rejoicing. Both were drunk. I was about to remove my shift when my lord ordered me to travel to his private rooms and retrieve one of his talismans: the ring with the glass stone.

Grateful that I was being issued a momentary reprieve from having to lie with the king's whore, I raced from his chamber and went below. It was not until I had returned with the ring and was standing outside the door to my lord's chamber that I pictured Anne's face on receiving the item.

This was the Queen of England. The finest jewels in the land adorned her pale, dry throat and bony fingers. She would be revolted by this pitiful bauble. My heart was filled with joy at the thought of her discomfort. She would have to pretend to admire the ring and its glass stone. To do otherwise would be to risk the wrath of her lover.

Upon my return, they regarded me with bemused expressions. Suddenly, Anne broke into waves of outrageous laughter. My lord smiled and motioned for me to come forward.

Anne bolted to a sitting position as my lord took the ring from me and slipped it on her finger. She shrugged.

My heart sank at her reaction.

"It may not look like much," he said. "Even so, it has a *glamour* all its own."

The whore's expression changed to one of concern. "What of those creatures you mentioned? The demons of Paradox?"

"My love, you have seen my work before. There is no threat with you."

"I meant to our guest," she said, eyeing me mischievously.

"A little vulgar magick never killed anyone who took precautions. Besides, there is no reason for her to stay, unless you wish it."

"Yes!" she cried. "Let the little dear stay. I wish to share this with her."

I started to move forward. My lord frowned and waved me to a corner where an ornate chair waited. I sat attentively as my lord, dark and magnificent, caressed the bony witch and began to pleasure her.

A few minutes later, my lord lay upon the queen, pounding his cock into the whore's gnarled hole. He yanked her into his lap and allowed her to thrust her hips against him.

The woman's eyes were closed. I watched as the ring worn by the whore seemed to shine. The object caught all available rays of light in the room and twisted them into spiraling, prismlike patterns. She seemed unaware that she and her lover were rising into the air until her feet left the bed.

Her eyes flashed open. Gasping in surprise, the queen looked down. To her credit, she swallowed her fear and rode my lord as if she had been born to make love in this manner, so much like a god. I might have been jealous of her, but I was too busy drawing conclusions of my own.

XXIII

After they had sated their passions and literally settled back down to earth, the lovers parted and the king's whore came to me. She seemed to hold me in a completely new regard. Glancing at my clothes, she asked me to describe my wardrobe.

I did as I had been commanded.

"Shameful," she cried, looking over her shoulder and winking at my lord before returning her gaze to me. "You will have a new wardrobe. Have you any jewels?"

"None that I own," I stammered.

"That shall change as well. I will be your mentor. Your guide. With my help, you will be remade."

I did not know what to say. My lord sensed my reticence and ordered me to thank the queen. I did so and she gave me a sisterly hug.

Her smile was warm, but her flesh was colder than ever before.

XXIV

The next few days were a blur. The queen was as good as her word. She watched as I was fitted for the finest gowns and my long hair was put up and hidden away in ornate caps. For a brief, splendid moment, I was adorned in what could only have been the crown jewels. Naturally, any pleasure I might have derived from such an honor was immediately frightened away by the hungry, insane look that spidered across the face of the king's whore.

My lord wandered in occasionally, He said very little and rarely looked my way. His gaze was only for *her*.

Boleyn spent many hours talking to me as if I were to be her confidant. She described her life at the castle with phrases such as "boredom" and "drudgery." The woman actually *shuddered* when she told me how she loathed her husband's touch. I found myself pitying our liege, who defied all that was sacred to make this evil creature his queen.

Anne filled my mind with endless details about her existence. On several occasions she stopped to question me about information she had given earlier, as if she were worried that I was not paying attention.

She said she loved my lord very much, but I knew better. The woman was incapable of love.

I act with a clear conscience.

XXV

My revulsion reached its peak when one night the whore asked me to undress. I thought she wished for me to pleasure her through some unspeakable means. That was not the case. Instead, she simply stared at me. For close to an hour she asked me to move this way and that; she even examined me with a magnifying glass, checking my flesh for minute imperfections.

"Perfect," she whispered. "You are so perfect. So much like an angel. It is good you cherish the gifts God has given you. Preserve them well. You do not have to share my fate and become old before your time; there are ways all the ravages of the natural world can be forced back."

Her hand rose to my breast and stopped before my nipple.

"Enjoy these times," she commanded. With that, she rose and departed. Her interest left me shaken.

XXVI

During this ordeal, I had to keep my mind from focusing fully on the matters at hand. I concentrated on the powers locked away within my lord's ring, his talisman. Clearly, that object had allowed the withered slut Boleyn to rise into the air like a goddess of old while she and my lord indulged their grotesque passions. I knew that the magick wielded by my lord lay within him, but I now saw that it was possible for him to lock away certain spells in repositories. That only made sense. He was often drained after performing a particularly difficult feat of magick.

The talismans I alone was allowed to clean each day held great powers; of this I was now convinced. The problem then became one of deducing how to make them work and learning what each might accomplish. For this I knew I would need time, and so I had to wait until the king's whore finally tired of me.

The opening for which I had been waiting came a week after I had first seen one of the talismans performing its assigned task. Boleyn did not come to the castle until very late on that day, and so I had time to clean the lower chambers fully. Alone where the talismans were kept, I slipped the ring on my finger and waited for something to happen.

Several minutes later, I was still waiting.

When Boleyn utilized the ring, she seemed to do nothing but concentrate and force her will upon the object. From her reaction when she was lifted up into the air, I deduced that she had no idea what strange power to expect from the ring. If she did not understand the ring's nature and was not willing herself into the air, on what did she concentrate?

Her pleasure. She was *feeling*, not thinking. Clearing her mind. Allowing herself to be open to each new sensation.

I squeezed my eyes shut and tried to recall the love and gratitude I held the day my lord gave back the life of my little friend, the mouse. That love was a perfect thing: pure, and like all pure things, easily corrupted. I tried not to think of what came later. Only that one, simple feeling.

I rose into the air.

XXVII

From my past observations, I understood the nature of the butterfly broach's power. At the moment, I did not want to think about how it related to the strange events of the last week. Instead, I examined the other talismans: the knife, the goblet, the splinter of wood, and the hairpin.

The splinter of wood seemed so much less formidable than all the others, especially the blade. My hand went to it.

Suddenly, there was a screech from above. I cried out as a demonic *thing* hurled itself from the darkness and sailed for my face. Golden eyes and sharp, tiny teeth filled my vision. Somehow I moved. The creature landed on the table holding my lord's talismans. The dented goblet teetered on the table's edge, then fell.

As it struck the floor, I saw that the "monster" was no more than a stray cat that had somehow wandered into the castle. One of the servants had probably fed it.

The cat was gray and white. Its dark eyes reflected the flaming torch lighting the spacious chamber. The insolent little beast hissed at me, and I swatted at it. A claw rose swiftly and scratched the back of my hand. Blood struck the table. Yelping in pain, I advanced on the cat and it bolted, flying off into the darkness. I wanted to catch it, to wring its damnable neck, but I knew I had to utilize my time here to the fullest. Keeping a close watch on the beast, I bent low and picked up the goblet.

I had not considered how greatly I had been focused on my rage at the animal until I felt the goblet tingle and looked down to see a strange mist pouring from it. A thick fog engulfed the room in seconds. I heard the stray cat scratching at the floor, then took a step in its direction. The mists parted, and I saw the animal stiffen and fall still.

This talisman produced a cloud of death!

Like a fool, I released my hold on the goblet, anxious to turn and run from this room before the poisons I released could also take my life. The moment it left my hand I understood my error. The fog had not been affecting me so long as I held the goblet. In that way I was protected.

Reaching for the sorcerous item I had dropped, I felt my lungs contract. I stiffened as darkness closed over me.

XXIII

I woke to find my lord crouching over me. A fury unlike any I had ever before witnessed burned in his eyes. I was surprised to find myself alive and was certain that condition would be rectified in a moment or two.

"Little fool!" he screamed as he grasped my arm and pulled me to a sitting position. "Do you have any idea what you might have done?"

I stammered that I did not and said that I had only meant to *clean* the objects. The cat knocked one over, I picked it up, and mists poured from it.

The muscles in his face twitched and his grip on my arm tightened, bringing a slight cry of pain from my lips. He did not strike me. Instead, he snatched the splinter of wood from the table and cried, "Do you see this? This might have ringed you in fire! Would you have liked that? To burn alive? For you would have. Your fear would have defeated you and the power would have charred you into a husk."

Shaking his head, he released me. "Why do I waste my words on the dead? You are never to come here again. I will tend to these objects. No one else."

Later, the king's whore stared at the bruise on my arm with

distaste. "You really must take better care of your magnificent body, child. Anything less is unthinkable."

I cried myself to sleep that night. Without access to my lord's private chambers and his talismans of power, I would have no chance of gaining the upper hand against my lord and the creature he professed to love. Worse still, I had no idea if he suspected me in the intrigue I had been plotting. I still do not know.

Time alone will prove the judge of that.

XXIX

You may ask why I did not simply run away. Having gone over my earlier entries, I see it is a curiosity. Rather than scrawl these notes in a margin, I will tell you here and now. I could travel only so far from this castle before I collapsed with a strange sickness. At that point, I was easily collected. I discovered this during my first week with my lord. His magick was worked upon me when I first arrived.

For so long I have been his, body and soul. My blood fires his arcane ways.

No more.

XXX

The morning after my disastrous attempt to pry loose the secrets of all my lord's talismans, I woke feeling certain I had no more than a few weeks to live. Rumor had it that the queen would soon be served with a writ of arrest. Soon after that, she would be tried and executed. Only I knew it would not be her head that fell from the block — it would be my own.

I told you the magick my lord worked upon the lion and the tiger. As I write this, I am convinced that my lord intends for Anne and me to switch places in a similar manner. That is why she has been thrusting intimate knowledge of her life into my brain with her constant lectures and quizzes. I will find myself the perfect duplicate of Anne while she takes my form. No one will listen to my mad ravings that I am not the queen, that I merely resemble her. I must find a way to stop her. If utilizing my lord's magick against him is no longer an option, I will find another way.

I believe I know where to look for an entirely new weapon. The queen is not a mage, but she knows a form of magic that was old when the world was young: deceit.

She is not the only one capable of practicing it.

XXXI

Many aspects of my life I take for granted, often forgetting how unusual they must seem to a casual observer. Allow me to clarify one of them before I continue. My lord chose no less than the Queen of England as his paramour. This was a dangerous enterprise, one nearly impossible to keep a secret. Nevertheless, the trysts between the whore and my lord have gone on for years with no one the wiser.

I have no knowledge of how she manages to escape the king without arousing notice. All I can tell you is this: When she is here, I am the only one who can see her in her true form. Why my lord granted no one else this power, I do not know. Also, no one sees her come and go. No carriage brings her. One cannot help but wonder how her presence here is achieved.

In any event, there is never a shortage of gossip in England. In our castle, the whore is always a topic of conversation. I went to the source of all gossip in our castle. Her name is Gerty, and I have had many disagreeable dealings with her in the past. In truth, she is the wicked creature who had been in my room on that long-ago, magical day, and had plunged a blade into my little mouse. Now I may deduce that she was looking for grist for her gossip mill.

As I said, all the household staff holds me in contempt. I am the mistress of the castle; thus I am above them. I am a whore and a plaything; thus I am beneath them.

That I am a person has never entered into the equation for even one of them.

Gerty told me what I wished to know. Rumors fly concerning the queen's lover, supposedly a musician in her court. Some even believe him to be Elizabeth's father!

Unable to hide my excitement, I told Gerty that I would win great favor with our lord when I shared this tale with him tonight. He was moaning the previous eve about his need for some proper amusement, and what could be more entertaining than the trials and tribulations of the king? Particularly as we all know how he loathes the man so dearly.

"Tonight?" Gerty asked. "You will not speak to him until then?"

"I have matters to which I must attend during the day. That is all right. Better to deliver this story at the proper time, don't you think?"

With that, I turned and walked away from Gerty.

Long past midnight, Gerty was still wailing from the wounds my lord inflicted upon her when she immediately told him the gossip concerning the queen, just as I knew she would. The woman did not implicate me. That would have only made her punishment worse.

That night, I felt my lost companion lay in his grave a little easier.

XXXII

My lord called for me, as I anticipated. I was terrified to answer his summons, but I went anyway. He took me to the courtyard, set me against the tree, and worked a bit of magick upon me with my blood *and* his. From his hurried explanation I learned the true nature of my imprisonment. Until then I had believed the invisible leash binding me to the castle had to do with the distance I traveled. That was wrong. Instead, it is the amount of time I spend away from the castle that determines the severity of the illness which strikes me down.

What a mockery! If only I had known, I might have chanced the gnawing sickness simply for a change of locales.

My lord assigned me a task. I was to find Mark Smeaton, the musician who supposedly warmed Anne's bed, work my wiles upon him, and learn the truth behind his rumored affair with the queen. I would have two days in which to complete this task.

I left the castle, my heart thundering in anticipation.

XXXIII

I will not bore you with my travails in England. Suffice it to say I felt as if I had been let loose in a wonderland, and I never wished to return. Some say that wishing makes it so. I have come to consider that the aforementioned notion might be, in fact, the very basis of my lord's magick.

That matters little, now.

I found the man. Bedding him was a simple matter for one of my charms. What followed next is not so easy to describe.

I have told you that I am an experienced lover. This is an irrefutable notion provided we are to discuss the mechanics of pleasuring a man or a woman — the techniques. Nevertheless, I have rarely enjoyed the act. Rutting is all I have ever known.

That night, I made love for the first time. Mark was gentle with me. Not out of fear or ineptitude, but because he wished to tend to my pleasure — *that* was more important to him than his own satisfaction. I have been in similar situations, usually when a lover cannot function despite every trick I have been taught to circumvent such an occurrence, but those incidents have always been a result of my lover wishing to compensate for his own shortcoming by eliciting a thunderous response from me.

With Mark, sex was shocking and unlike any experience I have ever known. I cried when we made love. I screamed so loudly when the first of countless orgasms ripped through me that my throat was sore for days.

But that was only a part of it. He played his music for me. Composed a piece before my very eyes and told me he was inspired by our love.

Yes, our love.

Until then, I was not quite sure of the word's meaning. I felt loyalty to my lord, indebtedness, fear, need — but these I had confused with love, or substituted for it. For the first time, I can perhaps understand what befell my lord. Being in love is both wonderful and terrible. There is no way for me to control myself.

How can I use this man if I care for him? Then again, how can I not?

XXXIV

Upon returning to the castle I gave my lord an account of the musician. I told him the man is indeed Anne's lover and gravely recounted the manner in which Mark Smeaton laughed about having Anne Boleyn right under the king's nose. Lies, all of it. My lord's fury was contained, and that was certainly a more frightening sight than when he releases his rage and has done with it.

You see, my lord has been willing to share his lover with his own father. That has always been part and parcel of his plan for vengeance. The idea, however, that she would dare to sleep with any others — that he cannot tolerate.

To my surprise, my lord encouraged me to see more of Mark. I protested, but he was adamant. He wanted the man happy and unsuspecting. At moments like that one, I could almost believe in the existence of God.

XXXV

Anne has been angry that her musician has been absent, seeing some little tramp. Enraged! My lord watches her closely. Suspiciously.

I am well pleased.

XXXVI

One night, Mark and I laughed about the queen. He loathes her. He is a playful one, my Mark, and on a whim he attempted a courtly flirtation with her. She chided him and said, "You may not look to have me speak to you as I would do to a nobleman, because you are an *inferior* person."

He protested, "No, no, a look suffices!"

My lover is not of gentle birth. He has risen only because of his talent with the lute. I hold him, stay close to him, and somehow feel pure when I lie beside him.

Even now, I close my eyes and see my lover's face, listen with my heart and hear his music, abide the invisible hands of a soft spring breeze and feel his gentle touch.

This is magic. True magic.

All else is a sham.

XXXVII

Thus we are brought full circle. It is midafternoon as I labor on this chronicle. This work is my only solace. In a few hours, Mark Smeaton will come here for the first time. Soon after Mark arrives, Henry Weir plans to torture my beloved and pry loose the secrets of Anne's duplicity.

I will see the mage dead first.

While I was away from the castle, I made other preparations. Poisons are simple to acquire.

All is in readiness.

XXXVIII

The day has passed quickly. The ointment is prepared. The gloves Anne Boleyn prefers me to wear at all times so as not to mar my flesh, even by accident, will protect me. The moment I touch the ointment to my lord's skin he will convulse and die.

Do not ask how I tested it.

A knock comes at my door. My heart is fit to explode. Merciful God, am I undone?

XXXIX

My mind is spinning. My visitor was Anne Boleyn.

Yet it was not.

I have learned how Anne leaves the castle without detection and arrives here without fanfare. My lord has made for her a double. It is her likeness in every physical way, but it radiated an aura of otherness that allowed me (and perhaps me alone) to identify it instantly. After all, it was my blood, not the queen's, that gave it life.

The double had a special chamber in a deserted wing of the castle. When Anne wished to visit my lord, she had only to find a secluded place, take out yet another talisman my lord had given her and work her will upon it. The double vanished from our castle and assumed the role of the queen while the real Anne cavorted with my lord.

I learned that it was the *double* who would die in Anne's place, not I. I had been mistaken.

For a single instant, I felt elated. Then I looked into the double's tear-filled eyes. Only then did I think to ask why she had sought me out.

"Do not go through with it," she said. "Your plan cannot work. Henry Weir is proof to all poisons, including the ointment you have purchased. He will not kill you. Your lover will be punished in your stead."

"How do you know of my plans?" I asked, terrified that my lord had somehow found out and he had told her.

Shaking her head, she whispered, "Your blood runs in my veins. We are sisters in all things. I have known your thoughts and your agonies for as long as I have been alive."

I did not want to believe any of this, but I had no choice. "If it is your head that will fall on the block, why has the queen been acting so strangely with me? She studies me, dresses me, admires me, and tells me endless details of her life at court. If I am not to trade places with her —"

"You are," the double said, "but not in the way you assumed. You see, through his magick, Weir can alter a person's memories or create them from whole cloth, as he has done with me. I possess Anne Boleyn's memories, but they are like a tale told to me about someone else. A fable pulled from a book. Yours are more immediate.

"As to why she has been reading you chapter and verse regarding her life, she wishes for you to sympathize with her, so that you will not mind giving up your life for her. She has, through the person of Henry Weir, attempted the same tack with me."

"I *am* to die, then," I said softly.

"Both of us, yes. You were half right in your assumptions. She wants your skin. Nothing else."

I tried to absorb all of this, but all I could think of was my lover already *en route* to the castle. He knew nothing of my plans. I had thought that when Henry Weir lay dead at my feet I would explain it all to him, secure the talismans, and perform the dark trick my lord had planned for me. In other words, I would change my lover's appearance to resemble Henry Weir's and alter the corpse to look like poor Mark. When Anne came seeking her lover, she would find him changed and wishing nothing more to do with her. Hence she would die on the block and my vengeance would be complete.

A new plan was in order, and there was little time to formulate it. The double spoke again.

"Why do you think Henry Weir's attempts to make Anne pregnant with a healthy male child have all been failures? Because it is your blood he has used, and your will is stronger than you know."

I stared into the double's earnest face. "Your duty was to tell our lord of my plans, not to come to me. Yet you did so anyway. Can I count on you further?"

The double nodded. "I have come here to show you where my loyalties lie. Until you gave yourself to the musician, until you knew love, I was too weak to act. Your courage has freed me. The bond we share has allowed me to take a part of your strength. I will do anything."

"Yes," I said, new ideas already forming in my mind.

The double looked directly into my eyes and said, "They tell me I have no soul, but can anyone be more soulless than either of them?"

I could not argue the point.

She began to cry. "I feel...I am lonely...I *need*."

Taking my shadow twin into my arms, I held her for a time, then asked what I had to of her. She readily agreed, and we hurried to our prospective tasks.

XXXX

This will be my final entry. You may wonder if I am writing it from the tower, awaiting execution in place of the scarlet queen, Anne Boleyn, or if I am in my chamber at the castle. I will allow you to draw your own conclusions. All will soon be clear.

Anne's double helped me in ways available only to her. I told you earlier that I was the only person in the castle, other than perhaps my lord, who saw Anne in her true form. Nevertheless, the staff understood that my lord's mystery lover was to be treated as if she were royalty.

My blood sister had no difficulty in gaining access to my lord's private chambers and collecting his talismans. Once they were in my hands, I knew my plan could not fail.

As to how I convinced Mark to travel here, I had told him that I held an honorable position at my lord's castle and it would bring me great favor with my master if he would come and play. He would also be generously rewarded.

Inducing Mark to take any gold for the performance was difficult, but necessary. He wished to do it simply as a favor to the woman he loved. If that aspect of his character had been revealed, if my lord saw him as anything other than a scheming wretch, my work would be nearly impossible.

Finally, Mark accepted the money. He said he would spend a fair amount on horses and liveries for his servants. I knew that would set the tongues of the gossip-mongers to wagging and would help to incriminate him all the more as Anne's supposed lover. After all, where would a musician who made only one hundred pounds per *annum* get the money for such an extravagance? From the queen, of course. For services rendered.

Soon the appointed time arrived. I had petitioned my lord for the honor of standing near when he put the musician to the question and later used his great power to tear the man limb from limb. I claimed that Mark Smeaton's touch had repulsed me and that I would gladly revel in his screams.

We were in my lord's vast receiving hall when Mark entered. He was unsuspecting of the treachery that waited for him. The moment my lord looked upon the smiling face of Mark Smeaton, he drew his jagged blade and cut my lover's throat.

I was too stunned to react. Mark fell, clutching at his wound, his eyes filled with mute accusation. This couldn't be happening, I told myself. It wasn't real. But it was.

"I'm sorry there wasn't more of a show, my bloodthirsty little harlot," my lord said as he looked down at the twitching form of my lover. "But he was unschooled, and the Paradox spirits would have come had I used my Art."

I felt my fingers close on the dented goblet, which I had

sneaked into the room earlier. My plan had been to use its mists to set everyone but myself to sleep. Instead, I hefted it above my head and brought it down on my lord's skull. He was so unprepared for this attack that he fell on the second blow.

I bent down over Mark and saw that he was dead. His eyes were open and staring. I screamed until my throat was raw, just as I had the first night we made love. Something moved behind me. My lord was stirring. Picking up the goblet, I willed its mists to appear. My lord fell to them.

Trembling, I covered the bastard's eyes with my free hand. The butterfly broach, pinned to my flesh beneath my clothes, performed its duty well. My lord shimmered and became a perfect duplicate of Henry Weir.

It wasn't long before the king's whore arrived, all in a rage. The moment she walked into the room she was engulfed by the mists I had released to ensure my lord's continued sleep. Had she been given the opportunity, I am certain she would have complained vigorously at having been summoned in this manner.

Her double, you must understand, also had the ability to trade places physically with Anne. Until this night, Anne had been unaware of that fact. My lord had wished to take no chances with his lover's safety. He wanted a means by which he could extricate her from any peril.

I knew what was happening at King Henry's palace. Earlier, I had used the butterfly broach for the first time. Anne's double no longer resembled her in the least. She looked, for all the world, like an ordinary maid. Her task had been to burst from Anne's chambers and cry that the queen had gone mad, that she had fled the castle and sought to escape England with her lover, Mark Smeaton. She would then lead the king's soldiers here, to the castle, where they would find Anne lying naked and asleep in Smeaton's arms. In truth, the sleeping man would be my lord. Both would be arrested and quickly executed.

We had planned it all so perfectly. Mark would have lived on in the form of Henry Weir, I would have married him, and Anne's double would have been given whatever form and whatever life she desired.

At least a portion of our original plan might have been salvaged if I had been able to keep my wits about me. Instead, the sight of Anne Boleyn lying helpless at my feet filled me with a murderous frenzy. I took the blade Henry Weir had used to kill my lover and savaged the queen. When I was done, I was covered in blood and the woman's corpse was all but unrecognizable. Her head hung from her shoulders by a thread. The act had been unsatisfactory without her screams. In any case, I was quite insane with grief.

Before long, the guardsmen came to my lord's castle and found him wearing the form of my lover. I had set him where he would be found easily. The carnage in the receiving hall went undiscovered.

My lord stirred to wakefulness as the guards were dragging him off. He seemed thoroughly dazed. When asked if he was Mark Smeaton, he replied that he was. A few seconds later, he muttered that he *believed* he was.

I watched this event from a safe distance.

My assumption is this: The magick was not meant to be utilized between the living and the dead. By transferring the form of a corpse onto that of a live man, more than the outer shell was given. Mark Smeaton's memories were somehow dragged into my lord's brain. This kept my lord confused and unable to draw upon his great power to extricate himself when he was brutally tortured on the rack and the knotted cord was pulled upon his eyes, blinding him.

He died like an animal, a fate that befit him.

Perhaps if Mark had lived, if my plan had been enacted, it would have all been for naught. My lord may have used his Art to countermand my feeble dabblings in magick and both Mark and myself would have died horribly. I have to believe my continued existence is what Mark would have wanted; I know that I loved him dearly and would not have hesitated to give my life for his.

In truth, these sentiments were first expressed by my blood sister, who will soon be taken to her execution. You see, the magic holding Anne's double in my form failed the moment I took Boleyn's life. She reverted to the form of the queen and was arrested in her stead. Magick, it seems, rarely works in the manner one wishes.

I have attempted to utilize the talismans left behind by my dead master to free her. With the butterfly broach, I changed my own appearance so that I could gain an audience with her. When I attempted to use it on her, it did not work. The butterfly broach had lost the essence of magick it held. It is used up, worthless as anything but a simple adornment. The goblet, too. The other talismans have power, but none that will allow me to save my friend.

We spoke for a time, until I could feel the enchantment holding me in my assumed form beginning to wear away.

This morning, I leave for the place of her execution. It is a private ceremony, but I promised my sister I would be there for her. There are gifts I possess without magick, and by utilizing them, I have secured a place in the audience.

From there, I know not where I will go. Another person might be concerned under my circumstances. I am not.

For the first time in my life, the choice is entirely my own.

Scott Ciencin authored the critically acclaimed horror trilogy, *The Vampire Odyssey*, *The Wildlings*, and *Parliament of Blood*. He is also the author of several best selling fantasy novels, including *The Night Parade*, *The Wolves of Autumn* and *The Lotus and the Rose*. Under the pseudonym Richard Awlinson, he penned the number one best sellers *Shadowdale* and *Tantras*. Currently, he is writing young adult horror as Nick Baron, with six books in the *Nightmare Club* series. Scott lives in Winter Park, Florida, with his beloved wife Denise.